Susan Carlisle's love affair with books began when she made a bad grade in mathematics. Not allowed to watch TV until the grade had improved, she filled her time with books. Turning her love of reading into a love for writing romance, she now pens hot Medicals. She loves castles, travelling, afternoon tea, reading voraciously and hearing from her readers. Join her newsletter at SusanCarlisle.com.

Born and raised just outside Toronto, Ontario, **Amy Ruttan** fled the big city to settle down with the country boy of her dreams. After the birth of her second child, Amy was lucky enough to realise her lifelong dream of becoming a romance author. When she's not furiously typing away at her computer, she's mum to three wonderful children, who use her as a personal taxi and chef.

Also by Susan Carlisle

Atlanta Children's Hospital miniseries

Mending the ER Doc's Heart
Reunited with the Children's Doc
Wedding Date with Her Best Friend
Second Chance for the Heart Doctor

Kentucky Derby Medics miniseries

Falling for the Trauma Doc

Also by Amy Ruttan

Winning the Neonatal Doc's Heart
Nurse's Pregnancy Surprise
Reunited with Her Off-Limits Surgeon
Tempted by the Single Dad Next Door

Discover more at millsandboon.co.uk.

AN IRISH VET
IN KENTUCKY

SUSAN CARLISLE

REBEL DOCTOR'S
BOSTON REUNION

AMY RUTTAN

MILLS & BOON

First published in Great Britain 2024
by Mills & Boon, an imprint of HarperCollins*Publishers* Ltd,
1 London Bridge Street, London, SE1 9GF

www.harpercollins.co.uk

HarperCollins*Publishers* Macken House, 39/40 Mayor Street Upper,
Dublin 1, D01 C9W8, Ireland

An Irish Vet in Kentucky © 2024 Susan Carlisle

Rebel Doctor's Boston Reunion © 2024 Amy Ruttan

ISBN: 978-0-263-32172-2

09/24

AN IRISH VET
IN KENTUCKY

SUSAN CARLISLE

MILLS & BOON

To Thomas

I'll love you forever

CHAPTER ONE

CONOR O'BRIAN STEPPED into the dim stable hall to a view of a female behind encased in dusty jeans, raised in the air and swinging back and forth. For the first time in a long time, he took a moment to admire the well-developed lines of a woman's firm bottom.

He cleared his throat to gain her attention and adjusted his focus. "Excuse me, but I'm looking for the owner."

The woman straightened then shoved the pitchfork she held into a pile of loose hay. With a swift practiced move, she flipped it off the fork over a stall wall. Dust floated around her in the stream of light coming in through the doors.

"Hello," he said louder.

She whirled, making her rust-colored ponytail whip round her head, the pitchfork held like a weapon. With a slim build, the plaid shirt, jeans and boots covered the curves he'd admired earlier. What caught his attention was the sparkle in her brilliant green eyes. Ones that reminded him of the countryside at home after a rain.

"Ho. Ho." He threw up his hands and stepped back. She stood almost as tall as he did. "I'm just looking for the person who owns the stables."

"What?" She leaned the handle of the pitchfork against

the wall then pulled white speaker buds from her ears. "Can I help you?"

"I'm looking for the owner." How long was this non-conversation going to go on? He was tired, having traveled all day.

She placed her hands on her hips and glared at him. "You found her."

His step faltered. This woman he hadn't anticipated. She looked more like a farmhand than the veterinarian he had been told she was. "I'm Conor O'Brian. I understood you would be expecting me."

Her eyes narrowed and her brow wrinkled. In a sweet Southern drawl she said, "I'm sorry. I don't recognize that name."

Had he been sent on a wild-goose chase? He had no desire to make this trip to begin with, but William Guinness, Liquid Gold's owner, had insisted Conor come with the horse. Someone who knew the animal well enough to see about him in the weeks leading up to the Kentucky Derby. Conor's siblings had encouraged him to make the trip as well. Now this.

"I was told that Gold would be stabled here for two weeks before moving to the racetrack barns."

The woman's face brightened. Her body relaxed. "Liquid Gold. Yes, the horse from Ireland. I wasn't expecting him until day after tomorrow. I should've guessed from your accent who you might be." At least she had expected the horse if not him.

She stepped forward and offered her hand. "I'm Christina Mobbs. Welcome to Seven Miles Farm and Stables."

He liked the name *Christina*. But they were not friends, so he settled on calling her by a more formal name. "Dr.

Mobbs, I would really like to get Gold settled. It's been a long trip. The flight, then three days in quarantine in Indianapolis, then the three-hour drive here. I think he needs something stable under his feet."

"Certainly. I have a stall ready." She walked farther down the hall and opened a stall door wide, then returned to him and moved beyond.

Conor stepped outside just behind her. He glanced at the countryside. It reminded him of home with its green trees and grass-covered rolling hills. At least that much he could appreciate about being here. Except he'd rather be in Ireland in his own home, being left alone.

Conor had pushed back about coming here but the knowledge that his brother and sister were worried about him had made him agree. They feared he had become too insulated and removed from life because of his loneliness and anger over losing Louisa and his unborn child. They had said they even feared for his mental health. Their idea was that with a change of scenery he might snap out of his depression. He didn't share the idea that a trip to the United States would change his mindset, but he had been left with little choice but to make the trip. After all, it was only for three weeks. What could happen in that amount of time?

Christina put out a hand as if to touch the large white truck and kept it there as she walked beside the matching horse trailer. "Nice rig."

"Not my doing but I agree it is nice."

"I'm going to need to see some papers before I let you unload him. Do you have a health certificate, import permit and blood tests?"

"I have them right here." He handed her the papers he had pulled out of his back pocket.

She flipped through the sheets, running a finger down each page. "Looks good. The training and racing certificates are even here." She handed them back to him and continued to the rear of the trailer.

Conor joined her there. Inside, he could hear Gold shifting his weight, making the trailer creak. After opening the back door wide, he pulled the ramp out and stepped inside. "Easy, boy. We're done traveling for a while. It's time to rest and get ready for the big day." Conor spoke softly, running his hand across the Thoroughbred's neck. "You have a nice stall waiting. Just for you."

Only with his equine patients had Conor felt like himself since his wife had killed herself and their unborn baby. Working with the horses eased his pain, or at least let him forget for a few minutes. With the horses, he dared to care.

"Let's get you out of here." He untied the halter rope from the bar in the trailer. Turning Gold, Conor led him out and down the metal ramp. He looked at Dr. Mobbs, who stood beside the driver, to see a look of pure pleasure on her face.

"What a fine-looking horse." Awe hung in each of her words.

"He is a handsome fellow. And fast, too." Conor could not help but speak like a proud parent. "I've been taking care of him since his birth."

"I would like to examine him before you put him in the stall." She stepped toward them.

"Why?"

She looked directly at him. "Because this is my place and if something is wrong with such an expensive piece of horseflesh, I want to know about it. I'm a veterinarian. I know what I'm doing. I also need to know Gold isn't carrying anything that might make the other horses here ill."

Conor straightened his shoulders. He wasn't used to anyone questioning his care of Gold or any other animal for that matter. "I assure you Gold is in fine health."

"Still, I must insist if he is to stay at Seven Miles."

She walked to the front of the horse, lifting his head with a hand under the horse's chin. "You are indeed a handsome fellow."

Conor watched as Christina looked into Gold's eyes, pulled up his lips to study his teeth and then ran her hand over his shoulders and back before doing the same to his legs.

She had a gentle but firm touch. Gold didn't take to just anyone; that was part of why William had wanted Conor with Gold, but the horse seemed content with Christina's attention. Did she have that effect on all males she touched? He pushed away that uncomfortable idea. What had made such a foreign thought flash through his mind? He hadn't thought of a woman that way since his wife died. Hadn't wanted to.

"I understand he was the highest point earner in the Europe seven-race circuit." She continued around to the other side of the horse.

"That is correct. That's why he was issued an invitation to the Derby race."

"You know no visiting horse has ever won the Derby." She looked at him from under the horse's neck.

Conor shrugged. "There is always a first time."

She grinned, taking his breath for a moment.

Christina had to admit the horse was in prime condition. Not unlike the man assigned to handle Gold, despite a sadness that shrouded him. It particularly showed in his blue eyes that held a hollow, haunted look. She had instated a look-but-don't-touch program after her no-good ex, Nelson had pulled his trick last year. After that horrible experience she didn't allow herself to trust anyone. She had considered herself a good judge of character until she'd been proven wrong in a very painful way.

When she stepped away from the horse, the Irish man said, "Now it's my turn."

She watched as wide, confident fingers repeated what she had just finished.

The horse's muscles rippled beneath his administrations. The animal stood still, obviously used to the man's hands.

All the while Conor spoke in a soft, low voice. His deep Irish baritone washed over her.

It made her think of the warmth of a fire on a cold, snowy night, pushing all the drafts away.

She hadn't had that in her life for too long. What did she have to do to keep him talking so she could bask in that feeling just a little longer?

Instead of finding an answer to her internal question, she stood there looking at him as if she'd never seen a handsome man before. Shaking herself figuratively, she redirected herself to the thoughtfulness he gave the horse's legs. He spent more time on them than he had other areas of the animal's body, giving them a thorough assessment. She watched, mesmerized. It always amazed her how so much weight and strength could rest on such thin supports. A racehorse full-out running was pure majesty.

Once again, Christina's consideration fell to the man doing the exam. The thick, dark waves on his head captured her interest.

A tense, blue-eyed look snagged hers, held. "He fared well for such a long trip."

"I would agree." She managed not to stammer.

The man squatted beside the horse. He reminded her of a Thoroughbred, slim and moving with slick, easy motions.

The driver of the truck stated he had to go if he was no longer needed. Conor removed his bag from the backseat and shook the man's hand. Minutes later they watched the truck and trailer rattle down the drive.

"Let's get Gold in his stall." She turned and entered the barn.

He followed with Gold on a lead.

A half an hour later they had Gold settled in a stall.

Conor stepped back from the stall gate. "It's always tough on a horse when it travels."

"Yes, and horses that are good enough to run the Kentucky Derby tend to be rather high-strung."

"Exactly. That's why Mr. Guinness's trainer wanted Gold to come a few weeks early. It gives him a chance to settle in. He can spend the time acclimating to the weather. Kentucky's humidity alone is far different from Ireland's."

"I imagine it is." One day she would love the chance to visit Ireland.

Conor continued, "I, on the other hand, am worn out. Could you show me where I will be staying? It's been a long day and the time change still has me out of sync."

Her head shifted to the side. What was he talking about? Her mouth twisted in thought. Dr. Dillard, the head veterinarian of the clinic at Churchill Downs, had said nothing about someone staying at her farm. She boarded and cared for horses. Not men she didn't know. "Uh… You're expecting to stay here?"

"Yes, I understood I would be staying near Gold." He looked around. "It doesn't look like there is a hotel on every corner, so I assume I'm to stay in the house."

"That isn't what I understood." But Dr. Dillard might have failed to tell her.

"I'm afraid that isn't going to work. I don't know you and it's just me here. I wasn't expecting to board you as well."

Dr. Dillard had asked if she would be willing to board Gold for two weeks. She needed the money and the doctor's goodwill since she wanted to work the Derby week at Churchill Downs. After what Nelson had done to her, she needed to prove to her peers she was nothing like Nelson and wasn't involved in his drug selling. The Derby only took the best veterinarians, and she wanted that seal of approval. She'd been working for the invitation to serve all year long.

"I will pay you twice what a hotel would charge me. Make it three times."

"You really want to stay here."

"Gold is my responsibility. I take that seriously. I need to be close by."

Christina liked a man who felt that kind of concern for those he cared about. Even a horse. She imagined that translated to people as well. Nelson had felt none of that in regard to her, and they had been together for four years. In fact, he had thrown her to the wolves to protect himself.

Along with Nelson had gone her dream of a husband and children as well. He'd destroyed all her business and personal dreams.

She didn't want it to get back to Dr. Dillard she hadn't been a team player. Enough that she wouldn't make any ripples by insisting he stay elsewhere. With her work at the Derby, she could make great contacts that would help her rehabilitation program grow. If Gold won the Derby it would also put her farm on the map just because he had stayed there.

And she could use the money. She was trying to build her business. That money could be put to good use. Part of her rehabilitation program was the water program she had developed and invested in. The heated pool for horses had put her back financially but it would pay for itself in a few years. Or at least that was the plan. She hoped one day Seven Miles Farm and Stables would be synonymous with the best place to take horses for rehabilitation and rest.

"Okay, but only twice the amount. Three times makes me feel dishonest."

He huffed.

They exited the barn into the afternoon sunlight.

Conor stopped and looked around the area.

She rested her hands on her hips and squinted against the bright spring afternoon sun. Did he see what she did? The beauty of the long tree-lined drive. The emerald green of the grass. The brilliance of the white wood fences. She loved the area around Versailles, Kentucky. For her, there was no other place in the world.

"It is pretty here. More than I imagined it would be."

Christina heard the sadness in his voice. "But you're already missing home."

"Something like that. This wasn't a trip I wanted to make." She had the distinct feeling his perceptive look missed very few details.

"You don't have to be here long. Only three weeks. It will pass fast. Especially Derby week."

"I'm counting on that." His face remained a mask, showing none of the emotion his tone indicated.

For some reason his attitude made her sad. But it wasn't her job to see about him; it was to board Gold. That was what she should focus on. She shouldn't see much of him. Her job had her keeping early mornings and late evenings. There was also her regular practice to see about. For the trouble there would be great gain. What could go wrong?

Conor watched the expression on Christina's face change from shock to thoughtful to acceptance.

He had Gold stabled, and he was ready to get some rest as well. All the traveling had left him tired and irritable. "If you don't mind, I really am exhausted. If you'd just point me in the direction of where I am to stay, I'll head there."

That shook her out of whatever was running through her mind and started her toward the barn's open doors to the outside.

Conor was quickly running out of good humor. He opened his mouth to say he would stay in the barn, but he thought better of it. "I assure you I am not an axe murderer. You are safe with me. I promise. I'm too tired to attack anyone."

"I wasn't thinking—"

"Look. I have no car. Until I pick up my rental tomorrow. I don't know anyone in the US. I don't know my way around."

She rolled her eyes. "I'm not scared of you. I want you to know I'm putting you in the extra room off the kitchen. It's little more than a storage room."

"That sounds fine. At this point I don't care."

Indecision flickered in her eyes.

What had made this woman so scared of men? "I promise I'm a good guy. I'll stay out of your way."

"Then come on up to the house. I'll show you your

room." She walked in the direction of the one-level sprawling brick house.

A black truck with supply boxes built on both sides of the bed had been parked near the back door. Conor followed her up the two brick steps into the house. They entered a pale green kitchen. There were dishes in the sink of the same color. On the wood table that looked well-worn lay a pile of envelopes. On the green countertops were the usual appliances such as a coffeemaker, mixer and toaster.

Somehow, this retro look suited her. Yet, he had the idea it wasn't intentional. More like modernizing the kitchen fell low on her to-do list.

She turned down a small hall off the kitchen and entered a room. "This way is your room, or that might be an exaggeration. It's more like a large closet with a bed."

He joined her.

She was busy stacking boxes against the wall so there was a path to a bed. "Sorry about the mess."

A small bed of sorts sat in a corner. There was also a desk and chair. The only item that leaned toward modern was a flat-screen TV on a stand.

"I'm sorry there's not more to it. I just didn't realize that I was gonna be boarding a horse as well as a man."

For someone who didn't want him staying with her, she apologized a lot. The room was so small he could smell the sweetness of hay and lavender on her. The scents of home. "I appreciate it." Conor dropped his leather bag to the floor. "Thanks. Beggars cannot be choosers. I'm not going to complain."

"The bed is made but I'll have to get you some clean towels." She brushed by him.

His body tensed. The reaction strange yet familiar. It had

been a long time since he felt anything for a woman. Conor didn't want to now. He wouldn't be unfaithful like his father had been. She needed to leave. He forced out, "Thanks, I appreciate it."

Christina grabbed a couple of towels from her bathroom closet and returned to the small room. She slowly approached, listening. "Conor?"

Hearing no sound or movement, she stepped to the door. She found him sprawled on the too-small bed, facedown. A soft snore came from him.

It had been over a year since there had been a man sleeping in the house. Until today, she had intended for it to stay that way forever. Nelson had made her hesitant about trusting anyone. Conor wouldn't be around long enough for it to matter. His money would be worth the chance.

After placing the towels on the desk, she took a blanket from the end of the bed and draped it over him. Apparently, he had had all he could take for the day.

Christina headed out the back door. There were still chores to do. Feeding the horses and securing the barn for the night must happen no matter what.

Who was this Irish stranger with the sad eyes now staying in her home?

The next morning the house was still quiet when Christina went out the back door at daylight to take care of the horses. Her guest had not arisen yet. She quickly scribbled a note stating, *Make yourself at home.* Then she left.

A bitterness that hadn't eased much over the past months filled her. She wouldn't be in this position of having a houseguest if it hadn't been for Nelson. Because of him, she was fighting to regain her good reputation and her aspirations and bank account. As if that hadn't been enough, Nelson had almost been the cause of her losing her veterinarian license.

One piece of paper had saved her, or she would have been working elsewhere. Not doing what she loved. That paper had proven she hadn't been the one stealing the drugs. She had to give Nelson kudos; he had been good at covering his problems. She'd no idea what he had been doing behind her back.

Worse, she'd believed he would be her future. Even the father of her children. Which she desperately wanted.

She had been deeply hurt once, and had no intention of letting that happen to her again on a professional or personal level. She kept any relationships on a superficial plane. She wouldn't permit another man to crush her like Nelson had. The fact she had managed to salvage her practice and her business was the only thing that had saved her sanity.

Even worse still, when she was down, all her mother could say was how disappointed she had been in Christina's judgment. Her mother reminded her in detail that Christina didn't dress like a lady or have a job where she could have pretty nails. That she lived in a man's world, and the list went on. That if Christina had tried harder, Nelson wouldn't have had to turn to drugs. All she had wanted from her mother had been her support, and there had been none.

Enough of those thoughts. She needed to get moving, there were chores to finish, then horses to exercise and more horses on her schedule to see. She finished feeding the horses and spoke to Gold on her way out. She would let Conor handle him. He really was a fine-looking horse. She couldn't afford to have anything go wrong with him in her barn.

Breakfast for her came before exercising the horses. Closing the kitchen door behind her, she inhaled the smell of coffee. She toed off her boots and left them lying beside the door. She padded across the kitchen floor with nothing but thoughts of her morning cup of coffee.

She pulled up short. Conor stood in front of the range with a fork in his hand. His hair looked damp. Apparently, he had found the bathroom. A worn jean shirt covered his wide shoulders, and the same type of jeans his muscular legs. His feet were bare. As enticing as he looked, she didn't care for how comfortable he appeared in her personal space.

He glanced over his shoulder. "I took you at your word and made myself at home. I haven't eaten since yesterday morning. I made enough for you as well."

"I'm surprised you found anything to fix a meal with." She moved to see what was in the pan.

"It was pretty slim pickings, but I do like a challenge."

Shame filled her. "I'm not much of a cook but I'll try to get by the grocery store today, tomorrow at the latest."

"If you'll tell me where the store is, I'll take care of that after I pick up my rental. It's the least I can do. Especially since you weren't expecting me."

Who was this man who just showed up and cooked her a meal then agreed to buy groceries? He wasn't like anyone else she knew.

"You have about ten minutes before it's ready. You might like to take a look in the mirror."

Christina's hair was a mess. That sounded too much like her mother. "I've been working in the barn, and this is my house. I'm sorry I don't look like I came out of a fashion magazine."

His hands came up in a defensive measure. "Ho, I didn't

mean to insult you. I just thought you might like to know you have dirt on your face."

She stomped to the bathroom and looked in the mirror. A large black smear went across her left cheek. Conor's statement had been a nice way of keeping her from going out on her rounds looking foolish. Most people wouldn't have been as considerate. She owed him an apology.

Conor looked up from where he was placing a mug of coffee on the table. "You look neat and tidy."

"I'm sorry I overreacted. Thanks for telling me. I'd have hated to spend all day with dirt on my face."

"No problem," he said as if he had already forgotten it happened.

She glanced around the room. "Talk about neat. You've made a difference in here in a short amount of time."

"I hope you don't mind. I wasn't always tidy. My wife made me learn."

Of course, he had a wife. A man who looked as good as he did, liked animals and was kind enough to help someone out and cooked wouldn't remain unattached for long. A woman would be quick to snatch him up. "I'm sure she misses you."

Clouds filled his eyes and he looked away. "I'm sure it's more like I miss her. She died three years ago."

"Oh, I'm sorry."

"She was a good woman who died far too early. I miss her every day."

The pain in his voice said it was more like every minute. What would it be like to have someone care that much about her? To feel that love and connection so deeply it would still bring sadness to his eyes after you had died.

Nelson had professed that love but in the end they were

just words. Their relationship had turned one-sided. His largest interest had been himself. Once she would have liked to have an unbreakable connection with someone, but the chances of that happening were gone. Now she didn't trust her judgment enough to let a man into her life.

CHAPTER TWO

CONOR COULD NOT believe he had just told an almost perfect stranger about his wife. It was the most he had shared about Louisa in years. Yet, he thought of her daily. Remained devoted to her even after she had done something as selfish as committing suicide. But he could never talk about the loss of their child.

That was something his father never gave his mother. Devotion. When his mother had been alive or dead. Conor had watched his mother slowly drift away, become a shell of herself in her humiliation over his father's public infidelity. As a boy, Conor had vowed to remain true to his wife. He had kept that promise even after her death. That conviction drove his personal life. When he made a commitment, it stood for something.

He had tried to keep his pain and thoughts over Louisa to himself. In an odd way it had felt good to let go of even one detail about her. Maybe that was what his family had been wanting him to do for the past few months. They saw what he needed even if he couldn't. But guilt rose in him. The worst was he had noticed Christina as a woman, causing the guilt to swamp him, but he could not help himself.

Like now, as he watched her move around the kitchen. Her actions fascinating him. He had missed that part of being with someone the most. Having another person around. The peace of knowing someone was nearby. Maybe that was it, the reason he had been comfortable enough to tell Christina about Louisa. He had nothing to worry about. It had nothing to do with attraction and everything to do with his needing someone to talk to.

"I must exercise the horses and then I've got some rounds to make this afternoon."

Christina's statement brought him out of his perplexing thoughts. "Mind if I get a ride to the car rental place? I understand it's not far from here."

"Sure." Having finished her meal, she pushed back from the table. "Leave the dishes. I'll clean up later."

"I'll get them today."

Christina shrugged. "I appreciate it."

"I'll be out to check on Gold in just a few minutes."

She set her dishes in the sink. "Thank you for breakfast."

"You're welcome." She headed out the back door as if she was already thinking about what she had to do for the day.

Conor wasn't sure he liked being dismissed or why it bothered him that she did so.

Fifteen minutes later he had finished tidying the kitchen as much as he could without invading her personal space. He pulled on his boots and walked to the barn.

Outside he took a deep breath, bringing the fresh spring air into his lungs. He scanned the countryside. If he couldn't be in his beloved Ireland, then this part of the world must be the next best place. He continued to the barn. Gold would be glad to see him. He had agreed to fill in as groom as well.

Gold's trainer would arrive by the end of next week in time for Gold to move to the barns on the backside of Churchill Downs. The trainer had other horses he worked, and he could not be away for weeks. Gold's trainer intended for the horse to have a couple of weeks' rest before he started serious workouts. The idea was to have Gold eager to race.

Christina walked one of the other horses back into a stall as he entered the barn. "That's a fine-looking animal."

She patted the horse on the neck and closed the gate between her and the animal. "Yeah, this is Honey."

The horse did have a coat that reminded Conor of warm honey.

"She's staying with me because of a torn tendon."

"That's pretty difficult to repair." Conor was surprised she was even trying. It was an expensive and long process, if it worked.

"It is, but that's what this farm is all about, or at least it will be."

He walked over to pet Gold's nose hanging over the stall gate. "I thought you just boarded horses."

"No, I'm working to build this into a rehabilitation farm for racehorses. I'm just boarding Gold as a favor for the track vet."

"I understand." He opened Gold's stall and entered.

Christina went to another stall. She walked the horse out of the barn.

Conor fed Gold before leading him outside to the paddock where Christina was circling the horse on a lead rope. As the horse went around the space so did she. Her movements were easy and graceful.

She glanced in his direction.

Had she caught him staring? He continued to the mechanical hot walker. After attaching Gold to one of the arms of the merry-go-round-looking contraption, he started the motor. Gold was led around, getting his exercise. Conor returned inside to muck out Gold's stall.

Christina entered the barn, tied the horse to the gatepost and proceeded to brush the horse.

Conor became caught up in her actions once again. Each stroke was smooth and careful. She made long ones across the horse's back that had him bowing his back. What would it be like to have her do that across his body?

Was he losing his mind? He hadn't had those type of thoughts in years. Why this woman? Why now? Maybe she should be afraid of him.

Conor held himself back from rushing out of the barn. He took his time returning with Gold. Thank goodness by the time he did Christina was nowhere in sight. He groomed Gold in peace, but still glimpses of Christina's attentions flashed in his mind as he worked. Was it wrong to be jealous of a horse?

For lunch Christina put out bread and sandwich meats. She ate at a desk on the other side of the room while on the computer. He sat at the table reading an equine magazine he was not familiar with.

She turned in her chair. "I'm leaving in about twenty minutes if you want a ride to the rental car place."

He closed the magazine. "I'll be waiting by the truck."

She asked as he climbed out of the truck at the rental place, "Can you find your way back?"

"Yes, I've been paying attention and I have GPS." It was the first concern she had shown him.

She nodded, a slight smile on her lips. "GPS doesn't always work well around here."

"I'll keep that in mind. Thanks for the ride."

Christina wasn't home when he returned. He spent the rest of the day getting settled into his small office slash make-do bedroom. He stacked boxes around and cleaned off a space on the desk for himself. Would Christina mind him doing so? She was so different from Louisa, but for some reason he found Christina interesting. He wasn't sure if he was comfortable with those feelings or not.

The next afternoon Christina pulled up her drive and circled into her regular parking spot behind the house beside Conor's red rental truck. She had been gone all afternoon doing rounds and hadn't seen him all day. He'd already left by the time she had returned to the house after seeing to the horses that morning. Her breakfast waited on the table. A carafe of hot coffee sat there as well. Where he had gone so early in the morning she couldn't imagine, but that wasn't any of her business. Yet, that didn't keep her from wondering.

She climbed out, immediately noticing the barn doors were open. She had closed them securely that morning. Maybe Conor had gone out there and failed to secure them since then.

She walked to the barn, entering with the late-afternoon sun streaming in from the other side.

Wind, one of her boarded horses, stood in the hallway tied to the post of a stall gate. Conor was squatted down on his haunches, looking at the horse's leg. He ran his hand along the leg, pausing at the knee joint.

Her concern turned to anger. What was he doing? This horse had been entrusted to her. He had no business touching him or having the horse out of the stall. Some of her boarders were temperamental and could easily run. What if one of them got away?

She started toward him.

He looked up. "Hello."

"What exactly is going on here?" She heard the bite in her voice. Did he? She stepped closer.

"He has a wound. I brought him out because the light is better."

"You could have just waited to tell me. This horse is in my charge. The owners don't like just anyone touching them."

Conor stood to his full height and squared his shoulders. "If I was the owner, I would appreciate help where I could get it."

"These horses' owners want a veterinarian seeing to their animal. Pardon me but not a trainer or groom."

Conor's eyes bore into hers as if he were speaking to a simpleton. "Many trainers and grooms are better equine caregivers than a veterinarian. That being said, despite your lowly opinion of me, I am a veterinarian."

Her brows went up. He was? She had assumed he was a groom sent over to see about Gold. It had never crossed her mind a veterinarian would have come all the way from Ireland with a horse.

"I am here at the request of the owner. I've taken care of Gold since he was a colt. His owner wanted me to travel with Gold since he can have a temper, and this is a new environment for him, but he knows me. I assure you I'm more than capable of taking care of Gold or any other horse you have in your stable."

"I'm…uh…sorry. I didn't mean to insult you."

"What about grooms and trainers?" His look chastised.

"Or them, either. It's just that I'm responsible for these horses and I can't afford for anything to happen to them on my watch. I guess I'm pretty proprietorial."

"I would say you are." His attention returned to the horse's leg.

That didn't sound like a compliment.

"But that can be a positive or a negative." He softened his earlier words. His deep Irish brogue went a long way toward easing her frayed nerves.

"Back to this horse." He touched the horse lightly. "The wound on his foreleg needs to be debrided and cleaned then wrapped."

"Let me have a look." Christina went to one knee and examined the leg. "This is pretty deep. I think stitches are required."

"I disagree. You are too quick to add something that isn't natural. A good cleaning with antiseptic and a bandage should do well. It isn't that deep. Let nature take its course."

She stood. "I should be the judge of that. I'm the one responsible for the animal, not you."

"Yet, I have some knowledge in these matters."

She placed her hands on her hips. "And you're saying I don't?"

"I'm not saying that at all. I'm just saying you might be overtreating."

His calm words only irritated her. "I don't agree. I would appreciate it if you would step away and leave me to this."

"What can I do to help you?" He coolly watched her.

She huffed. "I'm going to need some heated water. You can go to the house and see to that."

"Sending me off to get me out of the way?"

"Just pretend you're preparing for the delivery of a baby." Christina didn't miss the darkening of his face before he swiftly turned and stalked out of the barn. What had she said to upset him?

She would have to worry about his attitude later. There was work to do now. She went to the large enclosed room in the barn where she stored all her medical supplies and tack for the horses. After entering, she gathered bottles of saline, bandages, a tube of anti-infection cream and placed them in a cardboard box before going to the locked box that held her injectable medicines.

This was one part of her world she kept in order by the alphabet. And kept a count of. What was an S drug doing in the Ws? She must have knocked it out of place. Those types of occurrences she'd never questioned until Nelson's stunt. Now she found problems everywhere.

Had Conor been in here for some reason? He didn't even have a key. With a shrug, she returned the vial to its correct position and took out a vial of antibiotic. She also grabbed a syringe in a plastic cover. Picking up a bowl, she headed back to Wind.

Wind stomped as she set the box down to retrieve a four-legged stool and placed it nearby. "Easy, boy, this will be over soon."

Christina found the suture kit and opened it, removing the scissors. "I'm going to cut away the skin. Hold still and it'll all be over soon." She snipped pieces of dead skin off.

Conor entered the barn with a pan in his hand, but she didn't slow her work. Wind shifted to the right, but Christina held tight to his foot.

With a quick movement Conor placed the pan on the floor and came around her to hold Wind's head. He whispered to the horse in a low, smooth voice. Conor's gentle brogue rippled over her as well.

She did like his accent. What would it be like to have him whisper in her ear? She shivered just to think of the possibility. Where did that bizarre thought come from? It was not something that would ever happen, but still a girl could dream.

She'd had dreams but they'd been shattered. At one time, she had believed that there would be a forever-after between her and Nelson. They'd made plans to marry, and then she learned of his duplicity. At least this time she had been smart enough to put the house and farm in her name. Nope, she was better on her own. She would keep it that way.

Finished with the skin removal, she brought the pan close and dipped a rag into the warm water and washed the area around the wound, removing a piece of hay, dirt and grit. All the while she worked Conor spoke to the horse, keeping him distracted from what she was doing.

Christina patted the front thigh of the horse then picked up the bottle of saline and opened it. "This next bit might not be too much fun but hang in there, Wind."

Conor changed his stance, taking a more secure hold on the horse's head.

"There we go, boy," she spoke to the horse. Turning the bottle up, she let the fluid flow over the wound, washing any debris away. She continued until it was all gone, then looked carefully for anything in the wound. There couldn't be any chance for infection.

"You want a second set of eyes?"

"Yeah, sure. I could use a leg stretch, too."

"Then change places with me." He offered his hand to help her up.

She hesitated a moment, then placed her hand in his. A shock of electric awareness went through her. She quickly let his hand go. He moved closer to take her seat. Conor smelled of citrus, hay and grain. Like the countryside.

He handed her the lead rope before he stepped away from her. Lifting the horse's foot, he braced it on his knee.

Christina watched the top of Conor's head as he looked at the wound. Her fingers itched to touch his thick hair, but she resisted. Setting the foot on the floor, he took a seat on the stool and picked up the tube of ointment. "Nice job. The trimming and cleaning are excellent work."

Christina couldn't help but glow under his praise.

He glanced at her. "I'll finish if that's okay with you."

"I'm still not convinced that it doesn't need to be stitched."

Conor's look met hers and held. "Trust me."

Trust wasn't something that Christina gave easily, if at all. Nelson had destroyed that ability. "I'm just supposed to trust your word on this?"

"Yes." His tone didn't waver.

She couldn't have him messing around with her horses. "Their owners trusted me. If something goes wrong, I'm the one with her name and business on the line." What she didn't say was she had already had that happen and that one time had been enough. She was having to re-earn her good name.

"I'm telling you that nothing will go wrong. In fact, my way is easier on the horse. You try my way for twenty-four hours and then you can do it your way."

He made it sound like he was the one calling the shots. "If there isn't improvement by the morning, I'll be stitching him up."

Conor said nothing. He pulled on plastic gloves and smeared antibacterial ointment on his finger and applied it to Wind's leg.

The horse flinched, its skin rippling. Christina held the halter snugger. "Easy, boy, it's almost over."

Conor sat the medicine aside and picked up the paper-covered gauze and began wrapping the leg in a sure neat manner born of practice. He worked with swift efficiency.

"That should do it." He stood and stretched, raising his hands above his head.

Despite her best effort, Christina couldn't help but watch.

He finished and his look met hers.

She had been caught staring. Why he interested her, or why she even cared about him knowing she'd been watching him, she didn't know. Still, a tingle shot through her, and she looked away. "I'll give him a shot and put him in the stall then clean up. Thanks for your help."

"I don't mind putting things away. See to Wind." He patted the horse on the neck. "You are a good patient, boy."

"That you are." She ran her palm down the horse's nose then tied his lead rope to the post. She drew up the liquid from the vial.

"What're you giving him?"

"Trimethoprim sulfa."

Conor nodded. "That antibiotic should work well."

At least they could agree on that. She injected the needle into the horse's hip. "Before you go back into the stall, I need to see if I can find what caused this."

She went to the tack room. After finding a hammer and flashlight she entered the stall, searching for a nail or piece of metal sticking out. In a methodical order she searched for what might have wounded Wind.

"Got it." A small piece of metal that secured the bottom of the feed trough stuck out. "Wind," she spoke to him over the wall of the stall, "how in the world you managed getting your leg near this I'll never know, but it's the only place I see where you could have gotten hurt."

Conor joined her. "Show me."

She pointed to the spot.

Conor shook his head. "Horses never cease to amaze me."

Christina hammered at the metal to flatten it but it didn't lie against the wood as it should.

Conor put out his hand. "May I?"

"Sure. You're welcome to give it a try." She watched the muscles in his back and arms flex and release as he worked. Were they as hard as they appeared? These thoughts had to stop. Conor was her guest, not on her farm to ogle.

"How's that?"

"Uh...yeah, that looks good. I'll get Wind." She stepped into the hall, glad for the soft breeze blowing through it. Tonight it would rain. Taking Wind's halter she said, "Come on, big boy, I'll get you tucked away for the night."

Conor had the surgery items cleaned away, leaving a small bag of trash neatly tied up on the ground beside the stool and the pan on top. It was nice to have such an efficient man around.

"Anything I need to do?" he asked.

"I need to put the antibiotic in the refrigerator." She went to the tack room and placed the vial in the small refrigerator she kept there for just this reason. On her way out she picked up a folding chair and carried it with her.

She unfolded it near the gate to Wind's stall.

Conor stood behind her. "What are you doing?"

"I'm going to sit up for a while to make sure no heat sets in around the wound."

"You can't take the bandage off until the morning. The more you open it the less likely it is to heal well."

She cut her eyes at him. "I know that."

He lowered his head, acting contrite. "Sorry. I'm sure you do. I'll take the pan and trash in."

Twenty minutes later he returned with a basket.

"What're you doing?" She turned in the chair, putting the paperback book she kept in the tack room for these occasions across her knee not to lose her spot.

"I brought us something to eat since we missed dinner and I will not let you sit up alone with our patient." He placed the basket on the floor beside her. "I hope you have another chair put away somewhere."

"In the tack room behind the door."

Conor set up the chair beside her. Picking up the basket, he removed a thermos. "Tea. Hot." He placed that on the floor. "And ham and cheese sandwiches." He handed her one covered in plastic. "Can I pour you some tea?"

"Sure. Thanks for this, Conor. It's very nice of you."

The smile he gave her made her stomach flutter. "You're welcome."

They sat in silence for a few minutes before Conor asked, "Will you tell me what made you decide to become a veterinarian? A large animal veterinarian at that. We don't have many female large animal vets in Ireland."

"We're about fifty-fifty here. As to why, I imagine it was the same things as you. I love animals. I just gravitated to large animals and then horses in particular. Look where I live. It would have been hard not to care for horses."

"I guess it would have."

"Did you grow up on a farm?" Conor watched her face. He liked how expressive her features were.

"Nope. In town with one small dog. Much to my mother's chagrin, I loved horses."

"She doesn't like them?"

Christina rubbed her booted heel in the dirt of the floor. "It was more like she wanted me to be a girly-girl and I was more of a tomboy. Let's just say I didn't always measure up to her expectations. In fact, I still don't."

He took a moment to digest that information. Conor knew well the feeling of disappointment in a parent.

She put her cup down near the leg of the chair. "How about you? Did you grow up on a farm?"

"I did. But I didn't know what I wanted to do until I went to work during the summers, just to have a job, at a local veterinary clinic cleaning out cages. That's when my love of veterinarian work began." It also got him away from the ugliness between his mother and father.

"So what brought you on this trip? I've never known the horse's vet to travel with it and do groom work as well."

"My family encouraged me to come when I was offered this opportunity and Gold's owner insisted. He wanted somebody he could trust with Gold. What I did not expect was not to have a place to stay. I appreciate you giving me a room here. Actually, I have liked doing some physical work. It reminds me of when I worked at the clinic."

She grinned. "You're welcome. Please feel free to muck out as many stalls as you wish."

Conor chuckled. "Thanks for reminding me about what it is to do real veterinarian care."

For the next three hours she checked on Wind at least ten times. More than once, she entered the stall to study the bandaged area for any seepage. Placing her hand on the leg to see if there was heat in the skin caused by infection. He had volunteered a couple of times to do the exam, but she had refused.

They turned quiet and Conor watched as Christina's eyes slowly lowered after she leaned her head back against the chair. She would have a crick in her neck if she remained like that all night.

He studied her. She really was a pretty woman. Not in the goddess-or-movie-star-beauty way, but in the simple, fresh and natural sense. What really made her appealing was her caring heart for animals, her quirky, haphazard way of keeping house and her drive to go after what she wanted. What confounded him the most was that he even noticed those characteristics.

It had been forever since he had sat with someone in a simple setting and been satisfied. Even thoughts of Louisa were not hurtling through his mind. For once, he had to bring her up instead of her always being there. The idea made him both uncomfortable and relieved. He wanted to hang on to Louisa while at the same time it was past time to let her go. Was that how his father had felt about his mother?

He gave Christina's shoulder a shake. "You better go inside or you're going to fall out of the chair."

She mumbled, "I need to stay here and keep an eye on Wind."

"I understand that, but I think we can go inside now. Get a few hours of sleep. He will be all right until morning."

"I better not…"

"If it will make you feel any better, I'll check on him in a couple of hours. You need to get some sleep." He helped her stand. She swayed on her feet, and he placed an arm around her shoulders, pulling her against him. "You are dead on your feet."

"It's my job."

He started her toward the door. "That may be so but I can help. Now, stop arguing and let me get you inside to bed."

"To bed…"

The way she let the words trail off made him think of a fire, a soft bed and a warm woman against him. He swallowed hard. The guilt. He did not want that. Could not want Christina. More importantly, he wouldn't allow himself the chance of the pain that caring again might bring.

Christina took a moment to look at Wind. "You promise?"

"You have my word. Now, come on, sleepyhead." Conor guided her, arm around her shoulders, to the house, inside and down the hall to her bedroom. He'd never been in there. At the door, he flipped on the light.

She squeaked. "Turn it off. That hurts my eyes."

He did as she said. "Good night, Christina. Get some rest."

Christina murmured something and moved into the room.

Conor grinned as he walked to his little office bedroom. He shook his head. At the brief glimpse of her room, he saw clothes strewn everywhere. A pile of veterinary magazines beside the bed. It hadn't been made, and the covers looked pushed over to one side, as if she had been in a rush when she woke. The woman might be a great veterinarian, but she needed a housekeeper like no one else he knew.

Taking just his boots off then setting his alarm for two hours, he lay on his bed. He had a horse to check on. A promise to keep. The first in many years.

A buzzing sound went off sooner than he wished. He pulled on his boots and headed out the kitchen door to the barn. Fifteen minutes later he was on his way back to the house. Two hours later, after the sun had brought light to the day, Conor entered the barn again.

Christina was there in Wild's stall on her knees. Conor went to his haunches beside her. "What do you think?"

"I think it's better."

His voice took on a teasing tone. "Then I will not tell you I told you so."

She glanced at him, a gentle smile on her lips. "Thank you for that. I would've hated to hear it. We don't go in for the old methods much around here. Little patience or time. Thanks for reminding me that sometimes time helps more than anything."

Had that been true for him? Or had the passage of time just closed him further off from life? He stood. "You are welcome."

She picked up a roll of gauze and began wrapping the leg once more. "This reminder will come in handy when I plan rehabilitation for horses in my program."

He stepped to Wind's head and stroked his nose. "What type of horse issues are you planning to concentrate on?"

"Any that are leg related. I hate to see a horse put down when there's a chance that they can be saved. Maybe they won't race again but they still have value." She stood and patted Wind on the neck. "Just like this guy. He's worth the time and energy."

Conor patted the horse's neck as her hand passed. She stopped her movement, and he did, too. She quickly pulled hers away.

"I hate to see the waste of such a majestic animal." She picked up a feed bucket and moved to the trough.

"You know you can't save them all." He continued to stroke Wind while he watched her.

"Maybe not but I can try." She poured the feed into the trough.

By the tone of her voice, she believed deeply in helping the horses. Yet, the reality he well knew. "An admirable goal."

Done with the feed she picked up the trash.

Conor smiled and shook his head. Christina might not be a housekeeper, but he could find no fault in her care of the horses, her supply room, or the barn's cleanliness. "Come on. I'll fix us a hot breakfast."

They stepped out of the stall.

"Did you cook when you were married?" Christina asked.

"No. I had to learn after she was gone. Now I enjoy it."

"You know you don't have to cook for me all the time." She went to the gate and pushed it closed, locking it.

He started down the hall beside her. "I know but you're letting me stay here when you had not planned to have company, and I've got to feed myself so I might as well feed you, too."

"I have to admit your cooking is better than cold cereal but I'm gaining weight." She chuckled.

"From what I have seen you'll be just fine with a few extra pounds." He glanced at Christina, who met his look.

"Thanks. That's nice of you to say."

CHAPTER THREE

CHRISTINA WOKE TO the sun shining through the window of her bedroom. She jerked to a sitting position. She never slept this late. The horses would be starving. After being up late two nights ago, her lack of sleep must have caught up with her. The horses were no doubt stomping in their stalls to have their morning feed.

She flipped the covers off and popped out of bed. She didn't bother to remove the T-shirt she wore. Jerking yesterday's jeans on, she zippered and buttoned them and headed for the door. She would dress for the day later. The horses came first.

Not slowing down, she ran into a solid wall of warm, damp flesh. Strong fingers wrapped her upper arms, preventing her from falling backward.

"Umph."

She grabbed Conor's waist to steady herself. That only made the quiver running through her worse.

"Where are you headed in such a rush?" His sexy Irish brogue had deepened despite the spark of humor in it. The warmth of his breath whispered by her ear.

"Morning chores. Running late," she managed to get out.

"All taken care of. I saw to them all this morning when I checked on Wind and Gold."

"How is he?"

"Doing much better. I removed the bandage and checked him and reapplied it. He seems to be comfortable."

Unlike her. Christina stepped back, putting space between them. She now had a clear view of Conor's well-formed bare chest. He must have just finished his shower. She had been better off standing closer to him. She swallowed hard.

"I appreciate the help, but I'll just go out and check on him." She was used to doing everything by herself. She hadn't had help in a long time. Even then it hadn't turned out she could trust it.

"They've all been well cared for but I'm sure you'll want to see for yourself."

At least he didn't sound offended. More like impressed.

He shifted to the side, giving her clear passage. His look dropped lower. He cleared his throat. "I'll see to breakfast."

It wasn't until she pulled on her jacket, she realized he could see through her thin shirt. Even now her nipples remained at attention from being so close to him. Great. She couldn't do anything about it now. With a tug, she put on her boots. In the future she would be more careful.

In the barn she found everything just as it should be. Each animal looked well cared for.

She returned to the house to find Conor sitting at the kitchen table with a cup of coffee in front of him. At the chair to his right waited her coffee. There was also a bowl of oatmeal with toppings sitting on the table. He spoiled her. This attention she would miss when he left.

"I should get a shower before I eat." She stepped toward the door.

"Then your oatmeal will be cold." He sounded disappointed.

"Ugh, I'm not exactly adequately dressed."

His gaze lingered at her chest then came back to meet hers. Her nipples tightened. "I'd say you look just right."

"I still believe I'll change. I'll warm my coffee and oatmeal up."

He wore that slight grin she found so sexy. "If that's the way you want it."

She shivered. Should she be concerned about whatever was not being said between them? Yet, he had never once been anything but a gentleman. In fact, he looked irritated, she noticed. Maybe she was wrong. Her judgment could be off. Nelson had proven that. Still, Conor had been good to her and the horses.

Christina hurried down the hall to the bathroom for a quick hot shower and returned to the kitchen a short while later.

Conor still sat at the table, nursing his cup of coffee, with an *Equine* magazine she had received in the mail the day before open in front of him.

While she warmed her meal he asked, "What are your plans for today?"

"I've some patients to see." She pulled the food out at the beep.

"Mind if I tag along and see how it's done over here?"

Could she spend the entire day with him? She didn't say anything as she sat down to eat.

"This babysitting job is not quite as intensive as it could be. Gold is doing fine."

How could she say no? "I imagine it will be rather dull for you. It's simple basic veterinarian work. But you're welcome to come along if you want."

"I bet I will learn something. I'll straighten up here and be ready to go when you are."

"I've got to load supplies into my truck. I'll be about twenty minutes or so." She started toward the door.

"I need to collect my wallet and jacket." Conor went to his room.

Christina finished her breakfast and hurried out to the barn to get her supplies together. She was inside the tack room looking at the medicine box when Conor walked up.

"Is something wrong?" He came to stand beside her.

"No. I'm just doing my daily count."

"Daily?"

"Yes. I like to keep a close eye on my regulated medicines." Especially after what Nelson did. She couldn't take a chance on anyone ever stealing from her again.

"I also check the truck daily." She closed and locked the metal box attached to the wall.

He stepped into the hallway. "Why such vigilance?"

Christina joined him. "Because I can't afford any controversy. I've been working too hard to get my reputation back."

His brows came together and created a furrow. "What do you mean by that?"

"I'll tell you in the truck. I need to get going if I don't want to work late into the night."

They walked out of the barn.

"Stealing drugs is a real problem. Offenders are good at it." Nelson had been getting away with it for almost a year before she realized what he was doing.

"In Ireland it's the same. We watch ours closely as well. Those days of it just sitting on the shelf unattended are long gone."

She put the few items she needed away in one of the supply compartments on the truck.

He stood at the front of the vehicle. "Anything I can do to help?"

"No. I got it." She stored the medicines and IV needles in a locked bin. "Let me check the horses once more and I'll be ready to go."

"I now understand why Gold was boarded here. You are careful."

Her look met his. "I take what I care about seriously. Don't you?"

Conor did. To the detriment of his heart. Three years later he still honored his marriage vows. Something his father hadn't done. Conor believed in keeping his promises. Would Louisa have wanted or expected that of him for this long? Hadn't it been her choice to leave him? If he stepped out and had interest in a woman, would that be bad? He was tired of being lonely. He had not realized how much so until he'd started staying with Christina. But wouldn't that make him no better than his father? That, Conor wouldn't accept.

Conor climbed into the passenger side of her large truck. What had possessed him to request to go with Christina today? He wasn't sure if it had been out of boredom or being truly interested in the type of veterinary practice she had, or worse, the fact he just wanted to spend more time with her. That last thought gave him a prickly, panicky feeling.

Christina settled in behind the steering wheel. "I have a rather long day today. You're sure you want to go?"

Was she trying to encourage him not to go? "I am. How far do we drive to the first patient?" He buckled up.

"What I like to do is start at my farthest appointment and work my way home unless there is a serious case that needs to be seen right away. About sixty miles is my radius."

"That's half the distance across Ireland in some places. That can make for a long day."

She glanced at him. "Would you like to change your mind?"

"Are you trying to get rid of me?" He made a show of getting comfortable.

Christina started the truck. "Not at all."

She still hadn't relaxed enough for him to question her about the medicines more. He watched the countryside, glancing at her occasionally. She drove with determination.

Before midafternoon, they had stopped at three different farms all with long driveways and miles of wooden fence. At each, the owner or trainer was there to greet Christina when she stopped the truck outside the barn. She grabbed her bag and hopped out, ready to go to work each time.

With a wave of her hand in his direction she would say, "This is Conor O'Brian. He is visiting from Ireland." Her attention would then return to the problem with the horse.

Her efficiency amazed and impressed him as she went about the care of the horse, all the while talking and touching the animal as if they had been friends forever. Why did she insist on hiding all that tenderness behind gruff toughness?

They finished with one farm and were driving to the next. Christina hadn't said more than what was necessary the entire day. Being a veterinarian could be a solitary job but this was ridiculous. "Are you mad at me? Did I do something wrong?"

"Why would you think that?" She tilted her head in question.

He turned in the seat to see her better. "You haven't said over ten words to me in the last three hours."

"I've been thinking."

About what? "Maybe if you talk it out it would be better."

"I don't think that'll work." She slowed and made a left turn down a tree-lined country road with fenced green pasture.

"Try it. You never know." He looked at her profile. At least her jaw didn't appear as tight. Either way, Christina appealed to him. What would she look like in something feminine? He had certainly been aware of her breasts in the thin T-shirt that morning. More so than he'd been in years. Why Christina and why now?

"I almost lost my license a few years back."

He shifted in the seat, sitting straighter, his attention completely on her.

She glanced at him. "You aren't going to say anything?"

"No, I figured you'd say more when you were ready."

A small smile came to her lips. "I was stupid. Too trusting, really. I should have been doing the inventory of the medicines since it was my name on the line. But my then live-in boyfriend of four years, who I believed I would marry, had been stealing drugs. He was a vet tech and planning to enter veterinarian school. Then the authorities caught him selling and everything blew up. I barely retained my license. I'm still trying to build my good name back."

"So that's why you count the medicine daily. You blame yourself for his mistakes."

"That's pretty close to it."

He could hear the shame in her voice. "I'm sorry to hear that. It must have been hard to have believed in someone and have them let you down." How many times had he watched his father do that to his mother?

"It was."

Christina pulled into a small roadside park. Horses stood in the field surrounding them, swishing their tails in the bright sunlight. She faced him.

"I had just gotten the idea for opening a rehabilitation farm for racehorses and had started to look for funding. All the banks had gotten the word about what happened, so that was a no-go. Nelson, that was my ex, had not only destroyed my regular world but had managed to do the same to my dreams. That's why I agreed to take Gold so I could get in good with Dr. Dillard at Churchill Downs. I want to be one of the veterinarians on duty during the Derby. That's a prestigious position. It will look good on my vitae. I can also make contacts with those who might use my farm for not only rehabilitation but for horse holidays." She pulled two protein bars out of the pocket of the driver's door, handing one to him. "Break time."

His brows rose. He took it and unwrapped it. "Horse holidays?"

Her first smile of the day. "You know, a place to stay during downtime."

"That's sort of what this trip has been for me."

"How's that?"

Conor took a bite out of his bar and chewed slowly, trying to stall having to answer. Why had he said that about coming to America? After Christina had shared her own story, he owed her at least part of his. But he couldn't give her all. That, he wouldn't talk about. The loss of his baby was too painful.

"You have heard most of it. About my family wanting me to be here. Because they don't think I'm moving on after my wife's death."

"Are you?"

He'd never really thought about it. How like Christina to cut to the center of the problem. He would like to say he had started moving on but he couldn't. "I don't know."

She studied him a moment. "I bet you do."

"They thought I kept to myself too much. They wanted me to visit old friends, go to the pub, or come to their house for parties."

"But you didn't, did you?"

He shook his head. "Mostly I saw my patients and stayed at home. Then it became one patient. Gold. That might have ended if William Guinness had not insisted he wanted me taking care of Gold." Even to Conor that sounded sad. "I've been around more people since I came here than I have been in a year."

"I guess them pushing you to come worked."

He gave her a wry smile. "I guess it did."

Christina's phone rang and she clicked the hands-free speaker in the truck. "Doctor Mobbs."

"This is Dr. Dillard at Churchill Downs. I was wondering if you could come by and see me sometime today at the clinic."

Christina's eyes widened. Maybe this was what she'd been waiting on. "Sure, I can be there in about thirty minutes."

"I will expect you then."

She hung up. To Conor she said, "I hope you don't mind a trip to the racetrack. I need to obviously have a conversation with Dr. Dillard."

"I don't mind at all. Do you know what it's about?" His eyes held concern.

"I hope it's about me being on staff during Derby week." Christina pushed down her excitement.

"Why does that matter so much to you?"

"For one thing it's an honor. It also says that I'm a good enough veterinarian to be a part of that group." She started the truck.

"And you doubt you are good enough?"

"No, but others might." She wanted to move off that subject. She wasn't ready to go into why working at the Downs was so important to her. Instead, she shared the reason she could utter. She wasn't ready to go into how she had disappointed her mother. How her mother had thought Christina had dragged their name in the mud with the business with Nelson when it made the news. "It's a golden opportunity for me to tell other veterinarians about my new program. They will hopefully refer our horses to my farm."

"I get that."

"The Derby is the greatest event in Kentucky each year. It's like the English have Ascot. Hundreds of thousands will be there in person, and millions will watch it on TV."

"I had no idea it was so big. The racetrack is massive."

She glanced at him. "You've been to Churchill Downs?"

"Yes. I had to go see about a stable for Gold. Check out where he would be staying. I made arrangements to have him examined and tested before he could be boarded there. I also checked in with the vet clinic to make sure I knew exactly what was expected testing-wise."

Before now she hadn't thought much about what Conor had been doing with his days. "You've been a busy guy. And here I thought you spent your days planning my meals."

He grinned. "That doesn't take me hours."

She smiled. "I'm glad because then I'd feel obligated to feel guilty."

They took the wide highway out of the rural area into

the large busy city of Louisville. She entered the Churchill Downs grounds and drove around to the backside.

"You've been here before?"

"Numerous times." She pulled into a parking spot near a large building.

"Do you mind if I come in with you?"

"No, that's fine." Christina didn't wait on him before she headed toward the door of the Churchill Downs Equine Medical Center.

"I want to check out the facilities up close." He caught up with her and followed her into the building.

"Then I'll see you in a few minutes," she said over her shoulder before she spoke to the woman behind a desk just inside the door. "I'm Christina Mobbs. I'm here to see Dr. Dillard."

"Give me just a minute. He's seeing a horse right now." The woman walked down a hall toward the back of the building.

Christina took a seat in one of the two plastic chairs against the wall in the small reception area. Conor sat beside her.

She clasped and unclasped her hands. She couldn't help being nervous.

He said softly, "Hey, you have no reason to be so nervous. You'll wear the skin off your hands."

She narrowed her eyes.

"From what I've observed of your work you're as good as anyone I've ever seen. You're excellent with the horses, and your veterinarian work is superb. Don't ever let anybody make you feel any differently. It'll be fine." He placed his hand over her wringing hands for a moment.

That tingle she had when he touched her shot through

her again. She gave him an unsure smile. "Thanks for that vote of confidence. It's been a long time since someone encouraged me."

A barrel-chested doctor walked toward them. Christina quickly stood. "Doctor Dillard, it's good to see you again."

"You, too," Dr. Dillard said. He glanced at Conor.

She turned to Conor. "I understand you've met Doctor O'Brian."

"Yes. Good to see you again." The two men shook hands. "Doctor O'Brian, please feel free to observe wherever you like while I speak with Doctor Mobbs. Doctor Mobbs, if you would come with me. We'll meet in my office."

Conor gave Christina a reassuring smile before she walked away with Dr. Dillard.

Christina appreciated Conor's encouragement. She'd had little of that in her life and even less in the past few years. Now that she could look back at it realistically, Nelson hadn't provided that, either. She had been the one who kept the farm and their relationship moving. Nelson rarely offered her help or encouragement. She'd wanted marriage and children. He dragged his feet. Why she'd waited until he almost destroyed her entire world to distance herself from him, she would never know.

She certainly hadn't looked to her mother for praise. Her father said little to contradict her mother. To Christina's surprise, Conor's kind words were the most she could remember hearing in a long time. It took a stranger from halfway around the world for her to start believing in herself again.

"This is more a closet than an office but it's the best they could give me out here," Dr. Dillard said as he led her through a doorway.

"It's not a problem." Christina entered the room.

"Doctor O'Brian seems like a good fella. Thank you for being willing to board the horse he's overseeing."

"My pleasure." Conor really had been a good house-guest. She couldn't stop herself from enjoying having another person around. And he wasn't hard to look at, either. It was nice to have someone in her corner, too. A surge of pleasure went through her at the memory of his supportive smile. "Gold is acclimating well. Doctor O'Brian has been good help as well."

"When I spoke to him the other day, he said he was pleased with staying at your farm. I'm glad to hear that." Dr. Dillard cleared his throat. "Why I asked you here is to speak to you about joining the vet team during Derby week."

Christina's heart beat faster. "I would appreciate the opportunity."

He nodded. "You'll be doing different assignments leading up to the race days and on those you'll be stationed along the racetrack."

"I look forward to helping out." At least she would get a chance to watch the races. Some veterinarians would remain in the barn area, unable to see anything.

Dr. Dillard's eyes turned concerned. "Will you be able to handle your practice and farm while being here for a week?"

"I'll make that work."

"You'll need to be here before daylight and you'll be staying until after dark." Dr. Dillard wore an earnest look.

She straightened. "That won't be a problem."

"There'll be over forty veterinarians here on Friday and Saturday. We'll have a big responsibility here."

"I'll be glad to be one of them." She meant it.

"And we'll be glad to have you. By the way, next week-end on Saturday night my wife and I are hosting a cookout at our place for the team of veterinarians working at the Downs during Derby week. You should get an invitation in the mail this week. Why don't you bring along Doctor O'Brian as well?"

Christina wasn't sure she wanted to show up as a couple at Dr. Dillard's party but she really didn't have a choice. "I'll be sure to ask him."

"And I'll see you for the party and then on the Monday morning afterward for an orientation meeting here at the Downs." Dr. Dillard smiled at her.

She returned it. "I'll be here."

Christina left the office with a light step. She could hardly wait to tell Conor. She reached the front to find him talking to the woman behind the desk. He left the woman with a smile and joined Christina. She continued out the door and stopped out of sight of those in the clinic.

"Well, are you going to be working the Derby?" he asked, facing her, anticipation in his eyes.

"Yes." She threw her arms around his neck. "I am."

Conor's arms came around her, holding her tight against his hard chest. She absorbed his heat and strength for a moment before she realized what she had done. Letting go, she placed her hands on his shoulders and stepped back. He let his hands fall to his sides.

Her face heated and she looked at the tips of her boots. "I'm sorry. I didn't mean to do that. I was just so excited to tell someone."

"Don't be. That's the nicest thing that has happened to me in a long time."

She glanced up. Conor watched her with a warm intensity that made her belly flutter. "Doctor Dillard wants me to bring you along to a party at his house next Saturday."

He hesitated and looked away before he put more space between them. "Let me think about it."

She hadn't realized until then how much she had liked the idea of their going to a party together, despite her own reservations. Did he just not like parties or was it that he didn't want to go with her? Either way his answer shouldn't have bothered her as much as it did.

"Are we headed home now or out to more stops?" Conor looked everywhere but at her.

"I'm going to stop in and see if my cousin is here. She sometimes helps out at the human clinic." Christina turned toward a small white building down the dirt and gravel road that led farther into the backside. "It's been a while since I've seen her."

He fell into step beside her. "This is really some place. The spires are impressive. You told me it was large, but I had no idea."

He acted as if nothing had happened a few minutes earlier. If Conor could do that so could she. "I love this place. My cousin's parents used to bring me here occasionally. Not on Derby Day but on weekends just to watch the horses run. I am still amazed by the beauty and majesty of the Thoroughbreds' movements."

"You make it sound like poetry."

She looked at him. "Isn't it?"

"I've never thought about it, but now I have I couldn't agree with you more. One thing we do share is the love of a good horse. There's nothing like watching a morning stretch."

"We call it the Breeze. That's one of the many reasons I can't just let old racehorses go. I want them to have another life after racing. We all deserve a second chance."

His eyes met hers. Admiration filled them. "I think it's a very admirable thing you're doing."

She stopped. "Thank you for that. I needed to hear it."

"You're welcome. You should be praised more often. You are a great vet. You really care about your patients." He grinned. "The only thing I can find you fail at is cooking. And housekeeping of course."

That didn't even begin to hurt her feelings. She laughed. "Yes, I fail at both. Much to my mother's chagrin. She would like me to be a homemaker and mother like her. I don't care much for the homemaking, but I would like to be a mother."

His eyes shadowed over and he looked away for a moment before he asked, "Your parents live close by?"

"No, actually in Florida. They retired and moved down there. But my mother stays in touch with her friends here and seems to know all the gossip before I do." She stopped in front of the medical clinic, a building with the door in the middle and two windows to each side. She opened the door. "Callie works here."

He followed her inside.

"Hi, is Callie around?" Christina asked the man behind the desk. At the sound of a squeal Christina looked down the hall. Callie hurried in Christina's direction with her arms open wide.

"To what do I owe this nice surprise?" She wrapped Christina in a hug.

They separated.

"I've been over to see Doctor Dillard."

"And?" Callie looked at Christina with an anxious expectation.

Christina straightened her shoulders and smiled. "I'll be seeing you around on Derby weekend."

"Well, good for you. I'm not really surprised. I think you're more concerned about what happened than others are."

Christina huffed. "Tell that to the licensing commission. They seemed pretty uptight about it last year."

Callie waved a hand as if she could brush it all away. "That was then and this is now." She looked past Christina to Conor leaning casually against the wall. "Can I help you?"

"He's with me. Callie, this is Conor O'Brian. He's visiting from Ireland. He's staying at the farm seeing about one of the racehorses."

Callie's brows rose as she studied Conor a moment. "Hello."

"Hi." Conor stepped forward but stopped behind Christina.

"Staying at the farm." She had made it a statement instead of a question. Callie studied Conor keenly for a moment.

"Just while Gold acclimates to the weather and settles from the trip over." Why did Christina feel she had to justify Conor's presence? Because it had been over a year since she had anything to do with a man. It was time to get Callie's mind on something else. "How're you doing?"

"Well. Just getting prepared for the onslaught of people for the Derby. As much as I love the races it's super busy around here."

"This isn't even your place to oversee anymore," Christina said.

"I know but I help out when I'm needed. You're lucky to catch me here today. Langston is running a test today or I wouldn't be here."

"Langston is her husband, who works with preventing brain injuries," Christina explained to Conor.

Callie said, "I can't believe we live so close and don't see each other more."

"We'll have to do something about that. I hear you and Langston are really doing some innovative things with horse-and-rider safety." Christina liked Callie's Texas husband and appreciated his life-changing work.

"I like to think so. Only problem is we seem to work all the time, but we love it."

"Y'all are supposed to be on your honeymoon." Christina couldn't prevent the wistfulness from entering her voice. At one time she believed she'd be married by now. Maybe even have a child.

A silly grin formed on Callie's lips. "Sure, we are."

What would it be like to have someone act like that just at the thought of her? She looked at Conor, who stood with such patience, waiting on her. That wasn't a direction she should consider.

Callie spoke to Conor. "I hope you're enjoying your stay in America."

"I am."

"I'm sure it's quite different from Ireland," Callie said.

"That it is, but it has its appeals just the same." He glanced at Christina.

Callie's eyes brightened and she studied Christina a moment. "It does now."

Her face heated. Callie had fallen in love with her husband a year ago and she thought everyone should be in love.

A man holding his hand in the palm of his other one hurried into the clinic.

"I got to go." Callie stepped to the man and led him down the hall. "Be sure to pop in and say hi during the Derby."

"Will do." Christina pushed out the door.

Conor walked beside her on the way to her truck. "Did you and Callie grow up together?"

"We saw a lot of each other. Back then she was determined she was going to be a vet but changed her mind and now she does medical research with her husband on sports-related head injuries."

"That sounds like something beneficial to the industry. I do know there are too many head injuries."

They walked toward her truck. "They're doing some really great innovative work. I'm proud of them."

He reached for the passenger door. "I'm sure they are proud of the work you do or plan to do. Your plan for horses is to be admired as well."

How did this man manage in a few words to lessen the self-loathing she had felt for so long?

CHAPTER FOUR

CONOR APPROACHED THE BARN. He'd thought more than once over the past two days about what Christina had said about everyone deserving a second chance. Wasn't that what he needed, too? His siblings had accused him of not moving on. For so long he hadn't felt he could or even wanted to, but since coming to stay at Christina's a week ago, that had slowly been changing.

Conor wished he had a better idea of what caused Christina distress. He might be able to help. But why did it matter? This was someone he hardly knew, and he would be leaving in a couple of weeks. He had no investment here.

He entered the barn and walked through to the other side and out the doors into the sunlight. He found Christina bathing a horse. He stepped up beside her. "I figured I'd find you here."

She jumped and turned. The water hose she held soaked him from middle to his knees.

Horror flashed over her face. She dropped the hose and pulled the earbud from her ear. "I'm so sorry. You scared me. I didn't hear you."

He gave her a thin-lipped smile.

Then she doubled over in giggles.

The sound filled him with something best called happiness. He loved the tinkling sound. "Did you do that on purpose?"

Christina took control of her laughing and straightened. She looked at him and busted into giggles again.

Conor reached for the hose, but her booted foot came down on it before he could pick it up. She held it to the ground. He pursed his lips and glared. With a swift movement, he lunged. He would show her. Christina's eyes went wide seconds before he wrapped his arms around hers and secured her against his wet front. He held her there letting his damp clothes seep into hers.

"Stop. You're getting me wet." She wiggled, trying to get away.

His manhood reacted to her struggle. Something he'd experienced little of in the past few years until he had met Christina. It both thrilled and worried him. Yet, he didn't release his hold. He teased, "Who got who wet first and then laughed at them?"

She continued to squirm. "I didn't mean to."

"But you meant to laugh at me," he goaded.

She went still. Her gaze met his. He held it, watching her eyes shift from determination to awareness to questioning. Did she realize how aroused he was?

The need to kiss her had grown with having her so close, touching him; the days of being near her had compounded themselves into a need to taste her.

She blinked. "I did do that." The giggles bubbled again. "I'm sorry. You should have seen your face."

"I was too busy feeling my clothes being soaked." He tugged her closer.

Mischief filled her eyes. She said with complete innocence, "I didn't mean to."

His look held hers. He made himself not focus on her lips. "Maybe not but I'm still wet."

And desiring her. The feeling had been building for days. He'd pushed it down, shoved it away, but there it had been every time he was around Christina. Maybe if he got the unknown out of the way it wouldn't return.

Would she let him kiss her? What if she refused him? She had her own ghosts holding her back. Did he dare take the chance she would reject him? How would he know if he didn't try? He might regret it for the rest of his life if he didn't. There was enough of those in his life already.

His head lowered. His lips touched hers. He released her arms, his hands moving to rest lightly on her hips. Making her captive was not what he wanted. He needed her to want his kiss. Her hands ran up his chest to settle on his shoulders. An electric thrill shot through him at her touch. Christina wasn't pushing him away. She wanted it, too.

He deepened the kiss. Christina returned it. He pressed her closer.

Conor understood then how he had been fooling himself about not needing a woman. How quickly Christina had made his excuses lies. Every nerve ending in his body hummed with awareness of her. She made him feel alive once more.

She sighed and wrapped her arms around his neck, pressing herself into his throbbing length. Conor slowly kissed the seam of her lips. His tongue traced it, requesting entrance. Pleasure washed through him when she opened her mouth. He savored the warm moment, then plunged forward, eager for more. She welcomed him. His hands caressed her hips and circled to cup her behind, lifting her to him.

He would take all she would offer him. His body hummed

like it hadn't in too long, in ways he had forgotten existed. Christina had managed to make him push past his pain.

The whinny of the horse nearby broke them apart.

Christina looked as shocked as he felt. He had to straighten this out. Say something. Reassure her he wouldn't take advantage of her. "I'm sorry. That was inappropriate. I shouldn't have done that. Excuse me."

Disbelief turned disappointment filled her eyes. A flicker of hurt flashed in them before he turned and walked off, guilt washing over him.

Christina watched Conor stalk away, stunned. What had just happened? With him. With her. This wasn't something she'd seen coming. Or had she? Wasn't she attracted to him? She would be lying if she said she hadn't noticed his wide shoulders, his beautiful eyes, or how supportive of her he had been. And that list didn't include his accent that sent shivers down her spine any time he spoke. That had her thinking things she shouldn't. Before going to bed and in her dreams.

Still, she had never expected him to kiss her. Apparently, he hadn't anticipated it, either. Conor acted disgusted that he had kissed her, that he had made the first move. She didn't appreciate that at all.

Having been used before by Nelson and not measuring up to her mother's expectations enough in her life, Christina had no intentions of feeling that way again. Then along came Conor and she had opened herself up once more to rejection. He had slipped through a crack of crazy loneliness, and she'd welcomed him, basking in the feeling of being admired.

She picked up the hose and ran the water over the horse's back. Picking up the sponge, she soaped the horse down.

Maybe their interaction had been a bad idea but the kiss had been amazing. Perfect, in fact. His lips had brushed hers gently then he had crushed her to him as if he might never let her go. In a brief amount of time he had made her feel wanted, desired—necessary. It was as if he sensed what she needed and had agreed to gift it to her.

Then he had abruptly left her. Lost and alone. And not sure all she had felt had been true.

She took in a deep breath of air and let it out slowly. Conor hadn't been completely unaffected. His arousal had been evident between them. That gave her some sense of satisfaction.

A few minutes later she heard the sound of his truck being cranked then the tires over the gravel of the drive. He had left.

He did not return by that evening. She saw to Gold when she made her nightly round.

She had the light off in her room, but she wasn't asleep when Conor returned.

Conor came in quietly, went to his room. He must have taken his boots off because she heard his padded feet in the hall outside her door. His footsteps stopped there.

She held her breath. Would he knock on her door? Was he hoping she was still awake?

Long, lingering moments later, the shower in the bath came on.

Christina rolled her face into the pillow and moaned.

The next morning before breakfast Conor went looking for Christina. It was no surprise he found her in the barn. As he approached, she continued to brush the horse's leg.

From the tension in her shoulders, she was aware he stood

nearby. He swallowed hard being fully mindful that she deserved an apology for his actions, during and after their kiss. He shouldn't have done it to begin with and he shouldn't have treated her like she was a mistake.

"Christina?"

"Yes?"

"Can we talk? Clear the air." He stepped closer.

"There's nothing to talk about." She didn't even bother to look at him.

"You know there is."

She faced him. "I've been kissed before. No big deal."

Conor wanted to take her by the shoulders and shake her. Of course, it was more than a kiss. He could still feel the sweetness of her lips beneath his. Had dreamed of doing so again. He cleared his throat. "I shouldn't have walked off like that. I didn't mean to hurt you."

"Don't worry about it. I get it." She didn't look at him.

Conor didn't see how she couldn't worry about it. He had hurt her. "I said some things I shouldn't have. It's just that I promised to be true to my wife."

Her chin dropped and her eyes narrowed as she looked at him as if he had two heads. "I thought she had died."

"She has but I promised to be true."

A compassionate look came to her eyes. Her voice sank low. "Conor, she would want you to go on living. A kiss doesn't mean you're desecrating her memory. It doesn't mean you loved her any less."

He had made a promise he would always be true to Louisa. Not be like his father. But hadn't he used that to build a wall to protect his heart? If he let it down, he might get hurt again. He wasn't sure he could live through that again. Even for Christina.

Christina untied the horse from the post and led it out of the barn.

He watched as she released the animal into the pasture. She slapped the animal on the hip. "Go and have a good day."

The horse ran into the field with his tail in the air. Wouldn't it be nice if he could do that? Feel free for just a little while?

Conor came to stand beside her. "You care for them like they're your own."

"While they're here, they're my own." She looked at him as if that included him as well.

A lump formed in his chest. "Thank you for caring for Gold last night."

"Not a problem." She made it sound as if it wasn't. Is that the way she saw him, too?

"I know what I do with Gold is important but I'm thankful to you for reminding me of what it is to be a vet again. I've been babysitting one racehorse for so long I've started to forget what it's like to do the dirty part of vet care. The part that makes you feel alive."

"Well, I have plenty to do here to make you feel alive."

Conor chuckled. How like Christina to take him literally. "Let me check on Gold and give him a good walking and I'll be at your service. Are we good, Christina?"

"We are good."

She sounded like it, but he still couldn't be sure. He would just have to let time tell.

He spent the next hour seeing to Gold. Every once in a while, he caught sight of Christina swinging her hips as she listened to music and worked around the barn. She sang to the horses as well. He couldn't help but smile. Something he'd started to do more often since coming to America.

When it started to rain he brought Gold inside and put him in his stall. With that done he joined Christina in cleaning out stalls and replenishing hay. Every once in a while, she would remind him of something he'd missed. Still, he enjoyed the companionship, which he hadn't had in a long time.

Maybe now was the time to take a step forward. To move on with life. Couldn't he be friends with a woman and be true to Louisa at the same time? His family and friends, even Christina, had said it was time for him to move on. To have a second chance. Why shouldn't he start now? Christina had the kind heart to understand. He enjoyed her company. He couldn't think of anyone he'd rather spend time with.

He cleared his throat. It had been years since he'd done this. And after yesterday he wasn't sure she would agree. "Christina."

"Yes?" She turned to face him.

"I was wondering if you would like to go out to dinner this evening?"

Christina took a moment before she spoke. "I uh…don't think that's a good idea."

She had turned him down. He couldn't blame her after he'd stepped over the line. "Dinner. Nothing more."

"We shouldn't." She returned to using the pitchfork to spread hay.

"Probably not. But I'm asking you to dinner between friends. Something to repay you for letting me stay here. It would also give me a night off from cooking." All of that was true but he still couldn't help but want more. He liked her. Couldn't seem to stay away from her.

She turned. "I'm sorry. I shouldn't have assumed."

"Not a problem." Apparently, his statement about not cooking caught her attention.

She confirmed that a second later. "I'm sorry. I should have thought about all the time you've spent in the kitchen. I imagine you'd like a night off. Thank you. I would like to go to dinner with you."

The knot of anxiousness between his shoulders eased. He had no idea until then he had been afraid she might say no. Tonight he would try to make up for mistreating her the previous evening.

That evening Conor waited in the kitchen. He forced himself not to pace. He was out of practice when it came to going out with a woman even if she was just a friend. He had not been out alone with a non-family member in years. But this wasn't a date, he reminded himself. Yet, it felt like a date.

Christina entered the kitchen dressed in a floral sleeveless dress with a V-neck that showed a hint of cleavage. The fabric hugged her breasts and fell in waves around her hips. Conor's mouth went dry. He forced a swallow. She was lovely like a new filly in the field.

Her auburn hair flowed around her shoulders. Pink touched her cheeks as she ran her hands down her dress. "Too much?"

"Not at all. But you look like we might have to call this a date."

Bright spots of red formed on her cheeks. "I don't get many chances to wear a dress, so I thought I'd wear one tonight. My mother would be proud of me."

"I'm glad you chose a dress." His gaze went to her legs, which were trim and muscular. Just perfect.

"Thank you."

"After you." He directed her toward the door.

As they exited through the back door of the house, Conor took a moment to appreciate the soft swing of her hips. *Not a date*, he repeated to himself. "I'll drive."

"You're one of those guys."

"I guess I am." He opened her door and waited for her to settle inside his truck.

"That was nice of you but not necessary."

"You work hard day in and day out. You deserve to be treated special on occasion." He went to the driver's seat and slipped behind the wheel. "You smell nice."

"Not of manure and horse?"

"I have no problem with the smell of barn, but this suits you better." He needed to slow down, or he'd be right back where he was yesterday if she would allow him to kiss her.

She clasped her hands in her lap. "Are you going to spend the entire evening embarrassing me?"

"I just might if you continue to blush."

She pushed at her cheeks. "I've always hated the way my emotions show on my face."

"I rather like knowing how you're feeling." He enjoyed knowing where he stood with her. Where was the guilt he had been feeling over the kiss? One look at Christina in a dress had him thinking of other things.

"Conor, this is a friendly outing."

"You're right. We're going to be two people enjoying each other's company over dinner." He turned out of the drive.

"Where're we going to do that?" she asked when he pulled onto the main highway.

"I went through Versailles the other day and did not have time to stop. I thought we would go there if you had no objection."

She hesitated a moment then said, "That sounds fine."

He glanced at her. "If you'd rather go elsewhere, we can do that."

She placed her hands back in her lap. "No, Versailles will be nice."

Twenty minutes later Christina walked beside him down the main street of the quaint town with its brick courthouse in the middle of an intersection. The 1940s storefronts had been maintained with care. Hot pink flowers hung in baskets from the lampposts. A rosy glow fell over everything as the sun lowered.

Christina had covered her bare shoulders with a sweater while he enjoyed the warmth with his sleeves rolled up his forearms. He resisted putting his hand at her back. Yet, he remained close but not touching. He had already gotten in over his head where she was concerned. Was it from his forced proximity to Christina or was the attraction that strong?

He remained conflicted over his feelings for her, yet he couldn't keep his distance from Christina.

Christina, to his knowledge, had never made a movement he could have called a stroll. Tonight was no different. It was as if she were a horse pulling on the reins to go faster.

"If we don't hurry up, there might not be any tables. Then we'll have a wait."

"I'm enjoying the stroll with you." He wanted to spend as much time as he could with her. That way maybe he would better understand this temptation between them.

"What?"

"It's about slowing down and appreciating life. Something you find difficult, I know." He had learned to do that. Having lost someone special, he knew about appreciating time. He would be leaving Christina in another week and a half, and he wanted what time he could have with her. His footsteps faltered. That idea hit him like a kick in the chest. Since when did spending time with Christina become so important?

What about Louisa? Christina was right. Louisa would want his happiness.

From what he understood the week of the Derby would be busy. He would be lucky if he saw Christina at all. Sadness fell over him. They didn't have much time to explore what was between them. Did she want to?

"What makes you think you know me that well?" She sounded irritated by the idea he might see something she didn't want others to see.

"Because I've watched you over the last week and I've gotten to know you pretty well."

Her eyes widened.

Conor took her elbow to gently move her out of the way of a group walking toward them. "Now, where would you like to eat? It can be anywhere."

"There's a nice restaurant right down here on the corner." She pointed ahead of them.

"Then that is where we will go." It was the first time he'd used a firm tone with her, but he was not going to let her change her mind. The woman really did need to take time to enjoy life some.

She huffed. "You're not the boss of me."

"No, I am not, but you are my dinner date...uh friend.

I like them to have a smile on their face when they eat with me."

"Says the man that showed up at my farm a little more than a week ago looking like a thundercloud."

He smiled. "My brother and sister said something like that before I left."

She patted his arm. "With good reason."

They paused in front of the restaurant. It had matching front windows on either side of the dark wooden door. On both the windows was etched the word *Thoroughbred*. Above that was the figure of a horse stretched out in a run. In the corners were filigrees. Light from inside spilled out onto the sidewalk.

He held the door open for Christina. She balked at entering. "Maybe we should go somewhere else."

Was this about the same thing that had her hesitating on the ride over? Did it have to do with him or had she seen someone she didn't want to face? Her expression said she might be uncomfortable with the idea but she quickly recovered.

She inhaled a breath as if bracing herself before she stepped inside.

"Hey, Christina," the woman behind the hostess desk said.

"Hello, Jean. Do you have a booth available?" Christina asked with a note of forced brightness.

The woman smiled. "Sure. Just take a spot wherever you like."

"Thanks." Christina didn't wait on him but headed toward the far side of the room away from the door and traffic. She slid into a booth constructed to look like a barn stall as if relieved to get there.

Who was she hiding from?

He ran a hand down the smooth pieces of wood that made their booth. "These look like the real thing."

"They are from an old barn that was torn down near mine." She looked at the table.

"I like it. This old-world work reminds me of home." He took a seat on the red cushion and settled in front of her. "This is an interesting place."

A teenage waitress stood at the end of the table and handed them a plastic-covered menu.

During their meal a number of people casually spoke to Christina as they were coming to their tables or leaving. Each time she acted unsure when they approached then pleasantly surprised at their greeting. Just what was her problem?

Conor settled back in the booth watching Christina. "Apparently, you are well-known around here."

Her eyes flickered up to meet his look. "Yes. I grew up in Versailles. But that can have its disadvantages."

Those would be...? "True, but I bet it can have advantages as well."

She crossed her arms on the table, looking directly at him. "Have you lived in the same spot most of your life?"

"Yes."

"Then you must know what it's like for everyone to know your business good or bad."

"I do." His home was a place where everyone knew his pain. Like that his wife didn't love him enough to stay alive. That his father cheated on his mother. These memories walked daily with him. The expressions on towns-folk's faces held pity. The ones he hid from. Yet, it was home. "I've lived in the same village my entire life except for when I left for school." He needed a change in subject. "This is the kind of place that reminds me of a pub back home. But only quieter."

She looked beyond them. "It'll get noisier later. I've never been to a pub."

"Never? Our pubs are where the whole community hangs out. You couldn't live in Ireland without finding your pub. Have you ever thought about visiting Ireland?"

"No, but I've always wanted to travel. With the farm and horses to care for it's hard to get away. Maybe one day."

He turned the water glass in his hands. "I guess it doesn't ever let up. If you do come let me know and I'll show you around."

"I doubt that will happen any time soon. I'm trying to build up a business." Her voice held a wistful note.

"Why are you trying to do that instead of just having your regular practice? I would think it would be enough."

Christina let out a breath slowly. She leaned back against the booth. "Well, I sort of just fell into it. My ex-partner had the idea. When he left, I just couldn't close it down."

"But that doesn't mean that you don't need a life outside of here." He looked around the room.

She leaned back and pinned him with a look. "Is this the man whose family had to force him to come to America?"

The woman didn't mind hitting hard. "You have a point."

She smiled. For once that evening, she looked relaxed. "Tell me about Ireland."

He smiled. "I think you would like it. It reminds me very much of Kentucky with its rolling hills and green grass. The people are friendly. We've got stone walls, where you've got all these wooden fences, but we love our horses. We've got cooler temperatures."

She grinned. "You love the place as much as I love here."

"I do love it." But oddly, he hadn't missed it like he had when he had first arrived.

Christina stepped out of the restaurant to the streetlights burning. She had enjoyed her dinner with Conor more than she'd imagined. She had gone to extra trouble dressing and his reaction had been worth the trouble. Then to have his complete attention focused on her had heated her skin. More than once her heart had skipped a beat when his hand had brushed hers as they walked down the street or reached for something at the same time at the table.

She had to stop herself a couple of times from staring at his lips.

The only negative of the evening had been her reaction to going into the Thoroughbred. She had misjudged her strength in being able to handle returning. It had been a regular place for her and Nelson to join friends. Those who disappeared when she had been in trouble.

She'd had a choice to admit that to Conor or make herself hold her head high. The latter won. Being with Conor gave her extra reassurance. She was with a handsome man who would support and protect her.

How did she know that? Because he'd done nothing but show that since she had met him. She believed he was a good man. But hadn't her judgment been off before?

"A few people I've met have mentioned there is a small racetrack around here and that there is racing tonight. Would you like to go?"

She couldn't go there. The urge to shake her head wildly filled her but she didn't do it. What would she do if someone said the wrong thing in front of Conor? She would die.

"I don't know. I should really get home and make sure the horses are settled for the night."

"I can help you do that when we get back. I'd like to see how a race is run before the Derby."

She quickly released a sigh. "Okay, we can go for a few races."

In the car he said, "How about giving me directions."

"Turn left. It's only a few miles out of town. There's a large sign on the highway." They were walking toward the racetrack when she said, "These are the horses that didn't make the Kentucky Derby cut or probably never would but the locals coming here have fun watching the horses race. It's also a good place for the jockeys to learn and get experience."

She led Conor to the entrance where a woman sat at a portable table with a metal box at hand.

"Hi, Christina. We haven't seen you around in a while." The woman took the money Conor offered her.

Christina stiffened. She was surprised Emily sounded genuinely glad to see her. "Hello. It's nice to see you again."

They continued toward the stands.

Conor walked beside her. "Apparently, they know you here, too."

"Yes, I used to work here on the weekends." She led the way to a seat in one of the two metal bleachers going to the second row from the top. "I like to see. I love the horses, but I also love coming to the races. I've always enjoyed the small track. Sometimes I think they're more fun than the big races. Here you can really see the horses. And the crowd likes watching them instead of being seen themselves."

Conor sat beside her just out of touching distance but

close enough she could feel his heat. Her skin tingled with his nearness.

"Tell me about your races. I understand they're different from ours."

"There will be several races tonight but lots more on Derby Day, including the Derby. The horses run ten furlongs, or about one and a half US miles. Only three-year-olds run on a dirt track. These tonight will be very similar to those at Churchill Downs on Kentucky Derby Day."

"Do you bet much?" Conor looked toward the betting boxes.

"Almost never. When I'm working they don't allow it. Therefore, I make it a practice not to do it." She had already had a close call with the law once and she wouldn't give the racing commission a reason to question her behavior again.

"Christina." A woman called her from the aisle of the stands.

"Hi, Lucy. It's good to see you."

"You, too. How have you been?" Lucy sounded sincere.

"Just working a lot. How about you?" Lucy had been her friend.

"Busy, too. I was sorry about what happened to you. I haven't had a chance to tell you that. I should've been a better friend and believed in you." Lucy's look didn't waver.

"Thank you for saying that." Even now it was nice.

Lucy smiled. "Well, I better get back to work. I hope you come around more often."

Christina said to Conor, "Sorry I didn't introduce you. Lucy runs this racetrack."

She had been Christina's best friend, but Nelson's lies had fractured that as well. That, Christina didn't plan to dwell on. She'd been enjoying herself tonight. Conor had been a wonderful dinner companion. She didn't want to talk about the past and ruin the time they had together.

Conor looked out toward the track. "This reminds me of our local course at home."

Christina followed his gaze. There weren't any barns just horse trailers hitched to big trucks in a large lot off in a distance. The track was grass. It had been cut and trimmed. There was a well-used horse gate stationed across the track.

"Really? How is that? I understand your races are a cross between a steeplechase and a regular race."

"Some of them are." He leaned forward, resting his elbows on his knees.

"I have seen horses jumping on TV but I have no idea what happens in your races. I bet it makes for an interesting experience with the combo of jumping and running."

"It does." Conor intensely watched the activity in the area. He was a man who looked at the details.

"That certainly adds an element of danger to the event."

"It does but it also adds to the challenge." He commented without looking at her.

"I could see your point there. It sounds rather exciting." She would like to see one someday.

"We like to think so. We don't have such a large spectator area as Churchill Downs. Our seating is simpler. When the horses come up to the starting line people pour to the outside, and when they're not racing, they go inside under the stands to the bar and to place their bets."

"That's interesting. Our attendees pretty much live in the stands. You'll be amazed on Derby Day the number of people there. The pomp and circumstance involved, the traditions."

He looked at her and grinned. "I look forward to it. And Gold winning his race."

She had to admit she would be pulling for the horse. "Wouldn't that be exciting? You'll enjoy the Oaks race on Friday when the three-year-old fillies run. The stands will be almost as full and it's all day as well."

"But I guess you'll be busy."

Conor sounded disappointed she wouldn't be sharing it with him. It was nice to have someone want to share her company.

The announcer called over the microphone. "The horses are in the gate." Seconds later he announced, "And they're off."

The crowd stood. The horses ran around the first curve.

Christina went up on her toes in an effort to see better. When she wobbled, she grasped Conor's forearm so she wouldn't fall. His arm went around her waist when she climbed on the bench to stand on it. She spoke to Conor without looking. "Sorry, I can't see. I do miss having a large television screen like they have at Churchill Downs. I can't tell how they're doing on the backside."

Even in the distance the thunder of the horses' hooves could be heard. The horses came around the second back turn.

Christina stretched to see. She registered the tightening of Conor's arm. He wouldn't let her fall.

The crowd grew louder along with the pounding of hooves. The horses made the front curve and entered the part of the track in front of them. Unable to help herself Christina started jumping.

"They're coming down the stretch," the announcer said.

The crowd cheered as the horses thundered across the finish line.

Christina whooped then threw her arms around Conor's neck. His arms wrapped around her waist and held her. He grinned up at her with amazement sparkling in his eyes. Reality struck her. She pushed away from him and stepped down from the bench, pushing her dress into place. "I'm sorry. I should've warned you I get carried away."

He chuckled. "I have no problem with that. My arm may be bruised in the morning but it will have been worth it."

What must he think? After yesterday's kiss and her re-action and then she throws herself at him. She needed to put some distance between them. She patted his upper arm. "I'm sorry. I didn't mean to hurt you."

His arm squeezed her closer. "I enjoyed it. It's nice to see you happy."

During the next race she tried to restrain herself but didn't manage to do much better than she had earlier. Conor grinned then offered his hand to help her up on the bleacher and supported her once more. She looked forward to his protection with each race. Apparently, she wouldn't be suc-cessful in keeping her distance.

In the last race the horses rounded the last turn toward the finish line, one horse bumped another then another stum-bled into another before two horses went down.

Christina held her breath. She didn't see something like this often, but she had seen it before. It didn't end up well.

The jockeys moved quickly to get away from the horses. Jockeys still in the saddle continued for the finish line. The fallen horses kicked to stand while the racetrack staff ran onto the field. One staff member ran out from the sideline and grabbed the reins and tugged the most active horse's head, encouraging him to his feet. With one swift movement he stood.

The other horse lay on the ground, unmoving. In less than ten seconds a large blue screen had been placed so that the crowd couldn't see what was happening.

CHAPTER FIVE

CONOR ALWAYS HATED to see a screen go up. It didn't bode well for the horse.

Christina brushed behind him on her way down the bench toward the steps.

"Hey, where are you going?"

She pointed down.

It was then he saw her friend Lucy with her hand in the air, waving Christina down to the track. Conor didn't hesitate to follow. He made his way around people who had stepped out into the stairs.

He joined the women just as Lucy said with panic in her voice, "I could use your help."

She didn't wait on Christina to answer.

She followed, keeping pace behind Lucy. Conor was behind Christina as they hurried toward where the accident had happened.

Lucy said over her shoulder as they moved. "Our vet for tonight had an emergency and just left. The replacement is on the way but isn't here yet. It's a blessing you were here tonight."

They reached the track. There they went through a gate and loped across the grass track to where the screen stood. The need for it meant the horse would probably be put down. Unfortunately, accidents were part of the sport. An ugly part.

He followed Christina behind the screen to a scene he had expected. Christina went immediately to her knees beside the horse. She patted his neck. Fear filled the animal's large dark eyes. "Easy, boy, help is here. Easy."

Conor dropped down beside her. He ran his hand over the horse's back legs. Christina did the same on the front.

"I can't find a break here." She continued her examination.

Conor finished his. "I don't find one here, either."

Christina patted the horse's neck once again. She moved her hand over the horse's shoulder and along his back. "No obvious broken bones. Let's see if we can get him up on his feet."

"Let me get around on the other side so I can help push him." Conor moved opposite her.

Christina took the reins and stood. The horse kicked his feet. "Okay, boy, let's see you stand."

A couple of grooms joined Conor. "We're ready."

"Easy, boy. Slow and easy." She tugged on the reins. Conor pushed the horse. The men beside him did as well.

All the while, Christina continued to talk to the scared animal. Suddenly, the horse kicked and rolled and came to its feet. Conor stepped back to where he could see the horse's movements. He did not see a problem.

"Conor, do you see any issues?"

"No. He looks good to me."

"We'll give him a moment for his head to quit spinning." She stroked the nose of the horse, who settled before their eyes. "Now we're going take a little walk around," Christina said to the horse then led him in a circle.

While she did, Conor watched every movement the horse made for a limp or hesitation. With the next slow turn he saw it. "There it is. Right foreleg."

Christina stopped the horse. She handed the reins to a groom. "Slow walk."

The groom nudged the horse forward.

She stood beside Conor. "I see it now. Let's get it wrapped up and secure. Then he'll need X-rays."

An older man ran around the screen. He came to an abrupt stop. He demanded as he looked at Christina, "What are you doing here?"

Christina stiffened beside Conor. Who was this guy? Why was he speaking to Christina that way?

"Lucy asked me to help."

"We don't want you here. The racetrack doesn't need any more trouble because of you." He glared at her.

"I understand how you feel about that, but that's not the case here. I was vindicated."

Vindicated? What was she talking about? Conor stepped closer.

She glanced at him. He stopped. "Doctor Victor," she said to the man, "I'll go but first you need to know that the horse has an issue with the right front foreleg. It is barely detectable to the eye. X-rays will be required."

"I can handle this. Thank you." Dr. Victor turned his back to her.

Conor felt her tremble. "Christina, I think we're done here."

Her attention didn't leave the horse and the movements of the man, but she didn't argue. Conor took her hand and led her away. They walked out the gate to the parking lot. At the car she got in without saying a word.

He didn't start the car. Instead, he turned to face her. "You want to tell me what that was all about?"

"Not really."

He watched her a moment then nodded and started the car. He knew from experience that if someone didn't want to talk, he couldn't make them. He had been the same with his siblings. He pulled out of the gravel parking lot.

"You aren't going to try any harder than that to find out?" She almost sounded disappointed.

Conor glanced at her. "You'll tell me when you are ready."

"I guess you deserve some explanation."

She made it sound as if she wasn't convinced he did.

"It's not a nice story."

He looked at her again. "I've heard ugly stories before."

She started slowly. "About a year and a half ago all those people who spoke to me this evening had stopped doing so."

"Why?" That had to have hurt her.

"Because they thought I had been stealing and selling drugs. In fact, I almost lost my license. If I hadn't had the paperwork to prove I had followed the rules, I would have had the racing commission on me. Doctor Victor, the man who just came up, was on the board then. I came closer than I ever want to again to losing my license."

Now Conor understood the interaction between them. "So what happened?"

"My ex. Who lived with me for four years. Who had access to my medicines. Who said he loved me but pointed his finger at me when the authorities started asking questions."

Conor wanted to punch something on her behalf. The pain in her voice made her ex a prime candidate. "What was he doing with the drugs? Taking them or selling them?"

"Both. To make matters worse he gambled on the horses,

which is a no-no and was stealing to pay his gambling debt. What made it worse was I thought he loved me. That we were going to get married and start a family."

He winced. Marriage and family. What he had once wanted. But no longer. "I get why working at the Derby is so important to you now. It's your way of proving you aren't the person everyone said you were."

"Yeah. Regaining my good reputation is important to me in general but to my work with horses as well. People need to trust me. Horse racing is a small world. And to start a new business in it is difficult. What made me really mad was I was too stupid to see what he was doing. I trusted him. I can't trust my judgment anymore."

"I can see why. I'm sorry that happened to you." She had endured more than she should have.

"Things are better now. Even as hard as it was to walk into the racetrack tonight, it felt good to have people speak to me. I'm starting to rebuild my reputation."

"I haven't known you long but I think you are doing just fine. It takes time." He certainly knew that well. Three years later he had just started working through his wife's death. He took Christina's hand and squeezed it. "I know I would have missed out if I'd never met you."

Christina appreciated his warmth. Conor's words felt like a hot drink flowing through her. He made her want to believe him. She looked at his handsome profile. He was a nice man.

Conor continued to hold her hand. Gently, he rubbed the top of it with the pad of his thumb. "You have to be true to yourself. You know you are honest. You can't carry others' mistakes as yours."

"To say that is one thing. To live it is another." She relaxed in her seat, appreciating his reassurance.

"You shouldn't have had to deal with all that."

"I was the one that should have noticed or maybe subconsciously I did, but didn't want to know."

"Nor can you be perfect and all-knowing."

Her mother had certainly expected that of her. Do it better, be better, do it just so. Christina hadn't ever felt like she measured up. The thing with Nelson just proved she never would. Here Conor was telling her that she didn't have to do more than be herself. "Thanks for the vote of confidence. You have no idea what the means to me."

"Now I understand why you are so particular about counting your medicine cabinet."

"Yeah, I keep a strict count now. I take no chances." She wouldn't be put in a position of explaining herself again.

"Being super vigilant isn't a bad thing. What isn't healthy is obsessing over it. It's past time for you to move forward."

"You don't think I already know all of that?" Her words had a sharp note to them.

"Oh, I'm sure you do but you need to be reminded of it." He grinned.

They remained in their own thoughts the rest of the way home.

Conor pulled behind the house and shut off the car.

"I need to check on the horses." She was out of the car and at the back door before he caught up with her.

He called, "Hey, wait a minute. You're not running from me, are you?"

She looked at him, her eyes watering. "I don't know. Maybe I'm running from myself."

He cupped her cheek. "You have no reason to be afraid of me. I'm your friend, Christina. You can trust me."

And she knew she could. Christina loved the feel of Conor's skin touching hers. She wanted to lean in to his warmth and reassurance. But if she did, it would soon be gone. She couldn't let herself need it. "I know. Come on, we need to see about the horses."

He sighed, letting his fingertips trail across her cheek. "Yes, the horses."

It had rained while they were gone. They changed into their rubber boots and walked out to the barn. Conor went to see about Gold while she went through her nightly routine. He waited at the barn doors when he finished.

Christina flipped off the inside lights. Conor helped her close and secure the doors. The outside security light formed a subdued glow around them.

"You know, you're doing yourself a disservice. You have to know how amazing you are."

"Thank you. That was a nice thing to say. I'm the one who should be thanking you for your support tonight. For a moment there I thought you were gonna pick up a sword and shield. Maybe I should move away from here so I can leave it all behind."

"Take my word for it, it doesn't work like that. I've left a country behind and it is still here with me."

"You miss your wife, don't you?" Christina couldn't help asking.

"Every day."

What would it be like to be loved so completely? To know that another person had your back no matter what. That you were enough for them.

"I can say that it eases. But you do carry it around with

you all the time. Coming here helped. I didn't think it would, but it did."

"I'm glad. I just don't want to forget what can happen if you trust too much and mess up again."

Christina stopped, watching him. She had been so embarrassed in front of him tonight but instead of turning against her he'd stepped forward as if he would fight for her honor. More than that, he had listened, really listened to her. For that, she could kiss him. "Thank you for being a nice guy."

Placing her hands on his shoulders, she went up on her toes and gave him a soft kiss on the lips. She stepped back.

Conor looked at her a second before he pulled her against him. His lips found hers. She leaned in to him. As his lips applied more pressure, his hands moved over her back. Her muscles rippled under Conor's touch just as the horses did when she caressed them. The man had a tender touch.

His mouth released hers. Placing his forehead against hers, he whispered in a reverent tone, "Christina."

She liked the way her name rolled over his lips in his Irish brogue.

"Yes?" The word came out breathy.

"I know after yesterday I don't have the right to say this but I want you. Something I've not felt in a long time."

"Kiss me."

Conor didn't make her ask twice. She didn't have to ask. He gathered her into his arms and pulled her firmly against him. His mouth slanted across hers with more pressure than before. Her arms wrapped around his neck as she leaned closer. His hands circled and tightened on her waist.

"I don't know what you've done to me." He kissed her temple. "I've been in this fog for months, years, and all of a sudden around you it's sunshine." His mouth moved over her smooth skin to her ear. Taking her earlobe, he gave it a gentle tug. Christina made a soft noise of pleasure in her throat. The sound fed his desire. She tilted her head, giving him better access. He kissed along the long column of her neck.

This time she purred. Lifting her shoulder, she kept his lips against her skin. She ran her hands across his chest then up and over his shoulders as if memorizing his body with the tips of her fingers.

His mouth found hers once more. He kissed her deeply. She returned his kisses with enthusiasm. Conor loved her passion. He tightened his hold. She pressed against him as she ran her fingers through his hair. If he'd known Christina could kiss like this he would have kissed her sooner. She made his body pulsate. Like a horse waiting for the starting gate to open.

At this rate she'd drive him crazy. He had said he didn't want this. But he did with every fiber of his being. He feared he might be taking advantage of the fact Christina was there and available. No, everything about Christina urged him on. Pulled him to her. He was powerless to turn away. Her special appeal was part of who she was. A tiny feminine woman wrapped in dirty jeans and boots had awakened a craving only she could satisfy.

This lusty fervor for Christina he liked too much. He found her plush mouth again.

A drop of rain hit him on the forehead. It didn't dampen his attention or desire. He continued to sip on her lips. The rain turned steady and he broke away. "I need to get you out of the rain before we're both soaked."

"Like you were yesterday." She giggled.

He kissed her hard. "I will get you for that." He reached around her and opened the door. "In you go."

"Promises, promises." Christina stepped into the kitchen where the only light came from the hall. She moved to the kitchen counter. Her back remained to him.

He sucked in a breath until his chest hurt. "About promises."

She looked over her shoulder. "Don't worry. I don't expect any. I know you can't give them."

Conor released the air but found the pain had not eased. "I don't want you hurt. I will be leaving after the Derby."

"I know it."

Had Christina started second-guessing what had been happening between them? Maybe that was just as well. He wanted her but what she wanted and deserved he couldn't offer. For so many reasons. The least being he lived thousands of miles away.

"Coffee? Tea?"

What he wanted was her back in his arms, but he wouldn't say that.

The rain had turned heavy and lightning shot across the sky, making the dark room bright for a moment.

Christina jerked.

He made a step toward her.

"I'm fine. The thunder always gets me, but I love the rain. Which is good because I need to go check on the horses. That lightning will not have made them happy."

"Let me do that. I need to check on Gold. He can get wild-eyed quickly."

She started toward the door. "You don't have to do that."

He gave her an earnest look, his gaze fixed with hers. "Let me do something nice for you."

She stopped. "Okay. Thank you."

Walking to the door he said, "I enjoyed my evening with you more than I have anything in a long time. Thank you."

"Same for me."

Before he closed the door behind him he said, "Good night, Christina."

"'Night," she said so low he almost missed it.

Conor hunched his shoulders against the cool wind and rain as he hurried across the yard to the barn. He was grateful for the weather for bringing the temperature of his body back in line after kissing Christina.

The horses whinnied and shifted as he walked down the hall, checking inside each stall. Satisfied that all was well, he returned to the house. Inside again he turned off the porch light, leaving darkness. The hall light no longer glowed. He removed his boots and padded in socked feet to the bath.

"Are they okay?" Christina stood in her bedroom doorway with the light from her bedside table behind her. She wore a short, flimsy nightgown that the glow made transparent.

Conor swallowed. Those breasts he had been treated to a hint of days before were visible through the fabric. His blood flowed faster. His length had hardened. Why hadn't she gone in her room and stayed? He was torn between being glad she'd been waiting on him and fearing he couldn't stop himself from reaching for her.

Is this what his father faced when he'd been unfaithful to his wife and family? No, this wasn't the same. Louisa was gone by her own choice. He shoved his hands into his pockets. Even now his body vibrated with the desire to taste her, touch her, experience her. "I didn't mean to disturb you."

Her gaze met his, held.

The air turned thick. The rain pounded on the roof as his heart hammered in his chest. This was one of those crossroads in life where if he said or did the wrong thing he would live to regret it. So he waited.

"Uh…about a while ago… I…" She ran her fingers through her hair.

That made her nightgown flow around her. He could see the lines of her sweet body. "You…what? Tell me, Christina. What do you want?"

"I want you."

His heart kicked into overdrive. "I'm right here. All you have to do is reach out."

She took his hand, turned and led him into her room. Stopping beside her bed, she said, "Make love to me, Conor."

"Are you sure that's what you want?" He wanted no regrets for either of them in the morning.

"Yes."

"No promises. No tomorrows. Just now. Just feeling. I haven't felt in so long. I want to again. With you." He needed that so desperately, he hurt with it.

She looked toward the bed and nodded. He cupped her face in both his hands. Her eyes watched him, wide and unsure.

"We are going to take this slow and easy." He lightly brushed her mouth with his lips.

Her hands came to his shoulders.

He continued to kiss and caress and tease her mouth until her fingers bit into his muscles. His hands didn't leave her face as he deepened his kisses. He reveled in the soft, erotic sounds Christina made.

She returned his kisses. He ran his tongue along the seam

of her lips and she opened for him. Greeted him. At first, she hesitated but with one brush of his tongue she joined him in the dance. Even leading at times.

His manhood stood thick and ready. He wanted her now but giving her pleasure won out. Too much had been taken from her. She deserved to feel how special she was.

Her hands moved down over his chest, bunching in his shirt as his tongue stroked hers.

The fingers of one hand traveled along her neck, brushing the tender spot behind her ear then moving across the ridge of her shoulders to cup her bare arm. The other hand followed its lead. He ran the pads of his thumbs beneath the material of her nothing pajamas to touch the swells of her breasts.

Christina shivered. Her hands moved to his waist. She pressed into him.

His manhood throbbed, needing release. He swept a finger over her nipple. A burst of heat flashed through him when he found it stiff and tall, begging for his attention. His mouth left hers to travel over her cheek, down her neck. Cupping her breast, he lifted it and placed his mouth over it. Even with the material barring her from his mouth he continued to suck and tug at the tiny expressive part of her body. He looked at the material sealed over her beauty.

His fingertips touched her thighs. She trembled. His hand crawled under the short gown and over her hips, gathering the material as he went.

Christina stood still, only the rise and fall of her chest visible. Occasionally, there was a lurch and jump in her breathing. He revealed her breasts as if removing a silk drape from a famous piece of artwork with great anticipation and reverence. Unable to stand it any longer, he placed his mouth over a nipple.

Her breath hissed through her lips. Her fingers threaded through his hair, caressing him as he ran his tongue around her nipple to pull and suck. He held her at the waist with one hand and moved to the other breast, giving it the same administrations. His other hand found the edge of her panties and teased the skin there.

Christina quivered, her hands now resting on his shoulders. He left her breasts to kiss the hollow between them. From there his mouth kissed a line to the band of her bikini panties.

"Conor, it's my turn." Her words drifted around them, they were so soft. She tugged him upward.

He stood, his hands still exploring as he went.

The moment he reached his height, Christina's hands went to the top of his shirt. Their mouths met once again. All the while, her fingers worked the buttons from their holes. She pushed the material over his shoulders. He released her long enough for the shirt to drop to the floor. Before he could touch her again, she placed her palms on his chest, keeping the space between them.

Her fingertips dragged over his skin, sending tingling heat throughout his body. His nerves bunched and released as she went. He reached for her, and she moved his hands away.

"I'm not done admiring you. I've been thinking about nothing but touching you since I ran into you in the hall the other morning."

"That was days ago."

"Uh-huh." She kissed him just over his heart.

She had covered up that need well. "You never let on."

"I couldn't." She looked at him and grinned. "I didn't want to look like I was taking advantage of a houseguest."

This time he didn't let her stop him. He took her in his arms. "Take advantage of me any time you wish."

Christina giggled.

"I love that sound."

"What?" She gave him a perplexed look.

He grinned. "The sound of you happy."

Her hands came up his chest and circled his neck. "It's nice to feel that for a change."

He gave her a couple of quick kisses. "You should have that all the time. Now, enough of the talk. I want to explore you more." His hands found the hem of her gown and pulled it over her head. He let it go to land on his shirt.

Cupping her breasts in his hands, he kissed one then the other. He backed her to the bed, laying her on it, then joined her.

She pulled him to her. Pressed against her smooth skin, he found utopia. He rolled to his side and placed his hand on her stomach. Her skin rippled. His manhood twitched with need. Leisurely, far more so than he felt, he moved his hand down to her pink panties, slipping a finger beneath. His reward was the hitch in her breathing.

"These need to come off," he said before he kissed the dip where her neck met her shoulder.

She pushed at the panties then wiggled until she could kick them off her foot.

It might have been the sexiest thing he'd ever seen. The knowledge that what had been revealed would be his made him hotter than ever.

Christina pulled him to her, giving him a searing kiss. Her hands flowed over his back, causing his muscles to ripple.

His hand caressed the silkiness of her inner thigh before traveling to where her legs joined. He brushed his palm over her curls then went in search of her center. He found it warm and wet. Waiting for him. Slipping a finger inside her, he earned her whimper. Her hips flexed in greeting. Behind the zipper of his pants, his manhood ached for relief.

He continued moving his finger inside and out.

Christina lifted her hips, stiffened and keened her pleasure before she shivered and relaxed on the bed.

Satisfaction filled him. He wanted her to have the best pleasure he could provide. Conor kissed her lips, cheeks, eyes, tenderly giving her the attention and care she deserved all while holding her close.

Moments went by then she brushed his hair back from his forehead and looked into his eyes. "It's past time to take off your pants. I want you. All of you."

CHAPTER SIX

CHRISTINA COULDN'T BELIEVE what had just happened to her. She still basked in the waves of pleasure from her release. This was a new experience. Sex had never been as powerful between her and Nelson. And Conor hadn't even been inside her. Doubts rushed in. Would she be enough for Conor?

He stood and started removing his clothes.

She watched as his hands went to his belt. "Would you like us to get under the covers?"

His gaze remained on her. "I would like whatever you do."

"I didn't plan on this or I would have put on clean sheets."

"I don't care about the sheets," he all but growled. He removed his wallet and placed it on the bedside table then lowered his zipper.

Her mouth gaped at the size of him. She watched in anticipation as he pushed his pants down. Her mouth went dry. "Do you have a condom?"

He grinned. "I do."

"Are you always so prepared?"

"I try to be." He looked directly at her. "It has been a long time for me."

"Me, too." But he was worth waiting for.

When he shoved his boxers to the floor she sucked in a breath. He was all beautiful male.

He stepped closer to the bed. "Why all the sudden chatter?"

"I'm nervous."

"What do you have to be nervous about? You're beautiful and desirable." He pushed her hair off her cheek and cupped it.

"You're just saying that so I don't run off." The temptation to get under the covers grew.

His knee rested on the bed as he looked over at her.

She looked away. "I don't want to disappoint you."

"Just what makes you think you would disappoint me?"

"It's been a long time for me. I may not be any good." She just couldn't fail this man who had just given her so much pleasure. If this would be their one and only time, she wanted Conor to remember her.

He looked into her eyes. "I can't imagine how that would ever be true."

"More than one person has told me I don't measure up. Or I could be better." Her mother. Nelson. "It makes you doubt yourself."

He gave her an incredulous look. "At having sex?"

"At anything. My mother told me that. My ex stole from me, and I had no idea. This may be another area where I'm lacking."

"I tell you what. We will go slow. It's been a while for me also. We are in this together unless you would like me to leave."

"No. Please don't go."

"I'm not going anywhere unless you tell me to." He gave her the same gentling caress along her back she'd seen him give a fearful animal. He spoke her language. "I don't see how you could disappointment me in bed or out—ever."

He stopped her next words by sealing her mouth with his.

She ran her hands over his ribs, enjoying the firm male feel of Conor, to the expanse of his back. His hand cupped her breast, kneading it, teasing it. Her center tingled, and heated. His manhood pressed against her stomach. She wiggled.

Conor broke the kiss. "You keep that up and I'll be done before we get started."

She teased him with the movement of her hips. "I thought we had started some time ago."

Conor rolled away and picked up his wallet. He removed a little square package, making short order of opening it and covering himself. Returning to her, he took her into his arms again, giving her gentle kisses that had her wanting more and more.

She opened her legs in welcome. He settled between them. Rising over her on his hands, he entered her. She closed her eyes focusing on each movement of him inside her. He filled her and stopped.

Daring a look, she found Conor's face tight in concentration as if he were absorbing every second of their joining.

He pulled back, making her fear he would leave her, before he returned. His movements continued with deliberation until he had her urging him forward while she clutched the sheets and her legs trembled in desperation.

Heat coiled low in her, tightened, folded on itself and burst. She was flung into the air and slowly drifted on pleasure. In a dreamlike trance she drifted back to reality.

Conor increased his pace, pumping into her like his life depended on it.

She wrapped her legs around his waist, pulling him closer. He groaned and sank into her with force. She joined him in the push-pull moments. Conor stiffened, holding himself steady and roared his release.

If she wanted confirmation of her ability to please a man, she had it.

He came down, covering her with his hard, warm and relaxed body.

When he became too heavy she squirmed, and Conor rolled to his back. He pulled her close as their breathing returned to normal.

Conor listened to the rain with Christina's soft, warm body snuggled against his. Disappointment hadn't happened. Christina had been everything he'd ever dreamed a lover should be. He had missed this type of connection with a female. He'd not allowed himself the pleasure of a woman in so long. And to have this special big-hearted female next to him made his heart open again.

Christina sighed heavily.

He gave her a gentle squeeze. "Am I boring you?"

"No, I was just trying to figure out if I should ask you something or not." She ran her hand across his waist.

"You can ask me anything. If you are planning to ask if you were a disappointment then don't bother. You should have been able to tell I thought you were amazing."

"Thanks for that." She turned so he could see her face. "It wasn't that. I wondered if you would tell me about your wife. What happened to her."

Conor tensed. He didn't talk about that. The real story hurt too much. Christina waited. "You want to talk about her now?"

"Yes. I want to know about the woman so special you spent years in sadness after losing her."

It hadn't been just her. But he couldn't even tell Christina about the baby. The pain was still too great. He'd never said the words to anyone. Not even his brother or sister. He didn't want Christina knowing what he had done to his child. He wasn't sure he ever could tell her. He feared he would double over in agony just as he had when the doctor had said, "I'm sorry about the baby as well."

Conor cleared his throat and gathered his fortitude. Christina deserved his trust. She had earned it. "We had a little house in the village. A place we all grew up. Family and friends, and a busy social life. My practice was thriving. But one thing was missing. She always laughed and said she was the perfect childbearing wife. She would pat her hips."

Christina moved so she could look down at him. "Do you have children?"

He almost left the bed, but he forced himself to stay where he was. He would get through this. "No. It wasn't from the lack of trying. Sadly, we never conceived. Even after going through the medical system. As time went by, she became mired in sadness over the situation. Not emotionally strong to begin with, she took our problems particularly hard. She slowly disappeared on me. Becoming a hull of who she was because she wanted children so desperately. It became an issue in our marriage."

Christina's eyes turned sad with concern. "I shouldn't have asked you, but I understand her wanting them so much."

He could imagine Christina as a mother. She would be a wonderful one. Yet, their time together wasn't about creating a family. It was only for the here and now. Still, something nudged him to talk to her. To have her understand what happened between him and Louisa. "We had a horrible fight.

I told her I couldn't live like we were anymore. Something had to change. Because of me, the ugly things I said, she went out and saw to it by driving her car into a rock wall."

"Oh, Conor. How awful. I'm so sorry." Christina placed her head on his shoulder and wrapped her arms around his waist and hugged him tightly. "It wasn't your fault."

He wasn't convinced that was true. He'd said all those horrible things to Louisa, yet she'd carried the baby he had given her. Then killed herself because she didn't know. How could that not be his fault? For years he had lived with the conviction he should have known, should have seen the damage he had been doing to Louisa. Why hadn't he seen the mental state she was in? He should have noticed.

He'd helped to create it. Just by saying the words *I will leave you.* He hadn't meant them. He'd made a vow to stay with her in good times and bad. He had been and still was determined he would be better than his father. Threatening to leave hadn't been the answer.

Despite his carrying those doubts and guilts, Christina's tender reassurance made a difference. His load had eased by sharing his past with Christina. She had a way of making him think the future could be different. He started to believe that open wound might heal.

They stayed like that for a long time. Then slept.

Conor woke to Christina kissing his chest. Her hand brushed his chest hair lightly. He returned her kiss. Their lovemaking was silent and tender this time as if she wanted to heal his broken heart.

Conor woke with Christina still beside him. He watched the morning light slowly creep into the room. Soon, Christina's internal clock would have her up, ready to feed the horses.

She would push him aside to care for them. He would soak up holding her while he could. Right now, the idea of letting go of her soft, placid body made him want to squeeze her tighter.

He sensed the moment she woke. She gave him a soft smile before her eyes widened and she rolled away from him. "It's daylight. I have to get moving. The horses will be stomping in their stalls."

"I think they can give me two minutes." He couldn't believe he thought they could discuss something as amazing as last night and cover it in two minutes.

"There's nothing to talk about. You're a grown man. I'm a grown woman. We had a nice night together. We didn't plan it. It happened. Let's leave it at that. I enjoyed it and I hope you did, too. We both know that can't happen again."

Her detached attitude made him think of the time a horse kicked him in the ribs. Painful with a lingering ache. She was pushing him away. It was nothing worse than what he'd planned to do to her. She just beat him to it. Maybe that was how it had to be.

Or did it? He shoved his guilt away. He brushed his palm over her bare nipple.

She moved his hand away. "Don't start that. I've got to get to the horses. I've got a full day ahead."

"Christina, I didn't see you coming."

"Sometimes we don't see what we should and just get caught up in it. Other times we don't want to see it. I've been there and done that. I can't, I won't, do it again. It's too hard to come back from."

She climbed out of bed and started looking through clothes. Her room really was a mess. Just part of her charm.

"You sound like you're speaking from experience." Was

she thinking of the jerk who had stolen from her, damaged her reputation and broken her heart? Conor wasn't him. Or was he?

"We agreed to no promises. Just for fun. We both needed it."

He hated her sounding so flippant and callous. Yet, he understood why she lashed out.

"What's the deal with the promises, Conor? I didn't ask for any."

Did he want to tell her? The words came out before he could stop them. "The deal is my father ran around on my mother and me." He hesitated. "I promised myself I would never do that to someone I cared about."

Her look turned perplexed. "Are you planning to go to another woman tonight?"

"No. I'm talking about being faithful to my wife."

Christina's face softened. "Conor, you were a good husband, and I have no doubt faithful, but she wouldn't want you to be alone. I believe we both need to take a step back."

"But I didn't mean…"

She raised a hand. "It's okay. I'm a big girl. I've disappointed people and they have disappointed me. I just make a point not to get too close." She pointed at him then her. "This is not any different. Let's not get too invested. Put it down to a moment of insanity."

Okay, that hurt. "You do know you spent the entire night with me. There were moments of insanity, but they were earth-shaking ones." Why was he tempted to argue with her? Wasn't she offering him what he wanted without him being the jerk who walked out on her after one night together? "Neither of us disappointed the other."

She blushed and looked away. "You know what I mean. It was good but that was yesterday, and this is now."

He climbed out of bed and took a step toward her. "You don't think it could be good here, right now and in broad daylight?"

Christina's eyes widened. A little puff of breath came from the O her mouth had formed. "That's not what I meant. I thought you wanted the same thing as I. That we had an agreement."

"We did but I refuse to have you diminish what we shared."

"That's not what I'm doing." With jerky steps she moved around the room, picking up clothes then letting them float to the floor once more.

"It sure sounded like that to me." He pulled on his pants, leaving them unzipped.

Her gaze traveled over his chest to the opening of his pants. "I didn't intend for it to."

"Good. I'm glad to hear that. It's a time I will remember with pleasure. I would like to think you will, too."

Her look met his. "Conor, you should have no fear of that. It was everything a woman dreams of. Thank you."

Her words bolstered him but now she made it sound like their time together was an experiment in a lab. No emotion. Maybe that was the point; there had been too much emotion on both their parts. He hadn't been prepared for the connection between them. Had it been the same for her? He needed time to analyze it, adjust to it and accept it. She could need that as well.

"Conor—"

"I've got to see about moving Gold today. It's time for him to start working out where he will be running." The last thing he needed was for her to tell him how wonderful, how perfect, it had been and how it would never happen again.

Her eyelids lowered then rose again. "I understand."

"Will you check on Gold while I start breakfast? It will be waiting."

Half an hour later Conor stepped out the back door of the house and headed for the barn. Breakfast was getting cold. Christina had been gone long enough. Guilt had swept over him the second her sweet smell left the room. He had broken his vow to himself. His feelings roiled inside him. He couldn't sort them out, even if he wanted to. He shouldn't have taken Christina to bed even as pleasurable as it was. He had done her an injustice.

He wasn't staying in Kentucky. He wasn't any better than the guy who had hurt her. Conor wouldn't be around to support and care for her. He belonged at home in Ireland with his memories and his family.

She wouldn't leave Kentucky. Even if he dared to ask her. She was too firmly established here, in her horses, in her dream of starting a rehabilitation farm.

Bloody hell, he'd really made a mess of things.

To have acted on emotion instead of his brain was unforgivable at his age. He should know better. But her kisses, her body pressed to his…

His actions were so unlike him. He had always been practical, solid, thoughtful, yet Christina managed to make him throw out all his thinking abilities and go with feelings. The desire to live in the here and now became too strong.

Christina sat across the table from Conor. He silently sipped his second cup of coffee as if it was a normal morning instead of the one after an amazing night in her bed. She came close to groaning out loud. It had been she who had invited him in.

He'd come searching for her when she hadn't returned. She reluctantly agreed to the meal, but it had become a tense affair, making the food taste like hay.

Conor had been standing on the back stoop waiting, watching the barn when she had come out. She'd stayed longer than usual, needing to think. The moment she appeared he'd gone inside.

What had she expected? Hadn't she known the score before they made love? She was a grown woman. Hadn't they both agreed to no promises? Just the one night. Then why was she letting the idea that there might be more between them grow? She knew better.

Hadn't her past decisions proven that she didn't have what it took to last? She hadn't been good enough then and what made her think she was now? Could she ever keep a man like Conor?

He wasn't over his wife.

Somehow, her future didn't look as happy as it once had.

"Christina, stop it." Conor's bark jerked her out of her thoughts.

She looked at him over her mug. "What?"

"Thinking. I want us to remain friends," he came close to growling.

"We are friends."

His voice softened. "I certainly hope so." He sighed. "I'm going to Churchill Downs today. Gold will be moved there tomorrow. I have to make sure all is ready for him. He must pass inspection. I need to see if there is something more I need to do. Is there anything you need from there?"

Her chest tightened. She knew the day would come when

Gold and Conor would leave. It had been inevitable. What she hadn't expected was for it to affect her so. Maybe it was a good thing. She could start getting used to him not being there. Conor might as well leave for good now. At least she could start getting used to the idea because in a little over a week he would return to Ireland.

"No. I have to go Monday for orientation anyway." By then she would have moved past this dreary mood over Conor. She needed to make a good impression, and showing up looking sad and lonely wasn't going to be the answer.

"I'll be moving into a hotel in Louisville close to the race-track that Mr. Guinness has secured. I need to be closer than this to Gold. But I still plan to attend the party on Saturday night. Will you pick me up since you know the way?"

"I can do that." She looked into her coffee cup as if it had the answers to why her heart hurt.

"I'll be sure to let you know the information about where I'm staying."

The finality of it all saddened her more. But this was how she'd wanted it. He had agreed. It was for the best. She pushed back from the table, leaving half her breakfast on her plate. "Okay. That sounds like a plan. I need to get to work now."

That was what she should be worried about. Focused on. Her new business. She needed to make that her priority, and not worrying about Conor. Still, the thought of his kisses and caresses made her shiver. If she could force them into a box in her mind and close the top, she'd be better off. With some determination she'd get through the next week and then he would be gone.

She picked up her plate, cleaned it off and placed it in the sink. "Thanks for breakfast. I'll see you later."

Half an hour later she heard Conor's truck go down the drive. Her shoulders sagged. Why did she feel relieved and lonely at the same time? How had the man managed to matter so much in such a short time?

Conor drove toward Louisville and Churchill Downs thinking less about where he was going and more about Christina. What had happened between them last night hadn't been something he had imagined or planned for when he came to America. That might be the case, but he couldn't say he hadn't enjoyed being with Christina or that he wouldn't like to repeat the pleasure.

He wanted to respect the distance she had requested while at the same time he wanted to shake her and tell her they could figure something out. Maybe the problem was she had been the one to beat him to placing the boundaries.

Until recently, he would have said he would never be interested in another woman. That had changed because of Christina. Still, he couldn't give her what she wanted. A family. He couldn't go there again. But surely they could find a compromise because she had done the impossible, made him care again.

With little more than a week before the Kentucky Derby, the racecourse was already buzzing with more activity than it had been on his last visit. In just a few days, he would be a part of that. He would miss the calm, slow life of Seven Miles Farm and Stables. And Christina.

His work would really step up when Gold arrived tomorrow. The next day the trainer, along with his grooms and barn hand, would be there. It was Conor's job as the lead man on the scene to see that Gold was safely moved and checked into a barn. Today he would have a look at Gold's stable, but first Conor needed to check in with the clinic. It was time Gold really exercised. He needed to run and flex his muscles. The horse needed to get on the Breeze schedule.

Entering the clinic, he found the place busy as well.

Dr. Dillard came around the corner. "Hello, Doctor O'Brian. I was wondering when you would be in. It's about time to move into the barn, isn't it?"

"The plan is to do that tomorrow. Well over the hundred-and-three-hour limit for the horse to be on the premises."

"Indeed. Tell me, how has it worked out being at Doctor Mobbs's place?"

"Great. Gold seems to be in fine shape, and it's a quiet place to settle in." Conor did really love Christina's farm. If he lived in America, it would be the type of place he would like to have.

"Good to hear. Good to hear. I was wondering about sending others if necessary."

"I can't think of a better place." Conor meant it.

"How did you make out personally? I know the farm is a little farther from here than you would have liked."

"I made out fine." Was the man fishing for more than general information? Too fine, in fact. He had started to feel like it was home. "She was kind enough to rent me a room when I realized there was a misunderstanding about how close I needed to be to Gold."

"Well, I'm glad it worked out. I'm a little surprised she agreed. Christina has had a difficult time during the last couple of years. I'm an acquaintance of her uncle, who is also a vet. I felt the need to help her where I could."

"I know she appreciates it. She is an excellent veterinarian. I believe you will be pleased to have her on your staff."

"I believe you are correct. That's why I suggested her

place and have given her a position working here during the week. The man she got hooked up with dragged her name through the mud."

If Conor ever met that guy, he might do something he wouldn't be proud of.

"The program she is starting is worthwhile," Dr. Dillard continued, "I would like to see it flourish."

Conor would, too. "She has a wonderful place for it and she is excellent at that type of work."

"So I understand. Well, is there something I can do for you?"

Conor shook his head. "No, I just need to check in and see if there is anything required that I haven't already covered, then I'm on my way to check out the stall."

"I'll have someone call for a golf cart to take you to the barn. You'll need to plan to walk back."

"I can do that." He shook his hand.

The man nodded. "I'll see you Saturday evening, then."

Conor waited outside the clinic. Soon, a man in a golf cart pulled up. On the ride, he jostled along the gravel road between the barns and past the grassy area where horses were being washed and groomed. The man pulled to a sharp stop in front of a white barn with red flower baskets hanging from the porch. Gold would be installed in the second stall from the right. He got off the golf cart and the driver took off.

Conor strolled over to the barn stall, opened the door and entered. He checked the walls, the gate and feeding trough for any hanging wood, paint or any other material that could harm Gold. It all looked good and was spotlessly clean. Outside lay a strip of grass and a grooming area. Gold should do well here. Everything looked satisfactory.

He started his walk back to his truck. A golf cart came by and came to a sudden stop in front of him, throwing gravel.

The woman whom he had been introduced to as Christina's cousin looked at him. "Aren't you the guy that was with Christina the other day?"

"Yes. I'm Conor O'Brian. I'm staying at her place."

She looked around. "Is she here today?"

"No, I'm seeing about moving a horse I'm responsible for here tomorrow."

A look of disappointment came over her face. "Well, that's good. Do you need a ride somewhere?"

"As a matter of fact, I could use one back to my truck."

She patted the golf cart seat. "Then hop in."

Conor did and she took off like a shot. He grabbed the support bar holding the roof.

"Have you been enjoying your stay in America? At Christina's?" She glanced at him.

"Kentucky reminds me of Ireland. The grass, rolling hills and of course the horses."

"I have to admit I'm a little surprised Christina let you stay at her place."

Conor studied the woman for a moment. Was she trying to get at something? No, she was just making conversation. "Let's just say it wasn't her idea. She wasn't left much choice."

"She's remained closed off for the last few years, unfortunately. To everyone. Especially men."

"I understand she has good reason. I heard he was a real piece of work."

Callie studied him a second. "She told you about him?"

"Yeah, she told me about what happened."

"She must really like you. As far as I know outside of a

handful of people, she's never told anyone about what really happened."

Conor couldn't help but find pleasure in that knowledge. Yet, he still held out about the baby.

"I could tell by the way she looked at you the other day she really liked you." Callie made a right turn that almost slung him off the cart.

Christina looked at him a certain way? For some reason that made his chest expand. "I'd say we have become friends over the last two weeks."

"She hasn't let anybody close enough to be a friend in years. You must be somebody special."

He had no idea if that was true.

"I'm glad she has the job on the veterinary team. I know she really wanted that."

Conor was glad Christina was getting something she really wanted, too. "Yes, she puts great stock in working here during Derby week."

"Understandably. She had a difficult time and people were not kind to her, even though she wasn't the one found guilty. That jerk she thought she was in love with didn't do her any favors." Venom filled Callie's voice.

"That's my truck right up there. The red one." He pointed ahead of them.

Callie pulled to a halt beside the truck and he climbed out.

"It was nice to see you again. I'm sure I'll be seeing you around in the next week. Tell Christina I look forward to seeing her as well." Callie smiled.

"Thanks for the ride."

The visit to the track had been fruitful professionally but more so personally. It certainly had given him food for

thought where Christina was concerned. If he'd been trying to push Christina into the background of his life today,
he hadn't achieved that.

CHAPTER SEVEN

CHRISTINA WOKE AT the first ring of the phone and picked it up on the second. Truly, she hadn't been asleep. Her night had been spent thinking about Conor on the other side of the house.

She had known better and gotten what she deserved.

Conor was still hung up on his dead wife. He lived thousands of miles away. There was just no way a relationship between them would work. Apparently, he felt the same way. It didn't take him long to freeze her out.

He was a nice guy. But she'd believed Nelson had been, too. Her judgment of character had been way off. What made her think it wasn't the same with Conor? She couldn't afford to put her heart out there again and have it broken.

She ended the call. Scrambling out of bed she quickly dressed. She didn't get many midnight calls, but when she did, she knew it was an emergency. She never questioned whether she needed to go or not. People who owned high-strung horses recognized when there was a problem. Many thought they could handle things themselves so when they asked for her, she took it seriously. It wasn't something that would wait until morning.

She was in the kitchen pulling on her boots when Conor walked in wearing only sports shorts. He pushed his fingers through his hair making it stand up in places. He appeared rumpled and sexy. She looked away and pushed those thoughts from her mind. Now wasn't the time anyway. Later wouldn't be, either. Or she wouldn't let it be.

"What's going on?" His voice was low and gravelly with sleep.

"I have an emergency. I'm sorry. I didn't mean to wake you."

"In the barn?" His eyes turned anxious.

"No, it's one of my clients." She shoved her foot into the other boot.

"You're going off this time of the night by yourself?" He sounded genuinely concerned.

Maybe he did care more than he wanted to admit. "I've done it plenty of times."

"I'm going with you."

A little thrill of heat filled her chest, but she pushed it down. "That's not necessary."

"I'll be ready to go by the time you are." He headed to his room without giving her a chance to argue.

As good as his word, Conor arrived at her truck just as she was ready to go. She climbed behind the steering wheel. "You don't have to do this."

"Sure, I do."

She took off down the lane. They remained silent as she drove through the night.

Finally, he asked, "Where are we going?"

"The Owens' Farm. He has a horse down. He said she has been off her feed. He went to check on her before going to bed and found her on the floor." Christina gave the truck more gas.

"That's all the information you have?"

She glanced at him in the dim light. Even in it she could

make out the handsome cut of his jaw. "I know my clients well enough to know when they call it's something I need to react to."

"Okay, that's reasonable. How far is this farm?"

"We're almost there." She made a left turn into the gravel drive.

When Christina pulled up near the barn, Mr. Owen stood under the night-light with his hands in his pockets. He walked toward them. She climbed out and grabbed her bag from the side storage compartment of the truck. Conor joined them with his bag in hand.

"How's she doing?" Christina asked, falling in step with the older man on his way into the barn.

"Like I said, I came out to check on the horses before I went to bed. I found Joy laying on the floor of the stall. She had been kicking something awful. That's when I called you."

"Have you changed her food?"

"No, but I noticed she was off her feed yesterday and circling the stall more than usual. I thought I'd watch her another day, then this. I should have called you earlier."

The poor man looked so distraught she placed her hand on his arm. "We're here to help. We'll do all we can to make it better." She looked back at Conor. "This is Doctor O'Brian. Together we'll figure it out."

She never thought of it that way before, but they did make a good team. They played off each other's skills and experiences well. She enjoyed working with Conor. That was something she couldn't have said about Nelson.

They entered the barn, Mr. Owen directing them down the main hall to a stall on the other end. The horse was still on the floor. Groaning and twitching and kicking her feet.

"Mr. Owen, I need you to hold her head and speak softly to her."

When the farmer had control of the horse, Christina went to her knees beside the animal and placed her hand on the horse's belly. It was distended and hard. Conor came down beside her. He gave the horse the same examination.

"Will you do the general vitals while I listen for stomach sounds?"

Conor rose and picked up his bag. "I'll take care of it."

Thankfully, the horse had chosen to settle in the middle of the stall, giving them working room in the small area. Christina pulled her stethoscope from her bag. After placing the ends in her ears, Christina positioned the bell on the horse's abdomen to listen. The bowel sounds were just as she suspected. The horse had a bowel obstruction.

She put her stethoscope back and then started running her hand along the belly of the horse. "Mr. Owen, this became bad between when and when?"

"I was out here at eight. I came back about midnight. Just before I called you."

She looked out the stall door. "None of your other horses are having any problems?"

The man shook his head. "None that I can see."

Conor's look met hers. "Her face is swollen, and there is bruising around the eyes."

Were they thinking the same thing? As if Conor had read her mind, he nodded.

She took a deep breath. "Mr. Owen, I believe Joy has a large colon volvulus. You may have heard it called a 'twisted gut.' If we don't do surgery right away the intestines may burst. Joy will die if that happens."

Concern tightened the man's face. "I understand. So when is this surgery?"

"As soon as we can get ready."

The man's brows rose. "You'll be doing it here?"

She nodded. "Yes, we have no time to get Joy to a clinic."

The man's eyes widened.

"I need you to get me a large sheet that you don't want returned. It will have to go in the trash. Also hot water and soap. I need you to do so quickly."

Mr. Owen patted the horse's neck. "I'll go to the house right now."

"I'll get the supplies out of the truck." Conor moved toward the stall door. "You have this, Christina."

"Thanks. It's been a while since I've had to do serious surgery."

He gave her a tight smile. "I'll be here with you." Then he walked out of the barn.

It was nice to have another competent veterinarian there with her. In an odd way, Conor made a nice security blanket. She had learned to trust him, at least when it came to their work.

While he was gone she had brushed the hay away from the horse's belly using her boot. After that, she prepared a sedative so the horse would be calm and pain-free while they worked.

Conor returned with handfuls of supplies in a basket she kept in the storage area for such an occasion. "Check and see if I brought everything you need. I'll stay here with the horse."

Christina reviewed everything and found it well prepared. "Conor, talk this through with me. We are going to need to scab the incision site with soap and hot water."

Conor nodded. "The incision will have to be long. This surgery always requires a few more inches than expected just because you need to see so much of the area to find the problem."

At least her and Conor's discussion was calming Christina's nerves. "I need to give a bolus dose of antibiotics before we start."

"Agreed." Conor handed her what she needed.

She drew an amount up in a syringe. "Check me on this. I don't want to have any questions asked."

Conor studied the syringe a moment. "Yes, it looks correct to me."

She then went to the horse and gave her a shot in the hip.

Mr. Owen returned. "Here are two sheets. And the bucket has the water in it." He sat it on the floor and handed her the sheets.

Christina placed one over the wall in reserve. She laid one on the ground at the horse's belly and tucked in under her. Conor set out the supplies nearby. She was thankful for his help.

"Mr. Owen, I'm gonna need you to hold her head." The middle-aged man went down on his knees beside the horse.

She gave Conor a perplexed look when he left. He soon returned with a stool and placed it beside Mr. Owen. Conor was a good guy.

She pulled on plastic gloves then drew up a sedative and administered it to the horse. Soon, the horse had relaxed.

"Conor, will you prepare the incision area?"

He, too, pulled on gloves. He washed the area with soap and water. He then opened a surgical kit and removed the razor. After shaving the surgical area, he scrubbed it with antiseptic.

Conor moved to the side, and she took the space. He handed her the scalpel, and she made the incision.

"Should I go larger?"

"Another two inches. We need to be sure we can see everything." He watched beside her.

Christina did as he suggested. With the horse's abdomen open they went in search of the obstruction. She removed a handful of intestines. "Do you see it?"

"There it is," Conor said. "Down on the left."

She shifted the intestines so she could see. He was right. There was the twisted cord. "Let's get this resected and repaired."

Conor said, "Can you resect it while I hold it? Clip off on both ends at the same time. We don't need it to build up and burst."

She did as he requested. With that done, she took the scissors from her surgical kit and cut one end below the twist and then the other, and removed the piece of intestine.

"Excellent work."

Conor's praise washed through her. He handed her the needle and thread. She quickly stitched the two remaining ends together.

"I don't know that I've seen nicer stitches."

She smiled.

Working together, they slowly and gently returned the intestines to their place.

"Now, to get her closed up. You stitch and I'll pull the skin together." Conor handed her the needle and thread.

Together they worked until the incision had been sutured.

"While I clean up, why don't you check vitals?" Christina suggested.

"That, I can do." He washed in the bucket and started on the vitals.

By the time she'd cleaned up and he'd finished, the horse was waking.

"Mr. Owen, how are you doing?" Conor placed a hand on the man's shoulder.

"I'm well, and very impressed. You two working together is a show."

"A good one, I hope." Conor grinned.

"Certainly."

Christina had to agree. She and Conor did work well together along with doing other things well. "Thank you. We now need to get Joy on her feet. She needs to be led around for a while. Large animals don't need to lie on the floor. We need to work the anesthesia out of her system and get her organs active. Mr. Owen, you pull on her lead while Conor and I nudge her from behind."

The older man rose stiffly from the stool. She and Conor positioned themselves at the horse's back and pushed.

After a few minutes of encouragement, the horse wobbled to her feet and stood.

"Good job. Now, Mr. Owen, please lead her around in a circle. We need to get her loosened up."

She and Conor backed out of the stall.

The horse staggered but soon found steady footing.

Conor leaned against her. "Nice job, Doctor."

She grinned. "You, too. You know we're going to need to stay here and watch over Joy for a couple of hours."

"I do."

She studied the horse. "I'm sorry I can't send you home because I might need something off the truck."

"I wouldn't leave anyway." He sounded like he meant it.

She looked at him and smiled. "I guess you wouldn't."

Conor leaned against the stall wall. "We should encourage Mr. Owen to go to bed. He looks dead on his feet."

"I agree." How like Conor to show concern for another. The man got to her.

She entered the stall and took the lead from the man. "Why don't you get some rest? Conor and I have to be here anyway. We can take care of her from here. You may need to give her some attention after we're gone. So go."

Mr. Owen gave her a weak smile. "Thank you. I think I'll take you up on that."

She started walking the horse around the stall. Conor walked out with Mr. Owen but soon returned with a blanket and a couple of folding chairs.

"Go have a seat and let me have a turn." His hand brushed hers as he took the lead.

Her unruly heart jumped at the touch. She had been glad to have his knowledge and help. He had become a fixture in her life. It hurt to think about him leaving. Despite her better judgment, she would miss him.

Conor grinned. Christina had piled hay in the hallway then laid the blanket over it before curling up on it. Now she slept. This was becoming a weekly event for them to spend one night in a barn. Funny thing was he could not think of anywhere he would rather be except in Christina's bed.

He felt honored she trusted him to watch over the horse. When he had first arrived, she had mistrusted him at every turn. Slowly, her attitude had changed. He found it rewarding. His feelings for her weren't doing him any favors, or her, either. He wouldn't offer her what she wanted. He couldn't go there again. He couldn't take that chance again.

Yet, he smiled down at Christina. They were different, lived in different parts of the world and their lives were damaged. The negatives were too many.

She would be appalled to know that in her sleep she looked angelic. That her tough exterior had slipped and turned vulnerable.

He sat a chair near where she lay and leaned back against the wall of a stall. From there he could clearly see the horse tied in its stall. The animal would not feel like being frisky for some time. He set the timer on his watch to go off in an hour. He would walk the horse a couple of turns, letting Christina rest as long as possible. He would also do the driving home.

He continued to keep watch over her and the horse until light peeked under the doors of the barn. He shook Christina awake.

She opened her eyes and made a long catlike stretch. Which might have been the sexiest thing he'd ever seen.

"I didn't mean to sleep so long. You were supposed to wake me."

He shrugged. "You looked too peaceful."

Her attention went to the stall. "How's Joy doing?"

Conor liked that she had no doubt he would have taken care of the horse while she slept. "I've been walking her every hour. In fact, it's time for a walk now."

"I'll do it."

He watched carefully to see if the horse faltered or showed pain.

Christina smiled. "You know I could've done this without you but I'm glad I didn't have to."

He grinned. "That was a nice thing for you to say. I like knowing I'm needed. It has been too long."

She tied Joy up again. Picking up the blanket, she folded it then hung it over the back of the chair he had used.

"I'm surprised Mr. Owen hasn't been out yet." She started down the barn hall and in came the man.

"Good morning. How is Joy doing?" He looked toward the horse with concern.

"Great. Conor and I are headed home. You call me if you need me. I'll be back to check on her tomorrow. I'll be gone next week working the Derby but if you need anything you call me and I'll see that you get help."

"That's a big deal to get to work the Derby. I understand only a handful are picked."

"She got it because she is one of the best." Conor's voice held pride.

Christina looked at him and softly smiled, her eyes bright.

"My wife and I don't miss a Derby Day. We look forward to it every year."

"My family wasn't any different," Christina said. "It's an honor to be included as part of the staff."

"It's past due for you. You were mistreated a couple of years ago."

Christina looked down. "Thank you for that. I'm glad to have this opportunity but working ten to twelve hours a day will be tough. Few people realize how much goes on behind the scenes."

"I know they'll be glad to have you." Mr. Owen lifted a bag. "My wife has fixed breakfast for you. Egg sandwiches and a thermos of coffee. You can bring the thermos back when you come again. She said to tell you she would've invited you in but thought you might like to get home to your beds."

Christina took the bag. "Please give her our thanks."

Conor's stomach growled. "Mine in particular."

Christina said, "We'll give Joy one more look then we'll go. It's been a day. I need to get home and check on the horses."

She and Conor did their final analysis and headed for the truck, leaving Mr. Owen with instructions on how to continue Joy's care.

"I appreciate you helping out."

"Glad I was here to help. You were really good in there." He nodded toward the barn. "Impressive, in fact."

"Thanks. That's nice to hear."

Conor studied her a moment. "You haven't been told that before?"

"I didn't get much positive reinforcement from my mother growing up."

"You should be given it often." He meant it. Christina was an amazing veterinarian and equally amazing woman.

"I really appreciate it when I hear it." Christina placed supplies into the side storage bin of the truck. She yawned.

"You're tired. I'll drive home."

On the way to her house, she leaned back against the headrest and closed her eyes. When her head bobbed, he guided it down until it rested on his thigh. She sighed as she settled in.

Disappointment filled him when he turned into the drive. He would have to give up having her close.

Christina woke to warm, hard muscle beneath her cheek. She'd fallen asleep on Conor. She'd kept a number of long days but staying up all night wasn't her norm. With the Derby week ahead, she needed her rest.

It had been so nice to have Conor along tonight for the help and even the reassurance. She didn't do emergency operations very often and it was nice to have assistance, especially professional assistance. It had also been helpful to have somebody who took turns seeing about the horse.

She felt confident Joy would recover well. It might be touch and go for a few days, but overall, she would be fine.

When they reached her farm she hopped out of the truck. "I'm gonna go check on the horses. You're welcome to the shower first."

"I'm coming to help you." His firm tone stopped any argument. "I'll check on Gold as well. We're both exhausted and we can both go out there and get everything done in half the time."

In short order they finished caring for the horses and feeding them.

On the way to the house Conor kept pace with her. "Gold will be moving this afternoon. Thank goodness my plans were for later in the day. There is such an influx of horses at the Downs, so this afternoon appointment was the earliest I could get."

Sadness washed over Christina. She would miss the horse. More than that, she would miss Conor. She stepped on the stoop and turned to look down at Conor. "Thank you again for your help last night. I especially appreciate you staying up all night after I fell asleep on you."

"Not a problem. I was glad I was here to help."

She gave him a tight smile when she really wanted to kiss him. "I still appreciate it."

"I was glad I could be here for you."

"You're a really nice guy, Conor, and an excellent veterinarian."

"Thank you for the compliment. I'm not sure I wouldn't like the adjectives to be reversed."

"You are an excellent guy and a nice vet." Christina couldn't help herself. Her lips brushed his.

Conor's hands found her waist. "I think you can do better than that. In fact, I know you can." His mouth sealed hers before he pulled her against him, pressing her tightly against his hard body.

The kiss deepened. Their tongues tangled, searching and giving pleasure.

This is what she'd been wanting and missing since she had given her speech the day before. The one filled with lies. It would still be worth it to have him near, even if it hurt when he left. She would take advantage of what time they had for as long as he would let her.

Christina wrapped her arms around his neck and held tightly. She joined him in the kiss. The heat of desire spread through her. This man was honest and good. She could trust him. It has been too long since she had been able to say that. He'd proven himself.

Conor pulled away. "I'm sorry. I couldn't help myself."

"I'm not sorry at all."

He kissed her again. His need strong between them. "You know if we share a shower we could find a little more time to sleep."

She giggled. "I suspect that we would use it up in another way."

He gave her a deep, wet, suggestive kiss. "I suspect you're right. Let's go inside. I need to touch you."

His hand held hers as she opened the door. In the kitchen they kicked off their boots as if they had done the actions together their entire lives. Finished, she smiled at him. He returned it.

She took his hand again and led him down the hall into

the bath. Inside, she turned on the water. Her fingers went to the buttons of his shirt. Slowly, she opened them.

He pulled his shirt from his pants. She pushed it over his shoulders. It dropped to the floor. He chuckled. "I'm not sure this is a time-saving operation. But I do know if I don't take all the chances I'm given to be in your arms, I'll regret it. Forever."

Her hands went to his belt and worked it open. She treasured the intake of his breath when her fingers brushed his skin. Slowly, she unzipped his pants and maneuvered them over his extended manhood. With her hands at his waist she pushed his jeans to the floor.

He stepped out of them.

Her hands went to his underwear, but he stopped her. "My turn to undress you."

Gently, he pulled her T-shirt over her head. With it removed, he kissed the top of one breast then the other while he reached around her and daftly unhooked her bra. He pulled it away and dropped it into the pile of clothing on the floor. His hands made short work of removing her pants. "Honey, we will not make it to the bed."

She relished the deep, throaty sound of his accent as he nuzzled her ear.

"Mmm, that's okay with me."

CHAPTER EIGHT

CHRISTINA STRETCHED HER arm out across the bed. Her hand came in contact with a hard, warm body. A stream of pleasure flowed through her. Conor was there beside her.

She smiled, enjoying him and the sunshine flooding through the window. She could get used to this—waking up next to Conor.

She rolled enough in his direction to sneak a peek to see if he was awake. A blue gaze met hers.

"Good morning. Or should I say afternoon?" He grinned at her.

"It's not afternoon yet but almost. Have you been awake long?"

His hand brushed her breast. "I was just waiting on you to open your eyes."

A tingle flowed through her. "You were?"

Conor's hand moved to the curve of her hip as his eyes narrowed. "I was."

She rolled closer to him. "Is there something I can do for you?"

"Most definitely."

"Did you have something particular in mind?" She ran her hand over his bare chest.

"I do." His lips found hers.

She rose over him to straddle his hips. "Aren't you expecting a truck and trailer for Gold soon? Maybe this should wait," she teased.

His hands caressed the skin of her sides. "No, it can't."

"I should get to work." She moved to climb off him.

Conor held her in place, sliding her over him, filling her. "I don't think so. We both need to take time to enjoy what we have."

He left off *while it lasts*. But she was well aware of it. For a change, she would do just that. Her lips brushed his as she lifted her hips until he almost lost her and she plunged down again.

Conor made a sexy sound of pleasure in his throat.

She said, "I don't disagree."

Later, as they pulled on their boots, Conor asked, "Can we talk a minute?"

The last time that had happened she had said some stupid things, and she didn't want that to happen again. "I thought we had been. In more ways than one."

That brought a wolfish grin to Conor's lips that soon slipped to a wry tightness of his mouth. "I have to move into town. I can't be this far from Gold and the racetrack. With the security in the backside during the week before the Derby, I'm needed nearby."

"I get it."

He stepped closer. "I have a room at a hotel. Maybe you could spend the week with me there since you must be in town all week. It would make for a longer day to have to drive back and forth."

"I have the horses to see about." Even if she wanted to go, she had responsibilities and a business to consider.

"Can't you get someone to see about them?"

She leaned her head to the side in thought. "Maybe I could for a few days but not the entire time."

"At least say you will find someone for Sunday morning." Conor sounded close to begging. "That way you can stay with me after the party."

"I guess I could do that."

"I wish you would." He gave her sad eyes.

"I'll see what I can do between now and Saturday evening to get some help." She was already thinking of people she could call.

At 2:00 p.m. the truck and trailer to transport Gold rolled up her drive. Conor waited at the barn to meet it. Not soon after the truck stopped Conor led Gold into the trailer. Earlier, he'd collected all of the horse's supplies and placed them in his truck.

They both had examined Gold carefully to make sure he was well and fit. He would not be allowed on the backside unless he could pass the rigid Kentucky Horse Racing Commission list of protocols. Conor reviewed all his paperwork for shots dates and blood tests and how they were handled. All that information must be in order before Gold would be allowed on the property. After the horse was in a stall on Churchill Downs property, he would have limited access to Gold and only when security was around.

With Gold secure in the trailer, Christina joined Conor beside his truck. "I'll see you Saturday evening. Since I know the area better, why don't I pick you up at your hotel?"

"No. Once again, you are my date and I would like to see about getting us there. Please just plan to meet me in the lobby of the hotel at six. I've got it from there."

She started to open her mouth.

He gave her a direct look. "Christina, please do not argue with me."

"Okay."

Conor gave her a quick kiss on the lips as the truck and trailer started down the drive. "I have to go. I will see you Saturday evening. I'll call if I have a chance." He hopped in his truck and rolled down the window. "I will miss you."

She smiled, giving him a wave. A heavy cloak of sadness settled over her shoulders. This was just a taste of the feelings she would have when he returned to Ireland but on a larger scale. Then he would truly be gone.

She had brought this on herself. She'd have to live with that knowledge, but at least she will have had him for a while.

Saturday evening Conor paced back and forth in the lobby of the hotel in downtown Louisville, watching for Christina. He had expected her five minutes ago. Normally prompt, it was not like her to arrive late. Had she decided not to attend? No, she wouldn't do that. She had been working toward this opportunity to become a part of the veterinarian group at the Derby for too long. He pulled out his cell phone and looked at it. There was no text from her.

She must be nervous about being in a group of veterinarians who had judged her just a few years earlier. She worried too much about the past. She had proved herself not guilty and also qualified to care for racehorses.

With a release of fear, he saw her enter through the automatic sliding glass doors. She was a vision of loveliness, and she had no idea. Wearing a simple dark green dress, she appeared confident and dependable. She looked perfect to impress.

Little earrings dangled from her earlobes. The bit of shimmer had him wanting to bite at the sweet spot behind her ears. He had never expected to feel like this about a woman again. Especially for one who did not want him to. Going from not feeling anything for a woman to this intense need made his middle uneasy. Worse, he did not know what to do about it.

The more time they spent together, the greater the difficultly he would have in giving her up, yet he could not stay away from Christina. He kept reminding himself that this situation was temporary. After he left, he wouldn't be able to forget her. The past two nights alone had proved him wrong. He had been miserable without her. He'd quickly learned he would be willing to take any time she would give him.

Christina stopped when she saw him. A smile formed on her lips that had little to do with finding him and everything to do with her being aware of him as a man. His blood heated and his chest swelled. That sparkle in her eyes he would treasure for the rest of his life. She looked him over from head to toe.

Then she stepped up to him. Into his personal space. "You look very handsome." She ran her hand under one of the lapels of his suit.

He suddenly had no desire to attend a party but to have one just for them in his room. "Thank you. You look lovely, Christina."

"I love the way you say my name. Your accent is super sexy, making it more special." She gave him a quick kiss on the lips. He reached for her, but she stepped back before he could take her in his arms. Apparently, she was more aware of where they were than he. "We better go or we're going to be later than we should be. I had to change a couple of times."

"Was that because of me or the people at the party?"

"Both. Did I tell you how glad I am to have you going with me?"

"No, but I am glad to hear it. When Doctor Dillard mentioned it the first time, I wasn't sure you thought it was a good idea." He grinned.

"Okay, maybe I've changed my mind about you some."

He pulled her close for a moment and kissed her temple. "I'm glad to hear it. You know you really shouldn't worry. You are the most amazing person I know, inside and out."

"Do you say nice things to all the girls you go to a party with?"

He gave her waist a gentle squeeze. "Only to you. After all, I haven't been to a party in years."

"Well, I am honored to be with you tonight." She kissed him on the cheek.

He nudged her toward the door. "We have admired each other enough tonight to create cavities in our teeth with the sugar. We should go."

She grinned. "I was rather enjoying it."

"We can try it again later."

Outside the lobby door, Conor waved his hand and a car pulled up.

Christina looked from him to the car and back again. "What's going on here?"

"I rented a driver for the night."

"That wasn't necessary. You shouldn't have spent all that money."

Conor waved the driver back to his seat and opened the

car door for her. "You let me worry about that. I wanted to sit back here with you and enjoy the ride."

They settled into the backseat. She provided the driver with the address as they moved into traffic.

Conor took her hand in his. "I missed you. It's been too long. How are things? The horses?"

"I saw a couple of clients and spent the rest of the time in the barn."

"Did you find somebody to care for the horses tomorrow?" He brushed the pad of his thumb over the back of her hand.

"I made a few calls and found somebody I can trust. He's done it for one night before but he's willing to do it for three or four."

He leaned his forehead against hers. "So you will stay with me tonight?"

She gave him a shy smile. "If you still want me to?"

Conor pulled her hip against him. "Never question that I want you."

The driver pulled the car into the curved drive of a large redbrick two-story home with white columns and a wide porch across the front. The lights were shining in all the windows.

When the driver stopped at the front door, Conor climbed out and offered his hand. She took it. With a gentle squeeze he released it, closed the car door and offered his arm. Christina took it, holding tighter than necessary.

She was nervous about facing her colleagues. He was glad he would be there for her. She must have lived through an emotional ordeal for it to linger this long. But hadn't his wife's death done the same to him?

They entered the house and were directed along an elegant hallway to the open French doors at the back of the house. It looked out into a wide-open yard with a few aged trees. Among them hung white paper lanterns that lit the area along with lights from the house. To one side were four long tables laden with food, and also a man turning beef on a spit in the ground. Other round tables were spread out around the yard set for dining.

"Wow, this is beautiful," Christina said beside him.

"It does look nice, but the smell of meat cooking has my attention."

She smiled. "Always the cook."

"Hey, you haven't been complaining."

She hadn't. In fact, she hated returning to packaged food. "The only thing I can complain about is that I've gained almost ten pounds."

He leaned close. "And every one looks good on you."

"There you are, Christina. Good you could come." Dr. Dillard walked toward them. "And Doctor O'Brian. Nice to see you again."

Conor offered his hand. "Please call me Conor. Thanks for having us tonight."

Dr. Dillard shook it. "You're welcome. I understand you got your horse into the Downs stable without any trouble the other day."

"Yes, with a few hours to spare from those required." Conor took Christina's hand.

His attention went to the action for a moment before his look returned to Conor's. Dr. Dillard smiled. "We do have our rules for a reason."

"Understood. We have ours in Ireland as well."

Dr. Dillard glanced toward a woman waving at him. "My wife is calling. I must greet other guests. Please make your-

selves at home. I'll bring my wife around to meet you soon."
With that, he strolled off.

They moved to the drinks table and picked one then went
to stand under a tree.

"Do you know anyone here?" Conor asked.

"I recognize a few people but most of them I have no idea
who they are. People who work the race come from all over
the state. It's an honor to do so."

Soon, Dr. Dillard asked for the group's attention. He gave
a short welcome and stated that the party would be the fun
before the busy week ahead.

That drew a ripple of laugher from everyone. Conor
wasn't sure about what that meant but he was confident he
would soon learn. By then some of Christina's anxiety had
mellowed. For that he was grateful, but he remained close
to her anyway.

Dr. Dillard introduced his wife to everyone, and she gave
them directions on how to go about getting their food and
encouraged them to sit wherever they wished.

Conor and Christina lined up on one side of the long tables. Picking up their plates, they moved through the buf-
fet line. It was some of the most delicious-looking food he
had seen since arriving in Kentucky.

"I hope you like barbecue," Christina said over her shoulder.

"I love it."

With full plates, they found an empty table. They settled
into their chairs and started to eat. Other couples joined
them until there were only two places left. These were soon
taken by two men. As each new person joined them, everyone went around the table introducing themselves. Once
again, they circled the table with names.

After Christina introduced herself, one of the men gave her an odd look. "Aren't you the veterinarian who was caught selling your drugs a few years back? I'm surprised you were invited to work at the racecourse."

Conor felt and saw Christina stiffen. This could only be her worst nightmare.

"Yes, I'm she, but I was not guilty." Her fork made no noise when she placed it on her plate.

The man poked his companion with his elbow. "Don't you remember that case?"

The other man grunted and continued to eat.

The first man returned to the conversation. "Still, I'm surprised they considered you for this group."

"I assure you I've been officially vetted. And can do the job."

Conor had heard enough. Christina didn't have to sit here and listen to this and neither did he. "I believe you owe Doctor Mobbs an apology."

The man took another swig of the amber liquor in his glass. He huffed. "For speaking the truth?"

Conor stood. "For being rude at the dinner table."

Christina put her hand on his arm. "It's not worth it."

"No, it's not," the man said it. "Especially since I'm speaking the truth."

Christina looked around the table. "If you'll excuse me, it was nice to meet you all."

Conor had to admit Christina held her head elegantly high as she rose, but he knew the willpower it took for her to do so. Inside, she would be a mass of raw emotions. She walked away with her shoulders squared.

He glared at the bad-mannered man. "I know I'm from

another country, but I can recognize a drunk ass when I see one. You may not think so but you owe her an apology."

Conor caught up with Christina halfway down a path leading to a large barn in the fenced field behind the house. When he joined her he didn't say anything, he just fell into step beside her. Despite wanting to take her in his arms to comfort her, he resisted.

They continued walking. They were almost to the barn before she spoke. "I'm never going to live down what happened."

"From what I understand, you don't have anything to live down."

"But it keeps cropping up. My home is here. I don't want to leave. It wasn't even me yet I'm the one that carries the stigma."

"It's not fair. I agree with that. But sometimes life is not fair."

She gave him a troubled look. "I'm sorry. You know that better than I."

"We're not talking about me tonight. We're talking about you. I was proud of you back there. You held your head high and you didn't let it show how much it hurt. And you didn't let me get into a fight. By the way, I'm not sure I could've whipped him."

Christina gave him a weak grin. "You know I do appreciate you defending me."

"It's not hard to defend you because you know what you're doing."

They continued walking, entering the open doors of the barn.

Conor had learned early in his relationship with Christina that being in a barn was where she thrived. She renewed her energy. The barn was where she went when she needed to think. Christina didn't hesitate to enter. They were overdressed for the place but she continued walking and he didn't stop her.

A couple of horses' heads hung over their stall gates. Christina patted the first horse's nose.

The sound of an animal in pain came from the back corner.

Christina hurried down the hall with Conor right behind her. They found a horse lying on its side.

She didn't hesitate to go down to her knees in her dress beside the horse and give it a quick examination with her hands. "This horse is in labor and it's coming breech. We need to get this colt out immediately, or the mare may die."

Conor said nothing.

She looked at Conor. He had gone still as a post. His skin had turn ghostly. A haunted look filled his eyes. He appeared terrified. "Conor? I'm going to need help."

"I'll go get Doctor Dillard."

"There's no time. You'll have to help me. I'm gonna need your muscles if we're gonna get this colt into the world safely."

"I...uh..."

"Conor! Go to the tack room and see what you can find that we might need."

Conor blinked and seemed to rejoin her from wherever he had gone. He hurried away.

While he was gone, she placed her ear to the horse's bulging belly and listened to her steady heartbeat, hating that her stethoscope was in her bag at home.

Conor returned with an armful of supplies that included

blankets and a bucket. His skin had turned to a more natural color, but his lips remained a thin, tight line.

"I saw a water faucet just outside the doors. I'll get some." Taking the bucket, he hurried off.

When he returned to the stall, he sat the bucket in the corner.

She rose and scrubbed her hands. Conor continued to stand there looking at the horse.

"We have to see if we can turn it."

"There are already two legs showing." Conor's words were monotone.

"Still, we have to try. I need your help." Christina didn't know what was going on with him, but what she did know was she couldn't do this without him. He had to focus on what was happening. Whatever problem he had he could deal with it afterward. Right now, she needed his help. "Have you done this before?"

He nodded. "A couple of times."

"Then that's twice as many as I have. I'm going to see if I can turn the colt." She laid a blanket on the hay behind the horse before going down on her knees. She worked to move the colt but made no real progress.

The horse moaned.

"My arm isn't long enough to reach the head." She looked at Conor. His eyes met hers. She watched his stricken look turn to one of determination.

He removed his jacket and hung it over the stall wall, rolling up his sleeves as far as he could then washed his hands and arms before he said, "Let me try."

He helped her stand then he lay down on his stomach. "Watch for the contractions and let me know when one is coming. I don't want my blood cut off."

With relief, Christina placed her hand on the horse's belly and felt. Conor was back with her. "I'll try to give you as much notice as I can."

"If I can use those moments between contractions, I'll have more room. Timing is everything."

"I'll do my best."

Conor met her gaze. "I never doubted it."

Seconds later she said, "Here comes one."

He removed his arm. When the contraction eased he went after the head of the colt. "I need to find the nose. I'm going to shift the head so it's not hung. The colt is still alive. I can feel its heart beating."

"Contraction coming," Christina announced.

Conor removed his arm. "It's still breech, but I believe we can pull this colt out now. During the next contraction, you'll need to pull while I work the head." He put his arm inside again. They waited, anticipation hanging in the air. "Ready? Let's go on my call. You need to make this a steady pull but as quickly as you can."

She looked at him. "I'll be ready. Contraction coming."

"Now," Conor said.

Christina pulled the legs. Conor's face contorted while he worked through the contraction. She could see the behind of the colt.

"Gentle tug. The head is in the right place," Conor encouraged.

Christina continued the pressure. Soon, the colt slipped from the mother. She and Conor were both breathing heavily when they finished. They didn't take a moment to catch their breaths before they were on their knees beside the colt. Christina quickly grabbed a blanket and began working it over the small animal, cleaning its mouth and face.

Conor, more himself than he had been, still looked worried but he joined her in rubbing.

"He's not breathing. We need to get some air in him."

Conor went to work across the colt's middle section using circles.

Christina was busy continuing to clean the baby's mouth and nostrils. She placed her mouth close to the animal's nose and breathed out. After a couple of times, the colt snorted and its eyes opened.

She looked at Conor. Pure relief showed on his face. Far more than she would have anticipated.

"I'll get Doctor Dillard." He went to the bucket and cleaned up then left the stall.

She sat back against the stable wall to catch her breath and watched him go. What was the matter with him? She'd had to force him to help her, which wasn't like him. He'd jumped in when needed when they had worked together before but tonight...

The mare worked her way to her feet before the new colt wobbled its way to her side. The mother licked it in acceptance. It was amazing to see new life come into the world. Would she ever get to have that moment? Conor's face popped into her mind. What would it be like to have his child?

Dr. Dillard rushed up. "O'Brian said you've been busy out here. She wasn't due for another week."

Christina didn't even have the energy to stand. He had to help her.

"I'm glad you two were here." Dr. Dillard fussed over her.

She looked around and didn't see Conor amongst the growing crowd. "It was pretty exciting, but all looks well now."

"I understand the colt was breech. I'm glad you both were

here. I really appreciate it. This is my favorite horse. I have high hopes for this colt."

She went to the water bucket. "I'm glad we were, too."

"I heard about what happened at the dinner table. My apologies, Christina. That shouldn't have happened. He's been reprimanded. I put together a team and I expect everyone to work together. Saying stuff like that even when you're drunk isn't acceptable. You have more than proved your worth tonight."

"Thank you. And thank you for including me on the team and for your support."

Dr. Dillard's focus remained on the colt. "I'll see you at daylight Monday morning."

"I'll be there, sir." The crowd opened for her to walk through.

Christina moved away and headed for the house, searching out a bathroom and Conor. She looked everywhere and found him on the front porch. He stood with a shoulder against one of the columns, looking out at the night. What was going on? What had spooked him?

Shame filled Conor at his recent actions. He had failed Christina, his profession and himself. All of his feelings were tangled up in the loss of his baby. He could not think of anything else as he had watched the mare in labor. The horror of knowing his wife had killed herself when she'd been carrying his baby.

"Conor?"

The trepidation in Christina's voice only made him feel worse.

"Is everything all right?"

"I'm fine. Are you ready to go? If not, I'll call a taxi and leave the driver for you."

She went to him and wrapped her hand around his arm. "I'm not going anywhere without you. I'm ready to leave anyway. I'm a mess."

Soon, they were settled in the backseat of the car.

Christina held his hand while leaning her head against his shoulder, yet she said nothing. The driver maneuvered through the traffic. Before long, they were back at the hotel.

After the way he had acted, he dreaded asking when they reached the lobby, "Do you still want to come up? I'll understand if you don't."

She looked unsure for a moment. "I had planned to. If you still want me."

"I will always want you." That was the one thing he felt confident about. He led her to the elevator. "I'm sorry if I made you feel that I didn't."

The door to his suite closed behind them before she said, "I need a bath."

"You were wonderful tonight." He walked to the bar and took out a bottle of liquor. It was the first time in a long time. "I'm sorry I let you down."

"When?" She moved close but out of touching distance. "You defended my honor and helped in a difficult delivery. You have nothing to apologize for."

"I don't feel that way."

"Conor." This time she touched him on the arm. "Talk to me. Tell me what you were thinking back there. What upset you? For a few minutes there I didn't think you were going to help me with the colt."

"I almost didn't."

"Why? I know you're a good veterinarian, so it has to be something else."

He forced the words out. "Because it's too hard to watch a baby being born."

Confusion covered her face and she just looked at him. "I would think you'd be wonderful with babies. Of any type."

"My wife was pregnant when she killed herself."

Christina sucked in her breath. Her eyes watered. "Conor, I am so sorry." She wrapped her arms around him, pressing herself again him.

He returned her hug and pulled her against him, drawing comfort from her. They stood like that for a long time. Saying nothing and taking strength from each other. Slowly, his pain ebbed away.

"The colt brought back what had happened. Reminded me of what I had lost."

"You said nothing." She looked at him.

He cupped her cheek. "The hurt has eased since I met you. You have pulled me out of that dark place and forced me to go to work."

She smiled softly. "I did that?"

"Yes, you did." He kissed her and led her toward the bathroom. "And I intend to show you how grateful I am."

CHAPTER NINE

MONDAY MORNING, AS the sun brightened the eastern end of Churchill Downs, Christina stood at the back stretch of the racetrack. Her hands rested on the rail as she waited for the next group of horses to make their morning exercise run. Excited anticipation that came close, but wasn't quite equal to Conor's lovemaking, filled her. The exception heightened the thrill.

A warm body hers recognized immediately moved in close. She didn't have to look to know it was Conor beside her. She would miss him when he left. She didn't even want to think about it. Yet, the calendar days kept flipping by. Too soon, he would be in Ireland and she would be here. She wouldn't let herself think of him leaving.

That morning she had let him sleep and slipped out of bed. As much as she would have liked to remain with him, she wanted to make a good impression during the week of the Derby. She couldn't afford any mistakes.

Yesterday they had lounged around Conor's luxury hotel room. They hadn't even gone out for meals. Instead, they had enjoyed room service. They had watched TV, slept and then explored each other's bodies to their hearts' content. She had never felt more desired or satisfied. That day would be treasured in her memories.

"I missed you this morning," he murmured, leaning his head close to hers.

"I had to get moving. I needed to be on time." She leaned into him.

"I know, but that doesn't mean I liked waking up without you."

Unfortunately, that would soon be something she would have to get used to. "I'm afraid it's gonna be like that most of this week."

His voice held melancholy. "I don't even want to think about it. I hate the thought of it."

"We'll just have to take it day by day."

"So what do you have on your agenda? I'm not allowed to see Gold without someone in attendance, and he has to remain in the barn stall unless he's being schooled. I'm pretty much on my own except a few hours of the day."

She looked around at all the police officers within her view. "Security is tight around here. For the horses and the rest of us. I have to admit it's more substantial than I expected."

"I'll just be checking daily with the trainer and grooms to see if there are any issues. I understand that I can't do any care. I can only confer with the track veterinarians. Still, I'll be here when he runs and will run interference if necessary. In case there's any questions about his health and care."

She grinned. "Yes, those track vets can be territorial."

"I hope one feels that way about me." His gaze met hers.

Heat floated over her skin. "This one might."

"Might?"

"Are you looking for some admiration?"

"I'll take what I can get. Mr. Guinness will be here tomorrow. I'll be picking him up from the airport and having

lunch with him. Then bringing him by here in the afternoon. He will expect me to be at a meeting with the team
tomorrow night."

"Looks like we both are going to be busy this week."
Christina couldn't help but be disappointed she wouldn't
be seeing him. She needed to get used to it.

"Do you think you will have time to show me around
Churchill Downs today? I haven't even been to the stands.
I would like to have a look."

"You certainly should do it before Friday or Saturday."

"You mean that all this—" he waved his hand toward
the expansive grandstand on the other side of the racetrack
"—all of those, will be filled?"

"That and the end fields, and the center of the track.
There it's not so much about the races but mostly about the
bourbon. Personally, I'd rather see the horses run."

"I would as well."

The sound of horses racing drew her attention. Loud
enough that it created an anticipation in her chest. "Here
they come."

The thunder of hooves came toward them, then into view
as the exercise jockeys rode the horses at full capacity. They
went by and into the distance as they ran into the second
turn.

"When does Gold run?"

"He'll be coming around in just a few minutes."

"How does he look?" She wanted him to win for Conor.

"I'll let you be the judge."

It didn't take long before sounds of running and heavy
breathing filled the air. Soon, two more horses came around

the curve and before them. She grabbed Conor's forearm. "Gold looks wonderful."

"He does."

She clearly heard the pride in Conor's voice.

They watched in silence as the horses continued around the track and out of sight.

"I better get to the vets meeting." She turned to go.

He stopped her with a touch to the elbow. "Could you meet me for lunch and then show me around?"

"I'll text you when I know what my schedule will be."

"I hope I get to see you." He gave her a quick kiss on the temple.

"Me, too." She took a couple of steps and stopped again. Headed her direction was the rude man from the party on Saturday night.

"Excuse me."

Conor moved up beside her so he stood between her and the man. She stepped around him but stayed close.

The man cleared his throat. "I want to apologize. I was a jerk the other night. Bourbon loosened my tongue. I shouldn't have said what I said."

Christina didn't move. "I appreciate you coming to tell me. I hope we can work together without any problems."

"That's my intent."

She gave him a tight smile. "Mine as well."

The man looked sincere. "I heard about the colt delivery. Impressive."

"Thank you."

"Then I will see you around." His look flickered to Conor, who hadn't moved a muscle.

"I'm sure you will," Conor said in a tight voice.

The man gave them both a curt nod and left.

Christina looked at Conor. "That was nice of him."

"It would have been nicer if it hadn't happened." Conor released his fisted hands.

Her hand circled his arm. "I would like for it to be forgotten."

Conor spent the rest of his morning in the equine clinic, answering questions about Gold, then attended the track vet evaluation of the horse. Other than that, he was encouraged to leave the backside.

The rest of his week would consist of waiting and trying to catch a glimpse of Christina. Because he was associated with a horse that was racing, he was not allowed for security reasons to do any volunteer veterinary work. Which would leave him with time on his hands. He would have daily discussions with the trainer and the grooms and be at the track for any training, especially when Gold was running the Breeze or being schooled in the padlock. Other than that, he would be restricted by security.

Conor had volunteered to help out. He had seen Dr. Dillard briefly and offered to at least watch along the rail during the Breeze and at the padlock. To be a first responder. Dr. Dillard told him he would keep that in mind. Still, Conor did not anticipate being asked to help unless the man became desperate. Conor's problem was he missed being with Christina. Just the idea of not seeing her hurt.

Why had he let her matter so much? He hadn't planned on that happening. Hadn't thought it could. Despite his fear of being like his father, he had overcome it, and somehow Christina had slipped in and captured his notice. Something no one had managed to do since Louisa. He had never intended to care like this again, then came Christina.

A beep on his phone made him look. His heart jumped. Christina. She was through for the day and would meet him for lunch. She wrote she would wait for him in front of the equine clinic.

Christina greeted him with a huge smile that had him smiling like a fool back at her. It had only been a few hours since he had seen her. The woman had him acting like a love-struck teenage boy.

"I guess your morning went well." He liked seeing her so happy.

She continued to smile. "Very well. I'm going to enjoy this week."

"I'm glad to hear that." He squeezed her hand for a moment. "So where are we going for lunch?"

"There's a restaurant just off the backside. I understand from Callie they have some great burgers."

"Sounds good."

They walked down the gravel drive between the barns then crossed the road to a single-story building.

"I think you'll like this place. It's dark and has a lot of wood. It should remind you of a pub."

Something he hadn't thought of in days. Home. Interesting.

The lighting inside was dim. It took a moment for his eyes to adjust. The older building held wooden tables and chairs that had seen better days. Christina passed them up for a booth in the back. She slid in and stopped in the middle of the seat.

He waved her farther into the booth and took the space beside her. "I want to sit next to you."

"Maybe we shouldn't be so obvious."

He scanned the area. "Who here do you think cares? I certainly don't care if they know I'm attracted to you."

She grinned. "I like the idea that you are."

He took her hand and placed it on his knee.

An older man with a white apron around his waist came to take their order. They decided on hamburgers and fries.

Conor said, "Tell me how it went today."

"Really well. Not that we did anything in particular other than get orders and be reminded of how strict they are about the horses during Derby week security-wise."

"What are you going to be doing?" He rubbed the top of her hand with the pad of his thumb.

"The next two days I'll be helping with taking the daily bloodwork then watching at the padlock during schooling. The next day may be different."

"Then you're going to be everywhere."

The waiter brought their drinks.

"It sounds like it." She took a swallow.

"You'll be having some long days." He saw what little time he would have with her slipping way.

"I will. But I'm looking forward to it."

He squeezed her hand. "I'm glad this worked out for you."

"But I'll miss seeing you. Now, if Gold wins the Derby race we'll both be successful."

Conor was not sure that would make him feel successful about the trip. He already dreaded leaving her.

Their burgers came and they spent their time eating and discussing the horses that would be running.

"Are you off for the rest of the afternoon?" Conor asked.

"Yes, I can be your tour guide." She caught the drip running down her chin with a napkin.

He wished he could have licked it away. "I would like you to stay the night with me, too."

"I wish I could but I have the horses to see about." She ran her hand down his leg.

"I'll miss you."

She met his gaze. "I'll miss you, too. Are you ready to go? We'll go have a look at Churchill Downs."

"When you are."

She took out her phone and sent a text message.

"What's that about?"

"I got us a ride over to the stands. Otherwise, we would have a pretty long walk."

A few minutes later a truck pulled up in front of the restaurant.

"That's Carlos. He's one of the staff here. He said he would give us a lift." She climbed into the front passenger seat and moved over. Conor settled in beside her.

Carlos drove them back along the road they had walked earlier then veered to the left into a tunnel.

"I had no idea this was here." Conor looked around in amazement.

"Most people don't."

They came up into the sunlight on the opposite side of the track. Carlos stopped at the first gate on the grandstand they came to. Conor popped out then helped her down.

"Carlos, thanks for the ride. We'll find our own way back," Christina called over her shoulder.

He nodded and drove on.

They stood in front of the stands for a moment. "I've already told you about the twin spires, which are used as the logo for Churchill Downs. Come on, let's climb a few rows up so you can see."

Conor stood beside her, looking out at the track. "It is something. The big screens and hedges and the Winner's Circle."

"That, it is. As you can tell, we run dirt mostly here. But there is also a grass track. I understand you run mostly grass in Ireland. Both can be a mess on a rainy Derby Day."

"I can imagine. We have practiced Gold on dirt just because of this."

"The track is maintained carefully to make it as safe for the riders and horses as possible." He had seen the track groomers in action. They were a finely tuned and efficient group.

"Down there is where the starting gate is for a number of the races." She pointed to the right near the last turn. "A few races start near the first back turn. But I'm not telling you anything you don't know."

He smiled. "No, you aren't, but I enjoy hearing you talk. I love your enthusiasm."

Conor continued to listen and ask questions. Christina was in her element and loved the racetrack.

She spread her arms wide. "These stands will be overflowing on Derby Day. All to watch what they call the two greatest minutes in sports."

"I can see why they call it that." Conor couldn't help but be impressed.

"I have more to show you. Doctor Dillard made special arrangements so I can take you up to that balcony where you can see the entire track. Give you a bird's-eye view."

They went under the stands to the elevator. It took them to the sixth floor, where they stepped out into an open area with tables. She pushed through the glass doors that led to a balcony and walked all the way to the rail. "Isn't it gorgeous?"

He watched her. "It is but not as pretty as you."

Christina gave him a lopsided grin. "Thank you but you need to focus on the racetrack."

He put his hand around her waist and pulled her to his side for a little squeeze. "I'd rather concentrate on you." He let her go before she could complain. He looked at the track. "Yes, it is pretty. I still can't get over how large it is."

"It's impressive. Would you like to go see the museum?"

"There's a museum here?" He hadn't heard of it.

"Yes. It not only shows the past winners, but a short movie and history of the event."

"I would like to see it." He also wanted to make the most of the time he could have with Christina.

They returned to the elevator. The doors had hardly closed before Conor took her into his arms. His kiss had her gripping his shoulders to stand.

"I haven't had a chance to do that today and I will miss out tonight, so I'm making the most of this time alone."

The doors slid open. Christina watched him with a dazed look. He grinned. "Weren't you going to show me the museum?"

"What?" She blinked.

He chuckled. Her reaction to his kiss stroked his ego.

They walked the length of the stands and stepped out a side gate to where the museum was located. At the desk they showed their badges and entered the museum. They walked through what looked like a starting gate into the exhibit area.

Strolling along hand in hand, they circled the building,

looking at the trophies, jockey outfits and discussing the famous horses that had gone on to win the Triple Crown.

"Remind me what the Triple Crown is?"

"It's when one horse wins the Kentucky Derby, the Belmont and Preakness all in the same year. That's considered the Triple Crown. Only a few horses have managed to do it. And then they go out for stud."

"Which is not a bad job if you can get it." Conor gave her a wolfish grin.

She smiled. "Every man's dream, I guess. To produce many children."

The sadness covered his face.

Her eyes turned concerned. "I'm sorry. I said that without thinking."

"It's okay."

"Would you like to have more children?" she asked softly as if unsure of his reaction.

"I don't think so. It would be too hard to lose one again."

"But you might not."

It hurt to hear her so hopeful, but he had to tell her the truth. "I couldn't take that chance."

"I think children would be worth the chance." She tugged his arm. "Let's watch this movie. That's in the round. You'll like it."

A few minutes later, they were walking out of the museum. They stopped in front of the gift shop. A number of large women's dress hats hung on a stand.

"What are the women's hats about?"

"The women wear hats on Oaks and Derby Day. Some are very extravagant. It's part of the Derby's mystique and fun."

"I'd love to see you in one."

"I'd looked pretty silly wearing one while seeing to a

horse." She waved her hand up and down herself. "And one wouldn't go with my outfit."

"You deserve to experience some of the glamours of life." He would like to give that to her.

"Thank you, but I think this week is going to consist of blue jeans and boots."

He took her hand. "I guess you're right."

They returned to the track.

A golf cart approached. She waved it down. "Are you going back to the other side?"

"Yep," the woman said.

"Do you mind if we get a ride?" Christina asked.

"Hop in."

The woman dropped them off in front of the equine clinic. They walked toward her truck.

"I enjoyed my tour."

"I'm glad you did." Christina hesitated. "I guess I should get started for home."

"I wish you were staying with me. I'm sorry I can't go with you. I have to be at the airport early in the morning."

She placed her hand on his chest. "I understand." She opened the truck door.

He leaned toward her. "I want to kiss you, but I don't think this is the place for either one of us to have a public display."

Her gaze met his. "I know."

"Doesn't mean I don't want to."

"Same here." She brushed his hair back.

"Just the same, I'm going to give you a quick one." He took a step closer.

"And I'll gladly take it."

His lips brushed hers for a moment before he straightened. "I'm already missing you. I'll see you tomorrow."

"I'll make sure it happens." She offered him a small lift of her lips.

"You drive safe."

"Bye, Conor."

He watched Christina drive toward the exit. She stopped and waved out her window. She'd known he would be watching.

Christina finished taking what seemed like her hundredth blood test for the day, not to mention the number of daily records of medications that must be reviewed and overseen each day. This had to happen every day for each horse in the stables.

Now all of the competitors were securely on the backside, it had become a busy area. That would continue until Saturday evening after the last race.

She had expected such and loved the excitement of it all. It made her blood hum. Still, she was worn out each evening.

She hadn't seen Conor since she had left him the afternoon before last. She had been busy enough not to obsess over it, but when she did pause for lunch, she scanned the area, hoping for a glimpse of him. She should've anticipated it would be this way. But that didn't mean she liked it.

He was busy with Gold. Had responsibilities of his own. Mr. Guinness would expect him to focus on the race ahead. Understanding the situation didn't mean she didn't miss him. Painfully so.

Maybe it was just as well. She needed to get used to it. Soon, Conor would be gone. The problem was she had become used to him being in her life. There in the morning and again at night. Especially at night. That, she liked the best.

She had known it wouldn't last, but that didn't mean she didn't want to enjoy him while she could. Now their jobs were getting in the way. Not that either one of them could do anything about it.

That evening she drove home exhausted. She took care of the horses before going into the empty house. Where she'd found her home reassuring just weeks earlier, now she found it depressing. Lonely.

She headed for the bathroom too tired to bother with cooking a meal, not that she would have done anything more than microwave something. After a shower to wash off the dirt, sweat and manure of the day, she pulled on a shortie gown and climbed into bed.

She was almost asleep when her phone buzzed, notifying her of a text from Conor.

Come to the back door.

What was going on? She padded along the hall through the kitchen to the door. She flipped on the outside light, pushed back the curtains and found Conor standing on her stoop. She quickly unlocked the door and flung it back. "What are you doing here?"

Conor scooped her into his arms. His mouth covered hers in a deep, wet, hot kiss that shook her to the core.

Her arms went around his neck, welcoming him into her home and her heart. She missed him to the bottom of her soul. She returned his kiss, holding nothing back. Her legs wrapped his hips.

He stepped to the counter and sat her on it, then moved

between her legs. His lips traveled down her cheek. He nipped the sweet skin behind her ear. "I've missed you."

"I've missed you, too. What do you mean by coming to my house in the middle of the night and kissing me senseless?" She gave him a defiant look and a teasing grin. "I'm not gonna let you in my bed."

"Honey, I think you're gonna be glad that I came to your bed."

"You have a high opinion of yourself. Do you think you can just bust into a woman's house and make demands on her?"

He studied her face. "You want me to go?"

She wrapped her arms around his neck. "Don't you dare. I've missed you."

He grinned. "Prove it."

Christina kissed him with everything she had in her. She slipped her hand between them and ran it over his tight length.

"Okay, I believe you might have missed me." He picked her up again and started down the hall.

He said between kisses, "I can't believe that I've been in the same half a mile as you for two solid days and didn't even catch a glimpse of you."

"I know what you mean." She nipped his earlobe.

He pressed his manhood against her center. "Can I stay?"

"You can if you make sure the back door is locked. I wouldn't want another man busting in."

Conor growled. "There better not be another man wanting in. I don't share." He carried her to her bed and dropped her. "I'll be right back."

She lay back and sighed. "I'll be right here waiting."

* * *

The next morning Christina woke before daylight.

Conor groaned beside her, pulling her to him. "It can't be time to get up."

"I'm afraid it is. The one thing I do hate about running a farm is always having to get up early to see about the horses every morning."

He nuzzled her neck. "You picked the wrong vocation."

"You don't say."

He kissed her cheek and rolled away from her. "You stay here, and I'll see about the horses this morning. Sleep in for a change."

She looked at him in the dim light from her clock. "Don't tease me this early in the morning. I could turn on you."

He gave her a quick kiss. "Hey, I'm not kidding. You sleep and I'll be back in a little while."

"You would do that for me?"

"Sure. Keep the bed warm." She felt the breeze when he lifted the covers.

"That, I can do. I'll owe you one." She had already turned over on her stomach.

"And I plan to collect."

"Mmm."

He kissed her bare shoulder.

Just a few weeks ago she wouldn't have trusted him enough to see to the horses.

Conor returned, crawling into bed. They made love. It was poignant, slow and sweet. None of the rushed excitement of the night before.

"Each time it becomes more difficult to leave you," he said as she climbed out of bed ahead of him.

It hurt her heart to think about him leaving. She had

fallen for him hard even in the short amount of time she had known him. She couldn't imagine what the pain would be like in the future. Since she already knew there wouldn't be any tomorrows with him.

The next few days would be impossibly busy. That would be a blessing. There would be less time to think about her future without Conor. She had hoped to spend the weekend with him but instead she would be traveling back and forth from her house to Churchill Downs daily. Unfortunately, he had to remain in town those nights.

She had to break it to him sometime, that she wouldn't be staying with him. Now was as good a time as any. "I'm not gonna be able to stay with you this weekend."

"Why not?" he demanded.

"The person who I had lined up to see about the horses backed out on me. And I don't have time to call around and try to find someone else."

His happy face turned sad with his eyes downcast. "There's no one you can get?"

"Not that I know of right now."

He sat on the side of the bed looking dejected. "I hate for you to travel those extra miles when you could be closer. And with me."

"Our days have already been long and I'm sure they're gonna get longer. We wouldn't see much of each other anyway." She wouldn't be sleeping with him, either.

"That's probably true." He wouldn't look at her.

"I'm tied up all day today. Tomorrow is the Oaks. Then the Derby the next." What she left out was he would be leaving after that. "As much as I hate it, I don't think we need to have any interaction anyway. Us being together might come into question since Gold stayed at my place and we know each other. I don't want there to be any questions about my integrity."

CHAPTER TEN

"INTEGRITY?" HE LOOKED at her as if she had lost her mind. "You have to be kidding."

"There can be no suspicion of impropriety."

He stood. "Then I'll drive out here."

She shook her head. "I don't think that's a good idea."

"What are you scared of?" He jerked his pants on.

"I'm scared of being accused of tampering with a horse or race. My honesty and actions could be questioned. That, I can't take a chance on."

He faced her, his legs spread in a defensive manner. "Nobody's even paying attention and that would mean not seeing me. I'm leaving soon."

"You heard that guy the other night."

"He was an idiot." Conor's voice rose.

"No, he was saying what other people are thinking."

His chin jerked up. "So you plan to go through your life worrying about that."

"I have to get used to it. This is my chance to prove myself."

Conor's brows drew together. "Who are you proving yourself to?"

"My colleagues."

He glared at her with his hands on his hips. "You are a

great veterinarian. You did nothing wrong. Why do you think you need to keep telling people that?"

"Because I let them down." She found clean clothes.

"How did you do that?" His disbelief hung in the air.

"Here everyone in the horse-racing world knows everyone else or at least about them. I made them look bad."

His mouth fell open. "You didn't do it. Nelson did. You need to leave that behind and move forward. You. Were. Not. Responsible. You are a good and caring human. You have a business that is admirable. Just because your mother thought you did not measure up that does not mean that's a fact. I think you are wonderful. And enough for anyone. In fact, you are the most amazing woman I know."

"I appreciate that, but that doesn't change the fact that my name has been damaged, and I need to guard it." She headed for the bath.

He followed. "My point is it isn't about what happened with the drugs. It's about your self-esteem."

"It doesn't do much for my self-esteem to know that you can return to Ireland so easily or that I'm not worth staying here for. You act like you really care but you don't show it."

He looked confused. "What do you mean?"

"What are you going back to? You have family but a lot of people live far away from their family. You could stay here and help run the farm with me. It doesn't seem that you're having any trouble leaving."

He followed her to the bath. "Christina, I can't make that type of commitment. I gave all I had the last time. I couldn't live through a loss like that again."

"What makes you think you would lose me? Louisa killed herself out of despair. The loss of your child was an accident. I'm not going anywhere. This is your chance to start over. To find happiness. Here with me."

He filled the doorway. "Ireland. That's my home."

"You can make your home anywhere. Even here with me."

"I can't, Christina. I can't give you what you want. A husband. Children. I just can't do it again." He glowered at her. Why couldn't he get her to understand?

"I think you could. You're just scared. Maybe it's a good thing we can't see each other for the next few days. We can say goodbye here." She turned her back on him and started the shower.

The idea hurt him more deeply that he would have anticipated. He wanted to shout no, but he just couldn't offer her what she wanted. Now was the time to walk away from her. Even if it was another form of death.

Christina wasn't sure how their conversation had turned into an ugly argument that had gone so bad so fast. Had it been from frustration over not being able to see each other? More likely, it was over the fear they wouldn't see each other again after the race. Whatever it was, she had to learn to accept it was over between her and Conor.

She'd been awake most of the night after their fight when she should've been resting. Instead, she'd spent that time going through different scenarios of how to make their situation better. She couldn't afford to have any hint of impropriety. She had learned that the hard way. Negatives were eagerly believed, while positives were harder to earn.

She worked too hard to get this opportunity to assist during the Derby week. She couldn't fail. She was sorry that

Conor couldn't understand that. His reputation had not been called into question.

On Friday morning she drove onto the backside before daylight. Today would be the Oaks Race, all female horses. It would be a full day of racing. The backside was already buzzing with activity.

She had been given her assignment for the day the evening before. There were still a couple of hours before the first race. She and her partner teamed up to help with day-of blood tests. Each horse racing would have to be tested within thirty minutes of their race. This was to look for a number of medicines that could be used to enhance the horse's performance. Those were absolutely not allowed in the racing world. Horses found to have been using were immediately disqualified.

An hour before the first race she returned to the equine clinic. There she caught a golf cart along with three other veterinarians. The driver would drop them at their assigned position at the first turn of the racetrack. If there was an accident, it would only be seconds before she and her colleagues would be there to care for the horse. Other veterinarians would be doing the same along the mile-long track.

She carried medical supplies in her backpack, including different sized splints for the horses' legs, and pain medicines. Breaks and wounds were her largest concern during the actual race. There was much more to the two days of racing than many people thought. So much took place behind the scenes. It wasn't all about running.

In the distance she could see the stands filling. For once in her life she wished she could dress more feminine, to wear something besides her T-shirt, jeans and boots. She would have liked to look less masculine and more feminine, especially today when so many other women were dressed in their finest, including a hat. Many of them would wear pink in honor of the female horses racing.

Throughout all the activity, she never saw Conor. It wasn't from the lack of trying. She searched for him wherever she went. The chances of her seeing him would be almost nothing from her station on the rail. She was in a restricted area. He would not be allowed there.

Sadness washed over her. She'd known when she stepped out of the shower the day before and Conor was gone, that it was over between them. She had to keep reminding herself of that fact. It was for the best since he would soon be returning to Ireland. At least it wouldn't be a long, drawn-out romantic drama-like parting. That, she couldn't live through.

Friday evening she drove off the backside with a tight chest filled with disappointment. She had been around hundreds of thousands of people all day, yet she felt so alone. This, she should get used to because she would carry the feeling for months and years to come.

Her phone rang. She jerked it up without looking, hoping it would be Conor. "Hello."

"I was just checking in to see how you're doing?"

"Mama. I'm fine. Busy working at Churchill Downs." She put the call in over her truck speakers.

"You got the job?"

Her mother sounded so amazed it grated on Christina's nerves. "I did."

"Even after what happened?"

"Yes, Mother. And I did nothing wrong."

"No, but you should have realized what Nelson was doing."

"We've gone over this before. I'm not up to doing it again tonight. It's been a long day."

"What're you wearing to Churchill Downs? I hope you're wearing something nice."

"The last thing I need to have on while on the ground caring for a horse that is hurt is a dress."

"But it's Churchill Downs. All the women will have dresses and hats on," her mother whined.

"Except for those who have to work like I do."

"I have never understood you and those horses." Her mother's voice carried her usual disapproving tone.

Christina sighed. Here they went again.

"Why couldn't you have done something that didn't require you to get your hands dirty?"

"Mother, I want you to stop there." Christina raised her voice. "You have spent this entire phone call making me feel like I don't measure up. My whole life, in fact. I am a good veterinarian. I have done nothing wrong, and I refuse to act like I have. I'm good enough to take care of any horse at any time, and I love what I do. If you can't talk to me in a positive way then just don't call. I'm tired and I've had a long week. I'm not going to put up with it any longer."

There was a long pause.

"Christina, I think you're overreacting."

"Mother, I'm going to say bye now. Think about what I've said before you call again." Christina hung up. For once, she felt good about herself after talking to her mother. Conor had made her feel strong enough to stand up for herself. She wanted to tell him but that wasn't going to happen.

Because of him, her life would be different. Better.

Conor struggled to act enthusiastic about the Derby Day races. It would be a long day until Gold ran. That left him with a lot of time for his mind to wander. His thoughts were more on Christina than they were on what he should be worrying about—Gold. He and Christina had broken up. Wasn't that what he wanted?

Right now, all he needed was to see her. Just a glimpse. He missed her like he never believed he would. She was so close but so far away. Was she hoping to see him as well?

Over the past few days he had remained busy but not enough so that there was no downtime. That was when thoughts of Christina filled his mind. Was she as miserable as he?

He had not slept since leaving her bed four days ago. Gold's trainer and one of the grooms had even commented on how awful he looked. It did not help that he arrived early in the day, and Mr. Guinness required him for social events in the evening. All he could think about was how much he wanted to join Christina in caring for the horses. He would even help deliver a foal if he could do that with her.

Morning after morning he had stood beside the track, hoping she would join him to watch the horses run. He was disappointed. He had missed the look of expectation that came over her face at the sound of the horses running in her direction. Along with the adrenaline rush it gave him to bring her release.

Around horses and in bed with him she was beautiful. Expressive. In her element. She loved the sights, smells and the trill of horseracing. If he wasn't careful, he would start writing odes to Thoroughbred racing and Christina. There were probably already hundreds of printed poems about the Kentucky Derby. Christina deserved just as many.

What would happen if he decided to stay in America with Christina? His entire life had been built around being true to the one you love. He had seen what it was like when a husband wasn't faithful. It slowly destroys the other person and makes the family rot from the inside out. He had been true to Louisa but now she was gone. Could he be that devoted to Christina? Rebuild his life with her?

Mr. Guinness stepped up beside him at the rail. "You have stood here each morning. At first, I thought you were that absorbed in the horses running. But then I realized you aren't looking at the horses. You're looking everywhere but at them. Who are you searching for?"

Had Conor really been that pathetic?

"Is it the woman who boarded Gold?"

"Yes." Conor continued to search the crowd.

"So what is going on between you two?"

This was not a subject the two of them normally had a conversation over. "Right now, nothing. She told me not to have anything to do with her during the races because she didn't want there to be any appearance of collusion."

"Okay, knowing the security around here I can see that. So why the long face? After Gold's race, find her."

"There's more to it than that."

"And what is that?" When Conor didn't say anything right away, he continued. "You've worked for me for years and because of that we have become friends as well. After your wife died I, along with your other friends and family, have watched you become a shell of yourself. So much so that when your brother and sister came to me and asked me if I would send you over here with Gold I agreed to mess in your life. Not something I make a habit of. We were all worried you would never return to your old self. We all wanted you to have a fresh start. A chance to get away from your memories."

"I had no idea you were in on this."

"You would never have if you hadn't looked so happy when I arrived and now you don't. I would have never said anything. But I knew our plan had worked the second I saw you. This is what we wanted for you. Not necessarily to find someone but to move on past your grief and sadness. To start living again."

"I was that bad?"

Mr. Guinness nodded. "I knew by just talking to you on the phone. Just the difference in your voice said whatever this woman had done, you needed to grab hold of it."

"Being with her would mean leaving everything I've known behind in Ireland."

"You do realize there are airplanes. You can visit. Your family can visit you. Even Gold managed to get over here." Mr. Guinness grinned. "Do I dare to tread on our friendship enough to ask how you feel about this woman?"

"I'm afraid I'm in love with her."

"That's not a bad thing, Conor."

He thought for a moment. "No, it's not. In fact, I've never felt better about myself or life in a long time."

Mr. Guinness gave Conor a slap on the shoulder. "That's what I figured. Maybe you need to give your plans some thought. See what options you can come up with. Even as miserable as you are right now, you look far better than you did before."

"Now, we should concentrate on Gold. We need to go if we're going to walk him over to the starting gate. Maybe you'll catch a glimpse of her as we go."

Conor's chest tightened. Mr. Guinness and Christina were right. There really wasn't anything left for him in Ireland that he couldn't change. His clients had slowly drifted away, and he'd let them. He was down to Gold now. Here with

Christina, he could have a fresh start. They could build something together. If she would still have him.

He liked America. He liked living the lifestyle that Christina offered. So why wouldn't he stay? Because he was afraid. Of caring again and losing her, but if he didn't try then he would lose her for sure. He would have no more than he had now. Which was nothing. He knew well what nothing felt like. He didn't like it. Now he understood what it was to have Christina and he wanted that. He had to decide if it was worth stepping beyond his fear to take a hold of happiness.

Christina was worth that and more.

Christina remained in her position at the rail as the groups of owners with their families and those involved with the horses running the Derby race made their traditional walk from the barns to the starting gate.

She tried not to focus on Gold's group, but she couldn't help herself. She got a glimpse of Conor long before he reached her. Her heart fluttered hard enough she worried she might lift off. Was he as happy to see her as she was to see him? Was he still angry with her? Would he leave without telling her goodbye? The idea made her physically sick.

When the group came close enough, Conor's intent gaze locked in on hers. It didn't waver. In that moment it was only them. All the other stuff had fallen away. The thrill of seeing him buzzed through her.

Conor smiled. Concern filled his eyes but a hint of hope as well. She returned a small smile.

He didn't approach her. She appreciated him honoring her request they have no contact. Even though she longed to climb over the railing, run to him and wrap her arms around his neck to give him a kiss. She mouthed "Good luck."

His smile grew a little brighter as he continued past her on the dirt track.

Christina waited with building anticipation as each one of the horses was announced as they were put into the starting gate.

Soon, the track announcer said, "They're in the gate... and they're off!"

The horses came barreling toward her, spread out across the track. By the time they had reached her they had moved into a double line with a group in the middle.

Gold was in the group as they ran past her. She couldn't help but quietly cheer the horse and jockey on. She didn't dare be any louder.

The horses continued to run, picking up speed, and the crowd stood, hollering. From her vantage point she couldn't see even a screen to tell her how Gold was doing. She listened to the announcer as he called names and positions as the horses rounded the back turn. Seconds later the announcer said they're coming around the last curve and into the homestretch.

She heard Gold was in fourth place and the announcer then said Gold was making a move on the outside. He was in third place coming into the homestretch. The crowd was screaming louder. Gold crossed the finish line in second place.

Christina couldn't help but jump up and down. He had done so well. She was proud of the efforts of the horse, Conor and those who worked with Gold.

She wanted to run to the stands, wrap her arms around

Conor and congratulate him, but she had to hold her spot.
There was one more race before the day would be done.

Would Conor search her out? Or would he be celebrating?

The next forty minutes went by slowly.

She was exhausted and ready to go home by the time
the races were over. She slowly made her way to her truck.
Still no Conor. The horses were waiting on her. At one time
she would've hoped to spend the night with Conor, telling
him goodbye. Now she would be going home to an empty
house and bed.

She didn't know what she had expected. They were too
different. He from Ireland and she from the States. She
wanted a husband and family. He a good time while he
was there with no attachments. She was messy and he was
tidy. He could cook and she couldn't. She wanted to live
here and he had his life in Ireland. He was devoted to his
dead wife and she wanted him devoted to her. They weren't
meant to be.

CHAPTER ELEVEN

THE NEXT MORNING Christina crawled out of bed, fed the horses and returned to bed again. She was exhausted physically, mentally and emotionally after the past week. All she wanted now was to pull the covers over her head and stay that way for a few days, but with animals to feed and care for she couldn't.

She missed Conor with every fiber of her being. He was no doubt packed to return to Ireland. She had hoped, then prayed, he would call. The silence of her phone just added to her agitation and disappointment. She would have to learn to live without him. To be alone.

Working in the barn had been her therapy for so long and now he had ruined that. Memories of them being there hung in the air and settled in her mind. Neither reassuring nor comforting.

Tears stung her eyes. She blinked them away. Last night she had done enough of that.

A good day of rest and she would be her old self. Or at least that was the lie she kept repeating.

She brought this misery on herself. Had become too involved with Conor. Knew it while it was happening. Had told herself that and still, she walked into his arms and invited him into her bed. What had she been thinking? She hadn't been; she'd been feeling.

Rolling over, she clutched the pillow with Conor's smell still attached to her chest and buried her face in it. If she could just sleep today, then get up and start again tomorrow, maybe she could get her life back. With patience and taking care of the horses, the past three weeks would be forgotten. Then she could survive him not being there.

As much as working Derby week had meant to her, having Conor meant more. She had just realized that too late.

In the middle of the afternoon, she hauled herself out of bed. She had to get moving. She had to accept what her life looked like. Those weeks with Conor had only been a dream in the middle of reality. Now it was time to live in the latter once more. After pulling on her work clothes, she headed for the barn.

Cleaning out the stalls despite their not needing the attention would be a good distraction from her worries. She turned the music up and sang along at the top of her voice. The horses gave her a quizzical look but returned to their eating.

What was that noise? Her name? She turned.

There in the half circle of the sun coming through the large barn door stood the most wonderful sight she had ever seen. Conor. Her heartbeat roared in her ears. Her hands were sweaty and they shook. She murmured, "You're here."

"Where else should I be?" He studied her as if her answer was very important to him. "I belong here."

She staggered a moment, then planted the pitchfork into the ground to steady herself. "I thought you were leaving. That you were at least loading Gold to go home."

"No. We are both staying."

"Staying?"

Conor's mouth quirked at the corners. "As in not going."

"I know what *staying* means." She threw her shoulders back.

* * *

Conor liked this Christina the best. The one with color in her cheeks and eyes bright with determination. "Would you mind moving away from the pitchfork? It makes me a little nervous. We need to talk. I have a couple of things to ask you."

She placed the tool against one of the stall walls. "So talk."

He had hoped she might fall into his arms and welcome him back. But not his Christina. She would make him work for her. Make him bare his soul. "Gold is being put out to stud. Mr. Guinness wants me to stay here with him. In fact, I gave him the idea and volunteered for the position."

"In America?"

"Yes. In Kentucky. Mr. Guinness asked me to ask you if Gold could be stabled here. He would like me, with your assistance, to oversee the breeding program."

Christina's eyes widened and her mouth dropped, as if he was making it all up. "You would stay here? Stay in my barn?"

Conor chuckled. "Gold would stay here. I was hoping for warmer and softer accommodations."

"I…uh…"

He had never seen her this flustered.

"And where will you stay?" She looked at him.

He gave her a long, lingering look, hoping the desire he was banking did not burst into flames before they finished their discussion. "I was hoping in the house with you." His look bore into hers as he walked closer to her. "Except not in that tiny room off the kitchen."

"Then where?"

"With you."

"Is that what you want, to stay here?"

"I want to be where you are. I thought I left everything in Ireland. What I didn't know was I was coming to everything in America. You are my everything. You brought me back to life. Made me live again."

"You're willing to give up your home, your practice, your family?" She continued to watch him closely.

"I'm willing. I'll do what I must to be here with you. My life was empty and you filled it. I'll gladly do what I have to in order to have you in my life. My home was no longer home after Louisa died. I need to sell it and let somebody else create a life there. My brother and sister are there but I can visit them whenever we want. Which, by the way, I know you will like them and they will like you."

"You shouldn't have to give up everything for me."

"I see it as gaining everything. I can do what I love—caring for horses, helping you build your business and loving you the rest of my life."

She stepped back, shaking her head. "I'm not worth you giving up your entire life for."

He cupped her cheek, stopping her, and looked into her eyes. "Sweetheart, you are important enough and perfect enough just the way you are for me to flip my world. Never doubt that. You are perfect for me. The question is do you want me?"

Her gaze remained locked with his. "Of course, I want you. I've always wanted you."

"Not exactly true. I don't think you wanted me when I first showed up a few weeks ago."

She smiled. "I just wasn't ready for you then."

"And you are now?" He stepped closer.

She nodded. "Yes, because I love you."

He moved into her personal space. She smelled of something floral from her shampoo, hay and a freshness that was all her. He inhaled and savored it. "I love you, too. I never thought I would ever say those words again to a woman. Christina, you took something broken in me and put it together again. You are the glue that makes my life whole. I love you."

His lips found hers. She clung to him as if he were her lifeline.

They broke apart, breathing deeply. He maintained his hold on her. "We are going to find a good farmhand. One we can trust to see after the horses so we can sleep in, have dinner out and visit Ireland without worrying."

She looked at him with love shining in her eyes. "That sounds wonderful. By the way, I spoke to my mother the other day. She started putting me down again and I told her I wouldn't talk to her if she was going to do that. She still doesn't understand the choices I've made."

He chuckled. "I bet she won't understand you falling for an Irishman."

That look of strength filled her eyes again. "She doesn't have to understand. All she needs to know is I love you. If she starts giving me a hard time, I'll tell her I won't let her talk to me that way. Then I will politely hang up or walk away."

"I'm proud of you. But no matter what your mother says, remember I think you are just perfect the way you are. So much so I want to marry you."

"Marry me?" Her voice squeaked with surprise.

Would she turn him down? "I love you. Why wouldn't I want to marry you?"

"Because you said you wouldn't do that again."

"That was before I knew what it was like to almost lose you. I want you beside me always."

She hesitated a moment, looked away before she said, "What about children? You know I want children."

He swallowed hard. "I cannot say that I won't be terrified of losing you or one of our children, but I can't imagine a better mother. With you at my side I can do anything. I love you and I want what you want."

She threw her arms around him and pressed her face into his chest. "I love you, too. We will have the most beautiful children. I hope they all have your accent."

"If you will take me inside to check out that soft, comfortable bed of ours I'll whisper in your ear in my accent for as long as you like." He nuzzled her neck.

She grinned. "Promise?"

"Sweetheart, I promise to do that for as long as we live. I keep my promises."

EPILOGUE

Eighteen months later

CHRISTINA WALKED ACROSS the yard toward the barn. Conor hurried out, carrying their three-month-old son, Jamie. The baby bounced in his father's arms from the pace Conor set. Wide grins covered both male faces. Jamie obviously enjoyed his father's jostling.

Even at a young age, Jamie strongly favored his father. Christina had no complaints about that. Conor was an amazing and devoted father and husband. She had never seen a man more joyous or grateful than Conor when she had told him she was pregnant. Tears had filled his eyes.

He had to work at keeping his fear at bay during the pregnancy but that had become less evident after Jamie had arrived. Now Conor seemed caught up in the enjoyment of having a child, making the most of every minute.

When her mother and father had visited for the first time, Conor had run interference between her and her mother. He often interrupted her mother when she was about to say something negative and turned the conversation toward something Christina had done recently. Apparently, her mother had gotten the message and thought before she spoke further. Conor's desire to protect her only made Christina love him more.

She looked at her husband and her son. What had she done to deserve such happiness? "What's the hurry?"

"Gold's foal is coming," Conor blurted. "Buzz is with him right now. I was coming to get you. I didn't think you'd want to miss this."

"Of course I don't." Mr. Guinness had allowed them to breed Gold with a mare that had been hurt and rehabilitated on the farm. The mare's owner had no interest in her being returned so they had agreed to keep her. Conor had fallen in love with the horse. He felt she would be a good brood mare.

They all stood outside the mare's stall. Inside, Buzz, a stable hand who had quickly turned into an invaluable employee, softly spoke to the horse. They had hired Buzz so they could have a couple of mornings a week to themselves and soon learned he could handle more responsibility. Enough so they were able to visit Ireland.

Which Christina had loved. She had fallen for it and Conor's family. They had opened their arms to her and couldn't say enough about how glad they were to see Conor happy again. She and Conor were already planning a return trip to show off Jamie at Christmastime.

The horse fidgeted, stomping her feet.

"I better check her." Conor kissed Jamie's head and handed the boy to her then turned to go.

Christina grabbed his arm while holding Jamie secure in the other. "Hey, what about me?"

Conor grinned then pulled her hard against him. His kiss was slow, deep and held promises of later. He released her and her knees wobbled. That grin returned. "I've still got it."

She whispered, "I expect to see more of it tonight."

"You let me get this foal safely into the world and we'll celebrate during Jamie's nap."

Christina giggled and swatted him on the arm. "Go on. Jamie and I'll be right over here if you need help."

Conor entered the stall. She sat in the rocker that had been a gift from Conor's brother. He had made it after Conor had told him how much she enjoyed being in the barn. Conor had positioned it in the hallway so she could be close by while nursing Jamie or for occasions such as this one.

She spent as much time in the barn as possible working around Jamie's needs. The rehabilitation business had grown, and Conor had stepped in to fill her spot there. He had also received his US license to practice. They kept a few regular patients like Mr. Owen but mostly they remained close to home.

Soon, Conor joined her. "How are things progressing?"

"It may not be as soon as I first thought." Excitement filled his voice.

Conor had high hopes for this foal. Not that they had been planning to get into racing, but he wanted to give it a try. Just to see if they could do it.

"It might be a little longer than I thought. If you want to take Jamie inside, I'll come get you." He took a seat on a bale of hay beside her.

"Nope, we are happy right here." Jamie had fallen asleep in her arms.

Conor brushed his finger down her cheek. "You know when I came here I never dreamed I could ever be this happy. I love you."

"I love you, too."

"Conor, you better come," Buzz called from the inside of the stall.

Conor popped up. "Apparently, I was wrong. It's time."

Christina moved to the stall door. She watched as Conor gently guided the gangly foal into the world.

Delight filled his voice. "We have a colt."

She continued to admire her husband as he used handfuls of hay to clean the colt off.

After washing, Conor came to stand beside her, placing an arm around her waist and bringing her next to him with Jamie between them.

Together they watched the colt sway and bob until he found his footing.

"It never gets old watching new life come into the world." Christina sighed.

"No, it doesn't. It looks like a fine colt."

"It does." She shifted Jamie.

"Let me have him." Conor took his son. "Thanks for all these moments. I don't take them for granted."

"Nor do I." She wrapped her arms around him as she watched the mare nuzzle her new baby.

"Life is good." Conor gave her a squeeze.

Christina lay her cheek on his shoulder. "That, it is."

* * * * *

REBEL DOCTOR'S
BOSTON REUNION

AMY RUTTAN

MILLS & BOON

For all those who fight…
Dad, Gramma Marg, Sharon.

For those who won…
Theresa, Jennifer, Helen.

And those still in my heart…
Nanny, Mom, Barb, Dawn, Grampie, Aunt Dorothy.

CHAPTER ONE

IT'S SO SHINY!

Which was probably not the correct thing to think silently, but Madison was ecstatic. She was squealing inside and it was hard to contain her giddiness and remain professional in front of her new colleague. The lab she had been given for the next year was bigger than anything she had ever worked in. All the equipment was brand-new and state-of-the-art.

It even had that fresh, unused smell. Like a new car.

Only better.

The best thing? Her name, Dr. Madison Sullivan, was listed as the lead doctor on the outside of the lab. The last lab she'd worked in she hadn't been the lead researcher. Now she had a sparkling new lab and was an oncologist at a great research hospital.

It was a dream come true.

"What do you think?" asked Dr. Frank Crespo, head of the board of directors, following her discreetly. He was not a medical doctor, but he believed so much in her research that he had reached out and offered her this position at Green Hill Hospital in Boston.

"It's amazing," Madison gushed. "When can I start?"

Dr. Crespo chuckled. "Now, but I want to take you to the oncology wing so that you can meet the rest of the staff and of course, our department head, Dr. Antonio Rodriguez."

"Right." Madison hoped that Dr. Crespo didn't hear the hesitation in her voice, because she was very familiar with Dr. Antonio Rodriguez.

Very.

Familiar.

She and Tony, as he'd liked to be called, had been residents together out in California years ago. They'd constantly butted heads and just didn't see eye to eye on how things should be done. However, when they did agree, things were explosively good.

Hot.

Electric.

The sex had been phenomenal. No one ever had come close to the absolute magnetic pull that Tony seemed to have on her.

If they weren't arguing about something, they were in bed together.

The times they did get along, they worked like an unstoppable team. The problem was Tony was too rigid and took too long to take a chance. He was always questioning her. It felt like he didn't believe in her. He didn't trust her judgment and it hurt.

Too much. And that's why she'd ended it when their residency was over. How could she think of settling down with someone who didn't believe in her abilities?

Not that he ever asked her or talked about a future. And she hadn't asked him about his plans either. Tony had always been so closed off with his emotions.

Just like her father.

It had hurt to let Tony go. In the end it was for the best. Career came before love, marriage or the baby carriage as the old song went. She'd accepted a job in Minnesota and he went back to his home in Boston.

She was a bit worried that she would be working with Tony again and that he'd be her boss. Tony was head of oncology, but she was hopeful that enough time had passed that they could work together. Green Hills Hospital, or GHH, was one of the best on the Eastern Seaboard for cancer and research. This was about saving people's lives by working to cure cancer.

She couldn't save her mother, but she could save someone else's loved one. A brief stab of sadness moved through her as her mind wandered to the memory of her mom. Her mother was her whole reason to pursue this medical field.

This new job at GHH was the next step in her journey. She just needed a good place to work, to research and to publish some more papers on her research into CRISPR-Cas9, an exciting new genome editing technology. When she got some more articles published, she was going to apply to work at one of the most world-renowned cancer research facilities in Europe and hopefully with her idol, Dr. Mathieu LeBret, a Nobel laureate and brilliant physician. He rarely took others under his wing, but she was hoping to be the next one. The research facility and Dr. LeBret had made it clear that she needed more credentials. At GHH she'd get what she needed.

She was so close to that reality and she wasn't going to let a decade-old heartache get in the way of that.

Not at all.

Nothing tied her down and nothing would stop her from making her dreams become reality.

"Well, I'll take you down to the oncology wing. It's just down the hall, not far from your lab." Dr. Crespo opened the door and extended his arm. "Dr. Rodriguez will be eager to meet you."

Sure.

The Tony she had once known barely showed any emotion. She seriously doubted the inflexible Tony had changed that much.

Madison reluctantly left her bright, shiny new lab. Dr. Crespo shut the door and they walked side by side down the winding hall that led out into a beautiful atrium which had a gorgeous garden in full bloom.

"This is our cancer garden. Patients, caregivers and even staff can find respite here. We also have memory plants and trees," Dr. Crespo pointed out.

"How lovely."

And it was. It gave a sense of peace in the sterility of the hospital, a place for those hurting to find solace.

He nodded. "Ah, there is the man in question. Dr. Rodriguez!"

Madison's heart skipped a beat and her stomach dropped to the soles of her expensive heels as Tony turned around from where he'd been standing in the atrium. It was like time had stood still for him, save for a few grays in the midst of his ebony hair at his temples. There were an extra couple of lines on his face, but he was exactly the same as she remembered. Stoic expression, muscular physique which seemed to be perpetually held stiff as a board. No smile on his face. He was just so serious.

His dark eyes fixed on her and a jolt of electricity coursed through her.

Her body was reacting the exact same way it always did when she saw him.

And she could recall, vividly, how his hands had felt on

her body, the taste of his kisses, every sensation he aroused in her. His broody exterior barely expressed any emotion, but he showed her through every soft touch, every tender caress how he wanted her. She melted for him every time. It was all flooding back to her in that moment as she stood there staring at him.

Dr. Crespo was blissfully unaware, and for that she was glad. She was annoyed that even after a decade she was still like a moth to Tony's flame.

Tony ripped away his gaze and smiled half-heartedly to Dr. Crespo.

"Dr. Rodriguez, I would like to introduce you to Dr. Madison Sullivan. Dr. Sullivan, this is our chief of oncology, Dr. Antonio Rodriguez."

Tony's eyes narrowed and the fake smile grew wider, but there was no warmth in his gaze. She wasn't surprised he was being polite, but it shocked her how it bit at her. This was the way he was. Nothing had changed, so it shouldn't smart like it did. She was over him.

Are you?

He held out his hand, as if it were perfunctory. "It's a pleasure to see you again, Dr. Sullivan."

Her hand slipped into his and she was hoping that she wasn't trembling. "Indeed, Dr. Rodriguez. A pleasure."

Tony pulled his hand back quickly and she nervously tucked back a strand of hair behind her ear. She was suddenly very hot and she could feel her cheeks burning.

She always flushed when she was angry or sad or happy. Whatever emotion she felt showed up in her cheeks. It was frustratingly hard to keep a poker face.

"You two know each other?" Dr. Crespo aske, in amazement.

"I did mention that," Tony replied stiffly. "We were residents together. We learned under Dr. Pammi out in California."

"I must've forgotten. Dr. Pammi is an excellent oncologist. Well, this is great then," Dr. Crespo exclaimed, clapping his hands together.

Madison swallowed the lump in her throat. "Yes. Great. It is nice having a professional acquaintance in a new place."

Tony didn't say anything but just nodded.

Curtly.

Big surprise. Not.

"I'm going to continue to show Dr. Sullivan around. Perhaps after lunch you can show her the oncology wing?" Dr. Crespo asked.

Tony's eyes widened briefly. "Sure."

Honestly, she thought he was going to say no.

He's a professional.

And that she remembered all too well. He did take risks, but only those that were well thought out. Tony liked to play it safe and he was a rule follower. Never made a scene, but defended himself when he was sure he was right. Whereas she'd always been a bit of an emotional, exuberant student. She and Tony had clashed so much. And if she made a mistake he'd point it out, which annoyed her.

Greatly.

She went on a path toward oncology research, and he threw his life into the surgical side of cancer treatment. They both attacked the dreaded disease using different approaches.

She'd been foolish to fall in love with him, but being with him had been such a rush. At the time, he made her feel alive and not so alone. It was refreshing after spending a very lonely adolescence taking care of herself and her grieving father.

She was a fool to have those little inklings of romantic feelings for him still. They weren't good together. Leaving him had been agonizing, but it was the right thing to do at the time.

She thought back to one of their characteristic interactions in residency.

"Why did you say that to Dr. Pammi? What were you thinking?" Tony lambasted her.

"Uh, I was thinking about all the research that I did! And how I was right in the end. It worked."

"It was risky," Tony grumbled, crossing his arms.

"And it worked," she stated, staring up at him. "Is this why you dragged me into an on-call room? To yell at me for getting something right?"

Tony sighed. "You just have to be careful. This is a highly competitive program."

"So?" she asked, shrugging. "I'm here to play and win. Don't worry about me. I'm strong."

Tony smiled at her gently and then ran his fingers over her face. "I know, but you're hardheaded too. You didn't have to call Blair a butthole."

Madison sniggered and slipped her hand over his. "But Blair is a butthole."

Tony rolled his eyes and then pulled her into his arms. "You drive me crazy sometimes. You know that?"

"Ditto."

She snuggled into him.

She felt safe with him. Especially in those few scattered moments he let his guard down. This was the Tony she loved.

"Could you meet me at the main desk in oncology in two hours, Dr. Sullivan?" Tony asked, interrupting the memory that came rushing back.

"Sure," she said, nervously. "Two hours. Yes."

"Good. Well, enjoy the rest of your tour at GHH." Tony nodded at Dr. Crespo and quickly walked away in the opposite direction.

Madison watched him striding down the hall, his hands in the pockets of his white lab coat, his back ramrod straight and other people getting out of his way as he moved down the hall like he owned the place.

That hadn't changed.

Tony always had that air of confidence. It's what she was first drawn to. It was clear he still affected her the same way.

Working with him again was going to be harder than she thought.

Tony had been completely off track all day and he knew the reason. It was because Madison was starting today. When he first saw the memo come through from the board of directors he thought about saying something, anything, to keep her from coming here, but that wasn't very big of him. It was petty he prided himself on being professional.

Madison was a talented oncologist and researcher; it would be completely foolish to deny GHH that expertise and talent because he still had feelings for her after ten years. Try as he might, no one had ever held a candle to her.

And he had tried to move on after she left him. Only, he couldn't.

He wanted to marry, settle down and have a normal life, something he'd never had growing up. Tony wanted roots. Except he fell in love with Madison, a wanderer.

Part of him hoped he could change her, but he'd been wrong and she'd left. For so long he'd wondered what had happened. He was sure it was him. He was too set in his ways. He had a path in his mind and nothing was going to deter him from that.

And nothing had.

The number-one complaint he always got from his exes was that he worked too much. It was true. Work never let him down.

Except that one time…

He'd forgotten that Madison was going to be starting today of all days. It was the anniversary of the day he lost his best friend. The one life he couldn't save. The one time he decided to take a risk, act like Madison always did, and it hadn't paid off.

Jordan died.

Even though it wasn't Tony's fault, it still ate away at him. He was reminded of Jordan every time he went to see his godson—Jordan's son, Miguel—who wasn't so young anymore. On the anniversary of Jordan's death, he always went to the garden and spent some time there thinking about his friend and replaying what he should've done over and over.

Not that it did any good, but it was a habit. He'd just plain forgotten Madison was starting and that he would have to show her around. Today was the day that she was walking back into his life.

Not back into your life. Remember?

And he had to keep reminding himself of that.

When they had been together, it hadn't been good for either one of them. It led to too much heartache, for both of them, and he knew firsthand what heartache looked like.

He'd seen the devastation in Jordan's widow's eyes and then he'd seen that absolutely soul-crushing and heart-shattering pain when his father eventually left his mother. His father had gambled away her future and then left them in ruin.

Trust was hard for Tony. That was also part of his problem. He just didn't fully trust Madison. She'd left him before and she was so willing to try anything. She was a wandering soul and he wasn't. He was settled here and he wasn't going to put himself through a tumultuous relationship with someone who was going to leave him again.

So no, she wasn't walking back into his life. And today was not a good day. He was struggling to compartmentalize everything, but he was a professional so he just had to suck it up and make it work. He wasn't going to be, as Madison used to call difficult people, a butthole in front of the board of directors.

A smile tugged at the corner of his lips as he thought of her calling many obnoxious fellow residents buttholes. Usually under her breath, but he always heard it. Except himshe never called him that.

When he saw her there with Dr. Crespo, it made his heart stand still, because it was as if time hadn't touched her. It was like the last time he saw her.

The only difference was, there were no tears of anguish and anger in her gray eyes. Her pink lips were as luscious as he remembered. Her blond hair was tied back in a ponytail, the same way it always was, with that tiny wavy strand that would always escape and frame her face. Her cheeks were flushed with a subtle pink and he had no doubt that her skin felt smooth and silky.

He briefly wondered if she used the same coconut shampoo. She always smelled like summer. She exuded sunshine and warmth, especially during the hardest times of their residency. She always cheered everyone up. And she always looked so darn cute in her light blue scrubs and neon sneakers.

Except she wasn't in her resident scrubs and trainers. She was professionally dressed in a white blouse and a tight pencil skirt with black heels that showed off her shapely legs. He recalled the way her legs would wrap around his hips. With aching clarity, he could still feel her skin under his hands.

How soft she was.

How good it felt to be buried inside her.

His blood heated and he scrubbed a hand over his face. He had to stop thinking about her like that. She was not his. Not anymore. It was going to take a lot of strength, but he could make this work. He had to make this work.

CHAPTER TWO

TONY HAD DONE his rounds and tried to put at the back of his mind all those memories and old feelings that Madison was stirring up in him. He focused completely on his post-op patients, making sure they were resting comfortably and managing their recovery well. There were a couple of patients that he was able to discharge and leave in the hands of the oncologist who would administer chemotherapy and or radiation.

After he did that, he made his way to the chemotherapy treatment room and checked on his patients there who'd recently had surgery. The room was always cold, so it helped him to wake up and shake off the ghosts of his past that were pestering him today.

It usually completely cleared his mind.

Except now. It was frustrating. In their short interaction, Madison had gotten under his skin just like she did when they first met.

It didn't matter what kind of wall he put up; she got through. He could keep others at bay, but she always weaseled her way through.

It was infuriating.

I can't think about her.

And he couldn't. Things changed since they were together. He was a different person.

Are you?

He had work to focus on. That was what he needed.

When he finished checking on patients, he spent some time in his office going over files and preparing to meet patients tomorrow, which was his clinic dayThere was a huge wait list to see him and he wanted to get to everyone he could. There was a reason people requested him and came to GHH; he was one of the best cancer surgeons.

You weren't good enough to save Jordan though.

Tony shook that niggling thought out of his mind as he closed his last file and made his way to the main desk to meet up with Madison.

There was part of him that wished he could put this off, but how would that look? It would be totally unprofessional of him to avoid her. At least if he got this over and done with now, she could go off and do her own work and he could continue with his.

They'd operate in the same realm, but not work side by side all the time. They weren't residents anymore. He spent most of his day in the operating room and he knew she had a lab to do research. Sure, they'd see each other for consults, but they would be working in different spheres at GHH.

If he put off their meeting, it would just eat away at him. It was best to rip the bandage off and do his job as head of oncology.

When he got to the main desk, she wasn't there.

Typical.

Madison had always been running late when they were residents.

"Dr. Sullivan?" Dr. Pammi called out, not looking up from her clipboard.

"Here!"

Tony looked back to see Madison dashing up the hall, her lab coat fluttering behind her like a cape. He just shook his head as she skittered to a stop beside him, out of breath and tying back her blond hair.

Dr. Pammi didn't even looked flustered as she continued to take attendance.

"You're always late. That looks bad," he groused out of the corner of his mouth.

"Thanks for the warning, Grandpa," she muttered, rolling her eyes.

Tony leaned over and whispered, "You weren't calling me Grandpa last night."

Madison's mouth dropped open and then she slugged him in the arm.

"Dr. Sullivan and Dr. Rodriguez, is there a problem?" Dr. Pammi asked.

"No," Madison responded quickly. "There was a fly on his arm."

Dr. Pammi cocked her eyebrow, her lips pursed together. "You two are on scut."

Tony smiled at that memory. He'd been super annoyed at the time, especially to be assigned scut duty with her, but they had made it work. They always bickered, but they had so many good times too. Until the end.

Time healed all wounds, or so the saying went, but with her unwillingness to settle down they just weren't good for each other. It was for the best when it ended and he had to keep telling himself that.

Tony's stomach knotted and he tried to lock away all those memories. This wasn't the time or place to reminisce. Only, he couldn't help it. She was haunting him today.

Dr. Crespo was walking with Madison toward the main desk. Well, at least that explained why Madison was late.

"Sorry for keeping her, Dr. Rodriguez. We got a bit waylaid with the board of directors. They're very excited about the research that Dr. Sullivan is going to be doing here," Dr. Crespo explained.

"Oh?" Tony asked, intrigued. "What research is that?" He was curious. He knew that she had come to GHH for research, but didn't know what she was actually studying.

"CRISPR-Cas9," Madison responded. "I have some testing I would like to explore. Clinical trials and the like."

Tony swallowed a lump in his throat. "That's...ambitious."

CRISPR-Cas9 was fairly new and there was a lot they didn't know about the groundbreaking technology. It was a hot topic in the medical world. What Tony knew of it made him wary. There was a lot of risk involved, and when she said that she was going to test it, he immediately resisted because it reminded him she hadn't changed.

Not really. She was still taking risks.

When she was a resident she was so gung-ho about clinical trials and always eager to join them. Most times it would blow up in her face and she'd be devastated.

Clinical trials were important but she never took the time to really think of the implications.

I'm sure it's different now.

"Ah," he responded, because he wasn't sure what was left to say. The logical part of his brain was telling him that she was making a mistake and that CRISPR-Cas9 wasn't safe for his patients, but if his patients wanted to sign up for medical trials, he couldn't stop them.

Even if he wanted to.

"This time it'll work, Maria. I swear," his father lamented.

Tony had crept downstairs because his parents were fighting again. His dad had obviously come back, but when his dad did come home, it always made his mom upset and he never stayed around for long.

"We're saving that money, Carlo," his mother sobbed.

"It'll pay off. You have to trust me."

"I don't though," his mother said softly.

Tony was relieved she said it, because his father couldn't be trusted. He gambled everything away.

"You love me though, Maria. Don't you?"

Tony's fist clenched. He was annoyed his father was once again using love to manipulate his mom.

"I do," his mother sighed. "Take it."

"Ah, Maria. I promise it'll be better this time. I'll make so much that I can buy you that house and we can put Tony into a better school."

"Sure..."

"Dr. Rodriguez?" said Dr. Crespo.

Tony shook the memory away, banishing the agony of his past because there was no place for it here. "Sorry," he apologized.

Madison's lips pressed together in a thin line, her gray eyes going positively flinty as she narrowed her gaze at him.

"I have to get back to the board of directors and I'll leave Dr. Sullivan in your capable hands, Dr. Rodriguez." Dr. Crespo turned to Madison. "Great to have you on board. I am so excited to read your research as you publish it."

"Thank you, Dr. Crespo. You've been too kind," Madison responded tactfully.

Dr. Crespo walked away and she turned to look back at Tony, crossing her arms.

"You're a butthole. You know that, right?"

"What?" Tony asked as he tried to hold back the smile of amusement.

She'd called him a butthole. It was kind of endearing she was still using the same insult.

"Don't patronize me, Dr. Rodriguez. I saw that look on your face when I said what I was doing research. Surprise, surprise—you have misgivings. Well, I can tell you that this is the future of cancer treatments. The ability write cancer out of DNA. I don't care how you feel about it. We're not residents. All we have to do is work together and be civil."

"I totally agree," he responded.

"Then why are you smirking?" she asked hotly.

"Butthole?" He chuckled. "Really?"

Madison tried not to laugh, because she was still annoyed with him. When she mentioned what she was researching and that she was going to be offering medical and surgical trials based on her research to patients here, she saw that Tony instantly became protective. And she knew why.

CRISPR-Cas9 was newish, and there were a lot of unknowns surrounding it, and Tony wasn't a risk taker. That much hadn't changed, but it irked her. He deserved the title of butthole, because she knew what she was doing.

She had learned from her mistakes over the years. To excel at something always involved a learning curve. Each misstep hurt and she worked hard to improve. She carried those scars with her, which was why she was so good at her job.

Tony always was more cautious. It took him a long time to decide. She got that; he was a surgeon. She respected it. But she didn't make her decisions willy-nilly like he assumed.

Everything was so thought out. This was solid research. If it wasn't, she wouldn't have been here. She wouldn't be making huge strides in the treatment and the eventual cure for cancer. This is what she had been working toward her entire career.

If she was successful here at GHH and published, then she would finally be able to make her dream come true and work with Dr. LeBret in France. Dr. LeBret was her hero and he was willing to try new things and to take risks. If she got his attention and could work with him, benefactors could potentially offer her way more funding than she could get here. Ultimately, she coulc save more lives.

It annoyed her that Tony had misgivings. Even after all this time.

Tony was being stubborn, but seeing his eyes twinkle at being called that special name she used brought back all those memories where he had teased her about it in the past. It had been a private joke between them, and Tony was not a whimsical, lighthearted person with just anyone.

He was with me. Sometimes.

"I stand by my decision," she replied, haughtily crossing her arms. "I know what I'm doing and I don't need your approval."

"Good," Tony said. "Because you're not going to get it. I have my practice and you'll have your practice. We just have to be professional. That's it."

"That's all I want. I can assure you of that."

Which was true, but his finality still stung her a little bit and she didn't know why. She was not here to rekindle anything with him. That was the last thing on her mind.

Except it also wasn't.

Right now, in this moment, she could recall every touch, every heated glance and every kiss just as vividly as she could recall the way her heart had broken into a million pieces when it ended.

"Paging Dr. Rodriguez to treatment room three. Dr. Rodriguez to treatment room three," the PA sounded.

Tony frowned. "It's pediatric oncology."

"I'll come with you," Madison suggested. "You were going to show me around the department anyways."

Tony hesitated for a moment and then nodded. "Let's go then. Try to keep up in those heels."

Madison snorted and fell into step beside him as they quickly made their way through the halls. "You don't have to worry about me. I can keep up. In fact, I'm going to run the Boston Marathon in my heels."

Tony rolled his eyes. "Why do you do that?"

"Do what?"

"Make light of things," he groused.

"Because you're too damn serious sometimes. Butthole." She grinned at him and he groaned under his breath, but there was a slight smile playing on the corners of his lips. It gave Madison a brief sense of hope that this could actually work. That they could just leave the past in the past and work together. Maybe even be friends. Which was what she wanted. They were older and wiser.

It wasn't too long a walk to treatment room three. As they put on masks and surgical gowns, a pit formed deep in her stomach. She'd dealt with sick kids before during her residency and at previous hospitals, but she never got used to the idea that cancer would wreak havoc on a child's body, that cancer altered little lives.

This is why you do what you do, the voice in her head reminded her as she girded her loins to take that first, tenuous step into the treatment room.

She had to keep reminding herself of that when she saw five small bodies buried under blankets and hooked up to IVs, but it was the faces of the parents that always got to her.

The parents were trying to be so brave, but she could see the anguish that was lurking behind those eyes. Even though she wasn't a parent, she felt that to her core. She had seen that look on her father's face every day that her mother had treatment, and she was pretty sure that it had been reflected back to him in her own eyes.

You've got this. Remember why you're here.

She still felt the keen pain of watching her mother fade away slowly and then her father. He shut himself away from the rest of the world and she was alone.

Always alone.

Focus.

Madison nodded to herself, steeling herself and compartmentalizing all those feelings. She followed Tony past patients to the very corner of the room where there was an Isolette. She kind of skidded to stop when she saw a tiny baby in the incubator.

The mother was standing off to the side in a gown, looking terrified as Tony spoke to the nurse quietly.

Madison made her way over to the chart and smiled at the mother. "I'm Dr. Sullivan. May I look at your child's chart?"

"Of course," the mother's voice quavered. "Her name is Gracie. She's six months old."

"She's beautiful."

Gracie's mom smiled from behind her mask. "Thank you."

Madison flipped open the chart to read about Gracie's diagnosis. A neuroblastoma had developed in the adrenal gland. The tumor had been removed and the previous oncologist had ordered a high dose of chemotherapy, along with treatment to increase stem cell reproduction so he could harvest it for transplants. The transplants would help fight the disease.

It was a common cancer among infants, even though cancer in infants was rare. This was the reason Madison was so invested in her research. Neuroblastomas developed in the fetal cells at the embryo stage. If she was successful with her research, then one day they could eradicate this type of cancer in children before the child was born. Then there would be no need for heartbroken parents, hurting children or shattered souls.

Tony came over to the Isolette with gloves. He didn't acknowledge the mother, beyond a curt nod. Madison groaned inwardly. He was a great doctor, but his bedside manner still sucked.

Definitely a butthole.

She glanced down as Tony gently examined the baby. He was so gentle with his patient, who didn't stir much as he touched her. And then he gently caressed Gracie's head. It surprised Madison and her heart melted seeing him so tender with the littlest of patients.

"How is she, Dr. Rodriguez?" the mother asked, with trepidation in her voice.

"Her blood cell counts are down and we want to get them up so we can harvest stem cells to continue treatment. I'm going to order some platelets and that should alleviate the problem," Tony responded brusquely. "I'm going to monitor Gracie closely, but I have no doubt this treatment will work. She's been strong and responding well every step of the way. As you know, Dr. Santos has left GHH, but Dr. Sullivan is our newest oncologist. She'll be monitoring Gracie's chemo and radiation."

The mother looked over at her. "And what do you think, Dr. Sullivan?"

Madison was a bit stunned she was being asked for her opinion. She hadn't even had a chance to go over the file properly yet. She glanced over at Tony, whose eyes narrowed for a moment. She knew she had to be careful. If she wanted their work relationship to go well, she couldn't step on his toes the first day, especially when she wasn't familiar with the patient. But she was a doctor too. A damn good one and one with opinions. She did agree with the previous oncologist's treatment though.

"Stem cell harvesting and high-dose chemo is a well-known treatment for this type of aggressive neuroblastoma. I agree with Dr. Rodriguez and Dr. Santos."

The mother's face relaxed. "Thank you both."

"Have me paged if anything changes." Tony pulled off his gloves and began to walk away.

Madison set the chart down and followed quickly behind him.

They left the treatment room and disposed of their gowns and masks.

"Thanks for backing me up in there," he said. "I thought you might start spouting off on some new research thing. Dr. Santos and I consulted closely before I did the surgery."

She cocked an eyebrow. "Well, stem cell treatments are cutting-edge. You and Dr. Santos are doing the right thing. I'm not here to get in your way, Tony. I'm here to work."

And she meant it. She just wanted him to leave her alone so she could do what she needed to do in order to advance her career.

Tony nodded. "Good."

"You could be a little bit warmer though," she suggested, dumping her surgical gown in the linen basket.

"Warmer?" he asked. "I'm warm."

Madison snorted. "You can be. I do know that, but you were very businesslike with your patient's family. It's a bit... standoffish."

"I'm fighting for their lives. Trust me, when I win over cancer, I'm right there celebrating with them. And I win a lot."

"I know. I've followed your career a bit."

"Have you?" he asked, surprised.

"Of course. You're good at what you do and so am I."

Tony worried his bottom lip. "Maybe we should go grab a drink after work and talk about the parameters of our working relationship and what people around here should and shouldn't know. I've worked very hard on my reputation here."

"No doubt."

"So we should clear the air," he stated. "Maybe meet at Flanagan's at seven?"

Madison wanted to say no, but they needed to talk about the rules and how to navigate working together again.

"Sure. Send me the address."

He nodded. "Let's finish this tour then so you can get back to your lab and you can get caught up on all of Dr. Santos's patients. Or rather, your patients now."

Madison nodded and followed him, shocked by what had just happened. Maybe this was a mistake. But it would be smart to lay it all out. Maybe then they wouldn't butt heads so much.

She could handle a drink with him.

Right?

CHAPTER THREE

TONY HAD WHIZZED through the rest of the tour with Madison after they arranged to meet for a drink down the street at Flanagan's, where everyone from GHH met. He didn't know what had come over him asking her out like that, but after she had gone back to her lab and he got back to his work, he decided that it was a good idea.

It was better to be out in a public place to hash things out. He had nothing to hide, even though he was a pretty private person. He'd heard that from partners in other failed relationships that he was too aloof, too focused, introverted.

Cold.

Thankfully, none of his patients called him that. Although Madison was right; his bedside manner was a bit brusque.

Sure, he was professional, but he did care about his patients. He was so devoted to them. It was why so many people came to see him at GHH. The survival rates for his patients were higher than for any of his colleagues patients.

Except Jordan.

He'd lost other patients. He was a surgeon; it happened. Each one stung, but when it was his best friend? That had destroyed him.

Tony shook that thought away as he glanced at the picture on his desk. It was a picture of him and Jordan when they had been kids. Their arms were around each other, and they were laughing at Jordan's twelfth birthday party.

He smiled and he picked up the photo. He missed him so much.

At least there was Miguel, his godson. In Miguel, Tony could still see his best friend. He loved spending time with him, though it was getting less and less as Jordan's widow had found love again and was planning to remarry. Miguel adored his new soon-to-be stepdad, who was a decent guy.

Tony was happy for them, but he missed Jordan.

He was lonely.

And whose fault is that?

It was his. It was easier to push people away. It always had been.

Tony groaned. For one brief second he thought about canceling the drink with Madison, but he wanted to make sure that it was strictly business they were attending to when they interacted. He didn't want all those old feelings that had been muddling around in his head today to resurface. Or rumors to spread.

Madison was his past. GHH and his career were his future. That hadn't changed.

Kind of lonely, don't you think?

He scrubbed a hand over his face and finished with his paperwork. After doing a quick round on his patients, he packed up his stuff to head for home so he could change and then meet Madison at the bar for seven.

Thankfully, he didn't live too far from GHH.

It was summer and the sun was still up. June was his favorite month. As much as he loved Boston, he really hated the cold and dark of winter. Not that he did anything during the summer, other than spend a night or two in Martha's

Vineyard, where he now owned his late grandparents' cottage. But he'd only bought it last fall and he just never found the time to visit. Work was his life.

Maybe you need to take a trip out there?

It was a thought. He'd put some distance between him and Madison.

Uh, isn't that running away?

He couldn't do his work from his home in Martha's Vineyard. There were no virtual surgeries like in science fiction.

He was a grown man and this was getting silly. He just had to face this whole thing head on.

He unlocked the front door of the redbrick condominium in Beacon Hill, overlooking Boston Common. He greeted the doorman with a wave and made his way to the elevator, swiping his card for his penthouse two-bedroom condo.

Not that he needed two bedrooms, but he had bought it years ago when the building was new and the prices weren't so astronomical.

The elevator doors opened and he made his way into his condo, which was sparsely decorated with modern furniture. The space was cold and sterile like him, or so he'd been told. He just found it functional. He learned from a young age not to get attached to things. Especially to possessions that could be pawned off.

He dropped his satchel and coat before making his way to the shower. He undressed and as he stepped up the spray of hot water he closed his eyes, bracing his arms on the wall in front of him, trying to relax.

Instead he saw her.

Madison.

He remembered the time they shared a shower in the locker room at the hospital, late at night. Her body slick as he held her. Her legs wrapped around his waist and her back pressed against the tile wall.

Dude. Stop.

Tony groaned. He had to pull himself together. He quickly cleaned up, got dressed and then headed to the pub where he'd be meeting Madison. En route to Flanagan's he couldn't help but wonder where she was staying in Boston. Or for how long. And that was the kicker. She had nothing tying her down and he knew that for a fact.

Madison had said that she was keeping tabs on him over the years, but he had been keeping tabs on her too. Tony knew exactly how much she had moved from facility to facility around the country, and he didn't have high hopes that she would stay at GHH long term.

He had a hard time trusting someone who didn't have any roots. Especially since his father had had that wandering foot. He recalled the pain when his father abandoned them. He had no interest in someone who was always looking for the next new thing. Someone who couldn't settle.

Though he hadn't understood at the time his relationship with Madison had ended, now he knew it was for the best.

Was it?

When he got to the pub, Madison was nowhere to be found, which didn't surprise him at all. She didn't have Dr. Crespo to blame for her tardiness this time. He took a seat in a corner booth and ordered a pint of the featured IPA on tap.

As he settled back into the seat, he saw a pair of shapely legs through the window that was open to the stairwell that led down to the bar. The memory of those legs from the shower flooded his mind as he admired her through the window. He recognized those heels immediately. She was still dressed in her work clothes.

Tight white blouse, tight pencil skirt, black stiletto heels. It all accentuated her womanly curves. Curves he was all too familiar with. His blood heated and he curled his fist around his beer to keep himself from reaching out to touch her like he wanted to do.

Focus on the task at hand, Tony.

Madison breezed into the bar and saw him. She made her way over and then slid into the booth across from him.

"Sorry, I had some trouble logging into my GHH account. I had to wait for the IT guy to come and fix it for me. Hard to do research when you can't even access the online library database," she said quickly.

"I'm sure," he agreed, swallowing a lump in his throat.

"What?" she asked, looking at him curiously.

He shrugged. "I didn't say anything."

"I thought you were going to give me heck about being late. You always did."

"Don't put words in my mouth," he replied.

"Then don't have those words written all over your face," she teased.

Tony rolled his eyes. "You drive me around the bend. Seriously."

"Aww…" she replied sardonically. "I'm glad things haven't changed too much. Lighten up, Tony. We can be friends and friends tease each other."

"Not my friends," he muttered.

"Oh, come on. Jordan does."

His heart skipped a beat.

She doesn't know today is the day Jordan died. She doesn't know he's gone.

And he didn't want to tell her. Tony cleared his throat. "You're right."

He didn't want to talk about Jordan tonight.

Madison didn't seem to notice his reaction. She was too busy looking at the menu. When the waiter came back, she ordered a glass of white wine and then folded her hands neatly on the table.

She sighed deeply. "You wanted this drink to talk. Let's talk."

He nodded. "Right. I did. I wanted to discuss our working relationship and how we can manage together without... without..."

"The fighting we used to do?" There was a twinkle in her eyes.

He nodded again. "Exactly. I'm the head of oncology and it's my department. I hope you'll respect my wishes. You can't call me a butthole in front of people."

"I won't and I didn't. Look, I've changed, Tony. I'm professional and you have to trust me."

"I would like that." Only he wasn't so sure that he could fully put his faith in her.

She'd left him. She'd broken him.

"You have to meet me halfway, Tony. I'm going to work here at GHH."

"For how long?" he asked, finally getting to the point. It shouldn't matter to him how long she planned to stay. He shouldn't care. Except he did.

He wanted to remind himself why, and maybe if she told him the time frame he could get her out of his mind.

Her gray eyes widened. "What?"

"How long?"

Madison didn't know how to respond to that. Part of her wanted to say however long it took to get more work published and noticed by Dr. LeBret, but she didn't want to share that with him.

Sure, they had been residents together, lovers even, but that was over a decade ago. Even though she had known him intimately then, now he was just an acquaintance and she didn't trust him either. It was hard to depend on someone who didn't put their faith in you. It was hard to be with someone who never fully let you in.

"I don't know my exact time frame, but I'm here for now," she replied and hoped that was a good enough answer for him.

"Okay." Although, he didn't really seem to like that response either.

The one thing that had always driven her nuts about Tony was the inability to read his emotions, which ran hot and cold. He worked so hard to shut everyone out and he never told anyone why. It wasn't her business any longer. They weren't together. And she had to keep reminding herself of that.

All she wanted was a simple working relationship with him. That was it.

It was completely frustrating to her that she'd been thinking about him every second since she returned to her lab. Heck, she'd been thinking about him since she signed the damn contract to come to GHH. She'd convinced herself it would be fine but, so far she wasn't living up to her own promise.

Right now, she kind of felt like that meme of a dog sitting at a table, surrounded by flames, drinking his coffee and saying that everything was fine. This was fine.

Was it?

"Well, Dr. Crespo knows we previously worked together.

Do you think he'll tell anyone else?" she asked, trying not to think about Tony or how he was making her feel in this moment. She had to maintain this professionality. That's what she wanted.

"People will know, but it shouldn't amount to much."

"And if it does?" she asked.

"How so?"

"We have a past. What if rumors fly?"

"Let them."

Madison was a bit surprised at how unbothered he was by that. "Wow."

"What?"

"You're so nonchalant about it." The waiter set down her glass of wine and she took a sip of it. "Especially when you seemed so concerned earlier."

Tony shrugged. "We don't need to explain ourselves. As long as it doesn't affect our work. We have to be professional. No arguing in public like we used to do."

"I can be professional. I assure you."

"Good," he responded quietly.

"Can I get the same promise from you?" she asked.

Tony cocked an eyebrow. "What do you mean?"

She was a bit taken aback by his feigned innocence. She knew exactly how he felt about her research; it had been written all over his face. He didn't trust it. He didn't trust her.

"I stand by my research," she responded firmly.

"I'm sure you do."

"Are you?" she questioned.

"Well, you did jump around. Your name was attached to some failed trials…"

"That was ten years ago, Tony. Those were mistakes. I admit that."

He frowned. "I just don't want to play cleanup."

Her spine straightened. "I don't need you to do that for me. I told you before and I'll say it again, I stand by my research. It's sound and I don't have to prove it to you."

"Very well," he acquiesced.

"Are you going to stand in my way during clinical trials?"

"No."

"You don't say that with much confidence."

"I will protect my patients," he replied firmly.

"And you think I won't?" she asked hotly.

"Just be careful. Risks are… They don't always pay off. If I don't think it's worthwhile for them, I'll let them know."

"I'm sure you will," she responded sardonically.

"What's that supposed to mean?" he asked.

"Risks need to be taken, Tony, or medical advancements won't happen."

He opened his mouth to say more when his phone went off and glanced down. "It's Gracie. She's not responding well to the platelet transfusion. She might have a post-op infection."

"Maybe I can help?"

Tony cocked that eyebrow again. She could tell that he wasn't sure. From his expression he wanted to tell her no, but she was replacing Dr. Santos.

"Fine." He pulled out some money and placed it on the table. "Let's go."

Madison nodded.

She was frustrated that they hadn't finished their conversation, but right now that didn't matter. A patient needed them and he wasn't keeping her out of the loop. They were her patients now too. He wasn't shutting her out.

Small progress was still progress, and a little life was in their hands.

CHAPTER FOUR

WHEN THEY GOT back to GHH nurses had moved Gracie's Isolette into a private room, which was standard practice. Gracie could be fighting an infection, and there were a lot of other children in the treatment room who could also be susceptible to fevers and viruses. They couldn't put their other patients at risk.

Madison followed Tony as they put on disposable gowns, gloves and masks. Tony was the surgeon and if it was a post-op infection then he would have to take point on it, but she could suggest medicine that wouldn't counteract the chemotherapy they were using to help fight it off.

Gracie's mom was standing off to the side. Her eyes were wide behind her mask and she was wringing her hands. Madison understood that desperation and helplessness. She had seen it time and time again, but she felt it on a deep level too.

She'd seen the same desperation in her father's face as her mother died, and then he shut down, leaving her not physically but emotionally alone. She'd had to grow up fast then. So Madison wanted to comfort Gracie's mom, but there wasn't much that she could say to her right now. Not until they knew more about what was going on.

Tony opened the Isolette and was gently examining the baby. He was so matter-of-fact with patients, but watching him handle that delicate sick baby took her breath away. Madison stepped closer to him.

"Post-op infection?" she asked in a hushed tone.

"Indeed," Tony responded. "She'll need a dose of antibiotics, but we have to find out the strain of staph infection that's wreaking havoc with her."

"I'll draw some blood and get it off to the lab." The nurse in the ICU pod handed her what she needed to do a complete blood panel, but Madison also wanted to check Gracie's neutrophils level, because she had a hunch.

It wasn't uncommon for patients getting high doses of chemotherapy and radiation to have neutropenia. Neutropenia was often the cause of why people fighting cancer would get infections. It also made it harder to heal especially after surgery.

"Her wound is red and leaking," Tony remarked under his breath.

Madison collected her specimens and sent them off with the nurse. She then carefully palpated Gracie's abdomen right over her spleen to see if it was swollen, because a spleen could sometimes be a culprit in neutropenia.

Tony watched her. "Well?"

"It's enlarged. I'm going to have her blood tested for neutrophil levels as well. If she has neutropenia I want to start her on injections of G-CSF."

G-CSF, or granulocyte colony-stimulating factor, helped the bone marrow make more of the neutrophils that could be lacking in Gracie's blood. The platelet transfusion wasn't working. The baby already had an infection and they needed to get her through her chemo before they could harvest stem cells.

"Are you suggesting another stem cell harvest? Dr. Santos has done that."

"I'm aware."

"Should I remove her spleen?" Tony asked quietly.

"No. Not yet," Madison said. "I wouldn't mind getting a tiny sample of bone marrow. For now, let's get her infection under control. She can't take too much strain."

"Agreed."

Madison turned to the nurse. "Start her on a course of general broad antibiotics until the lab confirms what infection we're dealing with. Keep me posted."

"Yes, Dr. Sullivan," the nurse said.

Madison walked over to Gracie's mother, who was standing there terrified. Tony was removing the bandage and re-dressing the surgical wound.

"Is my daughter okay?" Gracie's mom asked.

"She has an infection. We're going to start her on some antibiotics and stop the chemotherapy until we get that infection under control."

Gracie's mom nodded. "Okay."

"It's common," Madison assured her gently. "Chemotherapy kills off cancer, but it can kill off the good things too."

She wanted to tell Gracie's mom that her baby would be fine, that there was no reason to worry, but Madison couldn't do that. She had learned that she couldn't deal in absolutes when it came to cancer. All the things she wanted to say, words that she herself had wanted to hear when her mother was fighting her own battle, she couldn't utter to Gracie's mom.

She hoped the little bit she told her was enough to calm her down and give her hope, because hope was all you could cling to in moments like this. Although, those words had done little to help her father...

"Daddy?" Madison asked, creeping forward. "I have dinner."

"Not hungry," her father muttered, not moving from the bed.

"You've got to eat." Madison set the tray down.

Her father rolled over. His expression blank. "Thanks, Madison, but not now."

She swallowed the painful memory away, not letting it in to affect her as she smiled gently at Gracie's Mom.

"It's common," she stated again.

Gracie's mom nodded, but she was still wringing her hands. "Okay, Dr. Sullivan. I understand."

Madison reached out and squeezed her shoulder. "I'll keep you updated every step of the way."

"Thank you," Gracie's mom said, choking back her emotions.

Tony motioned with a nod to follow him out of the room so they could discuss things further. Once they were out of the ICU, they disposed of their gowns and gloves. They found a small meeting room outside of the pediatric intensive care unit and Tony shut the door.

"Exciting first day," Tony said, dryly breaking the silence.

"Indeed. I wouldn't have minded a dull day," she replied softly.

"I understand." Tony then pulled out a chair for her. It was a small act, sort of chivalrous.

She sat down, her back brushing against his fingers. The simple brush, the heat she could feel coming from him, sent a shiver of anticipation through her. Madison remembered the way his hand would fit in the small of her back. How he would tenderly touch her secretly as they did rounds, so no one else would know. It had thrilled her, sharing those private moments with him.

And it led to heartbreak, remember?

They may have had those tender moments together, but outwardly around the other residents he was closed off. She never knew the real him.

Did he know the real you?

Madison cleared her throat and leaned forward, breaking the momentary connection. Tony removed his hand and made his way to the other side of the table, sitting down in one of the chairs. Obviously, he was putting distance between them, which was good.

"You mentioned a bone marrow sample?" Tony asked, getting straight back down to business.

"I would like to do one, but I also don't want to put too much strain on Gracie. I've ordered a CBC so we'll see what her neutrophil counts are before I order a bone marrow. Although, I'd like her to be over her infection. For now, I don't want her on the high-dose chemo. Not until this infection clears up. It's too taxing on her."

"Agreed."

"I had a chance to look over Gracie's file. Actually, I'm surprised that Dr. Santos didn't do chemotherapy before the neuroblastoma was removed."

Tony's lips pursed together in a thin line. "The growth was small. It was an optimal time to remove it. Dr. Santos consulted me and I felt it was a good time to do the surgical removal."

"I know that you're planning a stem cell transplant. What about a tandem SCT?"

"Is this why you were suggesting G-CSF injections?"

"It is. If she takes well to it, it might mean less chemo after the fact."

Tony frowned. "That would most definitely take a toll on Gracie. I don't think she can handle it."

"The tandem stem cell transplant is hard, but I think she can benefit from it. Once she's over the infection we could do the first transplant from the harvest Dr. Santos has done. I have no doubt that her bone marrow has been killed off, which is why she's in neutropenia."

"One stem cell transplant is hard enough, but a tandem? Why should she be put through that again?" Tony argued.

"Are you confident that you got all of the cancer?" Madison questioned as she got a little heated.

This was where the problem always lay when it came to them. Why did it have to be so black-and-white with him? Why couldn't he see that you didn't always have to cut out the cancer? Why couldn't he see other courses of treatment?

It was obvious that sometimes he did see them. She read the file and Dr. Santos's notes. But why, when it came to her, did he question it? Why couldn't he trust her? Even after all this time and her own reputation, why didn't he believe her?

Stem cell transplants, or SCTs, were common. And it wasn't even a huge risky she was taking. She'd successfully done SCTs on infants as young as Gracie before.

Surgery was great to get rid of cancers. But it didn't always solve the problem and took its own toll on patients.

Like her mom. The surgeon hadn't thought before they cut and it had been detrimental, pointless and just prolonged the agony.

"Why are you questioning my surgical abilities?" he asked.

"I could ask the same about you questioning my treatment. I'm not some greenhorn, Tony. We're not residents. We've both been battling this disease for ten years. We're both well established."

Tony took a deep breath. "You're right."

"I know." She smiled briefly. "I'm not going to do anything to Gracie until I have the CBC back and she's overcome this infection. SCT is hard on a child and I won't put any more strain on her than I have to."

Tony nodded slowly. "Very well."

"Good. Thank you." She leaned back in the chair. "I want our professional relationship to work."

"I do too. I don't want our past to muddy the waters."

"I agree with that." That was exactly what she wanted. She had always liked working with him. She'd missed collaborating with him. Not the arguments, but real work.

But seeing him and working with him was already stirring up so much emotion that she had long thought was buried and locked away tight. She just hadn't realized that one simple consult on a case would stir up all these memories and all these feelings.

She'd known this was going to be hard and she wasn't wrong.

"How about we get some dinner, a late dinner, since our drink was interrupted?" he asked.

Her heart skittered to a stop for a moment and she tried to control her surprise. Sure, colleagues had dinners together. But as much as Madison wanted to, she knew that she couldn't say yes to him.

Not if she wanted to keep this professional relationship as the status quo for her time here at GHH. She wanted to ask Tony if he thought that was wise, given their past, but she didn't because she didn't want to talk about their past failings.

It was over.

It was done with.

Was it?

"Thank you for the offer, but I think I'm going to stick around here and wait for the lab results. Once I have all the information, I can formulate my plan of attack to help Gracie."

"Of...of course," Tony stammered.

What had he been thinking? First he invited her out for a drink and now he was asking her out to a late meal? What was wrong with him?

There was a part of him that was disappointed, but mostly he was relieved because he hadn't been thinking straight. She was so calm with Gracie's mother, so kind. He always did admire her bedside manner. She was gentle and such a lovely person.

Her consult with him was sound and he was mad at himself for letting his usual mistrust, the one that ran so deep toward anyone who was willing to jump headlong into the fray, creep in. He'd snapped. Especially after their talk about Gracie's treatment escalated and he got his hackles up. He didn't just think that cutting out the cancer would solve the problem. Why would she assume that?

When he was a resident, yes, he worshipped surgery a bit. He'd thought it was natural to cut out the problem, because he knew that medicine could take its toll. He was cockier when he was a student, but he learned—as that same surgical resident and then under the tutelage of Dr. Pammi and her team—that sometimes the best thing to do in cancer treatments was not to cut but rather to step away.

There were times he had to argue for this fact with his patients, who thought the solution was to have the surgery, but if the cancer spread, surgery would be pointless and harmful. And then there were times when the patients would ignore the advice...

"It won't work," Jordan insisted.

"It can," Tony said gently.

"I don't want chemo."

"Chemotherapy works. It will help and then when get you on the right medicines..."

Jordan grimaced. "I watched my own father go through that. It ate away at him."

"It won't be easy."

"I don't want that."

"Jordan..."

"No, Tony. There's this new treatment."

He balked. "New treatment?"

"It's more natural. It's a clinical trial..."

"And if I don't think it's in your best interest?"

Jordan sighed. "I'll go to someone who can get me in on it. Come on, Tony. You know all the risks, you know the odds. I trust you, but this is what I want. Please, get me in on this trial and support me."

"Tony?" Madison said, breaking through his thoughts.

He shook his head, dispelling the memories of Jordan. "Pardon?"

"Are you okay? You completely zoned out."

"Fine." Tony stood up. "It's been a long day."

"It has," she replied.

"You'll keep me posted about Gracie?"

She smiled sweetly. "Of course."

He nodded. "Thank you, Madison."

There was more he wanted to say to her. He wanted to apologize to her because he did want this working relationship to go smoothly. Only he couldn't get the words out.

He left the meeting room then to put some distance between him and Madison. He had to get control of all these emotions that were threatening to spill out of him. Baring too much could be a sign of weakness. His mother had been soft on his father like that, and his father totally took advantage of her. It was why he locked it all away, so no one could hurt him.

Madison won't take advantage of me.

But it was hard to rely on someone who never seemed to agree with him. Someone who had wounded him by ending things, someone who couldn't stand still and someone he continued to care for deeply.

Tony couldn't put his heart at risk again. He wouldn't let his guard down and be tormented over and over like his mother had done. His father was shiftless, never staying one place, and Madison couldn't seem to root herself anywhere.

He couldn't fall for her again. And he couldn't let another slipup, like inviting her to dinner, happen again either.

They worked together.

Nothing more.

CHAPTER FIVE

A week later

"TONY!"

Tony groaned inwardly as he heard Dr. Crespo call him from across the atrium. He knew exactly what Frank wanted, which was why he had been steering clear of him. He'd also been avoiding Madison, but that was for completely different reasons.

It had been a week since he'd let his own guard down and foolishly invited her out for dinner. Although he had been partly relieved she had turned him down, there was a part of him that was stung she didn't accept. Even after all this time, he still liked being around her.

He was falling into the trap again. It was hard when he kept reacting to her, thinking about her, like no time had passed at all.

On the plus side, she seemed to be keeping away from him too. Other than talking about patients and business, they didn't seek each other out. Which was good. It was easier to maintain professionality that way.

Dr. Crespo, on the other hand, was looking for someone to help with the annual summer fundraiser, which wasn't a surprise. He did it every year. It was for a good cause. There were several free clinics that the GHH supported, and this silent auction raised a lot of funds to help continue programs that provided first-rate cancer treatment to those who couldn't afford it. Tony tried to volunteer time at the clinics when he could, and he approved of the gala. He just didn't want any part of organizing or attending it. Socializing and making small talk with strangers was the worst thing in the world.

He also had a sneaking suspicion Dr. Crespo wanted him to donate something. A weekend at his home on Martha's Vineyard would be a perfect thing to auction off. He had no problem with it, but he hadn't spent a lot of time out there since he purchased his late grandparents' home. He wasn't sure that it could be cleaned up and ready in time.

"Frank," Tony acknowledged as he stopped and waited for Dr. Crespo to catch up to him.

"Just the man I wanted to see," Dr. Crespo said, out of breath.

"It's about my place and the silent auction, isn't it?" Tony asked, cutting to the chase.

Dr. Crespo's eyes widened. "You know?"

Tony snorted. "Frank, I know you've been thinking about it since I bought the place last fall."

Dr. Crespo grinned. "So? What do you think?"

"I haven't had much time to spend out there and get it presentable. I've been busy."

"Well, the auction is in two weeks. You have time."

Dr. Crespo is too damn optimistic.

Tony chuckled. "Do I?"

"Come on, Tony. You know it's for a good cause. You're always at the free clinics and you know the need is great."

Tony sighed. "You're right. I'll have it all set for a weekend at the end of the summer."

"Good. You can talk to Dr. Sullivan about it."

Tony's stomach knotted. "Why would I talk to Dr. Sullivan about this?"

"She's collecting the items for the silent auction and volunteered to be our auctioneer."

Of course she did.

Tony kept that sardonic thought to himself. Madison did like to throw herself in and help out. It was endearing, but when she moved on, it left a lot of people in the lurch. He was all too familiar with being let down. Not only by his father, but by Madison and by himself.

He'd left himself down by not fighting Jordan harder on taking the traditional route of treatment. He'd helped him get on that clinical trial, took a risk and lost his best friend.

"Okay," Tony agreed, because there wasn't much to say. Madison was in charge.

"Perfect! Thank you, Tony." Dr. Crespo continued on his way, most likely to track down other doctors about donations or spread the word about his place in Martha's Vineyard. Tony sighed because he didn't want to talk to Madison.

It won't be that bad. Think of this as an extension of work.

And that's what he had to keep telling himself. This was all business, he reminded himself as he made his way over to where she'd be. He knew that it wasn't her clinic day to see any new patients, so she'd be working on her research.

He actually hadn't been over to her lab yet. It was in a new part of the hospital and hers was the first one in that new wing. He grinned when he saw her name on the door and all her accreditation after it.

Dr. Madison Sullivan.

This was what she'd always wanted.

"What are your goals when we're done?" he asked, hold-

ing her in his arms and staring up at the ceiling of the on-call room.

"Goals?" she murmured.

"What do you want to do? Where do you want to work?"

She propped herself up on an elbow, her eyes twinkling in the dark. "Cure cancer, of course."

He smiled. "I'm serious. I have surgery and..."

"I am serious. I'm going to research every avenue. I want my own lab one day. That's a big goal of mine."

They hadn't usually had in-depth conversations.

They'd never really known each other.

Not really.

He knocked, peering in through the small window in the door. She looked up from where she was hunched over a computer and then waved him in.

"Hi," he said, suddenly awkward as he walked in the room.

"Hi back," she said pleasantly in that way that always invited people in. Her warmth had first attracted him, and even after all this time he was drawn to her, to her smile and the kindness in her eyes.

Focus, Tony. For the love of God. Focus.

"Sorry for interrupting you."

She stretched. "You're not. Just catching up on some reading. I swung by the pediatric unit and checked on Gracie, and her infection is almost cleared up. I was going to come and find you and talk to you about doing an extraction of her bone marrow. Maybe discuss SCT again."

"Right. Yes. We do have to talk about that."

"Isn't that why you're here?" she asked.

"No. I mean, yes." He ran his hand through his hair, trying to get the words out. "I do want to talk about that, but I ran into Frank in the hall… Dr. Crespo."

Her eyes widened. "Oh. I see."

"You're in charge of the silent auction."

Madison crossed her arms. "I am. I don't know why I volunteered, but I thought it might be a good way to get to know people at GHH."

"You mean get to know the board of directors," he responded dryly.

She cocked an eyebrow. "What's with the tone?"

"I didn't have tone."

"You so did."

Tony let out huff. "I don't want to argue with you."

"I don't want to either, but you haven't told me yet why you're here."

Because you won't let me talk! He kept that frustration to himself.

"I'm offering up my place at Martha's Vineyard. For the silent auction. A weekend." Why couldn't he form a coherent sentence around her? What was going on with him? It was highly annoying.

Her eyes widened. "You have a place in Martha's Vineyard?"

"Yes. I mean… I haven't spent much time there since I bought it."

"Then why do you have it?"

Fair question.

He didn't want to talk about his grandparents now, because that would inevitably lead into his tumultuous childhood.

Those were secrets and hurts he kept to himself. He'd never shared it with her. It was all just work and sex a decade ago. Those damn walls he built for himself to keep everyone out.

"I do want to spend time there. Work takes all my time and I haven't been there since I bought it," he replied hesitantly. It was so hard to talk about, which was ridiculous.

Madison leaned back in her chair. "I don't know if I can include it in the auction."

"Why not?" he asked through clenched teeth.

There was a smile tweaking at the corner of her lips, a sparkle in those gorgeous gray eyes, and he realized she was teasing him.

"I'm kidding around, but I wouldn't mind getting some pictures. Do you think you can take me out there? I can snap some shots and see what you're offering."

Say no. Say no.

Only he couldn't because it made absolute sense.

"Sure."

What're you doing?

"Great." She beamed brightly, seemingly unbothered by them spending time alone together outside of work.

It was for the hospital. All for the hospital. So, it was like work. Right?

"Good." He just stood there, still kind of in shock over agreeing to take her to his place in light of the fact that he had been avoiding her all week. "Well, I'll send you a text about a good time when we can go out there and check the place out."

"I'm free this weekend," she offered. "How about Saturday?"

Tony couldn't think of a reason to say no. He was completely blanking. "Sure. I mean you didn't want to have dinner last week, but a day away to my place…"

"That was different. I was waiting on test results and this is for the silent auction. It's business."

She had another point. "Okay, we'll arrange something for this Saturday. Do you need to speak with me about anything else?"

Madison smiled kindly. "You came to talk to me. I didn't summon you."

He groaned. He was getting so flummoxed around her. What was it about her? "Right. Well, I'll talk to you later then."

"You know, there *is* something else I need to talk to you about. I was going to book a meeting, but since you're here…" Madison motioned for him to take a seat on the other side of the work top.

Although he wanted to leave and not put his foot in his mouth again, he couldn't. He was the department head. He pulled out a chair and sat down.

"What do you need to discuss?" he asked.

"I have a new patient. Pretty sure she's got ovarian cancer."

"Pretty sure?" he asked querulously.

"The scans at the free clinic point to a large mass on her ovary. It hasn't metastasized to any organs. She's young, a mother of two young children."

"So she needs surgery?"

"Yes, but there's a problem. She doesn't want surgery. She doesn't want to lose her only viable ovary. I've gone through a lot of the pros and cons with her and I said there is an option to do an egg retrieval, because she's not losing her womb. She just wants to do chemo. That's it. She thinks it'll shrink the tumor and chemo will work, but if she has the surgery to remove the ovary, then she might not need chemotherapy at all. The cancer could be taken care of with one procedure. It just seems like a no-brainer."

"It does."

"I'm hoping you can talk to her. She was reluctant, but she seemed open to having an appointment with us both."

Tony scrubbed a hand over his face. "Did she give any reasons why she didn't want surgery?"

"Other than her fertility, she's terrified of surgery. She's also the kind that does her own research."

Tony grumbled inwardly. Just like Jordan had done. That damn clinical trial and Jordan's refusal of chemo. Tony had taken a gamble and went against his better judgment—and reluctantly agreed. He'd stepped completely out of his comfort zone for his best friend, and Jordan had died. If Jordan had just gone with the tried and true methodchemotherapy and radiation——he might be here.

No. He wouldn't. His cancer was too far gone. It wasn't my fault.

"If she's willing to talk to the both of us, then I can give her some facts," Tony responded.

Madison nodded. "Good. If anyone can convince her, you can."

"I try," he said softly. He was good at talking to his patients and helping them make informed decisions about their treatment, except Jordan. It still stung. He stood up. "I better get back to what I was doing."

"Thanks for the silent auction donation and for agreeing to meet my patient."

Tony nodded. "Of course."

Madison turned back to her work and he slipped out of her lab. He had managed to avoid Madison for a week and so far they were cordial. Maybe working with her wouldn't be such a bad thing.

Madison tried to put Tony out of her mind, but it was hard to do. She was slightly kicking herself for not going to have dinner with him, and she couldn't figure out why. She didn't want to strike up a relationship with him again, no matter how good the sex had been in the past.

Amazing sex was not something to build a relationship on. Which was too bad, because when Tony and her got together it was toe-curlingly good. That she did remember vividly. No one else had held a candle to the sheer electricity and the sparks between her and Tony. But marriage was based on trust and loyalty. Her parents had that and more. Still, it didn't mean anything in the end. Her mother died and her father was left alone and heartbroken.

It was vivid in her mind. As fresh as when it first happened. Her father's pain. It terrified her then. It still did.

There had been no time to grieve when you had to keep it all together for your remaining parent. If there had been a cure back then, her mother would be alive and her father wouldn't have shut the world out.

She wouldn't have been so alone.

Which was why she need to be focused on her work and on nothing else.

Things just had to be kept professional. She was doing so well, keeping to her lab in between her patients. Then she got it into her head to help Dr. Crespo out with the silent auction, not only because the free clinics were beneficial to her for finding people for medical trials, but also because she just wanted to give the chance to fight back to those who couldn't normally afford top-level treatment.

Her parents couldn't afford the best when her mother had been battling cancer. Part of her always wondered if her mom had had better care, would she still be here?

These clinics were good. She wanted to help others in financial situations similar to what she'd grown up in.

That's how she met this young mom. When she saw that mass, she knew it was a surgical case and she had to ask Tony to help convince the patient that it was the right thing to do.

Children needed their mom. Madison knew, because even at almost forty, she needed her mom too. It had been far too long since she had her. A lump formed in her throat and she wiped her eyes quickly before shutting her laptop.

Great. Now she was crying.

It was hard sometimes to do the work that she did, to face cancer and remember her mother, but she also wouldn't trade it for anything. It was what kept driving her, kept her working and focused.

"You okay?"

Madison looked up and saw Tony was back, standing in the door. He had changed into his street clothes and she looked around, realizing that he had left a while ago. She had been so stuck in her work the time had slipped by.

"Fine," she said, her voice wavering.

Tony slipped in the room and shut the door. "I don't think you are."

Madison brushed a tear from her face. "Just thinking about my mother."

And she couldn't remember if she ever talked to Tony about her. It was something she was so used to holding back. How could she grieve her mother in front of her father? She was so used to expressing her sadness alone.

Tony's expression softened. "Come on. We're going to

get a bite to eat and I won't take no for an answer this time. There's a little café not far from here. We can walk through the Common. It's a gorgeous summer evening."

As much as she wanted to tell him no again, she couldn't because dinner sounded great and she didn't want to be alone right now.

He's a friend.

"Okay." She packed up her laptop and grabbed her purse.

Tony opened the door for her and closed it behind them. She locked it quickly and then his hand slipped into hers. It took her off guard, but she didn't pull away because she liked the way his fingers felt against hers.

It was comforting.

It had been a long time since she had that feeling of comfort. Even though they argued, there were so many times she was sure Tony was the one. Except, he obviously didn't think the same of her, which had broken her heart. It was hard to spend a life with someone who shut you out.

You did the same too.

It had been hard to let him go, but it was for the best.

Was it?

"Uh, Tony?" she said, softly.

Tony looked down and his eyes widened when he realized what he'd done. "Sorry."

She squeezed his hand and then released it. "It's okay. Old habits."

"Yes." His expression was soft and there was a sparkle in his eyes.

Just like old times.

They walked in silence out of the hospital, but she was missing the feeling of his hand in hers. Every moment she spent with Tony, the more she realized that this working with him wasn't going to be as straightforward as she originally thought.

As she'd said, old habits. They were easy to slip back into.

CHAPTER SIX

THE LITTLE CAFÉ was just a short walk from the hospital through Boston Common. Tony was right; it was a beautiful summer night. It wasn't too hot and a warm breeze whispered through the trees. It was just the humidity that got to her. It was so different from California and her home state of Utah.

She had only ever passed through Boston via connecting flights, so she never got to spend much time here. It was nice just walking in silence with Tony so that she could take in all the sights. She was used to Tony's broody aloofness. He wasn't much of a conversationalist. He always seemed to keep things close to his chest.

He was definitely guarded and always had been. It just solidified the fact he didn't trust her with his emotions, his life. It cut to the quick. How could you have a life or a future with someone like that?

You couldn't.

She spent some lonely years, needing comfort and someone to talk to as a young woman. She couldn't let herself fall for someone like Tony, someone like her dad. If she ever married, she wanted to share a life with her spouse, not have to guess how they felt or tiptoe around them.

There was a burst of laughter from children who were enjoying an old carousel in the Common. Its top was painted a bright blue with white stripes and it played boisterous organ grinder music. She grinned when she saw it and thought of the old merry-go-round that her mother would take her on, before she got sick.

Madison would climb on the tallest and pinkest horse she could find, her mother would stand behind her, holding her, and they would both scream and laugh. Especially when she threw her hands up in the air. She had this sudden urge to run over there and take a ride.

"Look at that," she gasped.

"What?"

Madison pointed. "The carousel."

"Do you want to take a spin?" Tony asked casually.

"Why would you think that?"

"Because you pointed it out and you can't take your eyes off of it." He smiled. "So, would you like to take a ride?"

It was out of the ordinary for Tony to offer something like this. Past Tony would've rolled his eyes.

She nodded. "I think I would."

"Let's go check it out."

The carousel was just finishing a ride and Madison bought two tickets. She turned and handed Tony one.

"What?" he asked, shocked, staring at the pass in her hand like she handed him a bucket of spiders or something.

"It's for you," she offered, pushing the ticket at him.

"I'm not getting on a carousel," he scoffed.

"You suggested we check it out."

"You seemed interested. Not me."

Madison cocked an eyebrow and then forced the ticket in his hand. "If I'm riding the carousel you are too."

Tony sighed. "Fine."

"You're dragging your feet. Come on, you old curmudgeon."

Tony rolled his eyes, but there was a hint of a smile on his face as they climbed onto the carousel. Madison worked her way around until she found a big white horse with a blue saddle. It wasn't pink, but it would do. She mounted it and Tony reluctantly climbed on the brown horse next to hers.

"This is ridiculous," he muttered. His grumpy expression made her laugh softly to herself.

"Have you never been on a carousel before?"

"When I was a kid."

"You're such a—"

"Don't say it!" he said quickly.

Madison laughed. "I wasn't going to say that, but I was going to say you're too uptight. You always have been. You have to live a little sometimes."

Tony pursed his lips, but didn't look convinced. He was gripping the pole, his knuckles white as the carousel's music amped up and it slowly began its rotation. The lively pipe organ music blared and the lights flashed as the horses went up and down and around.

Madison released her hold and raised her hands in the air to let out a whoop of glee. Tony couldn't help but smile at her then, relaxing slightly. There had been so many times when they were together when she would try to get him to do something fun, but he would always complain or refuse to participate at first.

Then, when he would break down and try something a little outside of his comfort zone, he would have a blast. Tony was always just so afraid of something new, something different, and she could never figure out why, because he never liked to talk about things or get too deep. Madison was different. She'd learned from an early age to rely on herself, but she also knew how to have a good time.

The spinning slowed and then the carousel came to a stop. She let out a happy sigh, because it was exactly what she needed.

Tony clumsily slipped off the horse and cussed under his breath. She stifled a laugh.

"I'm too old to ride a merry-go-round," he mumbled.

"That's a shame." She slipped off the saddle, but her foot didn't hit the floor sure and she toppled forward out of her heels. Tony reached out and caught her, but her face smashed against his chest.

Great. Just great.

"Whoa," he said, gently righting her.

She stood barefoot pressed close against him. She forgot how much taller he was than her. His hands held her shoulders and she could drink in his scent of the clean musk he always wore. There were times she'd steal his scrub shirt and curl up with it in an on-call room, like a Tony-sized security blanket. Her heart was racing a mile a minute as she just stood there, being held by him, staring up at the man she had loved so much. A man she thought she had known back then, but didn't. Still, she'd fallen for him.

His eyes locked on to hers and her mouth went dry. Her body reacted, hoping for a kiss. It felt like time was standing still or it had no meaning, and all those years gone by seemed to mean nothing.

He reached out and gently touched her face, causing a ripple of goose bumps to break across her sensitized skin. Her heart was hammering and she closed her eyes, leaning in and melting for him as he captured her lips with the lightest kiss. Instinctively her arms wrapped around him, drawing him closer and not wanting to let go.

"You need to buy another ticket, lovebirds?" someone shouted.

Madison stepped away quickly. Embarrassed.

"We better get off," Tony said, taking a step back.

"Right," she mumbled. She bent down and grabbed her heels and dashed off the carousel onto the pavement. She made her way around to find a place where she could slip back on her shoes. She held on to a metal post for balance and to ground herself after that kiss.

What had she been thinking?

Her body was longing for more, remembering Tony and his touch well. It was like she was waking up out of a deep hibernation and her body was hungry for more.

"Let me help," Tony insisted. He took her shoes from her and got down on one knee, taking her foot in his strong hand as he slipped on her heels like she was a princess. A shiver of anticipation ran up her spine as she gripped the post tighter. The cold metal dug into her palm.

"Thanks," she muttered breathlessly.

"Well, what did I say about those ridiculous heels?" He got up.

Madison rolled her eyes. "You're impossible."

He smirked. "So you've said. Shall we grab that bite now?"

"Please."

A perfectly romantic moment, or what she thought was a romantic moment, was ruined by Tony's pragmatism. That was another reason why they weren't together. They were too opposite in so many ways, but then again they were the same in others. It was obvious they weren't going to talk about it.

Maybe that was for the best. Just ignore it and sweep it under the rug.

Sure. When has that ever worked?

They crossed the Common and headed out on Beacon Street.

"It's not far," Tony commented, breaking the silence.

"I'm not complaining. I told you, I can run a marathon in these heels," she teased, then spotted the bar made famous by *Cheers*. "Oh, hey, look! It's the place where everybody knows your name!"

Tony gave her a serious side-eye. "You would sing that, wouldn't you?"

"I don't understand why you wouldn't. It's catchy."

Tony sighed. "You're always the life of the party."

"And you're like a grandpa, but that's kind of insulting to grandpas who aren't so set in their ways."

Tony chucked to himself. "Not much has changed in a decade, has it?"

"Not really."

They stopped in front a small Italian café and Tony held open the door for her. It was a charming place tucked away past the corner of Brimmer and Beacon. Madison loved all the redbrick and the colonial vibe in this part of Boston.

Tony quickly spoke with the maître d' and they were shown to a private corner booth in the back. They both slid in and she accidentally bumped her hip against him when they met in the middle. Her pulse began to race at being close to him again.

"Sorry." She scooted over, trying to give him some space.

The maître d' left them a couple of menus before disappearing back to the front.

"This is…cozy," Madison remarked, hoping Tony didn't

sense the trepidation in her voice. She couldn't seem so nervous. It was just dinner out with a colleague.

Yeah, one I've seen naked and I just kissed him.

She shook that thought away and tried to concentrate on the menu in front of her, but all the words suddenly just looked like gobbledygook because all she could think about was how close she was to him, how he was affecting her again after all this time.

Holy mackerel. It's just dinner.

"I like this place," Tony said, offhandedly. "Good caprese salad."

"Maybe that's what I'll have."

"The chicken parm is excellent too."

Madison shut the menu. "You grew up in Boston, if I remember correctly. Since you know this place, you order for me."

Tony cocked an eyebrow. "You're letting me have control? You never trusted my menu suggestions in the past."

"I am now." She set the menu down. "We're friends, I hope, and I have to be able to depend on my friend."

She was trying to show him that she trusted him and that maybe, just maybe he could finally learn to do the same for her.

"Okay," he agreed.

"Okay we're friends or okay on dinner?"

"Both," he stated. "You're right. We have a past, we're colleagues and I think there's a mutual respect. I would like us to be friends."

"Good."

Tony didn't exactly say that he had confidence in her, but being friends was a start. The waiter returned and Tony ordered some wine to accompany their meal of caprese salad and chicken parmesan. It was a lot of cheese for one meal, but she didn't often indulge in Italian.

"I'm sorry about the kiss," Tony finally said. "I forgot myself."

"It's okay," she replied. She was trying to be nonchalant about it, to casually brush it off, and failing miserably.

"No. It's not. I shouldn't have done that."

"And I should've stopped you." Only she didn't want to stop it when he pulled her into his arms.

It was just like it was the first time all over again. And that's the way it always had been. She couldn't fall into that trap.

Unless he's changed...

Though she doubted it.

"I'm sorry I kissed you," he repeated. "I don't know what came over me."

"We both got carried away. It won't happen again." If she said it out loud it meant it was true. In theory.

"You're right. Let's talk about something else."

"Sure. What do you want to talk about?" she asked.

At this point she was willing to talk about anything but them and the feelings he was stirring up in her.

"What brings you to GHH?" he asked.

"Is this that conversation about how long I'm planning on staying?" she asked.

He cocked his head to one side. "In a way."

"I see," she replied stiffly.

"All we ever talked about during our time together was my goal of being a surgeon and your dream of research and finding a cure."

"Is that so bad?" she asked.

"No," he said. "I mean, it does explain all your hopping around from one clinical trial to another."

Madison frowned. "We're not going to bring that up again, are we?"

"No, but I'd like to know your goals. Friend to friend."

Madison sighed. "I need to have more published. My end goal, besides the cure…is I want to work with Dr. Mathieu LeBret at his research hospital in France."

She couldn't believe she was sharing that out loud with someone. She didn't have time for many friends and she didn't like people knowing too much about her aspirations. Her field was a competitive one.

"Wow. Dr. LeBret is a Nobel laureate. Those are lofty goals."

"And what about you?" she asked, hoping he'd open up and share something with her.

Tony shrugged. "I achieved what I wanted. I'm a surgeon, head of oncology. It's safe."

"Safe?" she asked, querulously.

He nodded. "Secure."

"Security is important."

"It's the most important," he replied fiercely.

Madison understood that, but she made her own sense of security in the world. She had to.

"What was the draw with the carousel?" Tony asked, changing the subject.

"My mother, actually." She smiled, softly twirling her finger around the stem of the wineglass. "She used to take me on carousel rides when I was young. I've been thinking about her a lot today, and just seeing that carousel in the park made me think of her."

"Your mother died of cancer, didn't she?" Tony asked.

She nodded. "When I was fourteen."

"What made you think of her today?" he asked softly.

Madison sighed. "That patient of mine. She just reminded me of her. Only, my mother didn't have the best team of doctors because we couldn't afford it."

"I'm sorry," he said, quietly. "It's one of the reasons why I really do support our hospital and the work in the free clinics. I try to donate as much of my time there as I possibly can between work and Miguel."

"Miguel? Who is Miguel?"

First the kiss and now talking about their goals and dreams. At least he had confirmation that GHH wasn't a permanent stop for her.

Whereas it was for him.

Then she opened up about her mother and it just slipped out about Miguel. Tony didn't want to bring up his godson, because he didn't want to have to talk about Jordan or his death. Madison had met Jordan when he'd visited Tony out on the West Coast. Everyone who met Jordan liked him, and in a lot of ways Madison was very free spirited like Jordan. What they both saw in Tony was still a bit of a mystery. Still, they all had a blast those couple of days that Jordan visited.

When Tony returned to Boston without Madison, Jordan lamented to Tony that he had let go of a good one. It was a point of contention between him and his best friend, because Tony regretted the end of their relationship.

Now he was annoyed that he let it slip about Miguel. Now he'd have to talk about Jordan. And it was hard to talk about it all.

As he looked into her eyes, he knew he had to tell her.

I might as well rip the bandage off.

"Miguel is my godson. Jordan's son," he stated, hoping his voice didn't break with all the emotion swirling around inside of him.

Her eyes lit up. "Oh! I forgot about Jordan and that he lived out here. We should arrange a dinner—"

"Jordan passed away five years ago from cancer." Just getting the words out was difficult. It was hard to even process it at all, and he was still angry that he took the risk and approved Jordan to take that experimental treatment. He went against the tried and true. He should've fought harder to get Jordan to see his side. That was the reason he was always so cautious now. So skeptical.

"Tony, I'm so sorry." Madison reached across the table and slipped her hand into his. Her hand was so smooth and delicate. He'd always liked holding it. It was why he'd grabbed it earlier out of habit. She squeezed his fingers and he held on tight. He'd forgotten how small her hand was in his.

He didn't want to let go or break the connection.

In fact, there was a part of him that wanted to continue holding on to her for as long as he could, even though he knew he shouldn't.

Treading a dangerous path.

Feelings like these, this sentimentality and recalling her and their time together, had made him kiss her. And that had been a complete mistake.

Why was it so easy to forget the walls he planned to put up to keep her out when he was with her?

Because I loved her.

It had broken him so much when she ended it. Even though it was perfectly clear they were ill suited to each other. He had what he wanted in life and she had no plans to stay in Boston permanently. Her time here at GHH was limited.

"Caprese salads," the waiter announced, returning to the table.

Madison snatched her hand away and folded both hands neatly on the table in front of her.

"Thank you," Tony said quickly to the waiter, trying to regain composure.

"Well," Madison said, brightly. "This looks great."

"It is. Believe me."

Her eyes narrowed as he said that and she grinned, but it wasn't a warm smile. It was almost forced.

"I do have faith in you, Tony."

A little pang of guilt ate away at him. How could she trust him so easily? He had such a hard time with that, yet she gave it so freely. But it was hard to put that faith in people who constantly disappointed you.

His father, who could never be relied on, had squandered his mother's money and broken her heart and his time and time again. There were so many times he helped his mother out financially, only for her to turn around and send it to his father.

And then there was Madison, who couldn't stay still, who took so many risks that he was too scared to pursue her, to believe that she wouldn't just hurt him again. That she wouldn't leave for something better, just like his father always did. It was clear to him all those years ago that she had the same kind of wandering soul. She was always looking for a new opportunity, whereas he stayed rooted in Boston. He made his own connections and chances without taking a risk.

Maybe I've grown stagnant here too...

Tony shook that ridiculous thought away.

There was just no way that he could ever put his heart on the line for her again, especially with an end in sight. It was only a matter of time before Dr. LeBret saw her talent and snatched her up. And he couldn't blame him, because sitting with her now, all of that worry melted away and he couldn't help but wonder why he was so adamant about locking her out of his life for good.

CHAPTER SEVEN

DAMN. HE'S NOT WRONG.

That was Madison's first thought as she took a bite into the dinner that she'd let Tony order for them. She wasn't too keen on letting other people do that. Actually, she didn't know what possessed her in that moment to allow him, but she was glad that she had because it was the most delicious caprese salad and chicken parmesan that she'd ever had.

Maybe that was because she spent so much time doing research that her dinners usually consisted of a cup of instant ramen noodles or a sandwich. She was all about convenience and a lot of times she forgot to eat. This dinner was like her taste buds waking up after a really long nap and saying, *Yes! Now, this is what we're talking about!*

Tony had a half smile dancing on his lips as he watched her. "You look like you've never had Italian before."

"Not this level of Italian."

Tony chuckled. "You can't exist on sandwiches forever."

"You know me so well," she teased. Except he didn't.

"Not so well. I didn't know you could run a marathon in heels," he joked. "Especially, when you can't even dismount from a wooden horse without falling over."

Madison rolled her eyes. "You really don't like these shoes, do you?"

"I never said that," he replied. "Just if you're going to

come to Martha's Vineyard this weekend to check out my beach house, then you'll want to wear sneakers or sandals. It's a bit of a walk."

"How long of a drive is it?" she asked. "If I have to rent a car..."

"You're not renting a car. I'll drive us."

A shiver of anticipation ran down her spine. She was kind of hoping that he would offer to take her there, but she didn't want to assume anything. She was so used to handling things on her own because she couldn't rely on anyone to do it for her. She took care of herself and a lot of the time if she wanted something done it was up to her. It was nice Tony was offering to drive. It would also mean spending more time with him outside of work. They'd agreed not to let the kiss happen again, but when she was around him, she forgot herself.

"You don't have to."

"It's fine. Friends, remember?"

She nodded. "Right. Friends."

They could do this. They had to work together and they couldn't let any pent-up attraction from the past come between them. Even if she secretly wouldn't mind that.

"And to answer your other question, it's a three-hour drive."

"Three hours?" she asked, stunned.

"It's a weekend escape."

"It'll be a long day," she lamented.

"You trying to get away from me?" he teased. There was a sparkle in his eyes again. He was relaxing and the tension she had been holding in dissolved. This was the Tony she fell for, but it was also the Tony he rarely let out.

She rolled her eyes and chuckled. "No. I just have work."

"We all do."

"Fine."

He nodded. "I'll be picking you up on Saturday early. Like six."

Madison groaned. "So much for sleeping in."

"You'll have to tell me where you're staying. I don't even know where you're living."

"I'm in a condo building, right across from the hospital."

Tony's eyes widened. "The Commonview?"

A knot formed in the pit of her stomach. "Yes. Why?"

"I live in the Commonview."

Of course he did.

Madison was subletting a place from another physician she was an acquaintance with who was working abroad for the next couple of years. Her lease was for a year and it was a perfect situation because the condo was furnished. Since she never settled in a place for long, she really didn't have that many items. She was minimalistic and liked to travel light.

"Do you?" she asked, choking back a piece of chicken.

"Are you subletting? It's a private condo building."

"I am. Do you know Dr. Ackerman? She's currently in Germany for the next two years. She heard I was coming to GHH and we worked out an agreement."

"I do know Sophie Ackerman. She's a brilliant cardio-thoracic surgeon."

Madison nodded. "I worked with her a few years ago when I was in Minnesota."

"We're neighbors. Legitimately, because I live down the hall from her."

Of course he did.

She hadn't seen him in the halls, but then again she rarely

went back to the rental. If she did, it was always odd hours, which would explain why she probably hadn't run into Tony.

Yet.

This was just getting weirder and weirder. What was fate trying to pull? Maybe it wasn't fate; maybe it was karma?

"Well then, that should make it easy on Saturday to leave at the ungodly hour in the morning."

"You wanted pictures." He grinne, deviously and winked. "This is what you get for agreeing to help out Frank for the silent auction."

"It's for a good cause," she stated. "Free clinics are vital."

"I don't disagree."

"I've already had some people sign up for my clinical trials."

Tony's expression changed, his back straightened and his eyes narrowed. "Clinical trials. Right."

"Yes?" she asked cautiously. "What do you have against clinical trials? A lot of our advancements in modern medicine are because of clinical trials and testing."

"We also don't want to play with people's lives," he said carefully without looking at her.

"Is this about all the clinical trials I joined as a researcher in our resident days? I seem to recall you had issues with it back then."

He softened. "No, it's not that."

"Okay then, what is it? I'm not playing Dr. Frankenstein here, Tony. I'm not trying to create life out of cadavers and electricity. I'm talking about an advancement in cancer research so that we can find a cure. I'm trying to put myself out of a job."

Tony sighed. "I get that. I'm just more careful."

That's an understatement.

She kept that snarky comment to herself.

"I know. You always have been."

"What's that supposed to mean?"

"Nothing," she said quickly. "I don't want to have this fight with you again. The same fight that we had when we were residents. I'm not going to put people's lives in jeopardy. I pride myself on my research, and these people are taking a chance on something when they don't have much to look forward to. When their options are limited."

"I understand that, but sometimes the tried-and-true methods are what works, not newfangled naturopathic things."

She was confused. "When did I mention naturopathic?"

"You didn't. It just reminded me of a patient. Sorry."

"You had a patient who joined a naturopathic clinical trial?" she questioned.

"Yes," he responded tightly. "I signed him up for it. It looked good on the surface, so I took a chance because my patient wanted it."

Since when did Tony let a patient sway him? And then it hit her who the patient was.

She cocked her head to the side. "What happened with Jordan?"

Tony knew that the conversation would loop back to Jordan, but he didn't want to discuss it. He didn't want to talk about it over and over again. Not that he ever really talked about it to anyone. He'd failed his best friend by not being able to convince him that the clinical trial was too big of a risk. He had his reservations about clinical trials in general, but Madison knew what she was doing. She may not stay settled in one place, but her research was solid. He'd read her papers and she was right; *some* trials gave patients who couldn't always afford health care a fighting chance. But he'd leave that to her, and stick with what he knew and what worked.

After all was said and done, though, he wasn't exactly sure that his preferred method would have worked, that the cancer would've been eradicated. That was one of the problems with being surgeon in oncology: cancer didn't deal in certainties.

"He died of cancer," he answered.

"I'm sorry to hear that," she said gently. "And he was the patient who convinced you to try the naturopathic path?"

Tony took a deep breath. "Yes."

"Not all clinical trials are risky."

"I know," Tony responded. "Look, I don't want to argue. I hate that we are. I promised that I wouldn't step on your toes here and I won't."

He was evading the question so he wouldn't have to talk about it.

Madison didn't look convinced as she poked at the rest of her chicken. "Okay."

"We can focus on Saturday and the trip to Martha's Vineyard. For what it's worth, I'm looking forward to it."

She smiled wanly. "Me too. I haven't spent much time on the East Coast. This will all be a first."

"You'll love it. You loved the beach in San Diego. You'll love the beaches on the East Coast too."

"I'm sure. Tell me one thing I have to do, apart from taking pictures of your place, one thing to try or see when we're there."

"Well, besides the ferry ride, I know a little place that has the best clam chowder."

Madison blinked. "Ferry ride?"

"It's on an island," he remarked. "Didn't you study geography in school?"

He was teasing and trying to relieve the tension. He knew he gave her grief about every clinical trial she'd leaped into in the past, but that was over. He wanted to trust her. He wanted to be friends for however long she planned to stay.

She rolled her eyes at his good-humored jab. "Yes. Do you really think this is a day trip?"

"Sure," he answered with confidence. "We'll probably get home late."

"That's fine. I'm not going to lie—I'm kind of excited about the prospect of clam chowder!"

He chuckled. "I know we had some good clam chowder in San Francisco that one time."

Madison cocked her head to the side and then grinned. "Right! I remember that now. In the sourdough."

"It won't be served in sourdough this weekend."

"Why were we in San Francisco again?" she asked.

"Dr. Pammi chose a couple of us to go to that medical conference where she was speaking."

"Right! Then we spent our free time down at the pier. Remember the chocolate? Heaven." She took a sip of chianti and Tony couldn't help but smile at her. There were so many good times they shared, in between the fighting.

It ached when it was over, but it had been for the best. He understood that now. He couldn't see it back then, but their dreams and goals were so different, which was something else they never really talked about. How could it have been love back then when they really didn't know each other?

Yet when he looked at her, his heart was lost.

* * *

They finished their meal and then split the bill. It was dark out, but the Common was lit up with those old-time streetlamps. You could hear the music and see the lights of the carousel, which was running. As they passed it he thought of her in his arms. She was so close. He had loved holding her in that moment. He could still taste her kiss on his lips.

He glanced down at her and caught her gaze. Her lips parted and there was a brief flush of pink in her cheeks. How did he put his heart in her hands, a woman he barely knew? It had been a risk for him, but he did remember how he loved being around her.

He'd had fun with her, however fleeting.

As they walked back to their shared building, there wasn't much to say. He was just enjoying himself spending time with her. It was just as magical as he remembered and he didn't want it to end. It felt like home, in a way.

He hadn't realized how lonely his life had become recently. There had been other women in his life, but it was so fleeting and scattered. Nothing had felt the same as this had. He fought the urge to reach down and take her hand in his again, but jammed them in his coat pockets so he wouldn't be tempted. They were all feelings of nostalgia she was stirring up in him.

There was a time limit to her life in Boston. This wasn't her endgame, but it was his.

They walked into the building together and rode the elevator up, both getting off at the same floor.

Madison lingered in the hall. "Thanks for taking me out

to dinner tonight. I wasn't sure that it was a smart decision, but I'm glad that I went and that you extended the invite."

"I'm happy you agreed. Friends, remember?"

She nodded and tucked back a strand of her blond hair. "Right. Friends."

"So I'll see you tomorrow? We have that appointment with your patient, right?"

"Yes. She's coming at ten. I sent you the file."

"I got it. I looked it over and I'll look it over again tomorrow."

"Thank you." There was another pink flush in her cheeks and she was standing so close to him. All he wanted to do was reach out and stroke her cheek. He wanted to pull her in his arms and kiss her. Drown himself in her sweet lips.

Don't do it.

Friends didn't kiss and that's all she could be—a friend.

Tony took a step back. "Good night, Madison."

She grinned sweetly. "Good night, Tony."

He watched as she walked down the hall to her apartment and waited until she unlocked her door and was inside.

It was one thing keeping his distance from her in the hospital, but it was another when she was right down the hall. So close, yet still so far away.

Tony had a hard time falling asleep that night, especially knowing that Madison was so close to him. He kept thinking about her sleeping in her bed. There had been so many nights that he would spend watching her sleep. She always had this thing about curling up on her side, with her hands tucked under her head. If he remembered correctly, she also had a penchant for kicking him if he spooned her too close. There were several times she got in a good blow to his groin.

The simple solution was not to pull her close when she was in a REM cycle, but he couldn't help himself.

The chance of pain was worth it for him, because he loved holding her close. So many things in his life were taken from him that pulling her tight made him feel like he could hold on to her.

Except, it hadn't worked.

Sure. I take chances on ball-kicks, but not anything else.

Tony gave up tossing and turning. He got up and went over the patient's records that Madison had sent him.

By the time he got to GHH in the morning he was exhausted, but coffee was certainly helping him function.

Thankfully, it was a clinic day for him and he didn't have any surgeries on the docket. All he had to do was see Madison's stubborn ovarian cancer patient, a few of his own patients, then do a round of post-op checkups. Tomorrow would involve some procedures. Then the day after that he and Madison would head down to Martha's Vineyard so she could get the photographs for the auction. He didn't have to complicate this. It was simple.

Nothing had to happen.

I'm way too optimistic about this.

He laughed to himself softly and downed the rest of his coffee before collecting the files he needed and headed to the small conference room where they would be meeting this patient from the free clinic.

When he walked into the room, Madison was standing with her back to him, in those high heels that showed off the shape of her calves. His gaze lingered and then slowly traveled up her body. He vividly recalled how she looked, and he remembered how soft she was, how she responded when he touched her.

His blood heated.

She was wearing a tight pencil skirt again that left little to the imagination. Her white lab coat was off and her silk turquoise shirt was sleeveless and he admired her toned arms. Her blond hair was pinned up and he recalled keenly how he used to kiss her long neck.

Focus.

Tony cleared his throat and she spun around.

"You look like hell," she remarked.

He frowned. "Thanks for the compliment."

"Did you sleep last night?" She picked up her lab coat and slipped it on.

"Not well."

"It shows. Do you think you'll be okay for this meeting?"

"I'll be fine." He tore his gaze away and grabbed a seat, setting down his files. "You're in a very critical mood this morning."

"Well, I'm worried about this patient," she replied quickly. "Sorry for being so condemning of the dark rings under your eyes."

Tony stifled a yawn. "I'll be fine."

"Have another coffee," she teased.

Tony rolled his eyes and the phone in the meeting room buzzed. Madison answered it and he heard her tell someone to send her patient in before hanging up. She went to the door and opened it as a very young woman shook her hand. Behind her was a young man that Tony could only presume was the patient's husband.

He could see the worry etched on the man's face.

"Jessica and Mark, this is my colleague and the head of oncology, Dr. Antonio Rodriguez."

"You can call me Tony." Tony stood up and came over to greet them with a quick handshake. "Pleasure."

"Why don't you have a seat?" Madison offered.

"Okay," Jessica responded quietly.

Tony pulled out the chair for her and the woman smiled up at him and perched on the edge. He got the sense the patient was on the verge of running and he wasn't a stranger to that. Cancer was a very scary thing—he understood that all too well.

"I'm scared," Jordan uttered. "You have to look out for Miguel. Promise me."

Tony sat down next to his bedside. "I promise."

Jordan looked up at him weakly. "You're mad because I didn't listen to you."

"I'm not mad." Although Tony was, a little, at that moment. He was watching his friend, lying in a palliative care bed, wasting away. "It was your choice. I just... I tried to advocate for you the best I could."

"Yes. You are mad. But Tony, nothing would've changed in the end. You know it. It gave me a small percentage. Just like this treatment."

"This treatment you took is too new. Chemo is..."

Jordan held up his hand. "I would've wasted away with that too. Don't be mad at me, Tony."

"I'm not mad."

"Just look out for Miguel. Please."

Tony nodded, fighting back the tears. "I promise."

Jordan closed his eyes and then slowly opened them again. "If you ever get a second chance at something...take it."

The words hit today as he glanced over at Madison, who was pulling out scans and talking to Jessica and her husband. Tony shook away the memories and tried to focus on the meeting, because he was here to convince Jessica to get the surgery.

"What stage am I?" Jessica asked. "I've been thinking a lot about this…"

"We've been talking and maybe the naturopathic method won't work," Mark piped up.

Tony's gut clenched as he heard them talk about considering alternative medicines. He tried not to react as he leaned forward to talk to them.

"To properly stage your cancer we would have to remove your ovary. It doesn't appear to have spread from your last scan, which is good. However, I can't give you a stage until we can do a biopsy." Tony didn't want to be harsh, but it was the truth. Scans only showed so much.

"An invasive surgery just for a biopsy?" Jessica's voice shook as she said it.

"Well, if we find cancer, we remove it then and there, and I can examine and see if it's spread anywhere else."

Jessica's eyes filled with tears. "We want to have more kids. Only one of my ovaries works and that's the one with the mass."

"Which is why I'm recommending an egg retrieval," Madison said gently.

Tony nodded. "It's a good option."

Mark looked worried. "I don't know if my HMO will cover that."

"I will make sure that it is covered," Tony stated.

"I've already talked to our fertility team here at GHH and they're willing to help out. There are clinical trials of different fertility drugs they could put you on. It will offset the cost," Madison interjected.

Jessica brightened up. "If I don't get the surgery…?"

"The cancer will spread and it will kill you." Tony was blunt, but he wanted to get the point across. He glanced over at Madison, who was frowning at him.

"What will happen?" Mark asked. "If the biopsy shows cancer?"

"We'll do a surgery and remove the ovary that has appeared on the CT scan. I will see if it has spread and then you'll have to go through chemotherapy. I may have to remove your other ovary, which is why we're suggesting egg retrieval, but there is a likelihood that I will have to remove your uterus."

Madison sat up straighter. "We can also do a round of hyperthermic intraperitoneal chemotherapy if it hasn't spread. It's a longer surgery, but delivering warmed-up chemotherapy straight into your abdomen will help."

This time Tony shot her an inscrutable look. He hadn't done many HIPEC surgeries before. Dr. Santos never mentioned it and he knew that it was a fairly new but innovative treatment that was done for abdominal cancers.

It was also expensive.

He wasn't too sure how the board of directors would feel about a HIPEC pro bono surgery. He was annoyed Madison had suggested it without consulting with him about what they could offer this couple, but on the flip side he had no problems with offering this to them if it was approved. He just didn't want to get their hopes up without cause.

"I would like to preserve what I can. If I don't have my uterus, then my egg retrieval will be useless," Jessica said. "I would like to hear more about HIPEC."

"It's a longer surgery. Bigger incision," Tony stated.

"I've worked with surgeons and done HIPEC on some of my tougher cancer patients. It can be expensive, yes, but there is a new dosage of chemotherapy we can try. I can get you on a clinical trial for that," Madison offered.

Tony was fuming inside. A new drug? Without board approval? Madison was just her same old rebellious self, jumping in without looking at all the facts. It was risky. All he could think about in that moment was how his father always leaped before he looked.

It always cost them.

Always.

"We have a lot to discuss, but I would like to do the egg retrieval as soon as possible so that we can get the surgery scheduled," Jessica stated. "I do want to fight this."

Madison beamed. "I'm so glad. I'll get you an appointment this week to see our fertility doctors, and if you're interested in HIPEC I'll get you on my clinical trial."

They all stood then as Madison shook Jessica's and Mark's hands. Tony did too, but didn't say anything else as Madison escorted them from the meeting room. He just waited until she came back in. She was all smiles, but Tony didn't feel like smiling.

Sure, he was glad that the patient was seeing sense about their surgery, but Madison had spoken out of turn. First the HIPEC, and now this new chemotherapy medicine she was researching? Was she going to get the patient to agree to egg donation so she could edit out the cancer gene through the use of CRISPR? It was all too much, too risky for his liking.

What if they couldn't even get approved for of this? They could've just given a patient false hope. He keenly remembered having hope like that dashed away by broken promises.

Madison spun around, arms crossed.

"What?" she asked, obviously sensing his mood.

"HIPEC?"

She cocked an eyebrow. "Haven't you done HIPEC before?"

"Actually, no. Dr. Santos would've had to be the one that worked in tandem with me and he never mentioned it."

"I've done it," she said.

"It's risky."

"It has great outcomes."

He frowned. "A new chemo drug?"

"Yes," she said, firmly. "Not *new* new. Not to me. I know my job."

"I didn't say you didn't."

Her eyes narrowed. "And this is where we butt heads. All the time."

"I'm very well aware."

Madison sighed. "If you don't want to do the HIPEC surgery, I will ask another surgeon. That's if she agrees to it."

"I'm the one donating my time to help minimize costs." He ran a hand through his hair. "I'm sorry."

Her mouth dropped open and then she took a deep breath. "I am too. I should've consulted you about the HIPEC. I guess I'm on edge because…"

"I questioned you and I had no right to do it."

She nodded. "I want you to be the surgeon on this, but we need to trust each other and work together." She had a point, but it was hard for him to trust her. He had to put it behind him. It would be unprofessional to do any less.

"Agreed. It won't happen again," he replied tightly.

"Thank you and I will consult you beforehand. I'm glad I can count on you."

He swallowed a lump in his throat. At least he was the reliable one, always there to pick up the pieces. "You can. I'll be the one doing the first step of the surgery. I'll be there with you."

"Good. I will take care of the medicinal part, because that's what I specialize in."

In that she wasn't wrong, but a part of him was struggling on how he could trust her judgment. What if she was rushing things again?

You're the surgeon. This is her patient.

And he had to keep that thought at the forefront of his mind while working with her.

He nodded. "At least she's open to surgery."

Madison's face relaxed and she smiled again. "Exactly. Her scans show that we probably caught it early. She can go through a fertility cycle—it'll take about a month—and then as soon as retrieval is done we can wheel her into surgery. It's going to take that long anyway to get her on the clinical trial and all the necessary financial approvals."

Tony nodded, resigned. He said he was going to trust Madison with this and he was. He was going to support her like a good head of oncology would. "Hopefully, it hasn't spread to her uterus."

"I hope not, but I try to look at the positive. It's all a risk."

The moment she said that, his spine straightened. How could she be so nonchalant about a risk? He just didn't understand that. The one time he gave in to the possibility of risk, Jordan had died. It wasn't his fault, but he was still blaming himself because he could've pushed him harder.

He could've made Jordan see that chemo might've given him a chance. He didn't listen to his own instincts and gambled on something he shouldn't have.

He had to remind himself that this was different. At least Jessica was open to surgery. There was nothing at risk here but the outcome for the patient. Not Tony's reputation or his heart. And they both would make sure Jessica understood what the surgery was about so she could make an informed decision. He just hoped this whole thing worked out.

"Well," he said, quickly. "I've got other patients to see. Keep me posted."

Madison nodded. "I will. And Tony, thanks."

He didn't respond. He just left the meeting room, trying to put some distance between her, his feelings and all the memories of Jordan and his father that were bombarding him today, because it was still hard to let go of the fear.

It was hard to put his faith in something that he didn't understand. Something unpredictable. Something that might cause pain. He'd had enough of that in his life. He didn't need any more.

It was hard to put his faith in Madison. But he was going to try. He could do this for her. She might only be here for a short time, but he wanted to make this professional relationship work. He wanted her as a friend.

Truth be told, there was a part of him that also wanted her to stay, but he knew that wouldn't happen, so he kept that to himself.

CHAPTER EIGHT

SOMETHING WEIRD HAD happened after she and Tony met with Jessica and Mark. Madison had pretty much figured it had to do with the fact she was signing Jessica up for clinical trials, but when she talked about the HIPEC procedure and the new chemotherapy, Tony had just become different. A wall went up and she had an inkling, once again, he didn't trust her.

That's when her guard went back up too, because she was falling into the same pattern they had followed time and time again. It had led them both down a path of heartache, and lots of arguing. She wasn't going to feel that pain again.

It took her a long time to get over Tony. It was hard for her to open her heart to anyone else.

Maybe because I didn't want to.

Madison had tossed and turned all that night. Sure, Tony had ruined her for a lot of other relationships. That was the easy explanation for why she wasn't married or had a family—and for why her work came first.

That focus on work was something she and Tony had in common, but at least he had some friends and family here in Boston. Madison's dad lived in Salt Lake and she tried to fly out Salt Lake to see him from time to time, but it was hard. She didn't fully forgive him for shutting her out for so many years after her mom died. Their relationship had never really recovered.

At least he wasn't alone. He'd found someone else when she moved away to college. He'd tried to reconnect, but she was always too busy with school and work. Madison had spent the last ten years moving around, getting closer to her goal in her cancer research and her dream of working with Dr. LeBret.

It was hard to make connection, friends, or even date when you were constantly on the move.

Yeah. That's the reason.

She had been so pleasantly surprised that what would've been a blowout argument in the past didn't turn out that way. They'd talked, apologized and agreed to move forward as professionals.

It thrilled her to see this change. This is what she was hoping for when she came to GHH, but there was a part of her that continued to be skeptical.

She had no time to dwell. Today was the day she was going to be in the pediatric procedure room while they extracted a sample of Gracie's bone marrow to determine if the neutropenia had killed off her marrow. If so, then they would have to do a bone marrow transplant.

Hopefully, Tony would agree with her that Gracie was a candidate for the tandem stem cell transplant, because Madison had seen this a few times in her various jobs as an oncologist and she was confident that it would work here too.

At least Tony hadn't been totally against that.

He's not against the HIPEC or the new chemo either.

It was nice to be able to collaborate with Tony, to have him trust her.

Madison took another deep calming breath as she pulled

on her mask and headed into the procedure room. Tony was there already and Gracie was sedated and prepped. He looked over as she came in.

"We're just about to get started, Dr. Sullivan," he said over his shoulder.

"Great. Dr. Santos did a stem cell extraction before her neuroblastoma surgery. Have you given any more thought to the tandem?"

"I have," Tony said. "I think it's a good idea. It does mean going through the chemo process again and potentially risking neutropenia."

"I'm aware, but at least she'll have a chance to recuperate. The high-dose chemo did do its job." Madison stood over Gracie's little body and looked down on her wistfully. She was so cute, so small, so sick. She was vulnerable.

When Madison helped little ones like this, it made her think of her longing for a family of her own, but the idea of her child getting sick and going through cancer, possibly dying, terrified her. She remembered the pain of losing a loved one all too keenly.

"Scalpel," Tony said to a scrub nurse.

All Madison could do was stand back and watch the procedure. Tony was so calm and gentle with the incision he made. He was so confident in everything he did, it was like he belonged in the operating room, but then she had always thought that.

There were times when he'd be in surgery with an attending and she would watch him from the observation room. Tony had no hesitation during surgery. It was a gift, almost like he was born to take control.

And she knew he studied meticulously, working endless

hours in the simulations labs to hone his craft. He was so sure of everything.

Except her.

He was always so scared of the unknown, but she was scared too. Scared of spending her life with someone else who shut her out emotionally.

Don't think about that now.

She tried to steer her thoughts back to the procedure. She watched every step that he took as he extracted the sample of bone marrow. It was like witnessing poetry in motion.

"There," Tony announced. "All done. Dr. Syme, please close Gracie up."

Dr. Syme, a young surgical resident, stepped forward and Madison followed Tony out of the procedure room into the scrub room. They peeled off their masks and protective gear to wash up.

"I'd forgotten," Madison remarked as she stepped on the pedal for the stream of water to start.

"Forgotten what?" Tony asked.

"How good you really are at surgery."

He smiled at her softly. "I like being in the operating room. I swear it's not a morbid thing, but I feel in control somehow. Other times...things are out of my control."

"Surgery can be risky," she replied. "I don't mean it as a slight. Medicine can be just as problematic too."

"I know you didn't. I think we can learn a lot from each other."

Her heart skipped a beat. "I do too."

She wanted to reach out and touch him, but resisted. When his arms had wrapped around her at the carousel, she'd felt so safe.

So secure.

She couldn't recall the last time she felt that way.

He just continued to scrub out. "So we're still on for Martha's Vineyard tomorrow, right?"

"Yes. I would like to get the pictures squared away for the auction in a couple of weeks. I hope you'll be attending?" She grabbed some paper towel and dried her hands.

"I suppose," he groused.

"You suppose?"

"It's a good cause. I just don't like the schmoozing. I'm not exactly charming."

"Oh, I wouldn't say that." Her cheeks flushed hotly.

Great. Just great.

This is the last thing she needed to talk about.

"Maybe you can give me some insider trading about what will be on offer." There was a twinkle in his eyes as he teased her.

Nice change of subject, Dr. Rodriguez.

"No way, pal. It's all secret."

"Figures."

They left the scrub room together and walked back to the main oncology wing. She had some more patients to see later in the day and she was aware that Tony had a couple of other procedures and some post-op patients to check on. She wasn't sure why she was hanging around him. Maybe it was the change. Maybe it was the prospect of having a friend again. She didn't make friends easily.

I've missed him.

"Have you heard from Jessica, the ovarian cancer patient?" Tony asked, breaking the silence that had fallen between them.

"I have. She set up an appointment with the fertility doctor, Dr. Page, for Monday. Dr. Page invited me to attend and I think I will."

"Keep me posted on that."

"Oh, I will. Have you thought more about the HIPEC?" she asked. "I can send you some information."

"I think I would like that. I haven't done really any, but I want to learn."

"And I appreciate that." Without thinking she reached out and took his hand, squeezing it slightly.

He glanced down and she realized what she'd done. She let go of his hand quickly.

He paused. "Well, I have some post-ops to check on before my next procedure."

Madison nodded. "I have some patients to see myself. I may head down to the free clinic if I get done with my work."

"Good. I'll be knocking on your door bright and early tomorrow. Try and get some sleep."

"Okay," she said softly. "See you later."

Tony nodded and hurried off to the postoperative wing.

Madison took another deep breath. Maybe it wasn't such a good idea to go with him to Martha's Vineyard tomorrow. Maybe she was just asking for trouble. She hadn't been thinking when she took his hand—it just felt natural.

The problem was she couldn't back out now. She had to go and get the pictures for the silent auction. She was caught between a rock, an island and Tony.

It was definitely a hard place to be stuck in.

True to his word, Tony was prompt and was knocking on her door at six o'clock in the morning.

Sharp.

Good thing she was also ready for him, because she was

used to his promptness. He hated when she—or anyone, for that matter—ran late; it was one of his pet peeves. She was sorely tempted to be a minute or two late, just to drive him a bit squirrelly, but she wanted to get this day over with because it would mean less temptation. The sooner she got the pictures of his place, the better.

"Good morning," she said brightly as she flung open the door.

Tony's eyebrows raised. "You're actually up?"

"Why are you so shocked? Have I been late once at GHH? I don't think I have."

"Well, you were late for the tour on your first day."

She frowned. "That was Frank's fault and you know it."

Tony was smirking, his eyes twinkling. "I know. I'm teasing. Come on, I booked a spot on the ferry and I want to make it to our boarding time."

"Sounds good." She reached back and grabbed a light jacket and a bag which had her camera and an umbrella. She locked her door and Tony looked at her gear.

"An umbrella?" he asked, touching the handle that stuck up out of the bag.

"It's supposed to rain. Haven't you looked at the forecast?"

He made a face. "It'll be fine. Besides, I'm not making you walk anywhere."

"It's better to be safe than sorry," she quipped. "Don't make fun of my extra baggage."

Tony chuckled at her little pun. "Fine. I won't."

They took the elevator down to the parking garage, and this was Madison's first time seeing Tony's sporty sedan. It was black with tinted windows, clean and shiny. It looked like it was fresh out of the dealership.

"You don't drive around much, do you?" she asked as he unlocked the doors.

"I used to do more driving. I took Miguel to a lot of activities, but Jordan's widow is about to get remarried and... his stepdad is a great guy." There was a moment of hesitation and he opened up the door for her as she slipped into the passenger seat.

Jordan had been a good guy. She could understand why his death was affecting Tony so much. She knew how close they had been—she'd seen it herself when they were out in California. Tony slipped into the driver's seat. They made their way out of the parking garage and onto the streets of Boston.

It was Saturday, early in the morning, so there wasn't much traffic on the roads. It was a bit overcast and a few drops of rain splattered on the windshield.

"I guess living across from GHH means you don't need to drive as much," Madison remarked, trying to quell the tension that had dropped between them when Tony had mentioned Jordan and his godson.

"Not really, but if I'm going to utilize the vacation house, then yes, I'll be getting more use out of the car."

"You should use the house. I mean, you must've bought it for a reason."

Tony shrugged as he navigated the streets to head out onto the highway. "It was a good deal. I have some happy memories on the island."

Madison was intrigued now. Tony never talked much about his childhood, his parents or anything from his past. He was a closed book. It was like he didn't trust anyone with his secrets.

"Oh? Your parents have a place out there?"

"My mother's parents lived there. I would go spend time with them when I was young. They died before I hit puberty and after that... Well, I was out on the island last fall and feeling a bit nostalgic when I found that their house was back up for sale."

Her eyes widened. "It's your grandparents' home?"

Tony smiled and nodded. "My great-great-grandfather built it. It started out as one of those gingerbread cottages that Martha's Vineyard is so famous for, and it expanded. You'll see. The previous owners did update the inside to make it a bit more modern, but it's still wonderful."

"I'm surprised you're not out there every weekend," Madison remarked.

Tony sighed. "Work and... It's a family home really. I don't have a family."

There was sadness in his voice, a longing, and she understood that keen pang of craving something more too. She wanted to ask him why he didn't get married; she was actually surprised he was still single. He was so adamant about roots. What had held him back?

Maybe me?

It was a stupid glimmer of hope that came out of nowhere, and she was mad at herself for thinking that. They had their chance, and it had ended.

She'd ended it.

They didn't work as a couple. Then again, she and Tony had never talked like this before. He never gave an inkling of ever wanting more and if he did, how could she lay her heart on the line for someone who never opened up to her, someone who never fully trusted her?

The answer had been simple back then: she couldn't.

Except now, the wall was coming down and she didn't

know what to make of it because she didn't believe it was down for good.

She'd been burned by this before.

Still, he was willing to work. They were arguing less. It was nice to really partner with him. Maybe things had changed?

CHAPTER NINE

TONY DIDN'T KNOW what had come over him when he started talking to her about the house. He didn't like to talk about his family, about how his mother had grown up well-off, but then ran away with a poor man his grandfather didn't really approve of.

His mother was cut off, but that didn't stop Tony's father from slowly bleeding her dry. His grandparents and his mother disagreed and became estranged.

However, the rockiness of that relationship didn't creep down to him. His grandparents took him for a week or two every summer, until they both passed away tragically in a car accident. That's when his mother had sold their family's home and his father had spent every last dime of that money. Even the money his mother set aside for his education.

It's why Tony had worked so hard to get into medical school and then to help provide for his mother, until she passed. His dad had tried to come back into his life before he moved to California to work with Dr. Pammi, but Tony had shut him out.

It was a longing for happier times that had brought him back to Martha's Vineyard last fall. Then he saw his mother's family home was back on the market. He had to buy it, but when he walked through the house after he bought it, it was so hard. It hurt so much.

A part of him worried that by coming back here, he'd be too vulnerable in front of Madison. He was never unguarded with anyone.

He was stunned that he had been talking about it at all with her. It also felt freeing to let it all out. She didn't need to know all the sordid details about his family's past, the embarrassment of his swindler father—that was his cross to bear. But he could share happy memories of his time here. It felt good to share and talk with someone.

He changed the subject to things about the island, the progress with the auction and patients. They made it to their ferry crossing time. They had to leave the car and head up on the deck before the vessel could depart from Woods Hole on the way to Oak Bluffs.

His place was just outside of Oak Bluffs, overlooking Nantucket Sound. He hadn't told Madison about one of the best things waiting at the end of this ferry crossing. The Flying Horses Carousel was the oldest operating merry-go-round in America. Tony had never thought much of it, but since the other night in the Common and witnessing how excited Madison was to see that carousel, he couldn't wait to show her the one on the island.

An image of her looking up at him on the Common carousel filled his mind. He adored that light of excitement in her eyes. And with that image came the memory of the sweet taste of her kiss, of all the kisses from their past. He could drown himself in her lips.

Don't. Get it out of your head.

They wandered around on the top deck. Madison was leaning over the rail with her camera out and taking photographs. It was windy and the water was a bit choppy for Tony's liking, but it didn't seem to bother her. She was smiling, her blond hair coming loose out of her braid and swirling around her delicate face.

It made his heart race a bit as he watched her longingly. All he wanted to do was take her in his arms again. She was the family he always longed for, but he just didn't trust someone who flew by the seat of their pants. He was too afraid to reach out and make anything happen. Which was why he was alone.

Sure, it was easy to blame work and the workload, but really who was at fault for that?

He was.

Madison turned and looked at him, smiling brightly, her cheeks ruddy from the wind. "It's gorgeous."

Tony nodded, beaming at her as he made his way over to the railing. "Sorry it's not sunnier."

"You can't control the weather. Or can you?" she teased, cocking an eyebrow.

"I wish. If I did, you'd have the perfect sunny day."

He braced his arms on either side of her, her back to his chest as the waves sent mist into the air. The sound was a bit tumultuous today, but he didn't mind in the least since Madison wasn't moving away from him. She just continued to snap pictures.

"I like the sea sort of stormy. I always have," she remarked.

"I remember," he replied.

And it was true. He did remember. She was from Utah, the land of mountains and snow, tall timber, but also farmland in the valley and red desert rocks to the south. There were lakes there, but he'd been with her the first time she'd walked the beaches in San Diego and seen the sea.

It had been a dreary day, but a group of them had time

off from studying and working nonstop under Dr. Pammi and went down for a beach picnic to take a break. The endless shifts of rounding and charting and such had taken their toll. The look of pure joy on Madison's face as she stripped off her sandals and ran out into the surf was something that he'd forgotten about until now.

Maybe he'd locked it away because that was a moment where he started to fall for her. Others had joined her with reckless abandon, but he had held back, just watching her splash happily in the surf.

Madison had joy. She knew how to live life.

It actually surprised him that Madison was still single. He thought she would've been married by now, but then on the other hand she moved around so much. Maybe she didn't want a husband or family.

It was something they never talked about before. Of course, there wasn't much time discuss any of that when they were studying, butting heads or falling into bed with each other.

When he was around her, all that worry he always carried since he was a kid seemed to melt away. It felt so right with her. But he couldn't have her, and he wouldn't hold her back.

She leaned back against him. "You afraid I'm going to topple over the side?"

"Well, you are from the mountains," he teased.

He stepped back and she slipped her camera back in her bag.

She shrugged. "I love something everywhere I've been."

"Really?" he asked.

"Sure. There's always something positive to look out for."

Tony had forgotten what a sunny kind of person she could be, just willing to jump in, both feet first, into any given situation. It was scary, because that was something he had never been comfortable with.

He'd never been able to just live in the moment. Most of the time, he would have to plan things out meticulously.

It could tend to be a bit tedious.

Just relax.

And that's what he planned on doing today—just relaxing and enjoying some time in one of his favorite places.

Madison was leaning over the railing again. "There's a lighthouse!"

He leaned over beside her. "East Chop Lighthouse. We're not far from the ferry terminal."

"How far is it to your place?"

"Not far at all. Just outside Oak Bluffs close to Jaws Bridge."

Her eyes widened. "Jaws…what?"

Tony chuckled. "You know, the shark movie. It was filmed there. That bridge is a great place for jumping off and swimming."

Madison shuddered. "No. Thanks."

"You've swum in the ocean before."

"I've waded out in the ocean. I didn't do surfing or snorkeling or anything like that. I don't like sharks." Madison shuddered again for effect. "I love the ocean, but I don't particularly like the idea of what lurks beneath."

"And here I thought you could find something positive about any place."

"Not sharks!" She shook her head. "No way."

He chuckled to himself. She was so endearing sometimes.

"I'll protect you from sharks. I promise we won't jump off the bridge, but we can take a walk over it so you can get some good shots of Joseph Sylvia State Beach. Beautiful white sand."

"That sounds like a plan."

The ferry pulled into the Oak Bluffs terminal. They went back down to his car and waited their turn to disembark. There was a bit of rain and it was sort of overcast, but it wasn't cold out. In fact, it was warm, even with the breeze.

As soon as they disembarked from the ferry, he drove over to parking.

"We're here?" she asked. "That's a short trip."

"I'm going to show you something you'll like. Especially since you went gaga over the Frog Pond Carousel."

Madison's eyes sparkled. "Seriously?"

"The oldest carousel in America that's still operating."

"Let's go!" She grabbed his arm and shook it.

They walked over to the Flying Horses Carousel. Madison practically squealed when she saw it. The Frog Pond carousel was cute, but this was the epitome of a merry-go-round. It had gilt and lights. The horses shone brightly under the lighting. There was painted scenery from 1879 and brass rings which, if you could grab one, would give you a free ride.

"It's beautiful!" Madison whispered. "I've never seen anything like it."

"It was originally in Coney Island and steam powered."

"We have to go for a ride." Madison was jumping up and down, clapping.

Tony laughed softly. "I figured as much."

They both bought a ticket and then got in the line to wait for the next ride. Tony decided this time, he wasn't going to even attempt to get on a horse; he would just stand next to Madison. She found a golden horse and climbed up.

"Worried about your hip, old man?" she teased.

"Yes." He winked. "I'm good standing here."

The operator shut the gate and the carousel started up, playing its joyous music as it went around and around and up and down. It had been thirty years since he rode this. His grandfather had brought him here once when he was ten, but he didn't enjoy it as much as Madison seemed to. Her eyes were closed and she had her arms outstretched.

At least today she was wearing sneakers and not heels, but he was slightly disappointed that she might not fall into his arms again. Instead, she wobbled slightly in her seat and gripped the pole.

"It's okay," he whispered in her ear, drinking in her scent. "I won't let you fall."

Then he held her steady, his arms wrapped around her waist. She looked back at him over her shoulder. Pink stained her cheeks as the flush crept up her neck and he could feel her trembling. Their gaze locked and his own pulse was thundering between his ears.

Kiss her.

Only he resisted.

He promised her it wouldn't happen again and he meant it. Although, right now in this moment, he wished he could take it all back.

The carousel ended and he stepped back, taking her hand and helping her down off the horse. They didn't say much to each other, but his pulse was racing, his blood heating, and he didn't let go of her hand as they exited the carousel. At least this time they didn't get scolded for lingering.

"How was that?" he finally asked, breaking the silence.

"It was wonderful," she said. "Truly. Thank you for bringing me here."

"You're welcome. Well, let's get to my place and get those

pictures in. The last ferry leaves at nine thirty p.m., but I reserved our tickets for seven thirty."

"That sounds great. I'm eager to see your family home."

They got into his sedan and the tension was still there—that sexual energy that always crackled between them. If this had been ten years ago, they would've been in bed by now.

But this wasn't ten years ago. They were no longer those carefree students of Dr. Pammi.

Their feelings were different.

Were they?

Madison wanted to say something, anything to Tony. She just couldn't think of a word to say. They had promised after that first kiss to keep things platonic between them, to be colleagues and friends, and they'd been doing a good job. They were working well together.

At least, that's what she kept telling herself.

She was completely deluding herself.

When he leaned against her on the ship and then held her on the carousel, she had melted inside. His touch had a way of making her feel totally secure. She didn't want to push him away, even though she knew she should.

Friends, remember. We're just friends.

Instead of saying something and possibly making it all worse, she focused on the scenery outside as Tony drove them away from the town of Oak Bluffs and down along a stretch of coast. She could see the appeal of Martha's Vineyard, even on a rainy, gloomy day.

There were green fields, trees everywhere and white beaches. The cottage homes were cute and quaint at first, but the farther they drove from the town the more lavish, large homes started to dot the countryside.

Modern style, barn style and farmhouse. She couldn't believe it. It was as cute as a button.

"There's the bridge," Tony pointed out and nodded.

She glanced over and saw the infamous bridge. No one was out jumping off it today.

Tony made a turn up a driveway that wound up a small hill.

"Here we go." He parked in front of a gate, rolled down his window and then punched in a code. The gate swung open. There were trees all around a circular gravel drive and she let out a small gasp as the white coastal cottage came into view.

"It's gorgeous," she exclaimed.

She was glad it wasn't one of those modern square houses. This house felt it belonged.

The gate automatically closed behind them, and Tony parked the car. She got out and followed him to the front door. He unlocked it and then punched in another security code.

Inside, it was a bit stuffy, and the few pieces of furniture Madison could see were covered in sheets.

"Did it come turnkey?" she inquired, looking around, her voice echoing in the empty house.

Tony flicked on a light. "No, this was some of my mother's stuff that she kept in storage. Pieces she saved after her parents died. I brought it all back when I bought it."

"So you've been back here more than once?"

Tony dropped his head and then grinned. "Okay, twice. I do have a maintenance company come and check on it and periodically clean."

"Well, we can't take pictures of it with all the sheets covering up the furniture. It looks like a haunted house." Which was a bit of an exaggeration. Whoever had owned it last had completely updated it, but they hadn't destroyed the beautiful woodwork. Wood trim moved through the house like a lifeline; it looked like it had been planed from driftwood and then stained a red cherry color...

Madison glanced up to see exposed beams and a beautiful banister that disappeared up a set of stairs.

She made her way into the kitchen, which was all modern with wood flooring, granite countertops, stainless steel and white cupboards. There was an old woodstove in the corner, possibly part of the original kitchen, polished and raised up on gleaming red bricks.

The back wall of the kitchen was all window and it led out onto a terrace that overlooked Nantucket Sound from on top of the hill.

There was a small pool and a hot tub. The backyard was open, save for a hedgerow which marked its boundaries.

Tony followed her silently. "Do you think this will work for the silent auction?"

"Oh. I think so."

"Great. We should get some pictures then."

"Yes, but first we clean and remove the sheets. And fair warning—we may have to find a knickknack store."

Tony's brow furrowed and he frowned. "Why?"

"You have no decorations, and we want this place to scream cozy romantic retreat at the auction."

Tony frowned. "Do I have a say in this?"

She grinned back at him devilishly. "Not at all."

CHAPTER TEN

MADISON REALIZED QUITE QUICKLY, without a doubt, that Tony was not having the time of his life going through little thrift stores in the village. She could tell by the sour look on his face, his exaggerated sighs, his groans and the way he dragged his feet, but he didn't try to stop her. It was kind of comical. Honestly, that made it even more fun for her. His grandparents' home was beautiful, but it definitely needed some added sparkle.

They had spent the morning cleaning and taking off all the sheets. She checked over the hot tub and the pool, which were both solid. Thankfully, the maintenance company Tony hired to clean and look after the place took care of those items. She had no doubt that in addition to the view, the pool and hot tub would be a big draw in the auction.

After that, she dragged him from store to store and gave him some helpful advice on items to buy, including towels for the bathrooms and better quality sheets—*not* bought at the thrift store.

Now Madison was getting a kick out of him grumbling behind her as she went through little knickknacks to bring some decorative beachy touches to his place.

"How about this?" she asked, picking a large wooden seagull off the shelf. It looked like someone had hand-painted it thirty years ago, back when folk painting and stenciling was the height of interior decorating, just like salmon-colored walls and teal carpeting.

He shot her an inscrutable look. "Do I have a choice?"

"Ye-es, but it would tie the whole look together."

"Your drawn out *yes* means I don't have much of a choice," he grumbled.

"You do. I'm just telling you it works. It's a look."

Tony glanced down into the cart. "What look is that? Crap on the beach?"

Madison chuckled and placed the homely seagull in the cart. "It's beachy."

"Crappy beachy," he mumbled, but a smile tugged at the corners of his lips.

She crossed her arms. "And you can do so much better?"

"I didn't say that!"

"We're almost done. Then we'll decorate the house. I'm telling you, rich city folks love this kind of stuff. Ooh, a butter churn!"

"How is that nautical?" he questioned.

She picked it up. "It's Americana."

Tony gazed down at the butter churn in disgust. "You're a brilliant doctor, Madison, but you suck at home decorating. I'm just going to put that out there."

She stifled a laugh.

It was good to tease and have fun with him. Right now they were just two people having fun, not worrying about anything. It was kind of freeing. It also reminded her of the way her parents had been. The laugher and the teasing.

The love.

Heat spread through her veins and she tried to look away so Tony wouldn't see her blushing. She placed the churn in the cart.

"Okay, I'm done. Let's get this out of here and then I'll take you to lunch. My treat, since I'm forcing you to buy all this…what you call junk, but I call treasure."

"Deal." He spun the shopping cart around and they went to the cash register to pay for their items. The local girl at the till gave the items Madison had picked out a curious look. It seems she agreed with Tony. They carried their purchases out to the car and Tony took them out of Oak Bluffs to Edgartown, down to the water that overlooked to the Chappaquiddick Point.

There was a tiny restaurant nestled close to the beach. It was rainy and getting rainier by the moment. She pulled out her umbrella and they dashed from the car into the restaurant.

"See," she said, shaking off the umbrella and closing it. "Always prepared."

Tony shook out his coat and rolled his eyes. "Sure. Rub it in."

"The weather app is very useful." She grinned at him innocently.

The little restaurant was pretty bare of people. There weren't many tourists out and about today, not that Madison could blame them. It was a miserable day. Thankfully, she had taken outside shots of the house before the rain had gotten any worse.

"Two?" the waitress asked.

"Yes," Tony responded.

"You can sit anywhere by the window," the waitress replied. "It's a bit slow today."

"Thanks," Madison said.

She followed Tony as they wound their way through the tiny tavern. It was completely nautically themed, with dark wood, captain chairs and wall-mounted fish. Nets draped from the ceilings. It was a little over-the-top, but that's what she liked about places like this.

There was a little booth in the corner where they wouldn't bump hips in the middle. She slid in and he slid in on the other side.

Their waitress came over and handed them menus and took their drink order before disappearing again.

"It's a shame it's so rainy," Tony remarked.

"Well, I'm just glad I got the outside photos done before the downpour."

"Me too. After lunch, we'll pick up our dinner at the market since our ferry doesn't leave until later tonight. I figure you'll need all that time horrifying my poor house."

She shook her head, laughing softly. "You mean improving it."

He chuckled. "Sure. We'll go with that."

"It's going to look good!"

"Okay…" he stated, grinning.

"You don't believe me, do you?" She was joking, but there was a part of her that was serious, because he just didn't seem to believe anything she said or did until she actually proved it to him.

"I do, I do."

Madison snorted. "You're *so* convincing."

"Okay, I'll trust you."

Her heart warmed when he said that and she reached across the table and took his hand.

"Thanks," she murmured.

"For what?" he asked softly.

"Trusting me."

"Trust is hard for me," he admitted.

"Why?" she asked.

"My childhood was a bit of an upheaval."

"I understand. Mine was as well. We have more in common than I thought."

Tony looked at her tenderly and he brought her hands up to his lips, brushing a light kiss across her knuckles, sending a rush of endorphins through her body.

You can't, Madison, a little voice reminded her.

Only she didn't pull her hand away. She ignored that little voice in her mind telling her that he was off limits, that he was just a friend. His kiss reminded her of all the times they had shared before. Not the arguing and not the work, but the moments she caught glimpses of the real Tony.

There was a time limit to all this though. She wasn't sticking around and she didn't want to hurt him again. She pulled her hand away, gripping the menu to keep her hands from trembling. She could feel the imprint of his lips on her skin and she longed for more.

"So," she said, clearing her throat and changing the subject. "Are you ready to decorate your house after lunch?"

"Just tell me how to make the weekend worthy of the silent auction. Should I put little mints on the pillows or...what?"

"You could offer up a gift basket full of things from the island. Other than that, they're getting a free weekend in a popular spot. Most people, I'm sure, dream of having a place overlooking Nantucket Sound in Martha's Vineyard."

"It is beautiful. I always loved my summers here as a kid."

She squinted and cocked her head.

"What?" he asked.

"I'm trying to picture you as a kid."

Tony rolled his eyes and the waitress came back to take their order. They both ordered the clam chowder and then

spent the rest of their lunch talking about nothing in particular. It was nice just being herself with him.

Why can't we have this?

She would so love it if they could.

True to her word, she paid for lunch, which she was glad to
do because he'd been right; it had been the best clam chowder she'd had in a long time. Rich and creamy, it just made
her heart happy.

They dashed back out into the rain and got into his car,
then headed to the market and grabbed some sandwich stuff
for dinner, as well as cheese, crackers and wine. When they
got back to his place, it seemed like the storm outside was
getting worse and there was a niggling part of Madison that
was wondering if they would be able to get back to the main-
land tonight. How bad did it have to be before a ferry was
canceled? To be honest, she was kind of nervous about traveling in choppy water.

"Shit," Tony groused glancing at his phone.

"What?"

"Ferry is canceled for tonight, maybe even into tomorrow.
There are winds of sixty-five miles per hour gusting off of
Cape Cod, causing high seas."

Her stomach knotted. "We're stuck here?"

Tony nodded. "Good thing we bought some bedding."

"Yeah," she agreed. "Speaking of that, maybe I'll throw
a load of laundry on."

She had to put some distance between her and Tony right
now. It was one thing to spend the day with him having fun,
but she had an out. They had ferry reservations—there was
an end.

Now, she was stuck here overnight with him.

It was too much temptation. She started the laundry machine, letting the whir of the wash and the hum of the dryer drown out the howling wind and lashing rain. Tony followed her into the laundry room. It was a tight squeeze and she could feel the heat of his body permeating through her clothes. She rubbed her hand absently thinking about the kiss.

"You okay?" he asked.

"A little freaked out about the storm and the fact we're trapped here." She spun around and faced him, gripping the dryer behind her, edging back as far as she could, but all she wanted to do was lean against him and have him hold her.

"Me too," he agreed. "Not the storm so much."

"Then what?"

"Being here with you," he said quietly.

She swallowed the lump in her throat. "Why is that?"

"I haven't stopped thinking about that kiss on the carousel at Frog Pond."

Her heart thumped, her body tingling with anticipation. "Well…try."

The truth was she hadn't been able to stop thinking about it either. Just being with him made her so happy. It broke up the monotonous loneliness of her life.

His dark brown eyes bore into her, searing her very soul, and her pulse thundered between her ears. The storm raging outside wasn't the only one—there was another howling in her heart. And she was trying to remember why she was holding back. When had she decided he was off-limits? She couldn't recall. Tony had changed and she was falling in love with him again.

He tore his gaze away and cleared his throat. "How long do you think the sheets will be?"

"A while yet," she responded, her voice trembling.

"Let's go have some dinner then. There's no use standing around here watching the laundry."

She laughed, the tension melting away. "You're right."

"Of course I am." There was a twinkle in his eyes.

"What happens when the ferry opens up? How will we know?"

"That eager to be rid of me?"

"No, just curious. Are we here a week? Do I have to re-schedule appointments?"

"As soon as the ferry is running again we'll get a notification." He held up his phone. "I have an app and everything."

"Good."

They walked into the kitchen and worked together to pull out the groceries they had bought. She focused on helping get sandwiches put together while Tony worked on a small charcuterie board.

Her pulse was racing as she watched him. When he admitted to thinking about their kiss, it made her think back on it as well. She was sorely tempted to do it again, to just melt in his arms, even one more time.

"What?" he asked, catching her staring as he set meat and cheese on a wooden board.

"That's like a perfect picture," she exclaimed as he adjusted a bunch of grapes. She grabbed her camera to take a few shots and set up two wineglasses next to it. Tony watched her, his eyebrows arched.

"It's cheese and grapes," he stated.

"And it sells."

He laughed. "You're way too excited about this."

"Excited about the auction?"

He nodded. "It's not at Sotheby's or anything. It's a hospital fundraiser."

"And a gala," she corrected. "I want your place to look great and get the most bids."

"Then you shouldn't have bought that fugly seagull," he mumbled.

"Maybe I'll bid on this place myself," she replied, smiling.

"A romantic weekend for two?" he questioned.

"Sure. Why not?"

"Who's your plus-one?" he asked, his voice dropping lower as he leaned over the counter.

A shiver of anticipation ran down her spine. "Do I need a plus-one?"

"No."

"Then, no one. Just me enjoying your place on my own." She grinned wickedly. "My own romantic weekend."

"That's a shame."

"Why?"

"I was hoping you'd bring me."

"What? This is your place."

"You're right. Maybe you don't need to bid."

"Why? Are you going to bring me back?" She held her breath, regretting the question.

"I would."

Her heart caught in her throat as he moved around and touched her cheek. It caused tendrils of heat to unfurl in her belly. She was having a hard time telling herself to resist him again.

"Tony," she whispered. She wanted to tell him that they shouldn't. Every look, every touch just reminded her of what it had been like before.

When it was just the two of them and no work in the way.

This time they were older. Maybe it could work…? So she didn't push him away. She just wanted more, her body trembling with need, recalling every moment when no one else had ever made her feel the way Tony did.

She wanted to be in his arms again. Maybe that would chase away the ghosts that had haunted her for the last ten years. The lingering longing had been eating at her since she'd ended it all.

Would it hurt?

He pushed back a strand of hair from her face, gently tucking it behind her ear. "When I'm around you, Madison, I forget myself."

Madison closed her eyes and leaned into his hand, not wanting the connection to end. She'd missed this. All of it.

"I do too."

"Do you ever think of me?"

"Always," she whispered.

"What do we do?" he asked huskily.

"Kiss me, Tony," she said, breathlessly.

"Are you sure?"

"I am. Aren't you?"

He nodded. "Positive."

Tony kissed her again and she couldn't help but melt into his arms like she had on the carousel. Only this time there was no one to stop them. His lips on hers seared her very soul.

Now was not the time to think. It was the time to feel. His tongue pushed past her lips, the kiss deepening, his hands in her hair as he cradled her head. He trailed his mouth down her neck.

Fire moved through her veins and all she wanted was him naked and between her legs. There was no stopping this moment. At least not for her. She wanted this again. Even if it was just for the night. Things had ended for them so quickly and she missed him after all this time.

Tony scooped her up in his arms and carried her into the living room as there were no sheets on the beds upstairs. She didn't care where this happened; she just needed it to happen now.

"What about protection?" he asked.

"It's okay. I'm on birth control."

They made quick work of their clothes so that nothing was between them. The only sound was their breath, her pulse racing with urgency, needing him.

Tony ran his hands over her skin and she trembled at the familiarity of his touch. How it made her feel safe.

"I've missed you," he said huskily against her ear as he explored her body.

Madison couldn't form coherent words. All she could feel was pleasure coursing through her as he touched her between her legs. She wanted to tell him that she missed him too, that she always thought of him, but couldn't.

"Oh, God," she gasped as he continued to kiss and lick her sensitive skin.

"I love touching you, Madison," he replied, his voice husky.

"I want…"

"What do you want?" He teased as he circled a nipple with his tongue.

"You," she responded, arching her back, begging him to take her.

Tony moved over her, his hardness pressing against her core. He slid into her and Madison cried out at the feeling of being completely possessed by him again. He thrust into her over and over. It felt so good. She was lost in the moment. It felt so right.

Tony moaned as he slid a hand under her bottom, lifting her leg up as he quickened his pace, sinking deep inside her. She closed her eyes, her body succumbing to the sensations of being lost in the arms of the only man she ever loved. The man who destroyed her heart and the one she'd had to leave behind.

Had anything changed? She wasn't sure, but she didn't care. All she cared about in this moment was him.

She came, tightening around him. She clutched his back and rode through the wave of pleasure before he followed close behind her.

As she lay there in his arms, she realized she'd made a big mistake thinking they could just be friends and that nothing would happen between them. But at this moment, basking in all the heady pleasure she had just shared with him, she didn't care.

What did I just do?

Tony couldn't believe what had just happened. When Madison begged him to kiss her and touched him, he was a lost man. Making love to her again wasn't the best idea, but he didn't regret that it happened. He just had to be careful with his heart, because he wouldn't be able to handle losing her again.

He didn't want to hold her back, but he didn't want her to leave and he didn't want to ignore this or how he felt about her.

"I'm freezing," Madison said, smiling up at him from the floor. "Your area rug is not particularly cozy."

He grinned as he ran his fingers over her, reveling in her softness.

The dryer buzzed from the laundry room.

"Well, I bet those newly dried sheets will help." He got up and dashed into the laundry room. He pulled out the fresh sheets and then put the damp ones from the wash into the dryer. He took the warm sheets out to Madison. She wrapped herself up in one.

"So toasty," she sighed.

He grabbed two pillows from the couch and cuddled up next to her. "I guess we need to talk about this."

He was well aware she'd jumped around from job to job for the last ten years and his work was rooted here. He couldn't leave here.

Why?

Madison sighed. "We do need to talk. Tonight was wonderful."

"It was." He rolled on his side. "Why can't we have this?"

"What, sex?" She grinned.

"More. Why can't we try again? I've missed you."

She smiled and touched his face. "I've missed you too."

"We can take it slow. Get to know each other."

They couldn't go back as just friends now. Yes, there was an air of uncertainty, but it could be years before she moved on again. And maybe by then she'd change her mind.

"I would like to take things slow." She kissed him again. "I've missed you. So much."

He leaned over and took her into his arms, pulling her across his chest as he stroked her back. "Then we take it slow."

"One thing though," she said, resting her head on her chin.

"Now you're demanding things?" he teased.

"We keep it secret at work. For now."

He nodded. "Good idea."

"And…"

"Wait, you said one thing."

She giggled. "Fine. Two things. Can we make a bed up? I don't want to sleep on the floor all night."

"I think we can make that work."

CHAPTER ELEVEN

Two weeks later

TONY MADE HIS way to the operating room board to see which room his procedure was assigned to. Today was the second stem cell transplant for little Gracie. The baby had been through a lot the past few weeks, but he was pleased with how she was responding. At first he'd been uncertain about the SCT because Dr. Santos hadn't recommended it, but Madison had been right.

He had a hard time focusing. He'd been having that problem since he came back to Boston from his place on the island, because he couldn't stop thinking about that night. It replayed over and over in his mind.

It was like a dream come true. They had spent all night and most of Sunday just curled up together, talking about everything and nothing. When the ferry opened back up, they headed back to Boston and at work they tried to keep their distance, but it was hard.

Every glance was heated with a promise. After their shift, they'd go out to dinner and end the night snuggled up in his bed.

Dr. Crespo remarked on Tony's exceptionally good mood. It was true. He was just living in the moment, instead of thinking about the looming deadline of the relationship, when he would have to let Madison go.

When they saw each other in passing since then, and every time he looked at her, his mind was flooded with images of their reconnection. He could still feel the silkiness of her skin, her breath in his ear, her nails on his back as she clung to him in the heat of the moment. It made him want her all the more. And every night he got to relive it. Their secrecy in the halls of GHH reminded him of the days they snuck around as residents.

Only this time there was no arguing, no hiding emotions. He could be himself with her.

He scrubbed a hand over his face and stared at the operating room schedule for the third time.

Since this was the final stem cell transplant for Gracie it meant that he'd be working closely with Madison today, on a day she was particularly lodged in his brain.

You've got to get her out of your mind.

"Morning," Madison said brightly, coming to stand next to him.

Her blond hair was pulled back tightly and covered by a scrub cap. Baggy scrubs hid her curves, but Tony knew every inch of her under those layers and his blood heated as he thought about it.

His body tensed. "You ready?"

"Yes." She nodded. "This will be good."

"What chemotherapy did you use this round?" he asked.

She cocked an eyebrow. "I used naxitamab-gqgk."

His stomach knotted, but only for a moment. It wasn't what Dr. Santos would have used, but Madison knew what she was doing.

"I'm aware that Dr. Santos didn't okay it for patients under one," Madison continued, as though she read his thoughts, "but this medicine has good results. Even for Gracie's age group. Her mother consented when I gave her the facts."

Tony nodded. She'd dealt with the medicine side. If Gracie's mother was consenting, then that was all that mattered. It was a moot point.

Madison would not put a child's life at risk. She was talented and she was careful with her choices.

She's not like your father. This is not a frivolous risk.

"Let's get this done." He headed to the scrub room and Madison followed him.

Madison didn't say anything as they entered the operating room, but there was nothing much to say. In the operating room personal relationships were put to the side. He had to focus on the task at hand. She kept quiet during the procedure. He thought he'd prefer it that way, but instead he missed her talking to him.

The procedure with Gracie went off without a hitch and the baby was doing well. He was positive that this was a good move. After Gracie had the all-clear, Madison left the operating room. He knew she had some research to finish.

She was no longer putting in the tedious hours at her lab. Instead they spent their nights together, but he knew she had work to catch up on and he wouldn't interfere with that.

He scrubbed out. As he headed out of the operating room floor, he got a page from the emergency room, which was weird.

He was a surgeon, but a cancer surgeon. It was rare that he had anything to do with trauma, but sometimes some of his post-op patients came back with an infection or something. He made the call down to the ER from a nursing station.

"This is Dr. Rodriguez. I was paged."

"Yes. We have a patient who was brought in from Harbor Middle School for fainting," the nurse said through the receiver.

Tony paused, trying to remember all his current patients. "I don't currently have any pediatric patients that have been discharged…"

"Not a patient. You're on their emergency contact. Miguel Diaz. The school tried to get ahold of his mom but she's not responding."

Tony's heart skipped a beat. "I'll be right down."

He had to go make sure that Miguel was okay. He'd promised Jordan that he would be there for his son. Even though Jordan's widow was about to remarry and Miguel liked his new soon-to-be stepdad, even though Miguel was twelve and sometimes acted like he didn't need adults in his life anymore, Tony wanted to be there in the emergency room.

The nurses pointed him to the curtained bed where Miguel was lying under the blanket. He looked pale and was a bit sweaty. Tony was a bit taken aback, because the moment he walked past that curtain an image of Jordan flashed through his mind.

"Hey, pal," he said gently.

"Tony, what're you doing here?" Miguel asked.

"I work here. Remember?" Tony brushed back a few errant curls off Miguel's sweaty brow. "Tell me what happened."

"I don't know. I was playing basketball and then my legs were hurting a bit, I got dizzy and I woke up here," Miguel responded.

The trauma doctor, Dr. Carolyn Fox, came in. "Glad the nurses called you, Tony. You're his godfather?"

"I am," Tony responded. "What do you think, Dr. Fox?"

Carolyn frowned and motioned to step outside.

"I'll be right back, pal," Tony said, squeezing Miguel's shoulder.

Miguel nodded weakly.

Tony stepped on the other side of the curtain, crossing his arms. "Tell me."

"His blood pressure was low and he had a high fever. I am worried about the achy legs though and the petechiae. I've asked Dr. Sullivan to come down and have a look because of the history in his family."

Tony's stomach knotted. They'd paged Madison, which meant they were worried. "Okay."

Dr. Fox smiled briefly. "I'm sure it's nothing, but…"

"I get it," Tony responded quickly.

"Dr. Sullivan can order the tests she wants, but I will say that his platelets were a little high when I got back the results of a CBC just now."

Tony felt like the world was spinning out of control. This is how it all started with Jordan.

Not Miguel.

Usually, he could keep calm and collected, but right at this moment he was struggling. All these different scenarios were running through his head.

Madison entered the emergency room and made her way over. She took a step back when she saw Tony, and he was sure that his expression wasn't the most hopeful. All he wanted was to pull her in his arms and hold her, but they were keeping their relationship under wraps and that would not be very professional of him. Still, in this moment, he needed that physical connection to calm his jangled nerves. He held back but he hated it. He needed her.

"What's wrong?" Madison asked gently.

"It's my godson, Miguel. Jordan's son," Tony responded.

Madison's expression softened and she turned to Carolyn. "His chart?"

Carolyn nodded handing her the chart. "I ordered a CBC when he was first brought in. You'll have the report there."

Madison quickly scanned it. "I see. Well, let me examine him and we'll determine what to do next."

"Have the staff keep trying to call his mother," Tony responded. "I'll stay with him until Bertha can get here."

"Sure thing," Carolyn said before walking away.

Madison turned to face him. "It's probably nothing. It could be a lot of things, an infection or mono."

"His father had cancer."

"What kind?" Madison questioned.

"CLL—chronic lymphocytic leukemia," Tony responded. "By the time it was discovered, it had spread and metastasized."

And then he refused all my suggestions of treatment and I put him in the damn clinical trial he wanted anyways.

"I see. Well, we don't know anything yet. How about you introduce me to Miguel?" Madison asked.

Tony nodded and they both headed back behind the curtain.

Miguel's color was improving, so that was positive, but Tony could see the petechiae clearly. He hadn't noticed it before when he came in.

"Miguel, this is Dr. Sullivan. She's one of my colleagues."

"I knew your dad," Madison said, brightly.

Miguel's face lit up a bit. "You did?"

She nodded. "He came out to visit Tony once, when we were students. We pestered Tony the entire time trying to make him do stuff like ride the roller coasters on the pier, let us bury him in the sand in California."

Miguel grinned. "That's funny! Dad always talked about getting Tony into trouble."

Tony frowned. "Yes. I'm sure he did."

Madison laughed softly. "You were playing basketball and fainted."

Miguel nodded. "I've been feeling a bit sick. Then I had this pain in my knees. It's been off and on for a couple of weeks. Mom said growing pains and a cold. Or the flu."

"It could very well be. Do you mind if I take a look?" Madison asked, setting down the chart and pulling on some rubber gloves.

"Will it hurt?" Miguel asked.

"I don't think so, but if it does you tell me. Besides, you have Tony here," Madison responded.

"I'm right here, pal." Tony sat down next to Miguel and held his hand. "It's going to be okay."

Madison gently palpated Miguel's legs and he flinched a couple of times. Her gray eyes were focused on him and she was giving him words of encouragement, telling him to breathe.

"I'm just going to check your neck, for lumps, like if you have a sore throat or something. Is that okay?" she asked Miguel.

"Yes."

"Thank you." Madison gently checked his lymph nodes and then his eyes. Tony realized by her expression and the firm set of her mouth that she was seeing the petechiae too. It was hard to miss. Except Tony had missed it when he first saw him—he'd been too overwhelmed by panic and memories of Jordan. Madison was so calm, whereas he felt like a wreck. He loved that she was so gentle with Miguel.

Then again, she'd always had a great bedside manner when they were residents, whereas he'd struggled. As a surgeon he tried to be better, but he didn't have as much hands-on time with his pediatric patients. Usually they were with their parents.

Madison still had that easy rapport with her patients. It was something he admired about her.

"Miguel?" Bertha pushed back the curtain. Behind her was her fiancé, David.

"Here, Mom!" Miguel said, brightly.

Tony stood up so Bertha could step in and hug her son, and then David hugged Miguel.

"What's wrong, Tony?" Bertha asked, taking the seat he just vacated.

"He fainted. He has some joint pain." He was trying to be careful, because Bertha would jump to conclusions and they didn't want to get Miguel worried. David placed a hand on Bertha's shoulder, giving it a squeeze.

"I'm Dr. Sullivan," Madison said, picking up Miguel's file. "I'm going to be admitting Miguel for some observation and run some tests if that's okay."

"Tests?" Bertha asked.

"If you want to chat outside, we can," Madison responded.

"I'll stay with him, Bertha," David offered.

"You okay?" Tony asked.

Miguel nodded. "Yeah, if I'm staying, can you visit my room later? Maybe we can play a game…?"

Tony nodded gently. "Of course."

Bertha followed them out of Miguel's bed, and Madison

led them to a small private room where they could chat further. She shut the door and Tony pulled out a chair for Bertha.

"What's wrong with him?" Bertha asked, her voice betraying a hint of terror.

"We're going to run some tests to find out. He was given a CBC when he was first brought to the emergency room and his platelets were elevated. I'm concerned about the joint pain and some bruising on his forearms. As well as the petechiae. His lymph nodes are also swollen."

"Oh, God," Bertha whispered, and she took Tony's hand. She was thinking about Jordan. It was hard not to.

"It could be an infection," Tony insisted, but he had a hard time saying it with confidence. Jordan's diagnosis was replaying on a loop in his mind.

"Tony is right," Madison agreed. "It could be an infection. I need to run some more tests, possibly a lumbar puncture, and for that, I need to admit Miguel. I'll find out the answer for you as soon as I can, but he'll be well taken care of here, Ms. Diaz. I promise."

Bertha nodded. "Thank you, Dr. Sullivan. And thank you, Tony, for being here."

"Well, I was in the neighborhood," he teased. "He'll be okay."

"I'm going to go back to see him." Bertha stood.

"I'll get him admitted. As soon as a room is ready, a porter will get you situated and I'll order some more tests," Madison finished as she opened the door.

"Thank you both." Bertha left the meeting room and Madison shut the door.

Tony just sat there. Jordan was in his mind and it was hard to contain all those emotions that he'd been bottling up for so long. His mother was gone, his father wasn't in his life and Jordan was dead. There wasn't much family around him.

All he had was Miguel and Bertha, but they were moving on too. He'd been happy for them, but now, the idea of Miguel being sick... It was too much to bear.

Then there was Madison. She was here now, but would she still be here in a year's time? Her track record spoke for itself.

"Tony?" Madison asked gently, squatting in front of him. "Are you okay?"

"No," he said stonily. "I'm not."

"Jordan?" she asked, softly.

He nodded. "CLL. Blood cancer—it's hereditary."

"It can be, but we can treat it. Tell me what happened to Jordan. All of it."

Tony nodded. There was no point in hiding it anymore. He kept his feelings locked up tight to protect himself, because he learned from an early age that feelings could be used against you. He watched his father use his mother's affection and feelings against her time and time again, but he was tired of holding this in.

He needed a release.

He needed to tell her.

Everything.

Madison's heart ached watching him slowly crumble in front of her. Seeing him so human and vulnerable with his godson made her soften even more. He was clearly hurting and she had never seen him like this before. Other than having met Jordan when he'd come out to California, she knew nothing about Tony's life, nothing about his history.

He was so closed up, but he was opening up to her.

She placed a hand on his knee, looking up at him.

"Tell me," she repeated softly.

"When Jordan was diagnosed with CLL, we found a small met on his lung and on his liver. The course of treatment is chemotherapy and radiation. Jordan refused."

"He did?" Madison asked. And then she remembered a previous conversation. "The naturopathic clinical trial?"

Tony nodded. "He wouldn't listen to me and, going against my gut, I got him on that clinical trial. He started a homeopathic treatment. Some new drug from another doctor that could clean the blood. I tried to convince him it wouldn't work, but he didn't care. I stood there and watched him die."

Madison rose to stand as Tony got up from where he was sitting and began to pace around the meeting room.

"So that's why you're so wary of clinical trials."

"If I said no, he'd find someone else to refer him. At least I could advocate for him. Maybe not treat him, but stand up for him during it. I know now it was all a mistake."

"You were trying to save him," she said gently.

"Chemo might've worked."

"There's no cure for CLL. You just live with it and maintain it," Madison stated.

"I know, but chemo would've prolonged his life. I shouldn't have agreed to the clinical trial, but I didn't want him going somewhere else. I took a risk. It failed." He shook his head sadly. "I failed him."

She realized that must've been incredibly hard for Tony, to even consider going against the grain of what he knew. He never did. He was steadfast and confident.

"You didn't fail Jordan," Madison responded.

"That's what Bertha says. We did both *try* to get him to see sense, but by the time he did, the cancer spread to his brain. There was no controlling the spread. It crossed that blood-brain barrier and he died. Slowly. Painfully."

Madison approached him deliberately and then put her arms around him. Tony resisted at first, but then his arms came around her, only for a moment before he stepped away, his back ramrod straight.

"It's not your fault. Jordan took the risk, not you."

"I should've pushed harder. I shouldn't have trusted his faith in something so foolish. I should know better. My father was always doing that. Chasing 'sure things' and squandering every last dime my mother had. He'd leave and only come back when he was out of money. Always taking a risk on our future." Tony's shoulders slumped. "It's hard to believe in anything, to try anything, when you've been constantly let down your whole life."

Madison swallowed the lump in her throat. She'd never known any of this. It explained so much about him. Her childhood was nothing like that, so she didn't understand what he went through, but she did understand the need for stability. For the first part of her formative years, she had two parents who loved each other and who loved her. She had this idyllic life.

Until cancer came.

Then she watched her own family get ripped apart. Her father shut her out. Madison had to step up to be that rock for him and for herself as her mother slowly and painfully lost her battle.

Surgery had been done, but that only made it worse.

After her mother passed, her father was heartbroken. She never wanted to feel that pain of loving someone so much and losing them. She couldn't even begin to process what Bertha and Miguel had gone through when Jordan died. What Tony was going through was something she just never wanted to feel, which was why she threw absolutely everything she could into researching and curing cancer.

Even at the risk of her own personal life. She flitted around the country and barely went home to Salt Lake City to see her father. The times she did manage to go home, it ached. The memories and the pain. The loneliness.

She had no real home.

Tony had stability here in Boston. He had a family in Jordan's family.

They had very different parents and childhoods, but they both had come to the same crossroads in life.

The only time she had felt somewhat safe and normal had been when she was with him, but it was hard to hold on to a love when Tony wanted to keep his roots and stay settled.

Maybe she had her own trust issues with regards to love…?

Right now, none of that mattered as she looked at Tony's back. All she could offer him was her expertise on Miguel's case, and herself. She could love him now and be his rock in this moment. And that was all. She was going to move on from Boston eventually to pursue her dreams and she was going to have to leave him behind again… There was no promise of forever.

Why not?

"You've got to believe in me though, Tony," she said carefully. "I'm going to do all I can for Miguel. Believe me."

He turned around slowly, his eyes laced with pain. "I know. And I do trust you."

He pulled her into his arms and kissed her deeply. She clung to him.

"It'll be okay."

"Just stay with me," he murmured against her ear.

A sob welled up in her throat. That was not something she could freely promise him right now, even if she wanted to.

CHAPTER TWELVE

IT WAS TEN at night, way past the time she should've walked across the road and collapsed into bed, but she had ordered a whack-load of blood tests for Miguel and some of them were coming in.

Bertha had gone home to get some of Miguel's personal things and he'd been admitted to the pediatric floor. Tomorrow he would have to have a lumbar puncture and a bone marrow biopsy. Tony had gotten one of the other surgeons to do that, as being Miguel's guardian ruled him out.

She hadn't seen Tony since their talk in the meeting room outside the ER. After he opened up, he'd been paged back to the operating floor and Madison wanted to get started on Miguel's tests right away, but she couldn't stop thinking about what he'd revealed. He had let down his walls and she got to see a bit of what made him *him*.

It explained so much. And she was appreciative that he shared that with her.

What she was worrying about was the future. Her plans hadn't changed, and it was hurting her heart to think about it all ending.

Maybe he'll want to join you when the time comes...?

She could only hope so, because while she didn't want to let go of her dreams, she didn't want to let go of him either. She wasn't sure if she was able to have both.

She stretched as the first couple of blood tests started to hit in her inbox. Dr. Fox had been right: there were issues with Miguel's platelet count and his white blood cell count was elevated. It could mean numerous things. Madison had also run some tests to check out his fibrinogen level, as well as prothrombin time and a partial thromboplastin time. These were used to check his blood-clotting levels, as sometimes leukemia caused issue with clotting.

There were no results about blasts in his bloodstream. Blasts were immature blood cells that were usually only found in bone marrow. The presence of blasts could mean leukemia. The BUN blood test showed that his kidneys were functioning normally, which was good.

She also ran a variety of checks for various infections and other diseases that could be genetic. She'd gotten a fairly extensive history from Bertha. There were autoimmune diseases in the family.

Tomorrow, Madison would feel a lot better. The lumbar puncture and bone marrow test would be done and the analysis could be run. The results would let her know what she was working with. There was nothing she could do but wait for the tests to be performed tomorrow. She hated waiting.

She shut her laptop down and made her way up to the pediatric floor. She should go home and try to get some sleep, but she wanted to make sure that Miguel was resting comfortably. When she came to Miguel's room, she heard the murmur of voices and peeked in.

Miguel was still awake and there, sitting next to his bed with a table between them, was Tony. There was a deck of cards. Madison grinned and leaned against the doorframe, watching them.

It stung her to think that Tony blamed himself for Jordan's death when it wasn't his fault. If Jordan had gone to another doctor, it could've been worse. She couldn't understand Jordan's reasoning for not listening to Tony.

She felt bad for him. She knew he hated that loss of control.

There are times I don't listen to him either.

And she grimaced thinking about those moments, from when they were students and she didn't take his advice. She'd learned from those mistakes, but in hindsight those were the times Tony had been right in the first place.

It was why he was a brilliant surgeon.

She turned to leave.

"Madison?" Tony called out.

She turned around and walked into the room. "Hi, just doing a round."

"I thought you'd be back at your place," Tony said.

"I was catching up on work and I lost track of time. The auction gala is in a couple of days so I was getting stuff organized." She didn't want to say she was waiting for tests to get Miguel's hopes up. She understood he was scared about the tests tomorrow and she didn't blame him in the least.

"Why don't you come play crazy eights with us until Miguel's mom gets back," Tony suggested.

"Yeah," Miguel piped up. "It's more fun with more people."

"Sure." She shrugged. "Why not?"

Tony got up and pulled over another chair to the little rolling table that was over Miguel's bed. Madison sat down and Miguel dealt the cards. It had been a long time since she played crazy eights, but she remembered a bit.

"You knew my dad too?" Miguel asked, placing a card.

"I did," Madison replied, setting another down on the pile.

Miguel nodded and then frowned. "You're also a cancer doctor."

"I am," she replied.

"What if I have cancer like my dad did?" Miguel asked.

Madison glanced over at Tony. She wasn't sure what to say. Tony's lips were pursed in a firm line. She saw the idea that Miguel could have cancer was hurting him.

"I'll treat it," Madison said, confidently.

"She's good. You can trust her," Tony responded, his gaze meeting hers briefly. Her heart skittered and a warm flush crept up her neck. She was so in love with him. Still.

How could she walk away from this? She wasn't sure.

"Ooh, an eight. I'm changing the suit to diamonds," she announced.

Miguel groaned as he pulled a card from the deck. "Oh, no."

They played crazy eights for another half an hour before Bertha came with things for Miguel. Tony said he would be there tomorrow and with him through all the tests. They both slipped out of the room together to try to let Miguel sleep.

"He's a good kid," Madison remarked.

"He is. He was part of the reason I was so glad to come home to Boston."

"I bet," she remarked.

"Jordan thought I should've brought you," he said quietly.

"Oh, did he?" Madison smirked as they continued to walk the near-empty hospital hall.

"He liked you."

She nodded. "He was nice, but I go where the research takes me."

Tony frowned. "I know, but don't you ever miss home?"

"Salt Lake?" she asked.

He nodded. "Yes."

Yes.

Only she didn't say that out loud. When she went back to Salt Lake, things were different. The heartache and memories of her mother were too real, and how her father had been, how he'd emotionally shut down for a couple of years. Home wasn't the same, which was another reason why it was so important for her to keep moving forward and hopefully get to work with Dr. LeBret.

"No. I mean, sometimes I miss Salt Lake, but I want to help in the fight to cure cancer." She swallowed the hard lump in her throat. "My dad checked out, mentally and emotionally, after my mom passed. Salt Lake...is kind of a painful reminder of my lonely childhood."

"I'm sorry." He pulled her close and she held him again.

"I guess we both have father issues."

"Yeah, it sucks," he admitted.

She laughed quietly.

Tony didn't say anything more. "Well, I'm going to head back to my place. I'll see you tomorrow?"

"Yes. Tomorrow. I'll be watching from the gallery and then waiting on the tests."

"Do you think it's cancer?" he asked.

She shrugged. "I hope not."

Tony nodded solemnly. "I hope not either."

The elevator dinged and he got on it with a quick wave. Madison sighed as the door shut. She did have a bit more work to do; she probably wouldn't be making it back to her lonely sublet tonight and that was fine by her.

Home was a lab.

And she was going to make sure she explored every avenue on the off chance that it was leukemia. She wanted to give Miguel a fighting chance.

For Jordan's sake.

For Tony's sake.

Tony was true to his word: he was there with his godson every step of the way through the lumbar puncture, the scans to check his lymph nodes and then the bone marrow transplant. It was all done while Miguel was under anesthesia, because it was a lot to put a young kid through. Even a kid at the age of twelve, who thought he was so big.

It was hard to stand off to the side and let another surgeon do the work. It was hard to let go of control as the head of the department, but he couldn't operate on his godson.

He glanced up in the gallery and saw Madison there. He understood her drive even more now. Both of them had fathers who'd left, in their own way. He hoped she'd come to his place last night, but he knew she was waiting on results for Miguel. The fact she was so invested endeared her to him all the more.

She was working on her laptop as she watched the procedure. Tony learned she'd put a rush on the diagnostics of the samples and approved it. Thankfully, GHH had a pathology lab that was second to none.

When Miguel was wheeled into the pediatric postanesthesia recovery room, Tony stepped back to let Bertha and David take over. As he was leaving the PACU he ran into Madison. She looked like she was moving in a hurry.

"The tests?" he asked, his heart slamming.

He knew the lab was good, but not that good.

"No. Not yet, but I got word from Jessica's fertility doctors that they're done with the egg retrieval. The mass has grown and there's concern about thickening in her uterine wall."

Tony cursed inwardly. It wasn't yet a month since they had first met with Jessica. The only way to properly stage her cancer was to do a biopsy laparoscopically so they could also check whether it spread.

"Is Jessica still here?" Tony asked.

"You're thinking of doing the biopsy today?"

"I am."

Madison crossed her arms. "You ready for the HIPEC?"

He groaned. He'd read all the stuff Madison had sent him. He was nervous about it, but he was ready to do it.

"If Jessica consented, then yes to HIPEC. If you are positive you can handle that, so can I."

She beamed. "We're going to have pathology hopping today."

"Indeed," he responded. "Shall we book it for today?"

Madison worried her bottom lip, which set him on edge a bit. "I'll get the medicines mixed. I'll be ready by the end of the day."

"Okay, I'll contact the fertility doctors and have them admit her. The last thing she needs is for it to start spreading to her other organs and making this whole retrieval a moot point. What about the paperwork for the clinical trials?"

"Already on your desk." She began to jog away, off to get the chemotherapy prepared.

Tony laughed to himself watching her scurry away. It seemed all the financial components and clinical trial details were squared away. There was no reason not to do it. With her by his side he had no doubt this would work. It would mean a longer time that Jessica would be under anesthesia, but if this gave her a chance to beat ovarian cancer, then it was something.

Tony got the operating room prepared and the staff all assigned. Jessica hadn't eaten anything to prepare for her retrieval, so they didn't have to wait a certain number of hours for her stomach to empty. Madison was already prepping her for the operation with all the preoperative antibiotics and fluids.

The other ovary, the nonviable one, was underdeveloped and it hadn't produced follicles during the retrieval procedure. Once Tony got in there, he was going to measure it under the care of the obstetrical team. If it had grown in size, then he would remove that too. He also planned to take a small biopsy of her uterus to make sure that the cancer hadn't spread.

He spent the rest of his morning reading to be prepared for the surgery. What he wanted to do was go and check on Miguel, but his godson was in good hands with Bertha and David. As much as Tony hated the idea of stepping back in his godson's life, Miguel was getting older and connecting with his soon-to-be stepdad more and more.

Tony would just be that fun uncle who came around sometimes. The prospect made him feel lonely. He'd come back to Boston because that was where he was from and he had Jordan, Bertha and Miguel waiting for him. Now Jordan was gone and soon Bertha and Miguel wouldn't need him as much.

Maybe Madison had the right idea. She didn't have anyone holding her back or tying her down. She had family back in Utah, but that didn't keep her from pursuing her goals.

What's keeping me here?

Tony shook that thought away and headed to the operating room when he was told that Jessica was prepped and ready for the surgery.

He scrubbed in quickly and saw that Madison was in there. She had the chemotherapy ready to run through the perfusion machine as soon as he was done removing Jessica's ovary. The porter from the pathology team was waiting and they were going to take the specimen to the lab right away to determine if the mass on it was cancer. Once that was confirmed, Tony would insert a catheter and the chemo would be run through the perfusion machine, which would heat the medicine, and they would start a wash of Jessica's abdomen.

When he entered the operating room he saw that Dr. Crespo and a few others from the board of directors were waiting in the gallery. A knot formed in his stomach. They were being put on display and an uneasiness settled over him at the thought of doing this procedure in front of an audience—especially when he'd be doing it for the very first time.

Part of him resented Madison for putting this on his lap, but the other part was kind of excited to try this procedure, to take the risk. And that was so unlike him.

His gaze locked with Madison's across the operating room as he took his place at the operating table. He glanced up at the colleagues in the gallery and nodded.

"Let's do this. This is Jessica Walters. Aged thirty-one. We're going to be doing a left laparoscopic ovary biopsy, as well as a uterine biopsy, to determine the presence of cancer. I will be making a small incision. If pathology determines the presence of cancer, I will remove the ovaries and any other diseased tissues. Once that is complete, I will be inserting a catheter for the hyperthermic intraperitoneal chemotherapy procedure with the assistance of Dr. Sullivan. Number four blade, please."

The scrub nurse handed him the scalpel and he made the necessary cuts. The abdomen was inflated with carbon dioxide. He dropped in the trocars to filter through the lights, cameras and laparoscope.

"Dim the lights, please," he stated over his shoulder.

The lights in the operating room were dimmed and he watched the video monitor. The ovary he was biopsying had a large mass, but it didn't look like a cyst. Measuring it, he could tell that it had increased in size since the last scan was done. He removed as much of the mass as he could and then biopsied some tissue from Jessica's uterus to see if it had spread, pulled it out and placed it in a specimen bag.

"Have pathology rush this, please," Tony stated to the porter who was in the room.

"Yes, Dr. Rodriguez." The porter quickly left.

Tony continued his examination and noticed the other ovary was indeed larger, which was not good. If the diagnosis came back as cancer, he would remove the rest of the diseased ovary, her fallopian tubes and the other ovary.

He just hoped the biopsy of the uterus was clean.

It felt like time was ticking by as he waited, but he knew that he was priority and pathology was working quickly.

The pathologist entered the operating room.

"Dr. Hilt?" Tony asked.

"Cancer in the ovary. It hasn't spread to the other tissue samples. Once you remove the ovaries and fallopian tubes, I can stage it, but since it hasn't spread to the lymph nodes or the uterus, I'm pretty confident it's an early stage."

"Thank you, Dr. Hilt." Tony glanced over at Madison and she nodded, but he could see the look of disappointment in her eyes. She might have been excited by the prospect of using HIPEC, but that didn't mean she wanted to hear her patient had cancer.

Neither did he.

His mind briefly wandered to Miguel. What if he had cancer? What if one day soon Dr. Hilt came in and told him that Miguel's labs were not good?

Don't think like that.

He had to put that out of his mind so that he could focus on the task at hand. Dr. Hilt remained in the operating room to take the ovaries and the fallopian tubes so he could do a frozen section and determine the stage of the cancer.

The biopsy of the mass had shown lesions and that was enough to have Tony remove the ovaries and other affected tissues. While he was in there, he checked other organs. Once he was done, he removed the laparoscope, camera and lights. The other incisions were closed and he fed a catheter into one of the trocars and out another one that remained, securing it. It would be a constant cycle through the machine.

Madison came to stand beside him. "I'm Dr. Madison Sullivan and I will be administering a dose of bevacizumab, carboplatin and paclitaxel which has been heated and will run through the perfusion machine to wash Ms. Walters's peritoneal cavity and hopefully kill any other cellular growth of cancer. This wash will take approximately ninety minutes. Once it is done, Dr. Rodriguez will close up and we'll be monitoring Ms. Walters's progress in the PACU. Please turn the perfusion machine on."

One of the nurses turned on the machine.

Tony could hear the whir and watched as the medicine moved through the catheter into Jessica. It would be a long time, standing here and waiting for the infusion to run its course, but they had already stood around while the pathologists ran their tests. They could wait for the chemotherapy wash to do its work.

Madison was now standing on the other side of the table, watching the machine. Their gazes met again and he smiled at her from behind the mask. She couldn't see the gesture, but he knew she understood when her own eyes crinkled. Madison was smiling back at him and it made his heart sing.

He had been scared about risking his heart again on her and he still was, but right now, sharing this moment where they were working together as an unstoppable team, he couldn't understand why he had pushed her away for so long.

Tony moved beside her and leaned over. "This is terrible timing, I get that."

"What is?" she asked, in a hushed undertone.

"Would you be my date to the silent auction?"

There were a few little twitters of laughter.

Madison's shoulders shook. "Poor timing, but yes. I suppose so."

There were a few more chuckles in the operating room.

"Great."

He knew the procedure was serious but he was sure patients could still feel emotions while they were under, and he wanted positivity in this place. What better way to get that than make a complete fool of himself and ask Madison out on a date?

"Well," she remarked. "So much for keeping it all secret."

CHAPTER THIRTEEN

"How do I look?" Tony asked, spinning around in his tux.

Miguel frowned. "Weird."

Tony frowned. "How so?"

Miguel shrugged. "I don't know. You're too fancy."

"He looks good," Bertha chided.

"Why are you dressed up, Uncle Tony?" Miguel asked.

"The big hospital fundraiser is tonight. I'm auctioning off a romantic weekend at my place in Martha's Vineyard. I have to wear a tuxedo."

Not that he particularly liked wearing a tux. He was way more comfortable in his scrubs. He also loathed the schmoozing aspect of it all.

If he wasn't offering up an item in the auction, he wouldn't go. But then again he did ask Madison to be his date.

"Well?" he asked again.

Miguel shrugged and went back to the game on his tablet. Bertha stood up and straightened his tie, tsking under her breath as she did.

"Tell me, Bertha…how bad?" he asked.

"You look good. Are you cleaning up nice for a certain doctor?" She winked and nudged him.

Tony rolled his eyes. "Maybe. Plus the board of directors will be there and it's a black-tie event."

Bertha snorted. "So romantic."

"What?" he asked.

"You can say it's for her. Weren't you two a thing before?"

"A long time ago," he answered gruffly. "And we are again."

"See, that's nice. A second chance."

Although, it wouldn't be much of a date. Madison was running the silent auction and she would be announcing the winners at the end of the night. She would be too busy to even look at him. Tony knew for a fact she was at the table with most of the wealthiest benefactors. He'd bought a plate at one of the other table before he asked her to be his date and before they got back together. A night of socializing wasn't his idea of a good time, but at least he'd be showing his support for her.

Usually, he'd purchase a plate but never show up. Work was more important. He could spend his night dictating or checking post-op patients.

You have residents for that.

Dr. Frank Crespo had mentioned to him that several members of the board hoped he'd be there. It was a big old sign to Tony meaning he should go. Frank said that a lot of well-to-do financial backers and board members were impressed by the successful ovarian HIPEC surgery that he and Madison had completed on Jessica Walters. The fact that Madison had found Jessica through one of the funded free clinics was also a bonus. He'd been proud to stand there with Madison in the operating room. He could make nice to benefactors with her for just one night, as long as he got to take her home with him.

Bertha was chuckling to herself. "She's cute."

He hadn't gotten to speak much with Madison after Jessica's six-hour surgery. He had been absolutely exhausted.

Once he made sure that Jessica was stable and recorded his operative notes, he went back to his place and crashed hard. Madison had kept him updated when Jessica came out of anesthesia, and she was doing as well as could be expected, but she was struggling with some pain and side effects from the wash.

When Tony had returned the next morning to check on Jessica, he found Madison curled up on a cot in her lab. A bunch of her research was lying on her desk, and he realized she had spent the night there.

He had woken her up and sent her home.

It wouldn't look good if the doctor in charge of the fund-raising gala was yawning and slugging back coffee the entire night.

Now, he was here for Miguel and Bertha's opinion on his designer tuxedo, which hhe bought a couple of years ago but hardly ever wore. He was glad it still fit him well.

"You should claim your happiness," Bertha said, running her hands down his lapels. "Jordan liked Madison and I do too."

"I know. Jordan lectured me about that," Tony grumbled.

Miguel wrinkled his nose. "Gross. Uncle Tony in love. It's bad enough you and David are always smooching."

"I thought you liked David?" Tony asked, chuckling as Bertha crossed her arms and raised an eyebrow.

"I do. He's awesome, but I don't need to see the smooching. Gross."

Tony and Bertha laughed.

Bertha sat back down in the chair by Miguel's bedside. "I'm waiting on the results of Miguel's tests," she sighed.

"Me too. I'm sure we'll hear soon. Take it as no news is good news." Tony straightened his tie. He was trying not to think about it. He didn't even want to entertain the notion that Miguel had leukemia.

Bertha cocked an eyebrow. "You forget. I've been here before. Waiting."

"I know," he replied. "Try not to worry."

But it was hard not to. When he looked at Miguel all he saw was Jordan and how he couldn't save his best friend's life.

There was a fast click of heels coming up the hallway. He turned just as Madison came swishing into the room, decked out in a tight-fighting, gray sparkly dress and with her makeup done. Her blond hair framed her face in big wavy curls. He had to do a double take to make sure that it was really Madison. He was so used to seeing her in scrubs or business suits, her hair always pulled back tight. Now it hung down just past her slender shoulders, like a golden waterfall that he wanted to push aside so he could press kisses to her neck.

She blinked a couple of times as her gaze traveled the length of him. "You look great, Tony."

"As do you," he said, clearing his throat. He couldn't tear his eyes from her. She was stunning. And she was his.

For now.

It suited her, but then he liked her in whatever she wore. It was all just a fancy dressing for the woman he cherished underneath.

Then he noticed the paper in her hand and his pulse began to race.

"Results?" he asked, pulling out his phone because he hadn't gotten a notification.

"Yes!" She handed him the paper to save him from logging into his GHH email. His hands were shaking, trying to hold back all the emotions that were threatening to spill out of him as he scanned the results.

He beamed with happiness and took a deep breath. "You're the oncologist, Madison. You tell them."

"You're sure?" Madison asked.

"Yes. You ordered the tests. You're Miguel's doctor."

Bertha was sitting on the edge of her seat. Madison turned to her.

"Not cancer," Madison exclaimed.

Bertha covered her mouth and strangled back a cry of happiness. Miguel was so happy, he had set down his tablet.

"What is it then?" Miguel asked.

"Thrombocytopenia, or rather immune thrombocytopenia caused from a mono infection. We also suspect you may have an autoimmune disease, so we're going to refer you to a geneticist and immunologist. The thrombocytopenia and mono can be cleared up with antibiotics and steroids. I'm going to discharge you in the morning. Does that sound like a plan?" Madison asked.

Bertha sobbed. "I would hug you both, but I don't want to wrinkle your nice outfits."

"Oh, you can hug me. I don't care," Madison said. Bertha flew into Madison's arms. Tony hugged Miguel as he bounced up and down.

Tony was thrilled with this news.

Not cancer.

Immune thrombocytopenia and mono was still serious, but mono could be cleared up and IT could be managed.

"I can't wait to go home!" Miguel said excitedly.

"I know, buddy." Tony rubbed Miguel's head. "It's great."

"Well, I have to go as I have to start the auction," Madison announced. "But I couldn't leave without giving you the results."

"I'm so glad you did," Bertha responded, wiping a tear from her eye. "Thank you."

"Yes. I better go as well. I'll come by tomorrow before you leave," Tony stated. He turned to Madison. "Shall we go?"

Madison nodded, her gray eyes twinkling. "I thought you'd never ask."

Tony held out his arm and she slipped hers under his. It was nice to escort her to the auction especially after it felt like a huge weight was lifted off his shoulders.

Miguel didn't have cancer like his father.

He wasn't in danger and Madison was on his arm. It was time to celebrate. Tonight was going to be a good night.

He was sure of it.

Tony couldn't tear his eyes off her all night. Every time she looked over at his table, she could see his dark brown eyes locked on to her and she didn't mind in the least.

It made her weak in the knees. It made her heart race.

And damn if he didn't look good in his tailored tux. It had been so impulsive of him to ask her out in the operating room. They had both agreed to keep their romance secret, but she'd loved that moment.

Everyone else in the OR had too. She had several young interns gushing about how romantic it was. And they weren't wrong. It was so out of the ordinary for him.

Every time their gazes met, she could feel the warmth, the flush of heat creep up her neck. A curl of desire was fluttering deep in her belly. There were people talking all around her, but she couldn't hear a word that was being said. All she could think about was Tony and how she wanted to tear that tux off his body.

She was so glad the results came in tonight before the gala and she was so relieved that Miguel did not have cancer.

For a moment when she'd seen Tony there with Bertha and Miguel, she'd been a bit envious. He was real around them. He had family and friends to support him here.

She had no one and that was her fault because she never settled. There was no time to do that when you were out fighting a silent killer every day.

She was honored to deliver the news and share that happiness with them. She'd forgotten, until that moment, what it meant to belong and to be surrounded by people who cared about you.

It had a been a good couple of days. The HIPEC surgery was a complete success and pathology had gotten back to her today determining that Jessica's cancer was a stage zero with the removal of ovaries. With the wash of chemotherapy, she would be pleased to let Jessica know she could ring the bell next week.

She was also able to fully discharge Gracie on Monday and now Miguel tomorrow. Miguel wouldn't be ringing the bell like Jessica or Gracie's mom would on her behalf, but that was more than okay. Thrombocytopenia and mono could be cured or at least managed, which was far better than cancer.

"Dr. Sullivan?"

She glanced up to see one of the wealthy benefactors looking in her direction from across the table.

"Mr. Morrison, sorry I was bit lost in thought. Thinking about some patients," she replied.

There was a subtle twitter of laughter at the table.

Oh, doctors, lost in their own world.

That was fine. She'd rather be in her lab or with Tony. This sucking up to people with money wasn't her idea of a good time. It was just all part of the job.

"It's okay, Dr. Sullivan. I was just saying how impressed we were with the gala you helped put together and the HIPEC surgery you and Dr. Rodriguez preformed yesterday. I understand from Dr. Crespo that it was a first for GHH," Mr. Morrison stated.

Dr. Crespo had a wide grin on his face and was nodding vehemently.

Madison swallowed the lump in her throat. "I will not disparage my predecessors, as HIPEC can be tricky. It's a long operation and it all depends on the health of the patient. We were fortunate to be able to perform it with our patient yesterday. I'm also thankful GHH has the amazing facilities to do so."

There. That should make them happy.

"And that patient came from one of our free clinics," Dr. Crespo piped up.

There was a mumble of excitement and nods.

"She did, and I worked to get her on a couple of clinical trials, not only for her cancer, but fertility," Madison confirmed.

"Excellent. Well, I can't wait for you to announce the winners of the silent auction. I'm sure I've won that weekend at Dr. Rodriguez's Martha's Vineyard house," Mr. Morrison said.

Madison glanced at the clock. "I think it's almost time to do just that. Excuse me, ladies and gentlemen."

She got up from the table and made her way to the private room with Dr. Crespo and a couple of other volunteers who were going to hold up cards with photographs on them. She had someone who was going to collect the checks from the winning bids.

After the auction was over there would be some dancing and cocktails, but really after the auction part was over, she was off the hook and she planned to take the complimentary hotel room she was given, order some room service and have her way with Tony for the rest of the night.

The butterflies in her stomach did a little flip as she thought of him and her in that king-size bed together. It was definitely better than the floor.

She made her way to the little stage in the banquet hall and turned on the microphone.

"Good evening, everyone," she said brightly. "I'm Dr. Sullivan and I want to thank you all for being here to support the GHH's free clinic initiative."

There was a round of applause.

"Now that we've had our delicious dinner and the auction has been closed, we're going to announce our lucky winners. We have some great items that were donated by fellow staff members and generous benefactors. So let's get started!"

As she gazed out into the crowd, her gaze latched on to Tony, sitting a couple of tables away. There were a few younger women at his table and for a moment she had a brief flicker of jealously course through her because she saw the way they were looking at him.

They wanted him.

Not that she was shocked, but she was a little green eyed. Then she saw that he wasn't even paying attention to them. His eyes were locked on her. Warmth spread through her as her body trembled, and she could feel the heated blush creeping into her cheeks.

Images of Martha's Vineyard and their frantic night on the floor of his living room flashed through her mind.

Get it together. Auction. Remember?

She tore her gaze from him and focused on the list of silent auction items. It was tedious going through each bid and congratulating winners. Her face hurt from smiling all night. Finally, they were at the end. Soon this would all be over. Tony's place was the last on the auction block and it had the most bids.

"The final item of the night is the one we've all been waiting for. A summer weekend at a glorious three-bedroom farmhouse-style home outside of Oak Bluffs, Martha's Vineyard. The house overlooks Nantucket Sound. It was generously donated by Dr. Tony Rodriguez."

There was applause and Tony stood hesitantly to nod his head quickly before sitting down. He was embarrassed about being called out.

"I got to tour the house myself and took pictures for the auction. Dr. Rodriguez's family originally built it and he just recently repurchased it. A weekend like this, in a private home, doesn't come up very often. It's a century home on the exclusive Martha's Vineyard. You're a short walk from a glorious white sand beach, or you have a heated saltwater swimming pool and hot tub at your disposal. Dr. Rodriguez also kindly offered a round-trip ferry crossing, and a romantic gift basket containing champagne and charcuterie for two. This was definitely our most popular item tonight. And the winner of this glorious weekend is Mr. Chad Morrison, with a generous winning bid of ten thousand dollars."

There were some gasps and a huge round of applause. Even Tony looked shocked. Mr. Morrison climbed the stairs of the stage and she shook his hand, giving him a quick peck on the cheek. Dr. Crespo shook his hand.

"Could Dr. Rodriguez could come up here?" Mr. Morrison asked. "I'd like a picture with him,"

"Of course." Madison waved. "Dr. Rodriguez, a picture, please?"

Tony nodded and climbed the stage. They all huddled together and Mr. Morrison handed the check over to Dr. Crespo, posing for the camera. Tony sneaked in behind Madison. She could feel the heat of his body against her bare shoulders. Then his hand brushed gently over the small of her back, just like it used to do when they were residents.

A secret touch.

That curl of desire was now a full-blown inferno raging through her. Her body was reacting intensely to that simple touch, her nipples hardening under her dress, her blood heating. But she plastered on her best fake grin as several photos were taken.

After the photos were done, Mr. Morrison, Dr. Crespo and Tony walked off the stage. She could see Tony was deep in conversation with them. Her job as emcee was almost done and she could escape.

"Thank you for your generous donations for our free clinics. The gala tonight has raised seven hundred thousand dollars," she announced.

There were more cheers and applause.

"The bar is now open—again all money is going to the free clinic—and there will be some dancing. Thank you again and enjoy the rest of your evening." She set the microphone down and Dr. Crespo came up to say a few words.

As she came down the stage stairs Tony was waiting. Her

heart hammered against her chest and he held out his hand, taking hers and helping her down the rest of the steps.

"Thanks," she whispered, her voice catching in her throat.

"I didn't want you to trip."

"I appreciate that." She was pretty sure her palms were sweating.

He didn't let go of her hand either, just held it, and she didn't pull away. A rush of adrenaline was running through her and all she could think about was him and her naked.

Oh, my God. I need to chillax.

"Dr. Sullivan and Dr. Rodriguez?"

Madison pulled her hand away quickly and turned around as Mr. Morrison came over to both of them with another man.

"This is Dr. LeBret. He's a colleague of mine from France," Mr. Morrison explained.

Madison's heart stuttered and she looked at the man. She knew exactly who he was. This was the physician she wanted to learn from, the man she wanted to be her mentor and someone she admired so much. She was trying to find all the words, but couldn't seem to.

"Pleasure." Dr. LeBret shook Tony's hand, but then took hers and kissed her knuckles.

"It's an honor to meet you, Dr. LeBret," Madison gushed.

"*Non*, the pleasure is all mine. I was visiting and Chad said I simply had to come and see some of GHH's work. I was there when the HIPEC was performed. Masterfully done, by both of you."

"Thank you, Dr. LeBret," Tony said stiffly.

He was there?

Madison's head was spinning. "I'm so glad you got to see it."

"I expect some great things from you both. Good evening." Dr. LeBret walked away with Mr. Morrison to greet some other people.

Madison grasped Tony's arm. "Can you believe that?"

"Your nails are digging into my flesh," Tony teased.

"Sorry. He's kind of an idol of mine. I've been following his research since my Bachelor of Science days."

Tony chuckled. "You told me. I had no idea he was in the gallery. Maybe he'll offer you a job…?"

There was a hint of reproach in Tony's voice and her stomach sank.

"I'm years off. I was told I need to publish more."

"Well, it's apparent he's watching."

"Not just me. The both of us," she offered.

"There's no point in watching me. I'm not leaving," he said quietly.

The little bit of excitement she was feeling fizzled away at Tony's admittance. Yeah, he wasn't leaving. He'd made that clear. Her plans were unchanged too: she would move on to Paris to continue her research if she got the chance. Tony was rooted in Boston and she wasn't.

The string quartet started up and couples were gliding onto the dance floor.

"Would you like to dance?" Tony asked.

"Okay," she responded.

She didn't really want to, but there were benefactors and colleagues watching, and she had to put on a good show, a brave face.

While inside her, a battle raged between the career she'd always dreamed of and the man she was once again falling in love with. The man she'd never stopped loving.

* * *

Tony was very well aware of who Dr. LeBret was. Everyone knew Dr. Mathieu LeBret was at the forefront of cancer research and a Nobel winner. If you were a cancer doctor and didn't know him, then you were living under a rock.

He was quite shocked to learn that not only was Mr. Morrison a friend of Dr. LeBret but also that Mathieu had been at the HIPEC surgery on Jessica. He'd been watching them, which caused Tony a little bit of uneasiness.

Madison thought she had to publish more before she'd get offered a job in France, but Tony had a sinking feeling that that offer was going to come sooner rather than later. Honestly, when he saw the gallery full of other doctors that Dr. Crespo knew, he was sure that someone in that crowd would put in a word about it. What he hadn't known was that the Dr. LeBret was in that gallery as well.

I'm going to lose her again.

That's all he could think about as they swayed slowly on the dance floor. She was in his arms right now, but he felt like it was fleeting and soon she'd fly away. Just like before.

It was a selfish thought and he knew that. This was always her dream and he wouldn't hold her back. So Tony just tried to focus on her in his arms—on her body pressed close to his, on the coconut summery scent that he loved to get wrapped up in. He gently ran his fingers over the exposed skin of her back.

She was so beautiful. He hadn't been able to take his eyes off her all night and he didn't want to now.

As they danced, he realized something had shifted between them. She seemed unhappy.

"Are you all right?" he asked.

"Fine," she responded, mustering a smile.

"You're not."

"Just tired. It was a lot."

"I understand. You ran it well."

She nodded. "To be honest, you didn't seem too excited about Dr. LeBret."

"Oh, I am. It's just…"

"Just what?" she asked.

He wanted to tell her he was falling in love with her, that he never had stopped loving her because no one held a candle to her. Only, he couldn't say those things out loud. She had a dream and he wouldn't give her a reason to stay behind.

He wouldn't keep her here because he wanted her to stay with him. Just like she shouldn't expect him to follow her. With her in his arms it was hard to think of the end, but with Dr. LeBret now aware of Madison's accomplishments it was difficult not to focus on the likelihood that Madison would have a job offer sooner rather than later.

This could very well be the last time he held her.

It saddened him, but he wanted good memories if the end was coming. If there was no future for them, then he only wanted her to look back on this moment with happiness rather than regret.

"We make a good team," he said. "A powerhouse."

Her eyes twinkled and she smirked. "I never thought I'd hear you say that."

"Honestly, I never thought I would. Can you imagine if Dr. Pammi saw us now?" he teased.

Madison giggled. "She'd have a stroke. I'm sure."

Tony chuckled. "Indeed."

"We do make a good team. I'm so pleased about Miguel's results."

He nodded. "Me too."

Tony spun her around and then pulled her close against him. His pulse was thundering between his ears and he could feel her trembling in his arms.

"Tony," she whispered.

"Yes?"

"I'm so tired of mingling."

Heat unfurled in his belly. "What're you suggesting?"

"Well, I've wanted to rip that tuxedo off you the moment I saw it. What I'm saying is I have a complimentary room upstairs."

The dance ended. There was a pink flush in her cheeks. He was so in love with her and it pained him to think that this might all end soon, but there was nothing to be done. Nothing had changed.

He held out his hand and she grinned, taking it and pulling him off the dance floor and out of the banquet hall. They jogged to the elevators and Madison swiped her keycard.

The elevator door opened and they stepped in. She pushed the button for the top floor, the doors closed and the elevator began to rise.

Madison pushed him against the back mirrored wall and kissed him. She claimed his mouth fervently and his body hardened under her touch. Her tongue pressed against his lips as the kiss deepened. He burned for her. He wanted to claim her again, like some primeval urge was overtaking him, and he wished there was nothing between them.

Tony crowded her against the opposite wall and began to hike up the layers of fabric of her dress until he found her skin, running his hands over her thighs, touching her and making her moan and grind against his hand.

"Oh, God," she gasped breathlessly against his neck, clinging to him. She wrapped a leg around his hips and he ground his erection against her, letting her know how much he wanted her.

It was taking all he had in him not press the emergency stop button and take her right there.

Tony nibbled her neck, cursing the longest elevator ride of his life.

When it came to a stop, they reluctantly pulled apart. Madison adjusted her dress and they got off, walking quickly down the hall to her suite.

She unlocked the door with a swipe of her keycard and then grabbed him by the lapels, pulling him into the darkened room, the door slowly shutting behind him.

Her arms wrapped around his neck as she drew him closer. A tingle of anticipation ran through him as he touched her in the dark. There were so many things he wanted to say, but couldn't right now. He just wanted to savor this moment.

He kissed her again, at first light and feathery, lingering in the sweet taste of her. He cupped her face, deepening the kiss again, and undid the clasp at the neck of her gown before trailing his fingers down her bare back to the second clasp and undoing the small zipper. She slid her arms out of the sheer part of the dress and he tugged it down over her hips where it pooled at her feet.

The thin sliver of streetlight cast shadows, but it allowed him to catch a glimpse of her. She hadn't worn a bra, just a lace thong. The dancing of the minimal light and darkness played across her skin and he ran his hand over the curve of her hip.

"So beautiful," he murmured, kissing her neck and shoulders. He ran his hand down her back, reveling in the silkiness of her skin.

Madison turned around and he cupped her breasts, dragging his thumbs over her nipples. She let out a small mewl of pleasure that sent a bolt of heated desire straight to his groin. She began to undress him, peeling off his jacket. Her fingers moved quickly over the small buttons of his shirt, thrusting it aside to run her hands over his chest.

Her simple touch fired his senses all the more. When her hands slipped below the waist of his trousers, he almost lost control as she stroked him and touched him.

"Madison," he groaned softly.

"I know. I want you too." She kissed him again. "I'm so ready for you."

They finished undressing and she pulled him down, spreading her legs so he could rest against her. His length pressed against her soft, wet core. She was arching her hips, making it hard for him not to thrust into her and take her like he desperately wanted.

He pinned her wrists over her head.

"Be good," he teased as he trailed his kisses over her body until he kissed her intimately, dragging his tongue achingly slow over her slit.

She cried out, her hands gripping his head as he held her hips down, controlling her movements and taking his time tasting her.

"Tony, please," she begged.

He chuckled huskily and moved over her. His arms were braced on either side of her head as their gazes locked. He kissed her and she clung to him as he thrust into her, finally claiming her. Except she wasn't his. Not as much as he wanted, but all he could focus on was the pleasure as he moved inside her.

Slowly.

He was in no rush, holding the only woman he ever

wanted close as he made love to her. She wrapped her legs around his waist and he quickened his pace, each movement firing his blood and making him want to forget how scared he was to even contemplate being with her again.

To forget his broken heart.

Madison came, crying out, her nails digging into his back, and he soon followed, giving in to the feelings he was trying to hold back and collapsing beside her.

She curled up against him and he held her. He didn't want this moment to end, but what future did they truly have together? Boston was his home.

Why? a little voice asked.

What was he waiting here for? His father to come home? No.

He wasn't sure.

"Should I go?" he asked as he held her. "You look so tired."

"No. Stay," she whispered, touching his face.

He kissed her wrist and then her lips, pulling her close. He might not have forever, but he had this moment. He had tonight and every night until she left.

CHAPTER FOURTEEN

Three days later

A BELL SOUNDED out across the atrium, signifying the end of a patient's treatment. Madison stood next to Tony, smiling proudly and clapping her hands. Even though the patient herself was too young to pull the bell, she was cradled in her mother's arms, her eyes open and looking highly confused. Her mother was crying and laughing as she yanked the pull cord with all her might.

Gracie tried to reach for the shiny bell, but then startled a bit as it rang out. Her mother comforted her and rocked her back and forth.

"Congratulations," Madison said, before turning to Gracie. "I'm going to miss you. Even though you have no idea who I am."

Tony snickered and shook Gracie's dad's hand.

"We're here if you need us," Tony said.

"I sincerely hope you don't," Madison added. "But I'll see you in a month for a checkup and then we'll space them out from there."

"Thank you both so much." Gracie's mom handed her daughter over to her husband, then stepped forward and shook their hands.

"Best of luck," Tony remarked.

This was the best part of the job as far as Madison was concerned. Her mother had never gotten to ring the bell and she got so emotional when she was able to celebrate that moment with her patients. Today it was Gracie and in a few days Jessica could ring that bell with all her heart.

Madison walked away slowly from the atrium, Tony by her side. Ever since they'd gotten back together it had been wonderful. It was like old times, but better. Now, she felt more like a partner to him. They were a team and yeah, they did work well together. They hadn't made any promises, and there was no need for long-term promises. She had no doubt they had time to figure it all out. She was planning on being in Boston for the next couple of years, at minimum.

Her plans hadn't changed, so while she was here, the two of them could figure out what to do and what their next move would be when the time came. For now, she was just going to relish this time together. She was hopeful he would come with her when she moved on, but she wasn't sure.

"You're very happy today," Tony remarked as they took the long way through the gardens. "I thought you had a bunch of grant proposals to write. I wouldn't be that upbeat if I had to do that."

She leaned into him, giving him a little shove with her shoulders. "I do, but I like when the patients ring the bell. I was just thinking of my mom and how she didn't get to do that."

Tony's arm slipped around her. "I understand."

They stopped for a moment and he sneaked a quick kiss.

"What're you doing, Dr. Rodriguez? We said we wouldn't do that here."

He grinned, his brown eyes sparkling. "I can't help it. Besides, everyone knows. Still, it's kind of illicit to make out with you at work."

"Well, I can't argue with that."

"No. You can't." He leaned in and stole another kiss. She loved it, but they hadn't really decided on the next step.

Madison wasn't sure what the future held; their paths were so different professionally. There was part of her that wanted to talk about it, hash it all out, but there was another part of her, a naughty side to her brain, that just wanted to enjoy the ride while it lasted.

"Paging Dr. Rodriguez and Dr. Sullivan to meeting room three. Dr. Rodriguez and Dr. Sullivan to meeting room three."

She cocked an eyebrow. "Meeting?"

Tony shrugged. "No idea."

"I guess we better find out."

They left the privacy of the atrium and headed to the meeting rooms. Meeting room three was one of the larger ones. Madison could see through the etched glass there were other people present already. She glanced back and Tony and he just shrugged again.

Madison knocked and heard a muffled "come in" from Dr. Crespo. She stepped in the room, followed by Tony, to see a few members of the board of directors sitting around the table, Mr. Morrison included. And then her gaze landed on Dr. Mathieu LeBret. His hands were folded neatly in front of him.

"Shut the door, Dr. Rodriguez," Dr. Crespo said.

Tony nodded and closed the door.

"Have a seat." Dr. Crespo motioned.

Tony pulled out a chair for Madison and then took the seat next to her.

"Dr. LeBret, you're the one who wanted to speak to them," Dr. Crespo said. "The floor is yours."

A faint smile hovered on Dr. LeBret's thin mouth. "*Merci*, Dr. Crespo. I've asked you both specifically, because I'm impressed by your teamwork. It's not often I see such a balanced yin and yang team of surgeon and oncologist. It was like watching a duet."

Madison glanced quickly at Tony. Her pulse had started racing and her stomach was in knots.

Oh, my God. Was this it? Was this the moment she'd been dreaming of?

"I've read what you've both accomplished over the years and that HIPEC was impressive. I know your old teacher Dr. Pammi well. Dr. Rodriguez, you're a skilled surgeon that everyone seeks out."

"I'm flattered," Tony stated. "I'm not the best…"

"No. I am," Dr. LeBret teased. "But I do recognize talent."

"Th-thank you," Tony stammered.

Dr. LeBret smiled. "Dr. Sullivan, you are a brilliant oncologist and you're willing to take risks on new treatments. You have proven yourself. I want you both working with me, before I retire."

"I…" she trailed off, at a loss for words.

It was everything she ever wanted and more because Tony was offered a position too.

Except Tony might not think that this was an amazing chance and she had the distinct inkling he could say no. How could she leave him behind?

She thought she'd have more time with him. This was happening faster than she expected.

If Tony did say yes, it would be amazing, but if he said no she'd have to leave him again, which was hard to contemplate.

Dr. LeBret looked at them both expectantly. "Well?"

"I'm at a loss for words," she managed to finally say, finding her voice.

"Think about it, but this is a once-in-a-lifetime opportunity. I wouldn't pass it up if I were you. I've already told the press that I'm here and retiring after I train you both," Dr. LeBret said.

"You've painted us into a bit of a corner," Tony snapped.

Dr. LeBret shrugged. "You two are the best. You'll make the right decision."

Tony glanced at her and she could tell by his stormy expression that he was not pleased with Dr. LeBret just assuming he would take the job offer.

Dr. LeBret and the other board members stood.

"The world is watching, Doctors." Dr. LeBret left the boardroom with Mr. Morrison, Dr. Crespo and the others trailing out. The message was clear. Dr. LeBret and the board weren't going to take no for an answer.

It was the opportunity of a lifetime.

Silence descended between them. The tension was absolutely palpable.

"Well," Madison said, letting out a huff. "I don't even know where to begin."

Tony snorted. "Same. It's quite the offer, but he's kind of egotistical."

"What?" she asked. "He's a Nobel laureate."

"So?" Tony shrugged.

"So?" she repeated, stunned.

He scrubbed a hand over his face. "I don't know. This is complicated. I don't even know what to think."

This was Madison's dream, but she knew it wasn't Tony's. She couldn't turn it down. Why couldn't he go too? It would make everything so much easier. There was a part of her that didn't want to leave him behind, but if he didn't want to go she would have no choice and it was tearing her to pieces. She worried her bottom lip and he was watching her.

"What're you thinking?" he asked.

"I want to go. You know I do. It was always the endgame," she said, trying to keep her voice from breaking and holding her emotions in check, just like she always did. "What about you?"

"I have a job. A good steady job here. Leaving is a risk— it's giving up so much."

She sighed. "Good doctors take risks. It's how we improve."

"Not all risks are worth improvement. Sometimes reliability and staying in one place to build a reputation is just as good."

"Is this about me following my dreams by moving around?" she asked, choking back the tears. "I don't regret any of my choices."

Tony frowned and didn't look at her, which gave her the answer that she needed. Nothing was going to change. He was staying here.

"Running from place to place won't bring you happiness," he stated roughly.

"I'm not running. I'm pursuing my dream. Why won't you join me and take this chance?"

"Why won't you remain here and finish out your contract?"

"I don't think there will be an argument about my contract from the board of directors. It's a feather in the hospital's cap for us to be offered this honor."

"And it's so much better moving from one job to the next

and never settling down. Always looking for the next good thing. How can anyone rely on that? You're running from something, Madison. You always have been."

"You have so many walls," she said quietly. "And you've never let me in."

"You have your own walls too. You put on a brave face, but you're pushing me away just as much as I'm pushing you away."

"How? I'm telling you that you should come to Paris—with me."

Tony's lips pursed in a firm line. "It's only about your career. That's all it's ever been."

"What do you mean by that?" she asked, angry now.

"I never knew how you felt. Ever. How can I take a chance with someone who is always moving on to the next big thing? Someone who always holds their emotions in check?"

"I loved you," she said as she choked back a sob. Tears were running down her face. "I love you."

The words came tumbling out before she could stop them. Yes, he was right: she locked her emotions away. She'd learned to do that so she could function and take care of her father. She had given up so much to keep her father alive in those dark years.

Emotions held you back and left you open to pain.

Keeping everything locked up tight had allowed her to pursue her dreams and get to this point. Except now, it didn't feel so much like an accomplishment. Her plans were still the same in spite of her declarations, just as he apparently planned to stay in Boston. How much of herself did she have to give up to be with him?

She thought things were different, but they weren't. How could she trust him with her heart? She didn't want that pain again; the heartache wasn't worth it. She didn't want to retreat into herself like her father had done.

She'd been pushed aside back then too. With no one to lean on, no one she could rely on, she had to be strong for herself. What pained her was she thought she could rely on Tony, but she was fooling herself.

She knew better.

Madison blinked back a few tears. She held her breath waiting for him to say something. Anything. Only he didn't respond to her and it stung.

"How can we be together when we're clearly on different paths?" he asked stiffly.

"You mean because I want to go with Dr. LeBret and you're staying here?"

He nodded. "Boston is my home."

"Why? You have no ties here."

"I have Miguel. I made a promise to Jordan."

"Bertha is moving on with David," she said softly. "Miguel is well taken care of. So the question is, why do you want to push me away? Why are you so scared of taking a chance?"

Tony scrubbed a hand over his face. He was still in shock that she'd admitted she loved him. There was never a moment in the past when she had told him that before. He didn't know how to really answer that.

He wanted to go with her. In theory it was a good idea, but his mind kept going back to his father. He wanted to tell her that he loved her too, that he'd always loved her. But at the back of his mind he wondered if Madison confessing her love was just a ruse to get him to agree to go to Paris. His father would always manipulate and gaslight his mother. Then Tony would have to go in and pick up the pieces of her life and shattered heart. Could he really follow Madison around the world?

What if her declaration was doing the same, using how he felt to go against his instincts, to go against the grain of what he'd always done, which was always the safe thing?

There was no one to help him when his heart was broken. Bertha had told him to seek out his own happiness.

He didn't know what to do.

She said she loved me.

He was so confused. He didn't know which way he was going. Why couldn't she stay here? It would be easier here.

Would it?

Tony sighed. Could he really take this risk?

Their gazes locked. Her gray eyes were filled with tears. Madison may chase after the next big thing, but she was steadfast and sure. She was educated and made good decisions. She owned up to her mistakes and never shirked her duties. She'd been right about the tandem SCT and the HIPEC. And maybe she was right about Dr. LeBret, who was willing to take a chance on them.

Tony swallowed the lump in his throat. "I love you."

A tear slipped out of the corner of her eye and she brushed it away. "Pardon?"

"I love you."

And he did. He'd always been in love with her. He just wasn't sure he could trust her and he wasn't sure he could follow her halfway across the world.

"I'm not sure I trust—"

"What?" she asked. "Me?"

"I'm just not sure." Tony stood up and walked away from her. His heart was aching. He needed to clear his head, because it felt like all his carefully planted ties were being up-rooted, and he was terrified at the prospect.

He wandered the halls trying to figure out what to do. He knew Dr. LeBret had told the whole world about the job offer. It should be so easy to make the decisions, but he was so scared. He went to his office and just buried his head in his hands.

There was a ding and he glanced at his phone to see the offer from Dr. LeBret's hospital pop up. It was very gener-ous, but could he give up everything here for that?

"Knock-knock!"

Tony glanced up to see Dr. Crespo standing in his door-way.

He groaned. "Frank, I'm so tired."

"I know. I'm sure you're mulling over that decision. Al-though, I think it's a pretty much done deal."

"How do you mean?" Tony asked.

"Mathieu announced it to the world. His hospital is doing many amazing things!"

"I know he's well respected, brilliant and I'm sure he's at the forefront of it all, but I haven't made a decision yet. It's not a done deal."

Dr. Crespo raised his eyebrows. "What's keeping you here?"

"Oh, thanks a lot, Frank," Tony chided.

Dr. Crespo shook his head. "That's not what I meant. Of course I'd rather have my head of oncology stay, but if I was your age and in your position I would jump at the chance to learn from Dr. LeBret. Besides, you'll be back and GHH will only benefit from you and Dr. Sullivan having studied in Paris. It would be such an amazing thing."

"Thanks, Frank."

He did have a point, but it wasn't helping him any and he was annoyed that Dr. Mathieu LeBret just assumed he was going to take him up on the offer.

Dr. Crespo clapped him on the back. "Try and rest."

Tony watched him scurry away, no doubt to speak to the press and gush to the benefactors about how he and Madison were stars. He could no longer just sit in his office. He was feeling a bit caged in. He wandered into the atrium and stood there, under the tree he had planted in Jordan's honor and at the bell Jordan never got to ring.

What is keeping you here?

Frank's question was playing over in his mind. Condos and property could be rented. Bertha and Miguel were moving on. He had no family here. All he had was Madison, so what was holding him back?

He glanced up at Jordan's tree and he thought about Miguel and his close call. Madison had stood by him through that whole thing. She had put him first in that moment. His father had never done that for his mother, or for him.

"I wish you were here, Jordan," Tony murmured.

He needed to talk through all these conflicting emotions. Yeah, maybe it would be easier if Madison stayed here in Boston, but it would only be easier for him in the long run. She wasn't like his father and he was foolish to think that.

Madison had had to be independent to survive since her mother died. She only had herself to rely on. If she didn't really love him she would just go to Paris, but she wanted him there, with her. It wasn't manipulation. She wasn't like that.

He scrolled through his contacts and hit Bertha's name.

"Tony?" Bertha asked. "Is everything okay?"

"Just checking in," he said, taking a seat on a nearby bench. "I know it's late…"

"No, it's fine. Miguel's in bed."

"I actually want to talk to you."

"Oh?" Bertha asked.

Tony sighed. "I would usually talk to Jordan about this."

"Lay it on me."

Tony sucked in a deep breath. "I promised Jordan I'd be there for Miguel, but I've been offered a job overseas."

"I heard about that on the news," she said. "It's amazing. A huge congratulations. So what's stopping you? It's with Madison, right?"

"Yes."

"I told you to seek out your happiness."

"The thing is, I promised Jordan…"

"Tony, you've been amazing to us since Jordan died, but we're good. David is here and you need to live your own life now. Of course, I expect to be able to crash at your Paris pad whenever I want."

Tony chuckled. "Of course."

"Take a risk on something, Tony. You deserve a chance."

Tony steadied the emotions welling up inside him. "Thanks, Bertha."

"Anytime. We love you and you're always a member of our family."

"I love you all too."

"Bye."

Tony ended the call and took a deep breath. It was like a huge burden was off his shoulders. His dad never kept promises, but Tony had kept his. Maybe for too long—the only promise he broke was to himself and his heart by pushing

Madison away. Bertha was right: they could always come home to Boston.

The job was for two years of studying and research. It was worth the risk.

And it was worth the risk to take on Madison, because he loved her and to move forward he had to learn to let go of the hurt and trust her with his heart.

Madison's stomach knotted when Tony walked away after she told him she loved him. He claimed she didn't open up, but it was hard to do that especially when she always had to take care of herself.

She'd spent a life swallowing back all her fears, her grief, her love, and instead just focused on her work. This was all to help others from living like she had, a life where a child had to become a parent to a father who mentally checked out. This offer was everything she wanted. Or so she thought. She never thought it would happen this soon.

All of her dreams were coming true, except it didn't feel like that much of a fairy tale, because Tony wouldn't go with her. Part of her wanted to turn the offer down, but it was hard to do that. This was her goal. The research she'd conduct at Dr. LeBret's hospital would be priceless. This was what she'd been striving for, for so long. She'd be able to really focus on her work with the CRISPR-Cas9 gene and explore other research proposals she had in the works.

It was only for two years; maybe Tony would wait for her? *You can't expect that.*

It stung. She was fighting back tears. Just when they were back together, she was going to have to leave, but she'd spent most of her formative years being strong for her dad. She was strong for her patients and other colleagues.

She had to make her dreams come true. She was pushing Tony away again, but expecting him to wait for her wasn't fair. And she was scared about entering into a long-term relationship with him. The idea that she could lose him again was too overwhelming.

Losing anyone she cared about was difficult, which was why she kept moving and didn't make connections. As much as he pushed her away, she did the same to him. What if she stayed here? Would it be so bad? She'd have Tony.

Her heart ached.

Tony doesn't trust me though.

And she understood it was hard for him to trust in someone after his childhood, but it was hard for her to stay for someone who didn't have faith in her.

She wandered down to the atrium because she had heard that was where he was. Sure enough Tony was sitting on a bench staring up at the night sky through the glass dome.

"Hi," she said tentatively.

"Hi," he responded. "Come sit with me."

She nodded and sat next to him, his arm resting on the back of the bench and then on her shoulders, and she laid her head against his shoulder.

"I'm sorry I walked away. I just needed to clear my head."

"It's okay. I understand."

"I needed some time."

Her stomach wrenched, because she had no doubt that he was going to tell her that he wasn't going to Paris. It hurt so much, but she couldn't let it hold her back. She sat up straight. "I'm going. I need to go."

"I know," he said softly.

"I love you, Tony. I don't want to go without you but… since my mother died this has been a dream of mine."

"I know. I remember."

"I love you. This is killing me to leave you, but I can't let this opportunity slip by. I'm not running from you or pushing you away." She swallowed, and her throat felt tight. "I don't know how you feel about long distance…"

"What?" he asked.

"What do mean *what*?" she retorted, her voice shaking.

"Why are you talking about long-distance relationships?"

"Because I love you."

He cocked an eyebrow. "I'm aware, but here's the thing—I do love you."

She shook her head. "You're a butthole."

He grinned and pulled her close and she pushed back at him.

"Madison, I don't want a long-distance relationship."

She crossed her arms. "So you want me to just stay here?"

"No."

She gave him a side-eye. "Then what, Tony? I'm not like your father."

"I'm very well aware of that."

"Then what?" she asked, exasperated.

"I trust you," he said.

Her heart skipped a beat. "You…you trust me?"

He nodded. "I do."

She brushed a stray tear away. "So what do we do? I mean, if you want to stay…"

Tony grabbed her hand. "I'm going with you."

Her heart stuttered and she widened her eyes in disbelief. *Did he just say what I think he said?*

She turned. "What?"

"What do you mean *what*?" he teased.

Madison slugged him in the arm. "Butthole, remember?"

Tony laughed and then stood up, tilting her chin back. "I love you and I know that we bicker a lot, butt heads, but I trust you. No, you're not like my father and I had to be a rock for my mother so long that I kind of became rooted, like a statue. Even though Boston is home, it's not saying we can never come back. I'm going to take a risk that's actually a sure thing and risk it on a rebel doctor—you. I'm going to Paris."

Madison stomach breathing, her pulse thundering in her ears. "You are?"

He nodded. "It's your dream. I won't hold you back. You don't need to be the adult for me to protect me, like you protected your father. I'm not leaving. I'm here and I love you. I want to marry you and I should've asked you that ten years ago."

A sob caught in her throat. "Marry?"

As in family?

Tony nodded and got down on one knee. "I don't have a ring, but I want to marry you and go to Paris with you. It's time to take a risk and follow my heart."

"I love you too," she whispered.

"So is that a yes?"

She nodded and he stood up, pulling her close. For so long she'd been alone and she thought it was for the best, thought that it was easier. But this was so much better. With Tony she really did have all her dreams.

She could finally have a family and another reason to keep fighting.

Fighting for forever.

EPILOGUE

Two years later

MADISON WATCHED A storm rolling in off Nantucket Sound as she walked along the beach. She'd left Tony in their house on Martha's Vineyard, still sleeping off the jet lag. They had spent two glorious years in Paris, but it was nice to be back.

After quickly getting married at city hall in Boston, they'd packed up and headed to Paris. It was amazing and everything she hoped for. Her first award-winning paper was being published, and Tony was now one of the lead experts on the NIR surgeries, as well as HIPEC. Under Dr. LeBret's tutelage they learned so much and had everything they needed at their disposal, but it was time to go back home.

Their visa had run out and GHH was excited to welcome back the award-winning superstar oncology team. The expert surgeon and the rebel doctor.

Though Madison didn't quite understand what she'd done to earn that label, Tony always got a kick out of telling people his wife was a rebel. All she could do was just roll her eyes and go with the flow.

"There you are," Tony said, walking up the beach.

"I like watching the storm," she remarked. "I've missed this place."

"Well, before I fell asleep and before you woke up, I made up the guest rooms for your father and stepmom."

Madison glanced at her watch. "Their plane should land soon."

"You told them how they have to make their ferry connection, right?" Tony asked.

Madison nodded. "I did."

"I put that fugly seagull in his room."

Madison giggled. "You're hoping he'll break it, aren't you? Because he had that long conversation with you about how he's a butterfingers. You think he's kidding, but he's not."

Tony shrugged. "Hey, it survived two years of being in a vacation rental while we were gone. It'll survive your dad. Maybe he'll like it and take it with him as a memento."

Madison laughed. "You know if it gets damaged or disappears we have to get another one."

Tony frowned. "Why?"

"It's a thing. Didn't you read reviews from people who stayed here? They all love my fugly seagull."

Tony groaned. "Maybe I'll just move it, so we don't get another one."

Madison grinned. "Maybe I'll get more of them and have a little family of them."

"No."

She loved teasing him. She was looking forward to this weekend. Her dad and stepmother were arriving from Utah and they were having a bit of a family reunion. It had been so long since she last saw him and her dad was so excited to meet Tony face-to-face. There had been many video calls, but her dad insisted he was going to walk her down an aisle of some sort since he couldn't be at their quick city hall wedding before they went off to France.

She'd had a heart-to-heart with her father about those years where he checked out. She forgave him and she was just glad that she wasn't running away from the sadness. She and Tony would fly out to Utah at the end of the summer so she could show him where she grew up.

"Miguel, Bertha and David are coming out tomorrow for the barbecue?" Madison asked absently.

Tony nodded. "I can't wait to see Miguel. Bertha says he's almost six foot."

"They grow fast. Speaking of which…" She trailed off. "There's something I need to tell you."

He frowned. "You got a job offer. Again?"

She snorted. "Always, but I want to return to my lab at GHH. I promised Dr. Crespo and signed the deal."

"Then what?" Tony asked.

"Well, our little duo might have to be put on hiatus in six months. You might need a new partner or lead oncologist."

Tony looked puzzled and then his eyes widened. "What?"

She nodded. "Yep. I'm about twelve weeks along. I just thought it was all that French food. Are you happy?"

"Am I happy?" Tony asked as he pulled her into his arms and kissed the top of her head. "I'm thrilled."

"There's more," she teased.

His body stiffened. "What?"

"Remember that hospital appointment in Paris before we left? I was violently ill and we thought I had a gallstone. Again, all the French food."

"Yes," he said cautiously.

"I had an ultrasound. That's how I found out I was pregnant, and that's how I know it's twins. Scans confirmed it. Surprise!" She ended with a shout, throwing up her hands.

Tony's eyes widened and then he laughed. "So a quartet?"

"Yes. We might need a bigger condo in Boston."

"I think so." He touched her face gently. "I love you, Madison. So much. I was a fool all those years ago."

"You mean a butthole, don't you?" She winked.

He chuckled again and kissed her gently. "Right. That."

"I love you too. Always."

And then they walked back to their home before the storm got closer, thinking about their future and their happily-ever-after.

* * * * *

*If you enjoyed this story,
check out these other great reads
from Amy Ruttan*

Tempted by the Single Dad Next Door
Reunited with Her Off-Limits Surgeon
Nurse's Pregnancy Surprise
Winning the Neonatal Doc's Heart

All available now!

COMING SOON!

We really hope you enjoyed reading this book.
If you're looking for more romance
be sure to head to the shops when
new books are available on

Thursday 24th October

MILLS & BOON

MILLS & BOON®

Coming next month

FESTIVE FLING WITH THE SURGEON
Karin Baine

'You don't want me to talk? I thought some women liked that sort of thing?' he teased her, whispering low in her ear, knowing the effect it had on her.

Her knees buckling, goosebumps rippling over her skin and a little gasp emitting from her lips were all things he remembered from their last time together, and he wasn't disappointed.

'Hmm, I'm of the opinion your mouth could be put to better use…'

The growl that came from deep inside his chest spoke of those caveman urges Tamsin appeared to waken in him. He'd never let himself get so wrapped up in thoughts of a woman that he'd brush aside all of his long-held reasons for avoiding commitment for something as basic as sex. Yet that was exactly what Tamsin did to him. All he could hope for now that he was lost to this chemistry was that things between them remained strictly physical. With any luck, a short fling over Christmas would give them both what they needed and they could move on in the New Year without fear of recriminations.

The knowledge that he didn't have to curtail his needs, that they'd gone into this together, eyes wide open, unleashed a part of Max he usually held back. Tamsin was getting more of him than anyone ever had.

Don't miss
FESTIVE FLING WITH THE SURGEON
Karin Baine

Available next month
millsandboon.co.uk

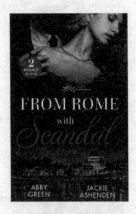

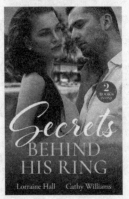

LET'S TALK

Romance

For exclusive extracts, competitions and special offers, find us online:

f MillsandBoon

X @MillsandBoon

⊙ @MillsandBoonUK

♪ @MillsandBoonUK

Get in touch on 01413 063 232

afterglow BOOKS

 Sports romance

 Sports romance

 Workplace romance

 Workplace romance

 One night

 Spicy

OUT NOW

Two stories published every month. Discover more at:
Afterglowbooks.co.uk

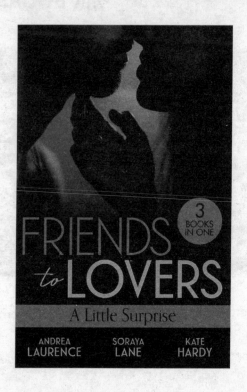

MILLS & BOON

THE HEART OF ROMANCE

A ROMANCE FOR EVERY READER

MODERN

Prepare to be swept off your feet by sophisticated, sexy and seductive heroes, in some of the world's most glamourous and romantic locations, where power and passion collide.

HISTORICAL

Escape with historical heroes from time gone by. Whether your passion is for wicked Regency Rakes, muscled Vikings or rugged Highlanders, awaken the romance of the past.

MEDICAL

Set your pulse racing with dedicated, delectable doctors in the high-pressure world of medicine, where emotions run high and passion, comfort and love are the best medicine.

True Love

Celebrate true love with tender stories of heartfelt romance, from the rush of falling in love to the joy a new baby can bring, and a focus on the emotional heart of a relationship.

HEROES

The excitement of a gripping thriller, with intense romance at its heart. Resourceful, true-to-life women and strong, fearless men face danger and desire - a killer combination!

From showing up to glowing up, these characters are on the path to leading their best lives and finding romance along the way – with plenty of sizzling spice!

To see which titles are coming soon, please visit

millsandboon.co.uk/nextmonth